Sheryn George is a journalist and lives in Sydney. She has been writing since she was six, but this is her first novel. (She tends to be a little slow to action.)

MISS LONELYHEARTS

Sheryn George

HarperCollins*Publishers*

HarperCollins*Publishers*

First published in Australia in 2004
by HarperCollins*Publishers* Pty Limited
ABN 36 009 913 517
A member of the HarperCollins*Publishers* (Australia) Pty Limited Group
www.harpercollins.com.au

Copyright © Sheryn George 2004

The right of Sheryn George to be identified as the moral rights
author of this work has been asserted by her in accordance with
the *Copyright Amendment (Moral Rights) Act 2000* (Cth).

This book is copyright.
Apart from any fair dealing for the purposes of private study, research,
criticism or review, as permitted under the Copyright Act, no part may
be reproduced by any process without written permission.
Inquiries should be addressed to the publishers.

HarperCollins*Publishers*
25 Ryde Road, Pymble, Sydney NSW 2073, Australia
31 View Road, Glenfield, Auckland 10, New Zealand
77–85 Fulham Palace Road, London W6 8JB, United Kingdom
2 Bloor Street East, 20th floor, Toronto, Ontario M4W 1A8, Canada
10 East 53rd Street, New York, NY 10022, USA

National Library of Australia Cataloguing-in-Publication data:

George, Sheryn,
  Miss lonelyhearts.
  ISBN 0 7322 7395 1.
  I. Title.
A823.4

Cover illustration by Alison Wallace
Cover and internal design by Jenny Grigg, HarperCollins Design Studio
Typeset in 11 on 15.5pt Baskerville BE Regular by HarperCollins Design Studio
Printed and bound in Australia by Griffin Press on 50gsm Bulky News

5 4 3 2 1   04 05 06 07

for all the Lonelyhearts out there...

CHAPTER ONE

Tick, tick, tick. That's the sound of women's spiked heels stabbing their way into the marbled foyer of Go Global Enterprises. That's where I work. *Biiiig* company. *Smaaall* paypackets. *Loooads* of profits.

But back to that sound. Just imagine it. Eight thousand people in the building, and seven thousand of them are female. That's a heck of a lot of pointy heels.

Our office building, the one that Go Global Enterprises has its gigantic flag on top of, is like a perfumed termite mound. We call it the Poisoned Palace. The floors are like the layers of an all-female nest, almost like the seven circles of hell, except this hell goes up, up, up to 140 storeys, right smack-dab in the middle of this skyscrapery city. Go Global Enterprises is like a separate world, with its own strange laws, languages and dress codes.

What do we actually do inside the Poisoned Palace? Oh. Forgive me. That's part of the sickness of working here – you think everyone must know because it's So Important Being In Media. All those spiky heels and the not-very-many blokes all join together and somehow produce loads of magazines.

Big ones. Small ones. Trashy ones. Sweet ones. Porn ones, too.

There are oodles of mags called things like *Oh Really?* and *Look Out!* which are basically lottery tickets stacked with appalling real-life stories:

> 'WE WERE SO HUNGRY, MY HUSBAND SERVED UP THE DOG!'
> 'MY GRANDMA GAVE BIRTH TO MY SON'S CHILD!'
> 'MY UNDERPANTS WERE BIGGER THAN THE NEIGHBOURS' CARAVAN!'

You get all this real-life drama, coupled with loads of opportunities to win stuff. There's usually some cash, a crappy car, an awful house in a place where no-one normal would want to live, some gardening tools, a new indoor toilet, weight-loss chocolates for a year, and perhaps a swimming pool in the shape of an elephant on offer.

Then there are lots and lots of puzzles and things: spot the difference; test your star knowledge quizzes; thematic crosswords based on Danielle Steele novels; and chess puzzles. (Yes, chess!)

The package is made irresistible because of the many peach-coloured bobble-jumper knitting patterns that are included. Throw in a bit of cooking to round it (and you) off – how to make big sponges, mainly.

And they sell literally truckloads of the things.

But don't get the wrong idea – it's not all downmarket. There are lots of other magazines at

Go Global Enterprises. There are smart, snotty fashion ones, like *Elegance*, which make you feel poor; then in-between, cool-young-thing mags called *Cheeky You!* and *Shopaholic!* which you open up and they go *sex sex sex orgasm orgasm aaah-aaah-aaah AAAH* and *buy this buy this come on get your credit card out!* These somehow manage to make you feel a bit unsexy and horny at the same time, depending on when and where you're reading them. (My ex hated them so I feigned disdain while getting a tingle in my pants. But that's another story.)

There's also a couple of blokes' mags. The biggest seller is called *Phwoar!*, which a bunch of male sex maniacs work on. They stack the pages with enormous blonde bosoms, barbecued sausages that look hilariously like penises, horrible boating accident victims and big red cars. *Phwoar!* makes me feel … puzzled.

And, secretly, between you and me, intrigued.

Then there's us. The 'jewel in the crown'.

Gossip!

Ta-daaa.

The *Gossip!* office always fizzes and pops, especially on Monday mornings. It isn't like the monthly mags, where you eventually do some work after moaning about being back at work until mid-afternoon. We're straight into it, week in week out. The deadlines are relentless, the competition fierce. What stories are breaking? Has Nicole cut her hair? Has a psychic made contact with Diana? Is William really having an affair with Chelsea Clinton? Fresh angles. The twist in the tail. Scoops teetering on the edge of smashing stories straight off the front page. Deadline is Tuesday night, which means on a Monday frazzled brains and fried nervous systems have exactly 24 hours before the blowtorch of *serious* pressure is applied once again.

I dumped my bag on my desk and, as usual, things fell out. Normal things. Two M.A.C lipsticks, called Scarlet Woman and Vivid; one Vital C Health Directions; and a magnesium complete. Sometimes I have lots more in my bag. It depends on what deficiency I think I'm suffering from. (This week, because I think I get period cramps from a lack of magnesium, I'm seeing if that supplement works.) Part of the joy of being health editor is getting free samples of everything you could possibly get in capsule form. Except hard drugs, you understand. I don't go there.

'Happy fucking Valentine's Day,' I muttered, looking around. The issue out that morning was our Love Special. Brides, proposals and big, evil split-ups. Perfect for Valentine's Day, don't you think? Usually a bestseller and awful to put together for me and Carla, 'cos Renata the advertising Evil Woman went completely bonkers round Valentine's Day.

Anyway, enough of that. I had to get ready for a meeting. Next-issue meetings mean we all pile into Geri's office with some ideas scribbled down on Post-It notes. Or thought up on the train. Or made up on the spot (like mine). Only something wasn't right. This morning, things were feeling decidedly slack. Chandra was reading her horoscope; Eleanor was hammering at a calculator; Carla, the fashion editor (and, bizarrely, my best friend next to Allison) was rearranging her treasured beauty cupboard. Our recently hired top reporter, Max, was laughing on the phone; and Craig, the art director, was looking at model cards. Tamara, the junior writer, was the only exception. She was reading through today's issue, circling things in red texta. (She was still kind of new. And it was her first real job. So she was still very keen.)

'Happy fucking Valentine's Day, fellow losers in love,' yelled Julie, our rock writer, early for once, walking past us to her seat in the corner, the *Gossip!* office equivalent of up the back of the school bus.

'Don't remind me,' I groaned. I didn't have any expectations, I kept telling myself. But I didn't want to take any chances. Valentine's Day? Sorry, *Saint* Valentine's Day. Saint Burn in Unloved Hell Day. Worst day of the year, as far as I'm concerned. In fact, I hardly notice it. It's not like it has ever done much for me. Saint Thanks for Nothing Day.

'Okay. Don't want to think about it, right?' she asked. I nodded, scowling.

'I said, don't remind me.'

'So, where's Geri?' Julie continued blithely. 'Maybe having a bit of sex and a sleep-in this morning.'

'I don't think so,' sniffed Chandra. 'She's never late.'

Too right she wasn't. So where was Geri?

As I looked around at our crowded, uncharacteristically subdued office on Valentine's Day, I realised something strange. Every single one of us loyal, quite attractive and rather clever *Gossip!*

women and men were single. Except for Geri. (Her husband's a horseback riding instructor.)

That's a bit odd, isn't it? (The single-ness of it all, not the riding instructor thing.) It's part of our general twenty-first century malaise, I suppose. Ah-ha, I thought. Idea for the meeting. Single stars – why they can't get a man ... Renée, Nicole, Dannii. I scrawled a few names down on my notepad, then checked my emails, feeling a bit smug at having a cool idea for Geri. It was so disappointing. So much spam was clogging up my in-box. I had 108 new emails since Friday night, and I could guarantee that only twelve would be at all interesting, or worth keeping. I deleted rapidly, until I came to one that looked promising. Something from Allison. My best friend. (And I mean it. She's the *best*.) She was probably emailing to tell me something that had happened in her office – people were always doing mad things on newspapers, like setting phones on fire or having sex in washrooms. I giggled in anticipation as I clicked open the email.

Check out the singles column in The Echo *then tell me I don't love you ...*

What? What had she done? My darling friend. We loved the singles column. There was something about other people advertising to find love that I couldn't get my head round. It intrigued me. As if you couldn't meet someone normally!

I reached over and snatched *The Sydney Morning Echo* from Chandra's desk. I scanned the columns, thinking there must be a new world record-beating horror entry today. Like:

MISS LONELYHEARTS

MAN WITH VERY HAIRY BACK SEEKS LOVING PARTNER. PREFERS BLONDE.

Distracted from the balding guy with a GSOH (Good Sense of Humour) and no income who wanted young girls for fun and games, I picked up my buzzing phone …

'Well,' Allison said with a laugh, a cheeky question mark in her tone.

'What?' I answered, puzzled.

'Third column. Check it out …'

'That's females. I'm female.'

'Hmn-mmm,' she mumbled, like she was about to crack the greatest joke ever.

'I'm straight, remember. Or I was the last time I had sex. Back in the last century.'

'Exactly, you idiot.'

'Still don't get it …' I said, looking over at Max's desk, where there was a scattered stack of pics of a soap star with a woman who wasn't his wife, but who was the brand-new star of his hit TV show. The shots were very chummy. Well, to be completely frank, he was licking her lungs out.

'It's you, Meg. That's you.'

There it was, staring up at me in black and white. I saw my life, *my life*, boiled down to a brief paragraph in a singles newspaper column …

> **26-year-old 160 cm petite and media-savvy brunette with green eyes, interested in health but essentially a bit lazy, loves music but not too loud, enjoys movies but**

> **on the couch, likes to laugh but wants someone to laugh with, needs cuddles, peppy conversation and a sexy excuse to launder my linen … Single forever, so well and truly Ready for …**

'Allison,' I gasped in shock. 'I didn't write this!'

'I know,' said Allison smugly. 'I did.'

'What the *fuck*?'

'It's so time you were over Ben …'

I could hear blood pounding in my ears. I knew my face was going violet.

'… and what,' I snapped, 'is going to help me get over *this*?'

'I dunno. Maybe a good shag? Anyway, Happy Valentine's Day!'

'Happy fucking Valentine's Day,' I shouted.

She hung up.

I ignored the blast of laughter from Julie and Eleanor and shrugged off the stares from Chandra and Tamara. I needed to read the rest:

> **… well and truly Ready for True Love and very big sleepless nights in. Write to Miss Lonelyhearts, PO Box 1235, email misslonelyhearts@echo.com**

Oh My God! My head slowly sunk to the desk. I closed my eyes. My hand still clutched the paper.

And damn, I could hear it again … *Tick, tick, tick.*

* * *

I slammed the paper down and wondered what the odd feeling in my tummy was. Apart from feeling really, really angry, I had to confess to something fluttery having a hoedown in my stomach.

Butterflies.

God, there was just the faintest hint of a thrill there. That hadn't happened since my housemate Dan raised his eyebrows up and down very fast at me once when I'd caught him taking a wee with the door open. (Yes, I know taking a wee isn't the normal term. I just don't happen to like the alternative, okay?)

He was extremely well-endowed, let's say. I would recommend him highly.

I stomped off to the tearoom, where Julie was busily muttering with Eleanor. That's where everyone goes for 'private' conversations, to bitch, or to cry.

I always get a shock when I see Julie, no matter how many times I see her, which is obviously a lot as I work with the woman five days a week. Her face always stops me in my tracks. Julie is absolutely gorgeous, in that rock-chick-type way. Her hair is thick, straight, sharp and slick. (I truly envy it. Mine is thick, curly, mad and … brown.) Her pale-blue eyes may be bloodshot, but they're always perfectly rimmed with kohl. Apparently she tumbles out of bed looking like this. I know, because she crashed on my couch once, or so she says. I know the truth. She actually is one of the many girls in Sydney who had decided she simply must sample Dan's amplitudinous penis.

Honestly.

Anyway, Julie was showing Eleanor the new diamond (diamond!) choker her latest love god had given her. For Saint Thanks For Nothing Day, apparently.

I was a bit dazed from my encounter with a description of myself in the singles column, and woozed past the both of them and started jiggling some herbal tea in my mug.

'Good weekend, Meg?' Julie asked.

'Weekend, yes, fine, thanks, nice, had one,' I said vaguely, squirting some more boiling water into my cup.

'What are you having?'

'Chai,' I said.

'What happened to echinacea?'

That was last week, during the cleansing diet thing. I'd done a three day detox. I'd been in a foul mood the whole time, but my skin was looking great.

'Chai?'

I hate mentioning the D-word around Eleanor. Eleanor is our managing editor, Julie's best friend, and she's about 200 kilograms. With beautiful eyes and a very scary cleavage. Which attracted Dan on one of those nights where everyone at the office ended up at my house, again – not the night Julie slept on the couch, obviously.

I want to make it clear that I really like Eleanor. The only thing that annoys me about her is that you practically can't get into the tearoom while she's in there. She fills the whole room.

'What do *you* think about it, Meg?'

'What? I think Julie's choker's great – err, intricate. Who's it from?'

'Paul, the guy from Lead Squirrel.'

'I don't mean *that*,' drawled Eleanor.

'What?' I said, sounding panicked. Did they know about the ad?

'Apparently Big Boss has been in the building since 6.00 a.m. – and Geri didn't know about it,' Eleanor explained, sounding concerned.

'So?'

'Duh, that means something major's happening – he's been huddled with the money people since six, there's usually a meeting with him and Geri at 8.00 a.m. every Monday and,' she paused for effect, 'he didn't keep it.'

'Well, why isn't she here if she's not in a meeting … ohhh. What's happening?' I said, twigging finally.

'She *is* with him. She's up on the 120th floor.'

'Oh!' That was where all the upper upper management CEO types with blonde wives and freshly pressed suits, wine collections and personal trainers lived.

'I reckon it's just a slap on the wrist about how much we've been running up,' said Julie wisely, picking away at her chipped black nail polish.

'Costs? But sales are great!' I protested.

'No, sales are okay. And ad sales are okay. But expenses are incredible,' said Eleanor sagely, looking at Julie. 'And your mini-bar expenses are shocking.'

'So, are you saying Geri's in trouble? Like, sacked trouble?'

There'd been some talk about us revamping. But we'd assumed we'd do it with Geri. It wasn't that unusual for editors to suddenly lose favour. Just as they seemed secure on their thrones, something usually happened. Some kind of coup, or revolution, or new management person would come along and shake the whole thing up. I'd seen it happen before, and I'd only been with Go Global Enterprises just under twelve months. A crushed editor would come trailing out of the building, escorted by security guards, carrying a sad little cardboard box of personal items. The horrible walk of death through the foyer to the front door, out to a waiting cab, with everyone staring, either looking horrified or smug while gleefully planning a promotion.

'But Geri's brilliant,' I protested.

'She is, but it's an advertising issue,' Eleanor said. 'And an image issue.'

Eleanor had a point. Like we'd all noticed that the magazine market seemed to be getting more and more ruthless about the ages and images of its editors. All the young predators coming up through the ranks were ex-beauty editors, so they were hand in glove with the women's magazines biggest money-spinners – the beauty industry. Not that I'm saying there's anything wrong with being young, pretty, smart, stylish and ambitious. It's just there should be more than one type able to make it.

Look at Eleanor, for example. She's got a head crammed with the best magazine brains I've ever seen in action. She can smell a scandal coming and predict where it's going. She can read, I swear, the body language of stars. Plus she can manage the staff and our budget. If Geri did take the walk of death, Eleanor should be her successor. But will she get anywhere? No way. Not in those clothes, not with that weight, not in this industry.

'If something is going to be announced, when will it happen?' I heard myself ask.

'By three o'clock,' Eleanor answered. 'That's usually the time they reach a deal for the payout.'

Like I said … Eleanor knows magazines. Now all we could do was wait.

CHAPTER TWO

When I got back to my desk, with my chai, Geri's office door was wide open. It felt horribly empty. No chubby arms flailing while she was making a cut-throat deal, no slamming down the phone and chortling, no barging out to light up a ciggie around the corner of the building. Nope. She and her conspicuously loud and always out-of-fashion print dresses were nowhere to be seen.

Chandra had a worried look on her face.

'Where's Geri, Meg?' she demanded. Like I wanted to say anything.

'I dunno,' I mumbled, sliding the section of the paper with my Miss Lonelyhearts description off the desk. It fell to the floor, and I kicked it under the desk, as far away from Chandra's X-ray eyes as possible. I wanted it completely out of sight.

'No-one knows where she's gone,' Chandra said, sounding a bit stricken.

'She's upstairs,' I muttered.

Chandra looked shocked. 'This is not good ... this

MISS LONELYHEARTS

is definitely not good,' she repeated ominously. 'And look what her stars say!'

Chandra based her life around what Madame Staria said. It's pretty funny, unless you're an Aries or a Scorpio, signs that she knows she's fated never to get along with.

Thank God she's not in charge. There would only be Air and Earth signs, all grovelling for her attention.

'See?' Chandra said, her pointer finger with its chewed-down nails poking the page in front of me. 'They're dreadful. So inauspicious.'

'Not good,' I agreed, ignoring her finger and actually looking at my own sign.

Pisces: A surprise for you sets off a new cycle of growth ... It's time to emerge from ...

'Hey!' she said. 'She's Gemini, not Pisces.' She gave me a funny look. '*This* is Gemini's.'

She started reading Madame Staria's prediction in a nervy undertone that nevertheless reached everyone in the office ...

> **Are you ready for a roller-coaster ride? Life's about to pick you up and throw you around, Gemini. Scared? Don't be – it's only change, and you're perfectly safe. Besides, you're one star sign that thrives on tempests – and you're certainly headed for the eye of the storm.**

'How can this happen to such a pure soul?' she announced, dramatically. We all shrugged. Julie rolled her kohl-rimmed eyes.

'I thought you hated Geminis?' teased Julie.

'Not Gemini-oxen,' countered Chandra.

Nobody else paid attention. Julie's Chandra-baiting was as familiar as Chandra's visits to her psychic. Who, secretly, I was desperate to visit. (Honestly. She sounds amazing!)

'But it says right here,' Chandra continued protesting to Max, Tamara and me, 'Mercury is retrograde thus we're all in for troubled communication ... and, anyway, Julie doesn't believe in astrology because she's a Leo.'

Julie threw a CD at her. It missed, but Chandra was still livid.

'That's it – HR will hear about that later.'

'Fine. I'll tell them about how you discriminate against your colleagues based on their stupid starsign,' Julie replied as she walked away.

'What did you say?' Chandra yelled at Julie's back.

'Ta-ta – off to interview Monkey Lode,' Julie said to the office in general, ignoring Chandra in particular, while swiping a crimson arc onto her lips. 'Don't expect me back too soon,' she winked.

'Yeah, bye.'

'See ya.'

We all watched with envy as she wiggled away.

'God, she has the life,' Tamara said. We all stared. Tamara never said things like that – especially in a jaded tone. We all smiled proudly at her. She was truly becoming one of us.

Apart from ignoring five calls from Allison, and three emails and two text messages, I spent most of the next few hours fantasising about what sort of guys answer a Lonelyhearts ad. I mean, maybe, just maybe they weren't all drop-kick rejects, right? I mean, maybe I'd meet some really nice, smart, funny, rich guy? Or a desperately shy maverick artist who was awesomely talented. Or …

'Where's your story?' Eleanor's voice thundered across the room. 'It was supposed to be in three hours ago,' she said sternly.

'Give me five minutes,' I said just as firmly.

'The layout was ready two hours ago. Just make it 1000 words and make the quiz 200,' she ordered. How did she know I hadn't actually started yet? I sighed and called up the document I'd been working on for the last week, about women addicted to shopping – something I'd never previously thought of as a disease, but there you go. Allison and I had put in a little research over the weekend. I added the vox pops I'd done with girls spending up big on credit cards, some stats, sighing with pleasure once the boring stuff was out of the way. Now for the quiz!

Doing the quiz for each story was my favourite part of the entire discipline loosely known as journalism – apart from the drinking and the socialising and the laughs and the time-wasting. I always wrote it with myself in mind – or at least to try and learn more. But no matter which way I worked it, the quiz usually made me look as though I was either in need of serious and immediate hospitalisation, or incredibly virtuous and healthy, a true role model for all fellow females.

While I *was* enjoying unearthing exactly when a penchant for January sales tipped over into a full-blown medical disorder (answer: February, when you tried to squish the phone bill onto the overcrowded digital mess that was your credit card) and was contemplating calling the story aspendicitis, the tension in the office continued to grow with every minute Geri's loud and messy presence was away from her conspicuously empty office. I almost expected someone in a cowboy hat to come in and drawl, 'it's too quiet'.

I filed my story to Eleanor's desk, saw Julie come back in, obviously a bit drunk, and sat back and watched as she blatantly made several calls to friends in New York and wrote up her interview before finally having a little rest on her desk. Julie's snores gave us the idea to send Tamara into Geri's office with Max, just to double-check she wasn't passed out on the floor (it was a long time ago but still, we'd wondered where she'd been that morning, too). By the time we'd done that the temptation to play got the better of us.

I mean, what else do you do when you think something terrible is about to happen?

You go to the smelly pub, that's what.

I must point out that our local is fairly disgusting. Don't go getting any glamorous ideas about stainless-steel bars and bleached wooden tables with tulip-shaped teal chairs, or soft leather booths with white kidney-shaped tables and flirtinis and cosmopolitans and apple martinis (Nicole's preferred drink) in irregular-shaped glasses served by impossibly handsome gay men with perfect skin and beautiful arms bulging out of too-tight tumescent T-shirts.

No, our smelly pub is a cross between a suburban sex shop and a 1950s Las Vegas gambling den where faded members of the Rat Pack could be spotted in the shadows, if you squinted hard enough.

The smelly pub employed about five barmen, all of varying degrees of revoltingness, with the exception of Fizz, my other lovely flatmate, who did about three shifts a week. They were all blokes. No barmaids. I think that's a little weird, actually. They all had great big beer guts (except for Fizz. He was tiny, and looked like a sinewy pixie). Today one of them, probably because it was really hot and steamy, was shirtless.

Julie's eyes narrowed, and Tamara clutched Max's nicely shaped arm. Chandra looked wistful. Eleanor was disgusted, and wasn't afraid to show it.

'Put a shirt on!' she shouted when she saw the sweaty tufts of hair sprouting from his sunburnt shoulders.

'Come on, love. You know you want me,' he winked.

Eleanor wasn't used to being on the receiving end of male attention, but somehow she resisted this charm offensive. Though, in fairness, however gutly our barmen were, they also were kind and avuncular, but not on your life, if you know what I mean.

Plenty of crusty old men and a couple of women cryogenically trapped in a rockabilly fashion moment from 1952 seemed to gravitate to our smelly pub – which meant we all felt wildly attractive, young and hip whenever we gathered there. It was one of the major things going for the place. Apart from the fact it was across the street and round the corner. So we could stumble back, but were never sprung.

It also meant Julie and Eleanor could smoke away to their hearts' content and their lungs' lament. They were both really proud of their disgusting hacking coughs, which they loved bragging about at work.

'I think I swallowed a rusty boat.'

'I have a dead dog in my throat.'

They were always making these kinds of comments. It's a smoker thing apparently 'cos I never got it.

Nearly everyone drank beer, except Chandra, and Julie, who always had a whisky chaser, and Carla, the fashion editor. And me. I don't drink at the moment, you see. I've given it up. Carla hasn't given up drinking. She just won't drink beer because it has so many calories in it.

'It's practically a three-course meal,' she'd say, looking at Max's brew with distaste.

She drinks straight vodka – calorie free, and she reckons vodka's guaranteed to leave her hangover-less.

'I was completely arseholed when I went to bed,' she'd chirp in the morning, as if she'd discovered some amazing health tonic.

Max sat down a bit nervously, staring at the shirtless barman. He was the star reporter, after all, and this was his first visit to the pub. I squished into the space next to him on the unsprung couch, feeling quite awestruck at this momentous occasion. The first time a new member of the *Gossip!* staff comes to the smelly pub is historically significant. One day he will have terrible stories about this place, I thought wistfully. We'll have to go into the toilets to see if he's all right, and cover for him if he doesn't come back to work, or supply him with chewing gum to cover his alcohol breath.

I sighed contentedly. It was great to have workmates. And I felt really safe and comfortable around Max. There was not a hint of sexual tension. He looked so cute, too, with his spiky hair and his neat clothes. He certainly had brightened up our girl-dominated office, without complicating things by being an available heterosexual man. I was very happy with the whole situation.

Though I wished Tamara could be wised up without having to literally out Max.

'Meg!'

I jumped. Max was looking at me, puzzled. 'Do you realise you've been staring at me with a funny look on your face for about a minute now?'

'Oh. Sorry. I was just thinking about how great it is you're here with us – at work, and now at the smelly pub.'

'Yeah? I wasn't sure I was fitting in. I mean, everyone's great. But, you know … Great bunch.'

'Excuse me,' said Chandra pushing past us, giving Max a funny look.

Max turned to me, eyebrows – nicely groomed – raised just a little.

'Don't worry about Chandra.' It was like sitting in front of a massive roast chicken dinner served with gorgeous crispy baked potatoes. I was about to get to tell my Chandra story.

Max snuggled in closer.

'She's obsessed with her horoscope, isn't she? Hope she doesn't find out where my Uranus is.'

I spluttered into my lemonade, lime and bitters.

'It's no wonder she's addicted to stars, really,' I explained kindly. It's very important to get the background briefing on your office workmates. Max was eager for details.

'How old is she, then?'

'God, I don't know. She never says. I guess … about forty.'

'Is that all? Demi Moore's in her forties and she doesn't …'

'But you can tell she used to be terribly pretty,' I said quietly as Chandra fiddled with a soft drink and whispered to Tamara. It was true. It just looked a little like she'd faded away.

'Mmmm. Needs a makeover. Anyway – why so bitter and twisted?'

'She used to live with a guy who was quite the football star. League, of course. But then she found out that instead of just sleeping with most of his fans, he was packing up and leaving her to live with one of them.'

I didn't bother telling him everything. That within a year he'd shifted cities, along with the new woman and their baby (he'd forgotten to tell Chandra her replacement was pregnant). Bastard.

'So – tragic love story. Thus the office fossil,' Max prompted.

Cruel, but true. Like an archeological site, Chandra had all of our history recorded within, layer upon bitter layer.

I caught Tamara's eye. She was staring at Max, and as soon as she noticed me she looked down, blushing. Oh-oh, I thought. Tamara's very sweet, but she hadn't sussed out why a successful Fleet Streeter would want to work in Sydney. She probably thought it was about the weather being hot and sunny.

She came over and sat on the other side of Max, who eagerly started a conversation about the latest episode of *Charmed*. She was in heaven. Well, I wasn't going to break it to her. Let her have her dreams.

I looked around at our funny group, on our grotty old armchairs with their falling-apart material, and thought how sad it would be if we all got the flick.

Everyone looked at me, aghast.

'Sorry, just thinking aloud – it's a bit like a farewell piss-up.'

'I'm not drinking,' said Chandra prissily.

Neither was I, but as if I'd boast about it. It was hard enough being the person in the office with the least hangovers ever.

'What we need to do is figure out some kind of wild publicity stunt to boost sales,' suggested Max. 'At the moment we're running what everyone else is running. See – here's the competition,' he said, pointing to the telly, where *Entertainment Tonight* was screening. 'Why buy us when you can get a fix at four-thirty every day?'

'You can't carry a telly on a train, Max,' Eleanor objected.

'But you can grab a paper – like *The Echo* or whatever it is,' said Carla, gingerly picking up a beer-stained copy abandoned on the table.

Everyone shuddered. *A newspaper.* I should know. I once worked on one.

'It's boring,' objected Max.

'It's got sections – lifestyle section things. People don't want to pay for a magazine when they can get them free,' Carla said.

'They're still boring,' Max insisted, picking it up and flicking through.

I cowered in my seat. I knew he was about to start reading the Lonelyhearts ads. They were the only un-boring bit.

'No – papers are boring. Look.' He flicked a few pages over dismissively. 'Boring, boring boring.' He threw it aside, doing massive mock yawns that showed off his English teeth.

Phew. He hadn't even noticed the singles section. I relaxed back into my comfy chair.

'Anyway. Saving our jobs. How are we going to do that – dress up like a sheik and interview the Big Boss …?'

'Not such a bad idea, Max, but he's our boss, remember, so it wouldn't run,' Eleanor said.

'What if we infiltrated a girl gang – or uncovered a brilliant scheme to murder someone famous?' Max was determined to find a solution.

'Or invented a scheme?' Tamara was equally as determined to support Max.

MISS LONELYHEARTS

'Or if we tried to murder someone famous, and one of you stopped us, and we become the heroes?' Now Max was becoming ridiculous.

My phone started vibrating against my hip. I excused myself to go to the toilet (fluoro-lit so junkies couldn't shoot up – so I'd been told).

It was a text message from Allison.

Rng me yu big spnk – hv ht nws

I rang her right away.

'What did you want?'

'This thing, this Miss Lonelyhearts thing I wrote.'

'Mmmmm.'

'You are going to so love me.'

'Why on earth would I want to do anything apart from throttle you at the moment? To be honest, Allison, this whole thing, it's – it's embarrassing – it makes me look so *desperate*.'

'Well, it doesn't actually, Miss Smarty Pants. Because no-one knows it's you.'

I sighed, and waited for her to start the persuasion game.

'And I know that you feel …'

'Humiliated,' I helped out.

'Yes. But you need to know something.'

'What?'

'It's going off.'

'What do you mean? It's only been in today.'

'No – it's going off.'

'Explain.'

'I've had over 100 emails and we haven't even started getting snail mail yet.'

'Yuk. This makes it worse.'

'It does *not* – they have no idea who you are. It says Miss Lonelyhearts, not Meg, 26, Pisces, LOVE WIMP.'

I said nothing. She was right, but I still thought she was wrong to do it.

'Listen to this: 29, doctor, single for two years; 33, businessman, with shares and three homes; pop star!'

'Oh Allison,' I sighed, exasperated. 'They're making it up. You should know that.'

'No, Meg, that's not the point. Look, we have never had this kind of response.'

'That's 'cos it's Valentine's Day, wouldn't you think?'

'Maybe a little. But I think it means you're the woman every man secretly wants. It must mean that. Look, I've got to go. I'm going to monitor this situation. I reckon it's a story, at least.'

'I am *not* a story. I can find my own men, thank you.'

She snorted. 'And who would that be then – George Clooney?' Then she hung up.

Honestly, she was supposed to be my best friend. I didn't even like George Clooney.

Everyone knows I want Gregory Peck.

Have you seen *To Kill A Mockingbird*? What about *North by Northwest*? *The Omen*?

Oh, never mind.

I sat in the toilets, looking at my phone, thinking, I'm the most wanted girl in Sydney?

I didn't even think guys in Sydney wanted girls any more.

CHAPTER THREE

When we left the pub, everyone else was nicely anaesthetised against the perils of something having happened while we were away. I was on edge. There are real disadvantages to not drinking, sometimes. I sat down at my desk and tried to look like I was busily doing work. In case Geri suddenly showed up. While we were worried for Geri, we were all a bit frightened of her too. It wasn't something you could put your finger on – it was a look she'd give, a twist of the lips, one raised eyebrow, then her attention, like sunshine, would turn away from you and you'd feel a little chill for a week. Or two.

But Geri's office was still empty and her door still open. Chunky handbag exactly where she'd left it.

It turned out we'd timed things rather well. Just as we'd all settled I looked up to see striding towards us, with a look of smug decisiveness, the new management guy with some tall, glamorous model and our publishing director, better known as Big Boss.

Yuk. The management guy was short and good-looking, with a taste for striped shirts. He was new, and was super-eager to make his mark. And it looked like it was about to get made – or sprayed, all over the *Gossip!* staff.

He cleared his throat, clapped his hands together, and called for our attention.

The office gathered around, including a few onlookers from across the hall at *Knitted Delights* and *Old-fashioned Homes*.

'I have just come from a very long and productive meeting with the former editor of this magazine.'

A collective gasp went up, right on cue.

'Geri, as you know, has done a tremendous job on *Gossip!*. Tremendous.'

We waited.

'We are still the market leader, and blah de blah, hmn frm ymn, blum.' His voice faded out. I felt a bit sick.

I couldn't believe Geri was getting shafted. I made eye contact with Eleanor, who, even though she'd sussed what had been happening before any of us, was still looking very shocked at just how fast you could get the golden kiss-off around here.

' ... while we all acknowledge Geri's *tremendous* contribution, I think after reflection you'll all agree that the time has come for a changing of the guard at *Gossip!*. Business times are tough – so I've made a tough decision, and I'd like you all to welcome the new editor-in-chief of *Gossip!*, Monica Drawmer.'

I watched in slow motion as Monica Drawmer swished forward, a bit like the Queen – if she were young and tall and an ex-model. And if she regularly popped off to Joh Bailey's for a blow-dry. Monica was a sensational forty-nothing, all fabulous salon-straightened streaked hair, slim stylishly dressed body, one faultless corporate package on career remote control. She greeted us all with a high-voltage lingering stare just a fraction above all of our unfashionable heads. The impact was immediate. So was the message. We were trolls, and she was our Queen.

'Not this one,' I pleaded very softly in case she heard. 'Not her.'

'I welcome the opportunity to work with you all.' It was like a frosty wind had blown over us. Like the Ice Queen from Narnia. Her voice was clipped, with an accent that was hard to place.

'Where's she *from*?' Tamara whispered.

'*Elegance*, you idiot,' muttered Julie.

'No, that accent.'

'Oh. She's English. I think. *Very* well-spoken,' said Chandra approvingly out the side of her mouth.

'Posh,' said Tamara, open-mouthed.

'Up herself,' said Eleanor. Not very softly at all.

I'd forgotten how … transatlantic Monica sounded. Like Elle crossed with Kylie and a Swiss finishing school.

'You should all know, and I say this with the agreement of our CEO,' here she turned and fluttered a pale hand at the publisher, 'that we are in make-it-or-break-it territory.'

She raised her voice, a bit like she was addressing the nation to announce the war against terror.

'I have no intention of replacing Geri – she had her style, and I have mine.'

Then it dropped again, to a soft conspiratorial whisper. 'I need to know, are you willing to embrace change and move forward with me? If you're not, you will have no place on my team.' She smiled, like a designer shark moving in for the kill.

'Or, to stop from going under,' Eleanor muttered.

'And if you don't,' boomed in Big Boss, who looked a bit impatient with Monica's Academy Award winner performance, 'one of you will go. Every week. Oh, and see the HR department rep, that balding guy, if you have any questions.'

Monica smiled, and turned to Big Boss. I just heard a fragment of what he said …

'And the whole magazine will go down, with you and the rest of them, if you don't get it back on top. This is a final warning.'

Monica Drawmer turned even paler. I met her eyes, wild, shocked, briefly, but averted mine. I didn't want her knowing I'd just seen how totally powerless she was in this situation.

Geri had already been and gone. Door closed. Chunky handbag not where she left it.

So that had been their opportunity to get her out of the building and avoid tearful scenes with distraught staff – and the TV cameras.

We didn't even get to say goodbye.

As soon as Monica disappeared into her new, Geri's-just-vacated office and shut the door, the rest of us shambled around, de-briefing, and dealing with the shock. Under the nerves and the upset, and the genuine concern for Geri, there was a kind of sick excitement rippling through all of us ... something big was happening – to us. To *Gossip!*. We were in the midst of a real drama. We were the stars of this crisis. And, being the media junkies and car-accident watchers that we were, it all felt a little unreal, and faintly ... stimulating. I know, it is a terrible thing to admit – but at least I'm honest. If that wasn't enough, underneath it all was bubbling my singles ad anxiety. What if people found out? What if Allison wrote a story? What if I got home and there were millions of men waiting for me?

I had to get out of there. My mind was racing and I needed to be by myself. I waited until Eleanor was concentrating on her computer screen and left. I wasn't in the mood to say goodbye. I crunched on a couple of magnesium tablets on the train ride, got out at my station, and walked through the Junction till I reached the streets of Bondi, with their multi-coloured, multi-hued, multi-multi citizens. It was after five in the evening but there was still plenty of bright, hot sunshine, with dark, streaky thunderclouds threatening to burst with rain the minute the clock hit six and the temperature, finally, dropped. I couldn't believe how symbolic it all was. Or, maybe, the clouds were there every night and I'd just never paid them attention before.

I got to my street, trudged up to my shabby, old, super-expensive semi, opened the gate, trudged a bit more, and opened the front door.

'Hello-ooo,' I sang out to my boys. I was looking forward to the reality check of Dan, Fizz and probably Eric to distract me. Eric wasn't technically living with us but, being best mates with Fizz, he was there practically all the time.

No music. No banging noises. No laughter.

No-one was home.

Bliss.

I plopped down on my favourite beanbag, and played with some beans as they dribbled out onto the wooden floor. Lovely and quiet. After a nice little doze I hopped up, ate some leftover sushi from the fridge, ran a bath and filled the bathroom with steam, the lovely hiss of Epsom salts hitting the water. The amazing smells of pure essential lavender and rose oil made it perfect. I poured a massive orange and carrot juice for myself in the kitchen and then chucked my clothes off, climbed in, and lay back in the just-too-hot-for-comfort water and sipped my juice slowly.

And started to think about Ben.

CHAPTER FOUR

There should be an equation – a calculation that tells you exactly how long it will take to get over a break-up.

For example: it could be duration times intensity multiplied by expectations – DxIxE=R (R being recovery, or the anticipated time it will take to feel something like normal again).

If I used this calculation my recovery time should be twelve months. But I wasn't sure how to factor in spending one night every six weeks or so having break-up sex. Which, mortifyingly, *he'd* insisted on stopping. I shifted in the bath to turn the hot water on.

Why did it still matter? Why did I still miss him so much? Think about him – every day. I didn't want to go out with anyone else. And I'd been pissed off about Valentine's Day, not because there were no secret admirers. But because I'd been hoping, more than a little, that he'd ring. Or write. Or … something.

I knew why I still missed him.

Because it had been great. Amazing.

It had been fantastic.

Why? I think it had to do with just how in love with me he'd been. He had always been super-cool, and then he'd fallen. Fallen for me, Miss Not So Super-cool. I genuinely thought he was amazing. Brilliant. Funny. And he really loved me. Came round at midnight. Wondered if we'd met before – in another lifetime. He'd had so many girls after him – so many. But he'd chosen me. And he was smitten. Then in love. Then we were planning a future.

One night we jumped into a cab on our way out. We snuggled into the back seat, smiling. Just happy.

'You are in love,' observed the taxi driver, smiling, looking sage.

We grinned. We hadn't actually said it to each other at that point.

'You should get married. This happiness – get married. You are so happy.'

I always think about that night. We *should* have got married. I mean, it was perfect. Everyone waits these days. I don't get what we're all waiting for.

Then one day he stopped being really happy and became distant. I couldn't figure out what was going on.

I knew Ben had gone out with some arty girl for a few years before he fell in love with me. But she'd left him to travel overseas …

She'd left him!

I didn't even consider she'd come back one day. But she did.

Ben sat me down one night when I'd cooked dinner and chosen a video for us and told me we needed to have a break ... a break! What does that mean?

After a few months of to-ing and fro-ing (and break-up sex) he'd told me that Freya was coming back and he needed to see how he felt about her and about me. He told me he'd thought she was his soul mate.

I guess I was in denial but then he told me one morning (after some more break-up sex) that Freya was flying in that day.

I know I should have been a grown-up but as we'd had sex at my house the same day she'd arrived, it didn't seem intrusive to ring him.

'Is she there?'

'Yes.'

'What are you doing?'

Bit of a wait. Then a throat clearing. It's a very guilty-sounding sound.

'Well, we've been having a bit of a talk, and you know, catching up, but she's pretty jet-lagged.'

'That doesn't sound very soul-matey.' It sounded a bit boring, actually. I wondered what she was wearing. Did she look beautiful to him? Did it all happen in slow motion? Was there a meltingly hot kiss? Did he know she was the one?

'Do you want to come over?' I heard myself asking.

'Well, I don't think that would be okay – she's just got here, Meg.'

'Do you want to go for a drink then – a bit later on?' If I could get him drunk, we'd definitely end up in bed.

'Please,' I whispered. A searing flash of self-hatred burned through me.

'Why do this, Meg? You've got to learn to let me go … give me some space.'

'You had sex with me this morning!'

'I need some time …'

'But why didn't you tell me she was coming back? Why did you leave that bit out?'

'You knew she was coming.'

'I found out this morning! We've been going out for nearly a year. Why didn't you say anything?'

'Because I didn't want to hurt you …'

I just clutched the phone. What could I say?

'Look, we should probably not talk for a couple of weeks,' he said after my deafening silence.

'Fine,' I snapped back, cool. I'd got him there. Besides, he always said that. And we always ended up talking. And the rest.

But, you see, this time he meant it.

I switched the hot tap back on, draining some cold out and throwing more lavender oil into the water.

Have you ever had a breakdown? Real depression? If you have, how did you know? Was there a moment where you went, this is it, it's happening, I am officially entering a nervous breakdown? Because if you did, I want to know how you knew. I mean, I didn't know. It seemed quite normal to spend most of the day sobbing into my computer. Then to make phone calls (to Mum, to Ben, to Allison) and sob into my phone. Then go back to sobbing into my computer. Then I would go to the pub, and sob there. After a few drinks, I would go home and not sleep.

I guess I had a clue that things weren't right when one day I couldn't get out of bed. The mirror provided a few clues, too. I mean, any other time I would have been excited about being so skinny. But I couldn't even get excited about having thighs that didn't touch any more.

I'm sure I would have pulled through. Eventually. But one horrible night, Allison came over and got really worried. So worried she rang my Mum. I mean, I'd been joking when I'd said I'd stick my head in the oven. It was electric for goodness' sake. What harm could I do in there?

But she thought lying still for three days and not eating anything or leaving the house or answering the phone or washing meant things had gone far enough. (Okay, okay. They obviously had.) There were a couple of other things as well. I was too tired to stop her, so I just lay on my bed, listening to the conversation.

'Hi, Mrs Tooley, it's Allison Mitchell here.'

'Hello Allison, love – how's your mum? I saw your dad the other day at the bank. Isn't he looking well?'

'Um, they're okay.'

'We haven't seen you for ages. When are you going to be coming around?'

'Um, Mrs Tooley, sorry to interrupt but Meg is very upset. I think you and Mr Tooley should come over.' Allison was practically panting with anxiety – even I could hear the worry in her voice, and I was huddled under the cocoon of my doona.

'Look, you have to come over – Meg is really, really upset.'

'But … but we're watching the tennis.'

'Please, come over. Please.'

'It's the Davis Cup!' my dad apparently yelled in the background.

It was only when Allison started to sob that my parents finally realised something a bit serious was happening.

They turned off the telly and drove for an hour to my harbour flat. Allison met them at the door and led them to me.

I was lying on the bed. 'What's wrong?' Mum gasped – obviously she thought being 47 kilos was too skinny. 'Is she on drugs?' she stage-whispered to Allison.

Dad, being practically minded, immediately said, 'Let's go to Sizzler and get you some food.'

I didn't have the energy to argue so Mum dressed me and they bundled me into the car.

During dinner, I ate very little. Mum and Dad looked at me like something had taken over their daughter, and they were trying to make out just what it was. Mum was beside herself.

'What is it, love?' she pleaded. 'What's wrong?'

'I think,' I said very slowly and very clearly, 'that I'm going to kill myself.'

'No, You Most Certainly Are Not!' she snapped, her mouth a thin red line, her eyes chlorine green with tears.

'Oh, love,' said my dad, starting his steak. 'Come home for a bit. You'll feel better.

Mmmmm,' he then said, eyes lighting up. 'This steak is great.'

I took leave from work and went to stay with Mum and Dad for a month. They fed me, and I swam in the pool, and sunbaked a bit. I still wept entirely too much.

'Mum, Meg's crying again,' my brother Tod would yell in a panicky voice.

'Is she?' my sister Karen would say, rushing in excitedly. She'd stare at me for a minute or two.

'What does it feel like?' she'd ask curiously. 'Does it feel like a knife going in and out of your heart?'

She wanted to be a psychologist. I really hoped she never made it – she'd destroy all her patients.

'Are you,' she whispered sympathetically, 'suicidal again?' Her eyes widened with anticipation.

'No, but I do want to kill someone,' I'd say meaningfully.

'I've never been in love,' she'd muse while I sobbed on my bed. 'Does it feel like this all the time?'

'Go away,' I'd tell her.

But, somehow, it was nice to have her there anyway. Even if she was incredibly annoying.

My mother would hug me tight.

'Just get angry,' she'd instruct. 'Anger is your friend. It can give you strength. Tears are repressed rage,' she'd recite like a lesson. 'You have to fight the disease to please.'

Yes, it's true. There was way too much *Oprah* being watched in our house. Not that I minded. She was a whole lot better than a counsellor. Mum, Karen and I would watch *Oprah's Change Your Life* TV together while my Dad tried to 'incentivise' Tod into doing more odd jobs around the house.

'I don't understand,' Dad would moan to me. 'I'll give him 10 per cent on top of everything he makes mowing people's lawns ... but he just doesn't seem interested.'

Dad was sweet, but sometimes he made a bowling ball look sharp.

Mum was wrong about me. I *had* felt anger, quite a lot, really. I'd imagine elaborate scenarios where Ben'd take me to dinner, and I'd be looking great, and in my imagination my breasts would be bigger, my hair wouldn't frizz and my legs were very long, like Anita Pallenberg's, which everyone knows is how she got Keith Richards. Anyway. Ben would do a double take when he saw me, instantly realise what an idiot he'd been, and would commence grovelling, desperate to get me back. Sick with longing. Smitten. But I'd behave coolly, impeccably, maddeningly indifferent, while he would beg me to come back, give a speech about how mad he'd been and how irresistible I was, incorporating all manner of pleading. Everyone in the restaurant would turn to stare at this man who had obviously made such a stupid mistake, and I would gently touch his hand, shake my head, and say something like, 'We can't go back. It's over. I wish you well.'

Or, I'd shut him up by flinging a bottle of wine in his face and giving a carefree little tinkly laugh as I walked from the restaurant, all onlookers bursting into frenzied applause and yelling thing like, 'Good for you' and 'You can do better' and 'Here's my number' and 'Marry me!' As I walked away I'd know I was never going to go back to him after the hurt and the humiliation, because I would be overflowing with self-respect and, well, self-control.

Revenge fantasies they were, yet they made me feel ... better, or powerful, at least in my head, at least for a few minutes. Positive visualisation, Chandra would have said. But really I was still way too in love with Ben to actually go through with any of it if I ever had the chance.

Instead, I asked life's great rhetorical questions. Like: 'Why did he dump me? *Why?*'

Like: 'Why doesn't he love me any more?'

Like: 'Who ate all my Tim Tams?'

Despite reciting things that Oprah would have been proud of, Mum wasn't really that much help in the philosophy department. She was practically the inventor of the treat 'em mean, keep 'em keen discipline. Why wouldn't she ... it had worked for her. She'd been with my dad since she was fifteen. Her one experience of insecurity was when my dad had told her, as a callow fellow sixteen-year-old, that he wanted to play poker with the boys at the surf club instead of taking her to the pictures on a Friday night. So she got one of the card players, some big hunky guy who was my dad's friend, to take her out instead. My dad's wondering where Bruce McTaggart is – and another friend has to tell him Bruce's out with his girl. My mother. What a minx.

Round one, Mother.

Of course, my dad has lived in fear of a repeat performance ever since. Thirty years of female terrorism, a son who doesn't like mowing lawns, one daughter breaking down and the other sunbaking topless in front of his surf club friends. At least his footy team's winning this season.

Obviously the fact that I couldn't stop crying – even after Oprah – was worrying, so the next thing I knew I was getting dragged off to see a counsellor. Mum thought I'd see some tough-love guru like Dr Phil. Ha!

This is how our conversation went.

Me: 'I am so sad *(sniff)* I can't believe he's gone – we loved each other *(choke)*. I can't think about anything else *(sob)*. If I can just get him back it'll all rewind and it'll be okay *(waaaaahhh)* …'

I looked hopefully through the downpour at the counsellor – male, thirty-ish – who nodded understandingly.

'Why did you love him?' he asked wisely.

Well, duh. We were in love. He loved me. I loved him. He made me feel so incredibly happy. He would look at other people and say, 'He doesn't love her, not like I love you.'

But the counsellor was okay. Though he was no Dr Phil. I mean, he suggested, for one, that as Ben had gone back to his ex-girlfriend that in fact he had a pattern, and therefore he was likely to want to gain closure with me. Which I took to mean that the counsellor was actually saying that at some stage, Ben would be compelled by his own love-life patterns to get back with me. At some stage. Once he'd figured out whatever it was he needed to figure out with his ex. The ex before me, that is. The ex that was now his girlfriend.

Oh. He also gave me antidepressants. And made me promise to cut down on drinking. And start eating. And to make at least one significant change in my life, to help me make the shift.

That's the day I saw the ad for the job at *Gossip!*. When I'd been with Ben it would have been exactly the kind of job I would have been a bit ... well, *embarrassed* to have. You see, he liked things that were serious. And stylish. He was really proud of me working on a newspaper. And *Gossip!* was undeniably, well, a bit tacky, I s'pose. But I couldn't stop looking at the ad. When I talked it over with Allison, I found myself getting twinges of excitement and goosebumps. I was experiencing a lovely emotion that hadn't been around my way for ages, it seemed. Enthusiasm. We'd been strangers to each other for some time.

Allison pointed out I wouldn't have to go to car-accident scenes any more, or try to talk to murderers' families, or do door-knocks – I'd be able to see films and read press releases and play in the beauty cupboard. Secretly, I thought, Ben would panic at losing touch with me. He'd realise that I was independent and he'd want me back, for fear of me drifting out of his life altogether.

Allison thought that part of my plan was a little, er, tenuous. You know, that we would inevitably get back together, because Ben was unable to let go of exes until he'd broken up with them at least twice.

I was determined that I'd be the girl he'd break up with once ... if you know what I mean!

Allison looked sceptical, but she hadn't said much. I knew she didn't like the idea of us getting back together at all. But she'd get used to it, when it happened. It made sense to me. I mean, we had hardly even started out. The relationship had so far to go. We'd talked about forever. It had felt like forever. 'Until I leave you' had never come into it. So, while I had to get on with my life, I also was, not so secretly, waiting.

Hanging in there was like being dragged for miles and miles behind a fast car with two people kissing in it, and one's your boyfriend and one's a freckly English-sounding twit. Even though you know you should let go, you hope they'll stop kissing and he'll jump out of the car, run to you, and as you hug in the road she tumbles over a cliff and the car bursts into flames.

No matter how many times I ran through this scene in my head, it hadn't happened. And it had been a whole year. So much for positive visualisation!

I opened my eyes. Still in the bathroom. Lord, I thought, standing up and reaching out for my special super-fluffy towel. I'd been planets away. It didn't make sense that Allison would decide I needed a Lonelyhearts ad. I mean, she knew Ben was the love of my life. She knew I'd never really got over him. She knew what the plan was, even if I hadn't talked about it that much, lately. Anyway.

I dried off, and wrapped myself up in another huge, fluffy white towel that I had stashed in my bedroom, lit the oil burner with some more lavender – it helps you to sleep, and it keeps the mossies away – took two valerian, three bio-magnesium, turned my lamp on next to my bed, and started to read *You Can Heal Your Life*. The fish tank in my room bubbled contentedly. It was a picture of quirkyalone peace.

Eventually, after a lot of affirmations, I fell asleep.

CHAPTER FIVE

Even though the world had gone mad, I got through the next day the usual way. I checked out my stars on Cainer's website. I took my vitamins. We proofed pages, made some changes, fixed typos and completely rewrote a story thanks to the star who had been about to celebrate her first anniversary but who overnight announced she was getting divorced. I wrote a quick piece about how alcohol had contributed to the break-up, and a quiz on how to know if it was ruining yours, and slowly we got everything away. Monica stayed in her office with the door shut and rang Eleanor when she had anything to say. It seemed she didn't consider this issue had anything to do with her.

It was Geri's swan song.

We wrote a loving farewell to Geri and ran a big pic of her on page three. We said she'd retired. Then we took a collection up.

'What should we get her? Some coke?' Julie said.

We were all stumped. I had no idea where you'd buy anything like that.

'That will really piss Monica off,' said Julie to Eleanor, pointing at our page-three tribute.

'I know, but Geri deserves it.' We all nodded. Plus we already knew we actually liked the idea of pissing Monica off. So we sent it to the printers.

After deadline was past – very smooth for a change – we all hung about for a bit. I was delaying going home. I hadn't even looked at *The Echo*. Okay, I had, but only to snarl at it. I didn't dare read anything.

I was hoping it would all blow over and no-one would ever know what Allison had done. I should have known better.

'Have you seen this piece your friend's done, Meg?' Julie asked. 'It's pretty good, really. For a newspaper.' She thrust *The Echo* at me, and I took it. Like it was radioactive. Wincing, I looked at page three.

'WHO IS MISS LONELYHEARTS?' screamed the headline.

BY ALLISON MITCHELL.

Oh no.

> In a world where relationships last less time than the food in your fridge, one woman seems to have found the secret of attraction.
>
> A Miss Lonelyhearts has racked up an incredible 2000 responses to her personal column ad in one day.
>
> The personal ad, published in yesterday's *Echo*, has had an unprecedented reaction. Flowers have been arriving at the paper's

offices non-stop, and staff are fielding calls around the clock.

Psychologist and social commentator Leslie Falkner believes it is Miss Lonelyhearts' combination of youth, attractive-sounding appearance, intelligence and vulnerability that has generated such a reaction.

'She sounds smart, and clever, but a little hurt. She's willing to move on, and willing to reach out.

'To many of today's men who are mystified by modern women, this ad spells out that she is looking for love, sounds like a great catch and is pretty to boot.'

One of the respondents, a Jon D, said the ad appealed to him because he felt he wanted to show her that guys are willing to have relationships.

'I don't want to meet someone at a club or something. She just sounded ... special, and funny. It was kind of brave for her to do that, too,' said the 27-year-old architect, pictured left.

I looked at his picture.

Oh my God. He was hot.

And what does Miss Lonelyhearts herself make of this?

If only we knew – so far she's playing hard to get. She failed to return any calls made by this reporter yesterday.

Bloody hell. Allison was so dead.

'That's not a bad piece,' said Eleanor thoughtfully, reading over my shoulder. 'We should follow up. What's she got that's so special? It could be good for a romance issue or something.'

'She must be a bit of a loser, don't you think, to … um, put an ad in?'

They both looked at me.

'God, Meg. If it wasn't for my job, I'd never meet anybody,' Julie said.

Eleanor just looked away. Oh no. Maybe she had put an ad in herself.

They both left for the day, and I sat there. I knew I was stalling. I'd already had the 'What time are you getting home?' SMS from Allison, which I'd ignored, and the phone calls, which I'd not returned. I was trying to delay the moment when I'd have to talk to her. My so-called best friend had interfered in my life, again – and I was meant to be happy about it. It was confusing. How could I actually want to set my best friend on fire? What if I said how I really felt?

By seven, it was time. Time to head home.

I turned the key, walked down the hallway and went into the lounge. No-one heard me 'cos the music – The Strokes – was shaking the windows. My housemates were sitting on the floor, surrounded by thousands of pieces of paper – some letters, some print-outs of emails.

'Isn't this *unreal?*' screamed Allison. She jumped up, turned the music down, and looked at me, smiling and flushed with excitement.

I walked straight past her, down the shady hallway, and out into the back yard. I sat on the steps, looking at the overgrown grass and the ants moving around the remains of a snail. A huge plane went overhead and I wished I was on it. Allison came out and sat next to me. She was holding a whole lot of letters.

'Aren't you just a *bit* curious?' she asked. 'Come on, look at this one. He's hot,' she giggled. She showed me a picture of a naked guy, lying on his bed with a rose between his bum cheeks. His bedroom was awful.

'Look at this one.' She showed me another. He was flexing pale, puny arms and sporting a bow tie. Naked. I felt the corner of my mouth twitching.

'What's with all the naked guys?' I demanded, shaking my head.

'Come on – there's actually a sociology degree sitting in the lounge room,' Dan said as he sidled up and sat down on the other side of Allison, I noticed. Casually. Hmmmn.

'Would you like beer or wine?' he asked.

'Water,' I said. 'And ice cream. No! Chocolate gelato. Lots of it.'

'Come on, Meg – at least let's get a laugh out of this,' he said and went back in to the lounge room.

'The boys,' Allison whispered to me, 'are completely immersed. Transfixed. Can't get them away from the letters. It's like they're watching some kind of human sexuality documentary.'

And it was. Even I couldn't stay in the yard ... curiosity got the better of me.

MISS LONELYHEARTS

'Some of these guys are weird,' said Dan, sounding like he was truly surprised.

Fizz just kept shaking his head.

'What made you do this – you're not desperate, are you?' he asked.

Allison hooted with laughter. I leapt on her, mock strangling her. Just a little too realistically for total comfort.

'She begged me to put it in,' Allison gasped, 'she was pleading with me: *I so want a rooooot.*'

'Shut up, Allison,' I said, climbing off, but not before thumping her – quite hard actually, on the thigh.

'Tell them!' I was getting very worked up about it all. Interesting.

'Okay, okay, *I* did it,' Allison admitted, laughing. 'Meg didn't know anything about it, *but* – I know she *needs* this.'

I shook my head. She was my best friend, but she truly was incorrigible.

'Anyway,' she said, getting all earnest on me, 'it's gone off – there's been this *massive* response.'

I looked at the piles of paper. She was right. There were *hundreds*, literally carpeting our scungy wooden floors.

'And it's not just these,' said Allison once she'd calmed down a bit. 'Look,' she said, dragging me into Dan's room.

'I'm, er, going through to make sure none of them are freaks,' Dan said, following us into the room. He was a bit embarrassed.

'It's probably best if you don't see any of these.'

'I have some at home, too,' Allison explained. 'The ones I thought you wouldn't be interested in at all.'

A horrible thought suddenly blossomed.

'Um. Allison.'

'Mmmm?'

'Diane hasn't seen them, has she?'

I have to explain. Diane is Allison's flatmate. But I just have a funny feeling about her. She's okay, really she is. She's just ... well, she's just a bit ... she sort of wants to ... well, she's unpredictable. She's sort of very peaceful, and natural, but there's something a bit ... like a hungry predator about her. I should really trust her more, I guess. She's Allison's flatmate, and after all, Allison really gets along with my flatmates. (Yeah, and she sleeps with one of them. Not that I'm supposed to notice.) So I should make the effort too. (I'm obviously not going to sleep with Diane, though.) And, after all, she claims to love Allison. And she does. A little too much.

No, not like that.

In that she kind of wants to have her life. I'm sure she fancies Dan. And I'm sure she'd love to be in on this. And Ali, who's smart as a whip, can't see that there's something dodgy about her, even though she seems ever so harmless and oh so nice.

Okay. Maybe I'm jealous. But really, I just ... Don't. Trust. Her. And I really didn't want her knowing about this. I can't explain why. I just didn't.

'Anyway,' Allison ignored my question while I pondered Diane's place in the life cycle of our relationship, 'there were heaps of phone calls.' She practically dragged me back to the couch. 'And letters.

Cards. Flowers. They've had to assign an extra person in the mailroom to deal with it. And set up a special phone line. You're a hit! The breakout star!'

'Must have been a *very* slow day in the newsroom,' I complained, giving her a gentle kick while holding the afternoon edition of *The Echo* and looking at the page again. This didn't seem real. Or maybe it just didn't seem that important any more. Maybe I was in shock. Maybe I was happy about it?

No. No way in the world.

'Don't you have anything better to do than …'

'Save your sex life from extinction? No –'

'It's not extinct!' I protested. 'I'm a quirkyalone!'

'Ha!' she interrupted. I grimaced. Okay, so it *was* extinct. And quirkyalones were a media myth.

'So,' she continued, 'now they want me to do a proper story. On you!'

I groaned and fell to the floor.

'But think! It's what everyone wants – good news.'

'Allison, it's my life.' I couldn't believe she was going to out me to the world as some kind of tragic reject desperate for love.

'It's okay,' she said, giving me a hug. 'I can do a story and not mention any names. About what this says about us, you know, as a country. A think piece. You don't have to get involved.'

I gave her a true glare and she grinned! That's the problem with knowing someone for so long. You begin to feel like you can get away with anything. And maybe she had a point.

Really, I felt quite curious. I didn't want to let anyone know – but surely, amidst all the responses, there had to be at least one good man.

'Okay,' Allison sighed, taking my silence for anger. 'Do you want me to get rid of them?' She looked straight into my eyes. I felt a flicker of alarm. She was serious.

'Come on, let's light a bonfire,' she said, grabbing a pile and heading towards the back door where the little-used barbecue was lurking.

'No!' I screamed at exactly the same time as Dan and Fizz started shrieking too. Dan flattened himself across the piles of letters. Fizz held his favourite letters protectively to his indie T-shirted chest with one hand and crash-tackled Allison with the other. I mean, Fizz hardly ever made a noise. What was going on?

'Really?' she grinned, rubbing her arm. 'Ow, Fizz, you big bully. Thank God,' she said, flopping back into an armchair and looking relieved. 'Because you wouldn't believe the strings I had to pull to get you in on Valentine's Day!'

We started to work our way through them.

At Dan's suggestion we set up three piles. One was for prospects with potential. The other was for rejects. The third was for possible police attention.

We read hundreds of letters. It seemed incredible that they could all have been writing to meet me – to have a relationship, with me.

Why was I so surprised? I mean, this was the modern world, after all. We were all disconnected, restrained, damaged, uncommitted, unable to sustain relationships.

Weren't we?

Yet, we were obviously dying to get involved with someone other than our personal trainer. Here was letter after letter from, well, mostly very normal-sounding guys, some who seemed okay. Actually, better than okay. Some sounded, I'll admit it, great. Really great. And solvent. And interesting! Musicians. Designers. Artists.

'Stop looking at all those arty-farty guys,' ordered Allison.

'I am not,' I protested.

'Yes, you are, I know you. What is it, anyway — you're great, you're creative, you don't need to hang with some arty-farty bloke — you'll only do it to show Ben you can pull an artist.'

Honestly, the things I let her get away with.

'Admit it — you're combing through looking for a Ben.'

'I am *not*,' I spluttered, provoked.

'Yes, you are. So scrap that idea immediately. Instead of a wanky tosser with no money and bad taste in music, let's find a guy with … hmmmn. A great car, for starters.

'At least!' blurted Fizz, excited.

'And his own house. And a boat and … and a holiday home!' added Dan.

Allison nodded. She was really on a roll now. 'No, no, we can do better than that.' She was *really* fired up about this.

'How about a home in Sydney, a one-million-dollar house at Belongil at Byron, and a romantic, ummmm, Blue Mountains getaway.'

'Yeah, that sounds good,' said Dan.

I kept quiet. This was getting *very* interesting.

So we read and we filed. There were some slightly suspicious ones, I have to say. But Dan kindly took control of those.

'Don't worry, Meg,' he said comfortingly. 'I know some blokes who'll do a bit of protection work if any of the funny ones get too near you.' He was probably referring to our neighbours, the drug dealers on the right-hand side.

'Oh God.' I flung myself back dramatically into a beanbag. A few more beans dribbled out onto the floor.

'What if I get a psycho-stalker?' I waved my arms about.

'You could get one of those anyway,' said Allison sensibly. 'This has got nothing to do with that. They don't know where you work, where you live, your name. Nothing.'

'They know about Miss Lonelyhearts,' I said to her, stressing out.

'But who is she, exactly? What details do they have? *Nada*. And there are about one million women in this city who could easily be her. So don't worry so much. No-one will ever find out.'

'I still think we have to make some kind of pact,' I said, suddenly.

'What?'

'You know. A promise. To keep me a secret … You are the only people who know,' I said to Allison, Dan and Fizz. 'Swear you won't tell. Not anyone. Come on, swear.'

They did.

'Fuck,' muttered Fizz.

'Fu-uck,' said Allison, grudgingly.

'Fuck?' Dan said, looking at Allison.

CHAPTER SIX

A record crowd was gathered outside the tearoom on Wednesday morning. We all needed a little pep talk before Monica's regime became official. Of course, it was Eleanor who gave us the background briefing.

'Monica Drawmer is,' Eleanor was saying conspiratorially to the entire staff huddling together to get that morning's goss, 'so single she can't recall what it's like to sleep with anyone apart from the cat …'

Everyone laughed a bit – so she wasn't perfect.

'She loves her cat,' Eleanor said meaningfully, looking at Julie.

Julie turned pale. She'd put her cat down a few months before because it had peed on her doona while a rock god had been snoozing off the marathon sex session he'd had with her beneath it.

'She's going to be desperate for immediate, obvious improvements and conspicuous change. She has to make it look like things are happening, even if nothing in the real world – figures, ad percentages – changes.'

Tamara shuddered and chewed on her little finger's ragged nail just that bit harder. Max hung a casual, protective arm around her. I really had to talk to him about that.

'She can't be that desperate – she's just been made our editor-in-chief,' said Max in cheerful cockney tones.

'Think again, new boy. She's just been demoted from the most glam job to the roughest, hardest ride you can possibly get.' I told you Eleanor knew everything.

'Why would that be happening, do you think?' Max asked.

'What are the circ figures?' Eleanor snapped back.

'They're down.'

So that's why Geri'd gone.

'They shouldn't be down, either,' Eleanor went on. God, she was good. 'The world's gone mad. There's been celeb divorces, star addictions, planetary upheaval, fairytale recoveries. We've got to find a way to get everyone into these things again – to feel they're important. Important enough to read *Gossip!*. *Gossip!*'s got to be seen to be about more than trivia – it's about making sense of the world we live in.' Everyone nodded. 'Because it's not about stars – it's about us. People. And tragedy. And comedy. Love, and sex, and death, and greed, and ambition, and whether good people finish first. The greatest themes known to humanity are in our pages.' She looked over us all. 'So why aren't we selling any more?' she asked, softly.

So why wasn't, I wondered again for the hundredth time, Eleanor running this place? Now, that was the question. I mean, she was, informally anyway. She was a born leader. I looked at the three chins quivering with passion, and knew immediately. The look. She just didn't have it.

We all waited for Eleanor to squeeze out of the tearoom so we could make our own cuppa. I made a chamomile tea to calm my pre-virgin meeting nerves. It was time to face Monica.

It is amazing how quickly things change. The week before the office had felt relaxed, interesting, exciting, chummy. Family. (Well, maybe I'm romanticising just a little.) Today it felt poisonous, like some kind of scary vapour was hanging in the air. I looked around. Chandra and three crawlers from the art department had already established themselves on the prime couch in the office, and all the chairs were taken, so I perched on the edge of the couch. (Big, flowery, fat cushions. Very Geri. So that wouldn't last.) Geri's photos of herself with hundreds of stars had come down and were lying in a pile on the floor, which the painters kept walking over.

Weird paintings lined the walls, ready to go up. One was an amazing portrait of Monica Drawmer, from her – oh no – from her modelling days.

'Yep,' said Chandra. 'She was a massive star in the … well, we'd better not talk about when it actually was.'

The portrait reminded me of Freya, Ben's arty-bitch, and I couldn't help but transfer a bit more of my lingering resentment onto Monica. Wanker, I thought. Who puts their own portraits up in the office? And where exactly was that thing going?

We'd find out after the redecorating was finished, I guessed, looking at the swatches of Tiffany blue on Geri's old desk. Soon there'd be no trace of Geri. Everything was changing.

Monica strode into the room and stood behind her desk, waiting patiently for the painters and decorators to leave. I think I saw one actually tug a forelock.

Well, she did look pretty aristocratic. But this was Australia. Oh. That's right. This was Australia.

'Welcome,' she said, with a glance at her slim, Piaget-dangling wrist. Time-keeping. Oh-oh.

Her suit said everything: Sonia Rykiel, expensive – more than two months of my salary – and very, very serious. Cream! Cream wouldn't last five seconds on me.

'Ideas,' she stated. 'You first,' she glanced at Chandra, who was trying to take a quiet slurp of her tea and failing. 'You're …'

'The features editor, Chandra Wright …'

'Right, Sandra. Go,' she snapped.

Chandra got up and started to leave the room.

'No!' barked Monica. 'Start sharing your … ideas, Sandra.'

Chandra slunk back to the couch, sat down, cleared her throat and began in a tight, high voice.

'I propose we make way,' said Chandra, rallying enough to shoot a meaningful look at me, 'for a brand-new esoteric column …' Dramatic pause. I cringed.

'Indian feng shui …' She looked up, triumphant. I super-cringed. Monica didn't waste any time.

'I'm over feng shui. It's tired, it's homework, it's bullshit,' she snapped, smiling a bitchy little smile at Chandra. 'It is not glam. It is not sexy.'

Chandra actually crumpled. My heart rate went up – and I felt all panicky despite the magnesium I'd taken that morning. I needed valerian!

'You – can you improve on that?'

That was me. God. Chandra didn't need to feel threatened.

'Um. I just finished a story on shopaholics.'

'That's a great way to win over advertisers,' Renata the advertising manager interrupted snidely. 'Make an illness out of consumption.'

Renata and I never did see eye to eye, but she always made me feel like I was being deliberately difficult. I didn't want readers to be suckers, that's all. So I did the brave thing.

I pretended she hadn't said anything.

'Anyway, I'd like to do a party frock workout for …' Silence. Complete vacancy of noise. 'But if you think it's too frivolous … I'm nearly finished.'

'No, no, finish the frock thing. And follow up the shopaholic thing, too.'

Relief flooded through me. 'All right.' Wow, she liked my ideas.

'Not bad. Pay attention, everybody. They're clichés, but they're just the kind of clichés these readers lap up. Anything else?' She looked at me expectantly.

'I want to do a revealing story on plastic surgery. A real exposé. One that will get us in the news.' I suddenly felt a surge of confidence. I mean, this was a good idea. A proper journalistic-type idea. 'One that ...'

'Enough. I get the idea. You're the ... ?'

'Health editor. Meg.'

'Health editor! God, it sounds like we're a hospital. Make that the ... beauty and fitness editor.'

I wasn't sure what to do. Was that a promotion? She was looking at me, impatient, like she thought some kind of response was appropriate. The options seemed to be freeze or nod. So I nodded.

'Next?' she snapped.

God, this was terrifying. You didn't know what was going on – and she seemed so ... impatient and disappointed by all of us. I s'pose she'd had a bigger staff on *Elegance*, probably people with, I don't know, PhDs in politics and fashion. Maybe editing *Gossip!* after *Elegance* was a bit like being told you could trade your Porsche in for a Toyota. Serious downgrading. Like being told your own personal Concorde was confiscated and you had to take the train to work.

'Eleanor?'

'I think we should follow this up,' she said, handing Monica a newspaper clipping. Monica unfolded it gingerly, a look of distaste on her lovely face.

'Hmn. Why?'

'It was in yesterday's *Echo*. It's interesting – what's she got that made so many men respond? If we could find out, we could all get a bloke. I suppose ...'

Oh, no – not the bloody Allison Lonelyhearts story thing. When would it end? I squeezed myself a little further over onto my fraction of the edge of the couch, hoping I wouldn't fall off. The precarious angle made my thighs bulge. Monica looked at me, or maybe my thighs, disapprovingly, before pointedly shifting her flinty gaze to rest on Craig, who nervously handed her the proofs for the next cover.

'That's not bad, Eleanor. Get someone onto it. You,' she said, pointing at the junior writer.

'Tamara,' squeaked Tamara.

'Follow that up would you?'

Subject closed. Nothing would probably come of it. And Monica had already moved on to Craig, who was awaiting judgment on his work.

'This look …' she proclaimed, waving the latest proofs, a super-busy cover with a sexy Pamela Anderson on it, with at least three more racy stories breaking out of the hot-pink background with big shouty letters, '… is stale. Is over. Is not us.'

Craig pulled his brown cardigan a bit tighter around his body in a feeble attempt to defend himself from the onslaught.

'Not only will I have to repaginate today, I will redesign this … out-of-date, irrelevant, tacky magazine. I will see this,' she waved a cover around like a club, 'dragged kicking and screaming into the modern world. Right. Now I know what we're up against, we are going to start redesigning, today. All production and design staff will meet in here at 10.00 a.m. Sandra, come back in here then, too.'

'Chandra,' she muttered. Monica glared at her.

MISS LONELYHEARTS

Chandra's face sagged even further. That meant her precious words would be cut for design.

'You,' she said, vaguely in my direction. I looked up.

Everyone rushed out, glad to leave me behind as official first sacrificial victim. Bastards.

'You stay. Shut the door,' she ordered.

'Plastic surgery is the most under-tapped advertising revenue base in this country. We need that money.'

Oh-oh.

'So, you are going to do a plastic surgery series.'

'Fantastic,' I blurted. 'I wasn't sure you liked the idea. I mean, you didn't say much.' Shut up, I thought, you hate her. But there was no denying the rush of excitement and relief flooding me. I hadn't realised how worked up I'd been.

'Not only are you going to write a fantastic story. About plastic surgery. Cosmetic advances ...'

What? Was I going to be promoted or something? This was unbelievable. I mean, I'd known it was a great idea, but this was unexpected.

'You are going to *get* plastic surgery!'

What? Perhaps I'd had a brain explosion.

'You are going to test the newest techniques.'

'Hahahahaha-oh. Oh. Right. Oh. Right-o. But, well, I'm probably not the best person. I don't have a very strong stomach,' I rambled, horrified at the idea of watching someone's face get cut off and stitched back on again.

'No. Haven't you been listening? *You* will have the surgery.'

'Me?'

'You will write a first-person piece that will be the envy of every magazine around.'

'But. Um. I – I don't want plastic surgery. I probably don't need it. I mean, I'm only twenty-six.'

'Are you saying no to the first assignment I give you? The one that's going to raise your profile and see you on current affairs shows around the nation?' She leant forward and looked me in the eye. Hers were cold. 'Make you famous?'

She leant back again, her voice dropping to a seductive wheedle.

'Besides, it was your idea – we're just developing it into something utterly new and absolutely newsworthy. The fact that you *say* you're only twenty-six makes it more fascinating.'

'I *am* twenty-six!'

'Even better. That's what we want. Not Cher – Jennifer Aniston. Not Jocelyn Wildenstein – Michelle Pfeiffer.'

Okay, that sounded better. Bitch. She was good. I sat back, chewing my lip, looking at her seducing me. She was dangerous.

'Meg, you have ideas.'

Oh, here we go.

'That's a wonderful, rare quality. But things are going to get very tough around here for people who won't go the extra distance for me.' God, she was using that speech-to-the-nation voice again. Is she saying this story would help me keep my job?

'Besides,' she said, looking me up and down in a way that didn't make me feel good. Not good at all.

'Are you really so perfect that you can afford to say no to a touch of self-improvement?'

I stared at her. Now this was getting a bit rude. A bit personal. She was utterly shameless.

'If I were you, I'd look at this as an opportunity – not an assignment,' she smiled tightly. 'I want an outline from you on your story one week from now.'

Isn't what she was saying illegal?

'I only want committed staff.'

Fair enough.

'Health is your area.'

Right again.

'You have to prove yourself to me.'

Maybe I do.

'This is your chance for a fresh start – in more ways than one.' She started to snigger at her own joke.

Can't say I joined in.

I stood up to leave. 'Don't close the door,' she snapped, smilingly. 'Open-door policy.'

Come on, say something, my inner goddess urged desperately. Oprah's voice echoed, merged with Mum's. Fight the disease to please. Say something. Tell her to shove off, my own voice pleaded. 'Tell her to fuck off,' Allison's voice urged. 'Go on – punch her,' Karen's yelled at me.

I didn't say anything. 'Oh, God you're pathetic,' I heard Allison say. 'Be supportive,' my inner goddess chastised her. 'This is a whole new experience.'

I was still standing there, riveted by my inner argument, almost waiting to be possessed by one of the voices. I was fascinated to see what one of them might get me to do. Except nothing really happened. I must have looked like a stunned mullet personified. I wasn't sure I could actually make my legs work.

'You can go,' she said, a bit louder, looking slightly worried, like I was a bit of a psycho. I eased my by now enormous-feeling bum out the door (being repainted Tiffany blue already) and emerged, shocked, into the hum of the office.

I sleepwalked back to my desk. Apparently I wasn't the only one feeling a little odd.

'What's all this?' I asked, wondering why there were about four bunches of flowers sitting on my desk. Chandra didn't answer. She was in no position to answer. Because Chandra was seething. She was slamming things around on her desk, which meant mine was shaking with the impact. All my vitamin bottles were rattling. One bunch of flowers fell over, drooling water all over my important documents (okay, over my free leg wax invite to We Believe.) I grabbed the rest to stop them falling off my desk. It was like *Poltergeist*.

'What's the point in being features editor,' Chandra glared at me, 'if she won't listen. Well?' she demanded.

'Er, not sure. No point at all, I suppose.'

'Everyone *knows* the esoteric sells, and feng is *hot*.'

I don't know about that. I drew the line when Chandra tried to feng my work corner for me.

You should see her work corner.

'And my name's not SANDRA!'

'It's Chunder,' said Julie, checking her face in a groovy compact mirror made of broken glass. 'You'd better shut up,' she nodded in Monica's direction. 'She can hear everything you're saying.'

I couldn't even enjoy the free-for-all that followed that one. I sat down and dialled Allison's number. 'Al,' I said, feeling desperate.

'Oh. You saw the Lonelyhearts story. Sorry, they were hassling me.'

'Al, my boss has just told me to get plastic surgery.'

'What a bitch – I bet she's not so hot-looking.'

'No, for a story. She says I have to test the newest techniques.'

'What?'

'And that I should look at this as a kind of opportunity for a transformation. You know, the ultimate makeover.'

'But you're twenty-six.'

'I know. And she wants the Lonelyhearts story, too.' I leant closer to the phone, whispering. 'Remember – you swore. Promise, even if someone gets a lead, that you won't tell them it's me. Okay?'

'Of course I won't. If anyone is doing this story, it's me.'

I said nothing, in that meaningful kind of way.

'*Joking!* Anyway. I have an idea for the plastic surgery thing. You'll do the story.'

'No way!'

'Listen. A *news* story! You just write down everything that happens. Then we find some hot-shot news journo, or a current affairs show, and expose her!'

'I don't know if I can wait that long. What if I lose my temper and ... stab her with that bloody nail file she kept pointing at me?' I started to laugh. I was still red-hot furious, but I suddenly knew Monica wasn't going to get away with it. And the elation was a total *rush*.

'That's better. Somehow, we're going to make this work for you. You won't have to get things stuck in your face or chop off your nose or get blow-job lips.'

'Brilliant! Thanks Al.' My voice dropped to a whisper. 'I've got all these flowers, too.' I don't know why I was whispering – everyone could see I was surrounded by giant boxes with thrusting blooms.

'Oh ... I got the courier to start bringing some over. There's bunches and bunches here.'

'Send them to a hospital or something,' I hissed into the phone. 'Someone will suspect something.'

'Everyone will think you're popular.'

'Everyone will think I'm doing the advertisers favours,' I muttered, seeing Renata striding through the office towards Julie, who looked like she was going to lose her breakfast. Allison laughed.

'Don't worry. I swore to keep you secret, remember? Bye!'

I stared at my screensaver. The beginning of a huge quaking rage was building inside. She wasn't going to sack me. She wasn't going to torture me either.

Cosmetic advances my *arse*. I was going to turn this into the story of a lifetime. Monica may *think* I'm going to get surgery but she had another thing coming. I was going to reveal them all for the charlatans they were.

And if Monica Drawmer thought I was stupid enough to be working away at the story she wanted, fine. All the better.

I popped an evening primrose oil and a magnesium (good for the skin, crushes PMT, calms the nerves) and started going through the pile of mail that gets dumped on my desk about 11.00 a.m. every morning, after the mail boys have had their ciggies and finally managed to sort it. As usual it was a combination of fantastic surprises – a pair of Sophie Kyron earrings as a thank you for writing a health piece on a model from her agents, all old and dangly and worth about $100 – and completely horrible stuff, like press releases on new breakthroughs for after-dinner wind control. Hair, skin and nail tablets. Didn't need those. (Good hair, skin and nails. It's my inner being that's shredded.) Invitations to pork launches. A back massager. And a sparkly invitation that looked quite promising.

Serendipity had offered up something at last. There was a plastic surgery field trip that evening … in the form of *Phwoar!*'s Sportsmodel of the Year awards.

Let, I thought, grim and determined, the games begin. I hit the speed dial.

'Allison, guess what we're doing tonight.'

CHAPTER SEVEN

It wasn't so much the white-blonde hair, the thickened, fleshy, life-of-their-own pouts, the startled eyes or the high-high heels that amazed me when I walked into *Phwoar!*'s Sportsmodel of the Year awards. It was the fact that these girls could stand at all with implants of that size.

Huge! Think pump-up scooters. Think gigantic loaves rising. Think beach balls. Think bouncy castles. Think ... well, you get the picture. I'm sure you've seen some of those people. Probably in my magazine, actually. But more often in *Phwoar!*. Sportsmodels are models who can't get regular gigs and who end up doing a lot of pin-up work. They're too lush and curvy and implanted and just a wee bit too, um, er ... Right. How to say it? It's not that they're trashy. They're just not at all likely to be in *Vogue* or *Elegance* ... you know what I mean?

'Where have they imported these women from?' asked Allison disbelievingly. 'California?'

'Mattel?' I suggested.

'Whatever, they can't be home-grown.'

Sydney wasn't that sort of place, I thought. *We* never boasted about plastic surgery. *Our* stars still had their original breasts. *We* still thought of massive oversized implants as an embarrassing Americanism. Didn't we?

'Are my breasts a whole lot smaller than I realised?' I asked Allison. Before my eyes, unreachable standards were suddenly being touted as just what every guy expected and wanted. The *Phwoar!* men were, no doubt, the kind of men who laughed at women like me when they removed their bra. Especially if it was a Wonderbra.

Big men. Drinking men. Sports-mad men who only noticed women if their breasts entered a room about five minutes before the rest of them showed up.

'Oh, *now* I get what a sportsmodel is,' Allison said, looking at the issue of *Phwoar!* she'd received in her showbag. 'They're bogans with great tits.' I nodded. She was blunt, but she was right.

My faith in our national identity as a small breast-loving country was shattered as I observed the women who were at the party. They weren't even in the competition — just knocking back the free cocktails and sushi, while wearing tiny bits of glittery material stuck together with sparkly body lotion.

We drifted backstage, went to the loo to reapply our lipgloss, and ran straight into one of the models shooting a vial of collagen into her own lips.

'Does it hurt?' I blurted out before I could cram my fist into my mouth.

'God no,' she said. 'I always carry this.' She proudly showed me a little tube. 'It's anaesthetic cream. Do you need some? You really shouldn't do your own without it,' she said, staring at my lips.

'I don't – they're mine.' I was feeling quite stroppy after Monica Drawmer's insinuations.

'You're lucky, then,' she said in a friendly tone. Her eyes drifted to my bosoms. Not very big, comparatively speaking.

I mean, I've never had cause for complaint. And no-one's actually formally objected to their size.

Asked for their money back.

Laughed out loud.

Told me to keep my bra on.

I was from the 'more than a handful's a waste' school of thought.

She rolled her eyes – and I swear I heard her think: *As if anyone would spend money on those.* You'd have to sue your surgeon. Claim you were undersold.

'You're not here for the contest.' It was a statement, not a question.

'You are?'

'Yep. I'm going to walk out Sportschick of the Year.'

'Oh. Why?'

'I win ...' she said, swivelling round and facing me, and ticking off a list of prizes. She then turned away and bent over right in front of me, revealing a very, very small G-string and everything there was to know about her perfect brown bum.

'What can you see?' she demanded.

I flinched, but bravely checked out the area she was offering up for examination. I was, after all, a professional.

'Er, everything.' That's great. Very snappy response. But what was I meant to be looking for, exactly?

'Is my, you know, looking all right?'

'Yeah – um, really nice, er, clean as a whistle. Not that I've seen that many, mind, so I wouldn't actually take me as the expert here ...'

'Thanks a million, she said, standing up and thankfully turning round. 'You wouldn't want to go out there with some toilet paper or something worse trailing out your date.'

'God no.'

'See ya.'

'See ya.'

'Hey – um, good luck. You know. With the prizes and the dancing and the bending over and everything,' I said. She smiled, and it was a lovely smile. Suddenly she seemed really nice.

'Thanks,' she said, and gave me a friendly little wave goodbye.

'Completely surreal,' drawled Allison. She grabbed my arm and led me out. 'That has to be the opening to your story,' she said urgently. 'That was brilliant.'

I quickly jotted down some notes in my tragic shorthand. 'Damn! I didn't get her name ...'

'Surely one of these guys can tell you. Don't you work with them?'

I looked to where she was pointing and, indeed, the boys from *Phwoar!* were all lined up, on stage. One of them looked embarrassed.

Nick Green. *Phwoar!* deputy art director, I'd seen him before, at the office Christmas party, and at the pub, and we said hi in the lifts. He was always so nice. And I'd looked at his bum. Small. And shoulders – wide. And his tummy. No gut to speak off. Tight. Black hair, in sort of cowlicks, and blue eyes, only dark. He was completely …

'He's gorgeous,' said Allison.

'He's a really nice person, Allison,' I corrected. 'I mean, does everything have to be about looks?'

She looked at me, eyes wide.

'And he's totally rootable,' I said, grinning.

That about sums him up: gorgeous, in a dark-haired, sleepy and blue-eyed, stubbly chinned, well-cut lips, manly, okay, *testosteronic* kind of way. Which does great things for me. Except he didn't look so manly right now. He looked, well, mortified. Sweaty, fidgety, uncomfortable. Like he'd rather be anywhere else.

And exactly like he didn't know where to look.

Which only made me like him more. Is there anything worse than a gorgeous man who loves being the centre of attention? Now, a gorgeous man who looks kind of uncomfortable surrounded by half-naked women – that's a different proposition altogether. That means he has a conscience!

I looked at him again. He would be hating this, I thought, a pang of empathy hitting me in the stomach. What was he doing up there anyway?

MISS LONELYHEARTS

'God the things you magazine people have to do,' Allison shouted in my ears. '*You* have to get plastic surgery – this guy gets to be embarrassed by strippers in front of his colleagues. What don't they make you do?'

Nick Green, embarrassed, his mouth set in a stern line, pushed the sleeves of his long-sleeved T-shirt back, revealing lovely forearms – they're a fetish of mine. I like them solid, and with muscles underneath. Strong, like they could hold you. His were lovely. He was gorgeous. Even if he was surrounded by strippers.

One by one the twelve models for the Sportsmodel of the Year award went nudely, almost, unless you actually count spangly things on a string as clothing, past the editor, the assistant editor, the ring-in celebrity nobody had heard of who was already very drunk, and all of the girls looked exactly the same.

I swear.

The shade of blonde may have been out by a fraction, but not much. I saw a curly blonde, a white blonde, and an ash blonde. A short-haired blonde, a rockabilly blonde, a sporty blonde, a blonde bob with 'Nola' written in silver studs on her ripped off-the-shoulder *Fame*-inspired white T-shirt. Actually, I thought she was Geri Halliwell for a second. But, obviously, she was Nola. I think. It might be the name of a stripper label. Sorry, sportsmodel label. There were other celebrity lookalikes, too. A Gwyneth, a Kimberley, a Madonna circa 'Vogue' and a generous sprinkling of Pamelas. One Jennifer Lopez – well, she was *almost* a brunette.

Not that I have anything against blondes. Nothing at all. I'm one of the true sisterhood – I don't normally hold blonde against anyone.

But these girls were *all* blonde. It was horrible. Then they started dancing, and that completely re-defined horrible.

Rod Stewart's 'Hot Legs' pounded out, and I felt myself start to giggle as the girl I'd seen in the toilets launched herself onto the stage, practically pole-dancing, sliding around and doing the splits and licking her lips, which were looking, I must admit, like the collagen had really done its job. One girl, the rockabilly, started break dancing. Somehow, despite the laws of physics and the cheap fabric, all of their bikinis stayed on. Polyester must be really, really strong. One bent over in front of Nick and he kept trying to avoid eye contact. Brown-eye contact, that is. She sat on his lap, facing him, and scissor-kicked his neck between her long, hard, brown legs, then bent over to face the stage, her hips winding around in a devastating corkscrew effect right in front of Nick's very red face.

The crowd went bestial.

Undoubtedly, my friend from the toilets was the winner, if the animalistic groans and screams from the assorted men who should have known better were any indication. Obviously, collagen had its benefits.

Great, I thought. And jotted down a few notes. She'd be a great contact for my story.

Well, except she looked gorgeous. Never mind. She was a contact. She might have a twin sister who'd been hideously deformed by a plastic surgeon, and maybe she was injecting her own collagen because she didn't trust cosmetic surgeons any more ... or maybe she was a doctor, or maybe ...

Okay, she was a contact. And a good one. It might lead somewhere. After all, she owed me a favour after I'd checked her behind for debris.

Nick looked like his neck hurt a lot. His face was extremely red. I made some more notes. This scene could be the beginning of the story. 'This,' I wrote with a flourish, 'is where plastic surgery can get you.'

A bit pleased with myself, I went to the bar and got a juice out of a bottle with at least ten nasty preservatives in it. Nobody does fresh juices at these places. I made a few more notes – the girls' costumes, their faces, their names and ages, and noticed a couple of big, scary-looking security guards checking me out.

'What are you doing, love?' one asked suspiciously, eyeing my notebook.

'Oh, I said, putting away my notebook, making a mental note to put them in my story, too. JOURNALIST ATTACKED AT NIGHTCLUB FOR PLASTIC SURGERY INVESTIGATION. 'I'm a journalist. I'm covering the event.'

'You're not meant to be taking notes. Have you got a camera on you?' One of them stepped forward. Though I'd laughed at him a moment before, now I felt scared. He was huge. And he wasn't happy.

'Guys, I haven't got a camera, and I am meant to take notes. I'm a journalist.'

'Your bag, love,' one reached out. 'And the notepad. Come on – hand it over.'

I clutched my bag and my notepad to my chest, and took a wobbly step back.

'Get lost,' I said, pissed off. 'I'm doing my job.'

I looked around for some help from Allison, but she was 10 metres and two million light years away with two of the hottest guys in the room. Typical. There would be many tales to tell tomorrow, no doubt.

'Hey,' said a voice. 'What are you doing here? This isn't meant to be a *Gossip!* gig.'

I turned around and saw Nick, grinning, still in an embarrassed kind of way, at me, running one hand through his thick, dark hair. I grinned back.

'Hi guys,' he said to the bouncers, who stepped back, looking uncertain of what to do next. I scowled at them, still clasping my notepad.

'We think she has a camera,' the biggest one said.

'She's fine, guys. She's with my work,' Nick explained, reasonable. But stern.

'I *was* fine,' I hissed at them. The big guys moved off to hassle some bloke who was getting a little too excited by the blondes. Nick looked at me and asked if I was okay.

'I'm fine,' I said.

'Really? Well, you looked a bit …'

'I wasn't scared. They're just …'

'Anyway,' he said, handing me a bottle of water. 'Why are you here?'

'It's a work gig,' I explained, opening the lid and taking a swig. 'I'm researching a story.' No need to tell him I'd been dubbed a great candidate for an extreme makeover by my boss. And that digging up dirt about plastic surgery gone wrong was my one way of wriggling out of it.

'God,' he moaned, dark hair flopping over one eye, 'I didn't think there'd be anyone else from the building here. I was hoping to keep this quiet.'

'Nick – there are TV cameras.'

'I know,' he smiled ruefully. Yum. I love rueful smiles. 'I thought I might have a lucky escape.'

'Nick, can I ask you something?' I said, dragging out my notebook.

He smiled. 'Sure.'

'What was the name of the girl with her legs around your neck? The one who won?'

'Oh,' he said with a laugh. 'Her name? It's, er, Fantasia Jones, I think.'

'No, her name,' I said, laughing with him.

'Oh. I don't know. She's Fantasia. I can grab her details from the event organiser. Most of the girls don't like using their real names – in case readers look them up, you know,' he explained. 'It's important for them to have their privacy.'

I must have looked a bit bewildered. How could you have privacy when you showed your private bits off? Then I mentally slapped myself. Everyone has the right to decide how they'll make a living. And whether they need to keep some things quiet. I waited while Nick went and talked to one of *Phwoar!*'s editorial assistants. He came back with a name and a phone number.

'My neck hurts,' he said, rubbing his shoulder. 'I wasn't told we'd be stunt props for exotic dancers.'

'Are you complaining? I don't get it,' I said.

'You know what it's like. Readers see one thing. We do the work. I didn't realise being a strap-on person was part of my job. I don't know that it should be something I'm doing for work.'

I couldn't have agreed more. I mean, I was supposed to be getting plastic surgery for a story. How bizarre was judging a sportsmodel contest in comparison with altering your face 'cos your boss doesn't like the look of it?

I wondered vaguely if Nick had a girlfriend. It wasn't the first time I'd wondered about him. The last time I'd wondered I'd even checked, and the word was he was seeing someone at work. But I had no idea who. 'He's taken,' Eleanor had said once when she'd caught me checking him out at the smelly pub. That was months back. And he'd seemed a bit ... well, a little sad. So I'd kind of backed off. Anyway, guys like him always had amazingly glam girlfriends – sportsmodel types, usually. Probably that, or someone he worked with at *Phwoar!*. There were some girls on the team. Editorial assistants. And a fashion person, I think. Or bikini co-ordinator?

Anyway, they were all young and drop-dead gorgeous and wore short shorts and nearly gave Big Boss heart attacks whenever he dropped into the office. Which was, I'd heard from Eleanor, rather frequently.

That was the thing with journalists. You inevitably ended up seeing someone at work because no-one else understood the weird hours, the dreadful pay, the undeniably addictive quality of the deadline – or got invited to so many of the same freebie gigs.

'Well, thanks for getting me Fantasia's number,' I said, ignoring the zing in my tummy that kept happening whenever Nick looked at me with those blue eyes. 'I've got to get out of here. If I hear "Hot Legs" one more time …'

'And they're bound to play "You Can Leave Your Hat On" any moment now,' Nick said.

I stopped as I heard the brass opening of Joe Cocker's strip saga starting up.

'Arghhh!' I screamed. 'I have to leave right now.'

'No, don't go,' he said. 'Don't leave me with these hair-removal queens.'

I laughed. No, I twinkled. Was I … flirting with this guy?

'No, really,' Nick said. 'I feel like an idiot here. I don't know what to say to them.'

'Why don't we both go,' I found myself saying. I think I was flirting … Immediately Paranoid Meg stepped in, bossing warm, Flirty Meg about. Who let you out? Shut up!

But she could not be stopped that easily, oh no!

'So … do you want to go for a coffee?' Nick asked.

'Yeah, love to.' Are you serious? Of course I didn't want a coffee – it was nearly eleven o'clock at night and I am an insomniac. But, well, I probably wasn't going to be sleeping anyway … 'I just need to let someone know I'm going.'

I didn't want him to get the idea I was abandoning my best friend, especially as this would not be the first night we'd split up before heading home. Oh no. I looked around for Allison, impatiently (I was keen!) and found her squished up in a corner booth with one of the male model lookalike feature writers *Phwoar!* seemed to employ. (The ones that aren't Travis Fimmel twins look like bikies. Yes, they do. Leathers, tatts, bulging muscles. No, I don't know why, they just do.)

'I'm going for a coffee,' I called out over the music (which by now had turned into ZZ Top's 'She's Got Legs') and Allison turned, her lovely face astonished. 'But you don't …' she started, before she caught sight of Nick. 'Oh. Have a great *coffee*,' she shouted over the music, before turning and whispering something in Travis's ear. He laughed. I gave her a wave, and blew her a kiss. 'Have fun. Bye.'

'Don't tell Dan,' she mouthed at me.

As if I would. I really did not need to get caught in the middle of their bizarre love affair.

Anyway, so that's how I found myself in the Craven with Nick, the big spunk, till very, very late.

It may have been all that caffeine.

It may have been my insomnia.

But it was more likely those blue, blue eyes.

I found myself feeling very awake, and very alive. A bit – *more*, in every way. I was making an effort, but it wasn't an effort. He was funny. I was funny. We had things in common.

I found myself telling him about *Gossip!*. About how I was the health editor, but wasn't exactly a picture of health. I told him about Geri, and he nodded his head and understood. Don't ask how he knew, he just did, okay?

Then he told me about *Phwoar!*

'It's a great place – the guys are fantastic and we have a good laugh every day. But ... it's weird, you know. Everyone thinks you're into these girls when you're not.'

Oh. I saw the light. The penny dropped. I tumbled. Dammit. Dammit! I excused myself abruptly and made a dash to my friend the toilet cubicle. I ripped up quite a few bits of toilet paper in an attempt to take the edge off my disappointment. Shit. He was gay. Of course – that's why everyone at *Phwoar!* was so good-looking, or so like a Harley Davidson club member. They were gay! Nick was gay, and working on a magazine for straight guys – how subversive! It all made sense now. Gay guys were always coy at first, till they'd sussed you out, but they were usually really friendly.

Oh shit. He was hot. And so funny. And kind. And sort of ... well, sweet. Sweet without being drippy. Wow. He was the perfect man.

Except for the gay thing.

Well, never mind, I told myself brightly. He's a great guy. You can never have too many friends, right?

After my realisation I felt a bit numb and I didn't hang around much longer. I pleaded fatigue, which was a big lie, and went home, and didn't sleep at all.

Somehow, underneath the insomnia, was a little voice of optimism that refused to fade away. He's approached you. Not every good-looking guy you meet is gay. It just seems that way.

He's gay, I argued with myself. There's nothing worse than false relationship hope. I knew from bitter experience. I convinced myself that it was silly to have fantasies about a gay guy, to feel this ... this ... crush thing blooming inside when it was destined to lead to misery and yearning and jealousy and a friendship where you acted like you didn't mind when he kissed his girlfriend ... or boyfriend.

I knew all that. Even pulling out my notebook and feeling like, yes, this could be the beginning of a very good story failed to stop the obsessive hamster on the treadmill of my mind.

He's gay!

But if he was, why wouldn't that damn zing fade? God, I was acting like, like ... Tamara.

CHAPTER EIGHT

'I wonder,' I panted to Carla, 'if you can OD on valerian.'

'That's an old lady drug,' she gasped. 'It went out in the seventies – and seventies drugs are not back. Not yet, anyway,' she frowned, sweat trembling on her upper lip.

We grunted and groaned for about a minute without trying to speak before she broke into one of my irregular moans of pain.

'My gran used to be on Valium ... are you having trouble with your nerves or something?'

'Not Valium, valerian. It's a herb, it helps you sleep, relax, *breathe* ...' I'd thought the last bit. I was too knackered to speak in anything but short sharp bursts.

'Anyway, how would I know?' she snarled as she pushed her legs through another cycle on the gym bike. 'You're the health editor.'

It's amazing that exercise sounds so much like sex, when exercise, everyone knows, is the unsexiest thing known to humankind. It gets sexy results, I'm not disputing that, but, my God! Tracksuits. Sweat. Seventeen-year-old editorial assistants from *Phwoar!* wearing short shorts. The mundanity of moving your legs round and round in never-ending circles and grunting around on all fours under fluoro lights, being strapped onto machines that force your thighs apart for the entire advertising department boys to see. Sweat. Stinky trainers. Treadmills. Sneaky perving. Showering afterwards, then having to get dressed in front of your friends or colleagues. Who were all younger/thinner/fitter than you, and had been since you were thirteen.

'Who thought this was a brilliant idea?' I gasped.

'It's important for us to be fit. Then we can do more free overtime and come in on the weekends without having a breakdown,' intoned Carla.

'It's just more competition and pressure, as far as I can see,' I grunted back.

What I didn't say was that exercising with my workmates was far too intimate for me. I drink with my workmates, I slave next to them, I sweat blood with them on deadline and I laugh about Chandra with them. But showering, sweating, *walking around naked*? Getting dressed with? Very close to swapping bodily fluids. Especially if people don't wipe down the machines. Soon we'd be checking out each other's toilet habits.

Carla and I were in the gym. Not just any gym. The work gym, in fact. The horrible truth, which we were actually working out, was enough to put us in a foul mood anyway, but we had no choice but to go there to work out for several important reasons:

MISS LONELYHEARTS

1. No chance of Monica Drawmer, Queen of the Southern Hemisphere Bitches, being anywhere in sight. She would never go to the work gym with us lower magazine life-form bottom-feeders.

2. To work off one week's fury and pent-up aggression at Monica Drawmer, previously mentioned Queen of the Bitches, before terrible violence against her could be done. We didn't want to go down in publishing history as the first women to murder their female boss. Slowly. With a nail file, an exfoliator, some glycolic acid and one perfectly aimed Manolo Blahnik stiletto.

3. To decrease circumference of thighs to increase my chances of enchanting Nick. In case he liked girls. I mean, I still didn't know for certain …

4. To hear the Tall Paul vs INXS single over and over very very loud – it was our work-out song *du jour*. (I still had a soft spot for Michael Hutchence. I couldn't help but feel it was so sad, such a pity that he was dead just when he was making a kind of comeback.)

5. To watch *The Bold and The Beautiful*. Geri used to let us watch it – or at least pretended not to notice we did. Not any more. Monica had *banned* us from watching it – and *ET*! Which just goes to show how completely and utterly clueless she was.

That's why we were at the gym. Not that Carla needed to actually be anywhere near a gym. She was twenty-four and an ex-model. Thin thighs. Snake hips. Large lips. Cheekbones. Perfect shiny black hair – no frizz, not ever, not even when it rained. Great look. Vintage meets pop art.

Carla had plenty of energy for the machines, because Carla was outraged. Monica had been vile to her in this morning's meeting, which made it three mornings in a row. Even Chandra was beginning to look happier now the pressure was off her.

Carla swung prettily off the bike and moved over to the large punching bag that hung from a nasty-looking butcher's hook welded into the ceiling. Venomously, she began to kick the shit out of it. *Thwack.* A great big dent appeared in the bag.

'That's for her saying my ideas are juvenile.' *Crunch.* The impact zone crumpled and the massive, heavy bag swung madly from its hook.

'That's for her being so up herself.' *Pmmmfmph.* Her Adidas had been transformed from fashion statements into killing machines.

Poooom. 'That's for the look on her face. She enjoys telling us off. *Bitch, bitch, bitch, fucking bitch,*' she sang as she belted the shit out of the poor innocent bag with her perfect size-six feet.

I stayed silent, admiring her nightclub bouncer performance. I was totally in agreement. She had every right to be pissed off. Monica Drawmer hadn't been picking on me – not for the last two days, which was a real worry. My theory was that the temporary reprieve from bitch rotation meant she thought she was going to get exactly what she wanted – and I wasn't so sure she wasn't. So far, all my research had unearthed, except for the fabulous self-injecting Sportsmodel of the Year, were happy women all delighted with their lipo, their new large lips, their gargantuan new chests or their freshly peeled skin.

It was time to ring Fantasia and get serious about this.

We dried off inside the shower cubicles, which is also where I put my clothes back on. I had vowed when I started going to the gym never to knowingly appear naked before my colleagues. I am self-conscious enough in a swimming cossie, thank you. I've spent years perfecting my walk down to the water with a towel around my waist, then timed it perfectly to drop it and run for the waves – known as the bum camouflage technique – and I wasn't about to get all naked and unself-conscious in front of people I had to see at the office and at the smelly pub every day.

Carla had no such scruples though. 'Can you see that?' she asked, showing me her perfect little boy's bum. She was pointing at something completely invisible on her peachy left cheek.

Why are women always doing this to me? I wondered. Why do they keep showing me their bums? I must give off mumsy vibes or something.

'It's a stretch mark,' she accused, giving me a tough little look. 'I'm sure of it. Which means,' she added ominously, 'that I've *put on weight*.'

I stopped drying my hair for a second. 'How? You don't even eat. Maybe you've been sucking in some nutrients by walking past the chip shop. Breathing in fat modelcules. Oops, molecules.'

'No,' she corrected, pulling on her Collette Dinnigan corset top (cheap, really, I'd been told, if you knew where the sample sales were). 'It's got to be those vitamin pills you gave me. I checked the label and they've got *other things* in them.'

Which brought me back to the valerian thing. I'd been taking a lot of them lately, but they didn't seem to be working. Which was very, very scary.

I wasn't sleeping much at all. There was a reason — or a few of them. The changes at work, this damn feeding frenzy of men wanting this Miss Lonelyhearts chick, and now the twangs of something that occurred when I looked at Nick, or thought of Nick, or caught a glimpse of Nick in the lift, especially when he did cute things like stretch and grin, and his shirt would pull out of his pants and reveal a gorgeous snaky line of sleek sexy dark hair stretching down towards everything that was *strictly* out of bounds to a neo-virgin like myself, a practically full-time and very devout practising celibate like me ... He made me swoon. That hair (dark, floppy, just a bit too long). His sleepy eyes (blue, like dark blue. Like the ocean with clouds over it). His slow grin. His look of ... genuine interest. Men who were friendly and enthused and eager weren't meant to be attractive — they were meant to be hideous. But he was attractive and gay, probably, or a male slut, I moaned to myself.

Which reminded me. I needed to do the office poll thing.

'What do you think,' I asked Carla, 'of men you can dance in front of in your underwear, offer your sexual bits up for speculation, and who then sort of shrug it off?'

'They're gay,' she said.

I must have looked a bit deflated, 'cos she popped her lovely slim arm around me and gave me a little squeeze.

'So,' I started, because I really wanted to be sure. 'Let me get this straight. If ten girls are lap-dancing around him …'

'Hmnnn,' she said, just like she was a psychiatrist.

'Ten girls who look like Pamela Anderson's skinnier, prettier younger sister. And he can walk when he gets up …'

'He's Not Interested In Women,' she concluded for me. 'At least, not women as we know them, Meg. Unless of course,' she furrowed her pretty pointy brows, 'he can't get it up. In which case, you're better off leaving that for some other girl to solve.'

'God, why aren't you the sex writer on this magazine?' I asked in admiration.

'Because I already get as many free samples of men as I like,' she said with a toss of her shiny hair and a little cat-grin. 'It's make-up and designer clothes that are really hard to come by.' She winked and said, 'Come on, let's get back upstairs. Something else might have happened.'

Clever girl, I thought, following her as we walked up the stairs – incidental exercise is very important. I was bursting with admiration for her. Only twenty-four, and already so wise, as well as perfectly sized.

How did she get to be so … *together* about everything?

I reluctantly dawdled back to my desk after the gym, having decided Nick must be gay and that I should stop torturing myself. I was, comparatively speaking for me, you understand, charged with resolve. Until ...

'Hey, didn't you go to this thing last night?' asked Julie, who was reading, actually, flicking through *The Echo*.

'What? What thing?'

I looked over her shoulder. There was a picture of the dancer we'd seen in the toilets shooting up collagen, a hideous close-up. She looked ... stupid.

'Oh! Yes. Not a good picture,' agreed Eleanor.

'Not a good look,' corrected Max.

Oh, Ali, I sighed. You wouldn't. No way. I scanned the headline.

THE *PHWOAR!* OF THE CROWD

Ali hadn't told me she was doing a story. She hadn't told me she was carrying a camera. She must have gone straight back to the office and filed at about 11.00 p.m. to meet *The Echo*'s deadlines. Then I saw the caption. 'Keep her away from heaters: Miss *Phwoar!* Sportsmodel of the Year shows why surgery among strippers, models and exotic dancers is reaching meltdown point.'

'Ali!' I said, feeling dizzy. 'That's my story.'

The phone rang. I grabbed it. '*Gossip!*'

'Did you see my story?' Allison said, excited.

'Your story? I know you never let a fact stand in the way of a good story, but that was my piece.'

'No, no, no, have a closer look, you're doing some kind of ... big thing, aren't you. I just did a small colour piece. And I had to come up with something to get them off my back about the Miss Lonelyhearts story. Seriously – the editor's screaming for more and this was the best I could do.'

She had a point. Sort of.

'Yeah, but Fantasia's my contact – and the caption summed up some of my story.'

'Oh that – but did you read the story? It's not about plastic surgery – the story's about modern man's need to have tribal activity. The photo editor chose the shot, and some stupid sub wrote the caption. Sorry.'

'But it makes out that she's …'

'Well, come on, we did see her shooting up collagen in the toilet. Hey, do you think they'll start doing fluoro lights like at your smelly pub so people can't …'

'Shoot up like they're junkies?' We were finishing off each other's sentences again. My pissed off-ness was melting.

'I notice you got another byline.'

'I was really pleased. One day I might …'

'Yeah, yeah, the picture byline.'

'It's important I get it before I'm thirty. Then I can get the gig on TV.'

I'd heard this fifty million times before, so I wasn't really tuning in.

'Anyway, Dan rang. I'm meeting you all at the smelly pub tonight. I can tell everyone about all your boyfriends.'

'Don't you dare!' I shouted into the receiver.

She'd hung up. I slammed the phone down.

I looked around. Everyone was getting back to work, or getting back to avoiding work. Monica was in a meeting. All I had to do was look busy and I had at least an hour to workshop my life on-screen.

'Okay,' I muttered to myself, 'so how do I start sorting out the mess that is my life?' I pushed aside some of the recent flower arrivals, and began hammering away at my keyboard.

Chandra looked up. I smiled feebly. She frowned.

First way to sort out life: Do not talk aloud to yourself, Meg.

Actually, the best method I had heard of whenever things were getting really bad was to write a list. Up until a few days ago I'd never read a self-help book. Well, technically I still haven't read one – I don't think five pages counts. I mean to, as research for my job, you understand, but what with Oprah and my mother and my father and my sister all quoting bits of self-help teachers to each other like it was a language I should have done at school, I hadn't really had to. I could just ... listen, and feel a bit sorry for them.

But the list thing made sense. It's something my dad, an avid reader of positive thinking and Dale Carnegie, advocated.

First you wrote the list. Then you wrote down what you could do about the things on your list. Then you wrote out the pros and the cons of each possibility. The pluses and the minuses.

I had always rolled my eyes on principle at Dad's 'you can do anything' speeches, but very, very secretly I agreed with him. At least about the list. It's just that I'd never made one before. But, given that I'd recently bought a Louise L Hay book, wasn't it about time I started to heal my life?

MISS LONELYHEARTS

It was amazing. Just by buying the book and leaving it in its trendy see-through bag next to my bed, the positive energy had osmosed through the plastic and through my hair, my skull and into my brain, and I was now open to thinking in a new way.

It was true, I thought to myself in a rush of post-gym endorphins. I can heal my life!

CHAPTER NINE

Fired with the fervour of a person who'd just discovered the fun to be had by thinking your life better, I started to make a list on my screen.

Okay.

I typed *Problems* in an energetic flurry. Then I underlined it. Then I bolded it.

No, I thought. That's too negative. Delete *Problems*, replace with ... *Opportunities*.

'No,' I muttered, 'that's New-Age sick-making speak.'

I swear I heard Chandra's shoulders creak as they moved together, then shifted a little higher. I think I heard the sound of teeth beginning to grind.

'Cross that out. Definitely *Problems*.' Julie was looking over my shoulder, her face about 3 inches from my screen.

'Piss off,' I whispered in a friendly kind of way.

'Oooh, secrets?' she said with a desperate lunge at my computer.

'Shhh! Chandra hissed at us both.'

'God, Chunder, it's not a library,' Julie fumed.

MISS LONELYHEARTS

'Some of us,' intoned Chandra like an aggrieved, potentially psychotic, social worker, 'are trying to concentrate.'

'On what – the position of Uranus?' Julie retorted.

No, not very funny, but somehow comforting. Chandra had been reading her horoscope on screen.

Good, Julie had snapped at her, winked at me, then wandered off to see what Eleanor was doing near the photocopier. At last! Free to continue.

Problem number one. I looked around furtively, trying to see if the scary editor was in her office. Nope. Obviously at some lunch getting pissed so she could come back and tell us to change everything.

I tapped in *Monica Drawmer*.

I toyed with the idea of bolding it and putting her name in 24-point type, but thought better of it. Someone – like the editor – would see it. She had very good hearing. Scary hearing. So she could probably see more powerfully than most human beings, too. She probably had hyper-senses, making her psychic or something.

Anyway. Description of problem.

Monica Drawmer is a bitch.

A powerful bitch. Insane? Better dressed than I could ever afford to be?

Was it that she intimidated me with her excellence? Professionalism? I asked myself, desperately trying to find a reason for everyone hating Monica besides her being an utter cow-faced bitch.

But there wasn't. It wasn't as if I'd never been bollocked by my boss before. Geri had been an angel when it came to encouragement, like a coach for your job, even though she had made me cry once or twice when she'd looked at me and said, 'You're twice the writer you think you are. Go and do this again. Give it the courtesy of a little time.'

And when I'd been through my chronic late arrival phase, she'd sent me home one day.

'Just go home,' she'd said when I'd turned up at 10.45 a.m. for the third time that week. 'Be off with you. I'm going to send you home every day you do it. Until you can get in here at 8.45 a.m., you don't need to bother coming in.'

'Am I sacked?' I spluttered, tears welling up, blinking furiously to stop them spilling over.

'No. Not yet. But you're being lazy. I didn't think I'd given a lazy girl this job. It's too important. If I've made a mistake, I will have to let you go.'

'God, she's ballsy,' said Allison, her voice tinged with awe when I phoned her in tears.

'Yeah,' I sniffed when I went over to see her at work. 'And I've fucked up my job.'

'It's easy to fix,' Allison said thoughtfully. 'Just prove her wrong.'

'How?' I moaned melodramatically.

'Well …' and she explained.

I got in the next day at eight-thirty, and pretty consistently ever after.

Geri never mentioned it again. But it took me ages to get the nerve to ask her for a pay rise. 'Oh Geri. I want you back,' I thought, getting a bit choked up. 'I want you back to rouse on me if I'm stuffing up. I'm young. I can learn.' I started to get carried away.

God, my attention span was even more goldfish than ever. Concentrate!

Problem with Monica Drawmer.

She wants me to get plastic surgery for a story.

Enough said, really. Looking at it on screen like that made my other selves start clamouring. Tell her to get fucked! they roared. 'Shush,' I said aloud again. Chandra's shoulders creaked and tightened up another notch, but she didn't say anything.

'God, you are so heading for cancer,' I muttered under my breath.

She turned around and gave me The Death Look.

Oh no – had she heard me? I was no good at all at bitchy self-assertion. I immediately suffered massive guilt and paranoia.

'Did she hear me?' I mouthed at Carla.

'Who cares?' She mouthed back. 'She's a mental case.'

Okay. Back to my list. I really needed to concentrate.

'Do you know,' I heard Chandra whispering furtively into the phone, 'that they're both Geminis?'

I stopped my list-making for a second to listen to whatever crazy conversation she was having now.

'Okay, so I mumble mumble mix the patchouli with the cat pee ...'

My ears pricked right up. Cat pee? 'Then some kitty litter ... okay mumble mumble sprinkle it around her desk mumble mumble,' she continued.

What was she on about now?

'I'm going out,' she announced abruptly, hanging up, then looking around in the style of a guilty criminal about to go into a police line-up, before shoving her wallet into her horrible big pink plastic carry-all that we once attached as a freebie to every issue of *Gossip!*. We were all too embarrassed to use it, but Chandra seemed to think it: a) shows loyalty, and b) is quite a handy size, really.

All defiant, she addressed us, taking a deep breath. 'I have to … do … I have to go. I'll be back … soon. Probably. Tell Monica I'm doing some research if she asks … if she gets back,' she added resentfully.

Wow. Chandra being unpredictable. Something to look forward to later. She'd been outdoing herself since Monica humiliated her in that first meeting. Plus it gave her someone else to loathe, apart from me. Though I knew she'd never forgive me for the Great Pay Rise debacle.

You see, I had received a pay rise six months after I started. Yes, despite the saga of the late arrivals. I must have done something right. But the point was, my pay rise was bigger than the pay rise Chandra received. I'd been there for five minutes. She'd been there for seventeen years. Payback, in the form of nasty looks and bitter tones, was inevitable.

But now she'd forgotten all about hating me. Ever since she'd found out that Monica and Big Boss were both Geminis she'd been obsessed with trying to change her negative karmic path with those astrological signs. When she wasn't bitching about Geminis, that is.

She'd bought all these dangly things to put around her desk to protect her from the brown spikes of negative energy she said emanated from Monica's office. They were driving Monica spare. I could see her flinch every time she walked past a plastic dragon and the picture of the Dalai Lama.

As soon as Chandra disappeared, someone walked over to her desk and poured water over the incense.

'Pong!' said Eleanor. 'She's losing it. She's completely twisted. She – ooh, what are you doing?'

'Working,' I glared, as scarily as I could. She raised one perfectly arched brow and sashayed off.

That's right. Problem number two.

Fancy boy who is gay.

Problem number three.

Best friend has set me up with hundreds of men I haven't been introduced to in a potentially humiliating act that has clearly indicated that there are dreadful flaws in our friendship.

So I'll need new friends, I thought tearfully. I can keep Carla, though she thinks I should stop wearing vintage to work. Or is that a friendship crime, too? I wondered. Maybe she's just jealous.

Problem number four.

Was cruelly dumped by one and only true love.

Problem number five.

Cockroaches are in the fridge.

Okay. Stop. Right. There. 'Focus, Meg. Focus,' I muttered furiously to myself. Carla giggled. Julie snorted. '*Focus Meg, focus,*' they chanted.

All right.

Okay.

Concentrating now.

The next thing I had to do was look at the pros and cons of each problem. Actually, is that right? Was that it? Or did I have to write the solutions, then write the pros and cons of each solution?

Or did I have to look for the good in all the problems – the silver-lining thing?

God, I couldn't remember. Maybe I could ring Dad, I thought, squeezing my sparkly stress ball. No. I had to do this on my own. It was part of growing up.

Right. Okay. Start with solutions.

Monica Drawmer.

Write revealing newspaper-irresistible story on how she's bullying her young staff into plastic surgery because she's a jaded old hag. Hack. Hag.

Problem with solution: might lose job and need the money and don't know how to do anything else.

Possible solution #2: *Get bad plastic surgery, sue doctor and make a fortune.*

That could be quite good, I mused. I could live in splendour in my rustic cottage for the rest of my life with a gorgeous sequinned silk bag, Fendi or something, over my head. Plus I'd have a really good reason for being single.

God. This list wasn't going all that well.

Okay. Possible solution #3: *Can expose her, keeping my nerve, keep job and make enormous sum selling my story to the tabloids.*

That was much better.

Next, I typed, feeling like I was really getting somewhere at last.

Boy problem. Ask Nick out, I wrote down. It was as if something had just guided my hands to tap that out. I hadn't consciously thought it or anything.

Just ask him out. Then you'll know. And if he is gay, you can laugh about it afterwards.

God, I was channelling some kind of inner emancipated sex goddess. Not likely.

Don't be pathetic. He can only say no. Ask him out.
No!
Well, then, prepare to be miserable for the rest of your life.
No!
Well, ask him out.

I was actually typing this down. Wow. Maybe I had some kind of John-Forbes-Nash-as-played-by-Russell-Crowe-type syndrome. Not that this was exactly like having two personae, and I wasn't actually seeing people or anything, or even being a mathematical genius, if my credit rating was anything to go by, but it was the only explanation I could think of that seemed to make sense.

Or maybe I wanted to ask him out. A lot.

Maybe this being timid thing, in fact being single altogether was just … a habit.

Exactly. It's a habit!

There they were, the words, straight from my other Self to the screen.

Just pick up the phone, dial his extension and see what he's doing.

Okay then. All the articles I'd ever done on panic attacks suggested I was actually having one.

I grabbed a leftover brown paper bag from lunch and practised a bit of deep breathing – not too much though or you hyperventilate even more – and started my mantra that I'd taught myself for moments when I couldn't breathe and my vision went fuzzy and I couldn't speak.

Yes, I did feel like a complete dickhead, so no, you don't have to worry that I was turning into Chandra. It's just that sometimes you grasp at straws.

'This is safe. This is a very safe thing to do,' I said under my breath.

'Hi!' I opened my eyes and felt my cheeks beginning to flame. Wow, it must have worked. It was Nick.

'What are you doing?' he asked, all smiley and friendly and gorgeous. Then he saw all the flowers.

'Wow, someone's popular.'

'Oh, them. It's just some research.'

I quickly tried to close the document with my list on it and swung my chair around to face him. Then I perched up higher just in case my list was still on the screen so he couldn't see my embarrassing conversation with myself. My chair wobbled under me and he grabbed my arm to make sure I didn't fall. Strong hands. Very strong. Mmmmm.

'I think you've frozen your screen,' he said helpfully. 'Look, you just hit …'

'Noo, don't,' I said desperately, blocking his view. 'It's um, important research. Secret project,' I added importantly. Phew. God bless improvisation classes at school.

I must really fancy him, I thought. I'm making a complete idiot of myself.

'Research.' He was grinning, with that one-eyebrow-up-one-eyebrow-down look that people make when they think you're amusing and you have no idea why. My list was shutting down. Phew. He was still staring at my screen. I felt completely flustered, and started shuffling papers around ... He was standing there, riveted by what looked like my email list.

Oh God. There were about eighty 're Miss Lonelyhearts' emails there.

'Well, come on then, a juice?' he asked. God, how boring did he think I was? No-one ever understands exactly why I wouldn't want to drink, no matter how filthy their hangovers or horrible the people they wake up next to are. It's just so normal to get pissed. I had a sudden inspiration.

'The pub?' I barked desperately. Anyway, maybe I could get some real info out of him after he had a few drinks.

'It's daytime,' he said and laughed. 'Come on, I'll get you a cake,' he suggested, his face going all sunny again.

'What kind of cake?'

'Carrot.'

'Make it a Portuguese tart and I'm yours,' I twinkled. Oooh, I was flirting. 'Okay.'

How cheesy was I? Why couldn't I be slick and cool?

But strangely, instead of bolting, he gave me one of those glances that looked like it was meant to convey that he thought I was funny. There was a little smile playing around the left side of his mouth. Nice mouth, I thought. Great skin, I thought again, eyes wandering all over his face. Loved great skin on men. It was because of all that exfoliating, Carla told me. Every time they drag that razor over …

The thought of him standing in front of his mirror in the morning with just a towel, a nice towel, clean and fluffy, possibly a dark, rich blue, dragging a razor over his stubble seemed to be almost verging on a possible sexual harassment case if I continued.

'Funny. I thought you were the health editor,' he teased.

'Of *Gossip!*,' I clarified.

'No, really.' He lowered his voice and looked around. 'Coming?' He looked a bit impatient. Quite stern. Hmmm. Sexy. I liked guys who became a little disapproving when you went a bit too far.

But what had I done? Hmmmn. A mystery.

'Sorry. You're serious. Okay. No problems. I could really do with a coffee.'

I looked up. Carla was staring at him. 'Gay?' I mouthed at her.

She shook her head. He turned away, and I noticed Julie silently pretending to have an orgasm, her face all mad.

I stifled a giggle. Not quite, and he turned around. Julie had to convert her pretend orgasm face into a pretend massive yawn.

'Gay?' I mouthed at her.

She shrugged her shoulders in reply. Then

MISS LONELYHEARTS

I noticed scary Monica Drawmer was standing behind me. Bitch.

'I'm just going to have a coffee with my associate,' I said to her, vaguely indicating Nick. Julie and Carla started to frantically pound their keyboards in fake work mode. It actually just signalled the gossip method had switched to email.

'Where's Chandra?' Monica asked bossily, spiking her way across the floor in ludicrously high heels. No good at all with our horrible scuzzy carpet.

'Out on a story,' I said in a sharp professional tone, at the exact same time as Julie said, 'She's in the toilet,' in a slack, why-would-you-care-anyway-bitchface tone.

'Tell her to come in, when she gets back,' she snapped at both of us. 'I can't believe this place.'

Tamara shrank into her desk as she said, 'God, I just know someone's going to be out next week.'

'I'm off then,' I said. Nick was staring at Monica. Disturbing.

'Come on.'

'Nice for some,' I heard the art guy who wears the brown cardigan mutter as I walked past.

'I'll be back in ten,' I said firmly.

God. Vikram the sub winked at me as I left.

You could never do anything in this place without it turning into a major display for the working public.

When I got back, everyone looked at me. But they didn't say anything. Okay, so it had been more like an hour. 'That Nick,' I said loudly to no-one in particular, 'has some great health contacts.'

I sat down and then I stood up again. Where was Chandra's desk? There was an enormous shrubbery-type arrangement where once had sat my colleague. Was this some kind of camouflage whereby some shrubbery would hide the gap left by the sacked one, giving the illusion that there were still plenty of people here, or that we were elite troops fighting an unseen enemy in the jungle ... or something?

Julie and Carla started spluttering. Max came up to me and said, '"Make it a Portugese tart and I'm yours?" Are you serious?'

'You like him,' said Julie.

'You *like* him,' Carla repeated.

'Of course I like him. He's a perfectly nice person,' I objected, crossing my arms across my front, uncrossing them, crossing my legs and turning huffily to busily tap at my PC, which wasn't on.

'And he's gorgeous,' Carla said.

'You think so?' I couldn't help myself. I was ridiculously pleased. Carla was notoriously picky.

'Oh, he is,' said Max, winking in a frenzied Benny Hill-type style.

'And he's *straight*!' I yelled, punching the air in victory. 'And we're going *out*!'

Everyone burst into warm applause. I did a little twirl and curtsied. My smile was beginning to hurt my face.

'I told you he was straight,' Carla said, like she'd never suggested he wasn't.

'No you didn't. You said he was probably gay,' I said, my face all screwed up in the I-can't-believe-you-just-said-that face people make when they've just heard something they can hardly believe.

'I hadn't seen him then,' she insisted. 'The second I saw him, my gay-dar was off. He's sooo straight.'

'Oh, he's not, you know,' Max hinted darkly. 'He's gay. He just doesn't know it yet.'

'What?' I demanded. 'How do you know?'

Max laughed. 'Gets them every time,' he chortled.

'STRAIGHT! He's STRAIGHT! And we're going OUT!' Wow, one coffee and this happens. No wonder I don't seem to drink any more – if coffee is enough to set me off imagine what alcohol would do! Though I was almost feeling like having a victory drink at the smelly pub.

'Straight straight straight,' I sang madly, plopping down at my desk and deleting the crazy files I'd worked on before.

If this problem could be solved, so could anything. Who knows? I might not even have to get plastic surgery.

As soon as the coffee buzz wore off I started to be able to hold a thought.

'Hey, what's happened? Who's redecorated?' I asked to no-one at all. 'Is Chandra in there? Where are you?' Chandra's desk was totally veiled with giant spiky plants and a huge ox.

'She was born in the Year of the Ox, and that cow Chandra has gone out to bloody Home and bought every feng cure she can think of,' said Julie with her nose all screwed up.

'Where is she now?'

'With Eleanor. Eleanor's encouraging her. She's hoping it will drive M round the twist,' said Julie.

'M?'

'Check out the door.' She shrugged towards the Tiffany-blue box that used to be Geri's office.

There was indeed a giant M on the editor's door.

'She thinks she's Madonna,' Julie drawled.

'She hasn't got a Guy Ritchie though,' I said, half to myself.

'She might,' said Eleanor thoughtfully, waddling past me and dumping a bagful of apples on her desk. 'I saw your bloke having a bit of a chat to her on his way back. And he is straight, by the way.'

I didn't respond. As if I was admitting to him being my bloke! I changed the subject.

'Where's Chandra?'

'Dunno. I was trying to help her choose some wind chimes and she muttered something about needing some space.' She nodded towards Monica's door. 'Did you hear she's thinking of changing the magazine's name?'

'To what?' we gasped.

'*M*, of course.'

Monica must have super-hearing, because even though we were semi-whispering, it was at that precise moment that she exploded out of her office. She stood before us, arms clenched by her side, teeth practically grinding.

'As you know, we have to make some sacrifices round here. Drake Norman will be through shortly to tell us of some very ... exciting plans for the future.'

'Oh God,' moaned Tamara. 'It's the first sacking.'

'Floor. Five minutes.'

'Oh God, she didn't deny it.'

'All right, who's here?' Eleanor stood up and started organising the troops.

'God she's great,' I said admiringly to Julie.

'I think we should call her Maximus,' Julie replied.

I couldn't help myself. I was crying with laughter. 'Cos she did look like Russell Crowe's red-headed bigger sister marshalling the forces.

'Look, smarties,' she said to us, oblivious to the cause of our hysteria. 'Let's get everyone together. Come on. We're supposed to at least support each other through this. Max, Carla, me, Julie ... Tamara, good. What about the art department? Okay, Brian, Craig, Ross ... all here. Subs desk: Amanda, Frieda, Norman, Vikram. Okay ... shit, that's right ... Chandra's not here.'

Big Boss strode into the room, with Norman Drake (the smug management guy) and Monica straggling behind.

'Hello, people,' he intoned.

'Where's Chandra?' I muttered. I knew she hated me and sometimes I wanted to set her on fire, but I didn't want to see her get humiliated again. At least not this badly. Not by Monica.

'I'm going to look for her,' I muttered to Julie, who stared at me, making throat-slashing gestures.

I wandered quickly through the offices, ducking into the toilets, looking under the doors. Then I heard a weird noise and, God, smelt an even weirder smell coming from under the storeroom door.

I walked carefully up to the door, sniffing suspiciously, like a beagle with a bomb alert bag.

It smelt a bit like pot.

I nudged the door open a crack.

There, crouching in a circle of white stuff, maybe cocaine, was a trance-like Chandra, muttering away, waving a stick of burning herbs around her head, a photo of Monica Drawmer stuck in a plateful of mud in the middle.

'Ahem,' I said, trying to gently awaken her from her occult zombie state. No response.

'Chandra,' I whispered.

She was still mumbling gibberish.

'Chandra!'

She started, maybe thinking that voices from another world were trying to make contact. She blinked a few times, stunned, her mouth hanging open.

'Chandra, there's a really big meeting happening. Come on. You can't not be there – they might notice.'

She suddenly got all stern and busy, stubbed out her herb thing, and huffily pulled off a purple robe with a giant silver pentacle painted on the front.

'What are you doing?' I said. 'Look, never mind.'

'How d-d-dare you interrupt a private religious ceremony,' she stuttered.

'Sssh,' I said. I could hear the Big Boss's minion droning away in the background. 'They can probably hear you.'

'I'm casting a spell,' she said. 'And if you hadn't walked in, everything would have been all right.'

MISS LONELYHEARTS

'God, whatever,' I snapped. She was really beginning to annoy me. 'I just didn't want you to get into too much strife. God. Play with your herbs. Get sacked. Or arrested. Set fire to the building. Anyway. Don't care. Goodbye.'

I slammed the door, face all red, feeling really pissed off. It was one thing for Chandra to be such a complete sulky bitch most of the time. But when I was trying to help her out a bit ... well, fuck her. She could get busted by someone else doing a stupid occult thing with poo or mud and cocaine or whatever it was in the beauty cupboard, I thought vengefully, stomping back to the meeting. Luckily, the bloke from HR was still talking.

'As you know, a week ago we announced that cuts were going to be made unless the performance of *Gossip!* could be turned around. And turned around fast. So today, I'm going to read the sales figures to you.

'We have sold 672 000 copies this week. Monica's first issue was ... up by 2000 copies on the previous week. Not quite up to expectations. The targets we set here are ... ambitious.'

Monica smiled weakly. She seemed to be about to be sick.

'But ... we must still make sacrifices. Monica's the first to admit that.'

That sounded exactly like a threat.

Chandra snuck in and stood at the back of everyone. She was a bit whiffy, her hair was all mussed, and there was a smudge of ash on her nose. Monica stared at her. A brief look of shock flickered across her face before she planted her inner-corporate-robot-trademark-fake-composed-smile back on.

'The second announcement we have to make today is that one of you is going to be leaving soon.'

Part of me felt excited. If it was me, I wouldn't have to get the stupid plastic surgery, and I could totally avoid any confrontation at all! Success!

'It is with great sadness that I announce,' he fumbled and shuffled a piece of paper, 'Vikram Boon will be leaving us …'

We all gasped. Chandra swayed, making a choking sound, and Vikkie caught her, gallantly.

We were all in shock.

Vikram was the best sub in the business. Okay, at least in the *Gossip!* office. How were we ever going to hand in sloppy copy again? Who was going to fact-check our stories? Write funny captions that also contained pertinent facts?

'Oh no,' moaned Julie, her head dropping into her hands dramatically. 'Not Vikkie.'

'We're going to have to work so much harder,' Tamara wailed.

And I'm still going to have to figure a way out of this stupid story, I thought. Damn.

Vikram, who had, I realised, been in and out of Monica's office over the last few days, grinned and waved at us.

'God, he doesn't look that sad at all,' I said to Carla.

'Redundancy payout,' Eleanor hissed through the side of her mouth. 'He's been here for seventeen years. Add it up.'

So that's why he looked so jaunty. And why Chandra looked so … devastated.

'Time to go, people,' Monica ordered as Big Boss and his boring lapdog made their way to the corporate bar or boardroom or whatever.

'Come on, Vikram,' announced Eleanor with a death glance at Monica Drawmer. 'Let's go to the smelly pub.'

He happily led us off. Leaving Monica standing there, looking kind of … annoyed, and … terrified?

CHAPTER TEN

Oh sorry. You want to know what *actually* happened with Nick.

You know how it is when something extremely significant takes place. It can take a while to tell anyone about it. It's so precious, and you just want to hug it to yourself for a while, see if it amounts to anything, so if it doesn't it's still perfectly preserved, and untainted by the humiliation of publicly deflated hopes. I'm big on avoiding shame and humiliation. In case you hadn't realised.

Anyway. I truly needed a bit of time before I told anyone about the details. I told Allison a few things. But no-one else has heard the full story.

Here's the whole thing. Just as it happened

He was so upfront. It was fantastic, but I found the fact that I liked him so much, so soon, a little intimidating. I mean, I was used to obsessing over Ben, and freaking out over being set up by my best friend. But here I was, feeling … drawn to someone I knew, but didn't know at all. I mean, that was unusual for me, you have to understand.

MISS LONELYHEARTS

'Can you keep a secret?' I'd asked him when we sat down. I was grinning like a ... well, like a loon.

'Sure,' he said, laughter in his eyes.

I leant in.

'My boss wants me to have plastic surgery.' I sat back so I could get a good look at the look on his face.

'What?' The look on his face was excellent! He was shocked. And a bit ... angry!

'She thinks it'd be a good story,' I explained. 'What do you think?'

'What is this? *Extreme Makeover*? Don't you dare touch a thing,' he said, kind of worked up. Kind of attractively worked up.

So I explained the set-up to him. And my plan to counterattack the evil editor.

'That's why I was at the *Phwoar!* thing,' I confided. 'I thought there would be some girls there who'd ... you know.'

'Well, I think you're right. We see a lot of girls with ...'

'Breast implants? How do you know?' I said, a bit aggressively. Whoa, girl! He looked embarrassed.

'They just look ... fake, you know,' he said.

I wanted to tease him about it. But I didn't. He was too cute. And I was a bit pissed off he was able to tell the difference between fake ones and, well, natural bosoms. What, I thought suddenly, would he think of mine? I flushed at my own thought. I tried to listen to him again, despite feeling flustered.

'I probably do have some contacts for you. There're some girls I know who said they were really unhappy with the jobs they had.'

'They tell you this?' I was surprised.

'Well, yeah. I cast for most of the shoots.'

'Oh ...' Yuk. Was he sleazy? He didn't seem sleazy. But best to check.

'Does everyone want your job?'

'They say they do – but they're secretly relieved it's me. Look, I know what you're thinking. "How can he do this job? Casting women to pose nude. Designing layouts."'

'It's not any of my business.'

'Well, it is. It's okay to ask. I mean, we're friends, right? And so ... no, I don't sleep with them. And no, I don't make them take off their clothes. Yes, I do have to look at nude shots of them, test shots. No, I don't keep any of the shots. And you know what? They don't really ... God, this sounds lame. They don't really, um, do anything for me.'

He rubbed his neck again. 'God, that sounds like I'm insulting them. I'm not. It's just not ... it doesn't affect me.'

'So ...' I said thoughtfully. 'Do you have a pulse?'

He threw his head back and had a really good laugh at that. I could see his Adam's apple moving through his beautiful skin, with the bits of man-stubble sticking out. Grrr. I wanted to rub my face against those stubbly bits. Like a cat on a scratching post. I suddenly felt like the best way for me to spend the rest of my life would be making Nick Green laugh. It was that satisfying. He stretched out his arm to me.

'I do. I swear I have a pulse. Feel it.'

I reached out my fingers, in slow motion. It seemed really very rude. And exciting.

I know! It *had* been a while.

I felt it, grinning shyly.

'And I swear I am in no way at all interested in those girls. And I don't mean "those girls" like it sounds. I mean,' he said, leaning in close, 'that I am in no way interested. Got it?'

'Yeah,' I said, feeling ready to move forward and kiss him, like we were in some old black-and-white movie. But before I could do something silly, like close my eyes and tilt my head back for a kiss, a look of uncertainty crossed his blue, blue eyes and he shifted back in his seat.

'So.' I cleared my throat. Time to be sensible. 'Some questions, okay?'

'Okay?'

'Do you have a girlfriend now?'

'What do you think? I'm insulted. I mean, I don't ask girls for coffee and let them feel my pulse when I'm with someone.'

'Oh. Okay. Right. I see.' I didn't at all.

'Okay, I have to ask this. Ready?'

'Ready,' he said, firmly, looking like he might laugh again.

'It's not funny!' I said, laughing a bit.

'Just ask!'

'Do you have a boyfriend?' I blurted out.

He laughed again. It was gorgeous. 'No! You?' he asked, looking serious again.

'No, no girlfriend.'

He laughed. Then looked earnest. 'No, come on. Tell me. Are you seeing anyone?'

'No boyfriend either,' I whispered. I suddenly felt very, very shy.

'Okay, now I have to ask something,' he said softly.

'So just ask.'

'What's with all the flowers?' he said in a firm, don't-you-bullshit-me kind of way.

'Oh.' I flushed. I hated lying. 'Just a story ... on Valentine's Day.'

'That was Monday, wasn't it?'

'Yeah, it's about post-Valentine's stuff-ups and how to get her back. All these companies sent, um, make-up bouquets for me to assess how guys can best make it up to their girlfriends, or potential significant others. You know, a "how to" story for guys.'

I really, really hated lying, but sometimes I was very, very good at it. He looked impressed.

'Actually, that's a great idea for *Phwoar!*'

'Well, you can't have it,' I said sharply, only half joking.

'Well, your mag is strictly for girls.'

'Doesn't mean guys don't read over their shoulders.'

'Seriously, I'm impressed. Let me know if you have any ideas for us.'

'You're the art director' – I deliberately left off the deputy – 'aren't you? I thought art people hated words.'

'Well, we do – but so many stories are, um, visual. Specially in *Phwoar!*'

'So they're not just about sex, then?' I hadn't meant to be provocative, but it just came out. Something to do with the way I'd said 'sex', then thought about having it ... with him.

We stared at each other, a bit too long to be considered not meaningful. I think it had something to do with the word sex. I felt hypnotised, but not really all that comfortable, and faintly aroused, but quite a lot like upending my chair and sprinting out of the coffee shop, too.

He broke the silence. 'So ... what are you doing this weekend?'

I thought of my shopping research that had to be done.

'Not sure ... maybe a bit of work ...'

'On the post-Valentine's story?'

'Mmmm ... but I have to work on a couple at a time, sometimes.' I was trying to make myself sound very busy and not at all at a loose end. 'But I'll be doing fun stuff, too.'

He raised his eyebrows. 'Anything special?'

'You know ... just stuff.'

God, that didn't sound very exciting.

'That sounds fun. Um. Would you ...' he started, brow all furrowed.

I waited for him to pop the question.

And waited.

'It's not a big deal,' he rushed on. 'Just a bit of a party.'

'Whereabouts?'

'Yeah, with the guys from *Phwoar!*. Saturday night. At the editor's place, in Bondi.'

'I live in Bondi.'

'There'll be other people there. Not from magazines.'

'Oh, normal people.'

'Not very.'

'Oh, good. So it might be fun.'

He laughed. God, I loved making him laugh. It felt good.

'Um … can I bring a friend?'

He looked a bit taken aback.

'My friend Allison. Just so I have someone to talk to. I mean, apart from you.'

He looked a bit perplexed. Had he been wanting to pick me up before the party or something?

'Er, yeah. Okay. Bring a few friends. Look,' he said, scribbling something down on a piece of paper. 'Here's the address. I'll be there early-ish, but most people will get there around nine, I think.' He handed me the bit of paper. I looked at it, and put it inside my wallet, along with all the other bits of screwed-up paper with important things on them. He stood up.

'Is it dressy?'

'Just … whatever. Whatever you want. It'll just be fun to have you there.' He squeezed my hand and little electric shocks zoomed up my arm.

'Yeah, I've got to get to a meeting,' he said, looking at his watch, which had sweet black hairs springing up around it. 'No, I'll pay,' he said in an alarmed tone as I reached for my wallet, and wandered to the counter. He squeezed my shoulder, gave me a wave, and walked purposefully off. Hmmn. Yummy.

God, he was nice. Why was he so nice? And was that a date he'd asked me out on? Or was he just friendly? If it was a date, wouldn't he have been a bit more … forceful or something? Or was being forceful something guys didn't do any more? Why wasn't everything nice and clear?

I watched his nice bum walk away from me. He had seemed interested … Like, interested, really, in me. And he'd invited me to a party. And I could take friends. There was only one thing to do. Have people round to my place to bolster up my ego and send me off into the night feeling like a social success story. A pre-party. The only kind to have.

I rang Allison.

'Guess what? Nick's asked me out –'

'Oh My God!'

'To a party. Saturday night. And I can take some people. So we have to have everyone over to my house beforehand, okay?'

'Oh,' she drawled. 'The old I'm-not-going-on-my-own thing?'

'Exactly.' Plus, if she came with me, nothing too much could happen. I felt … strangely guilty about how much I liked Nick. Like I was betraying Ben, or something. I know! I *know* it's ridiculous.

'Leave it to me,' she said.

I hung up. Yes! Everything was going perfectly. At last.

CHAPTER ELEVEN

By Friday morning I'd invited practically everyone I knew to drinks at my place, then on to the *Phwoar!* party. I almost rang people I'd been to school with until Allison pointed out they wouldn't all actually fit into my place. I invited everyone at work. And, even though I knew she'd come anyway, I even rang Diane and made a point of asking her over. She wasn't that bad. Maybe it was time I started being nice to her. Maybe even more of a friend. I almost invited Monica. I hovered around outside her door, wondering why I was doing this. Just as I changed my mind and was about to make a run for it, she looked up and gestured me into the room.

'Hi, come in,' she said, friendly. 'How's it going?'

Wow. I have never heard her sound so normal.

I sat down opposite her. 'I'm good … Busy,' I hurried to add.

'We're all busy,' she replied, sounding more like her normal self. The moment of warmth had faded, and frost was back. She leant in, closer. 'So, how's that cover story going? I'm excited about it. So are the advertisers,' she said, pointedly.

'Oh, it's, well ... good, really good.' God, how unconvincing was I. Obviously she was talking about the plastic surgery story. Obviously, I was working on it. But obviously I wasn't going to describe my interviews with people who weren't happy with their results.

'What exactly have you got?' she enquired. Nice one. She wants details. Time to feign innocence. When in doubt, act dumb. I smiled brightly, to throw her off the scent.

'I've got a great title – "Thirty seconds to Kylie's bum". I've found an advertiser's cellulite cream that apparently Kylie quite likes, not that she's got any cellulite I can see, and –'

'The plastic surgery story,' she clarified, losing patience. As if she was going to let me off the hook.

'Oh. Well, I've been researching it for the past few days and –'

'Research isn't going to get you anywhere,' she snapped, her voice a bit shrill. Did she know I'd been improvising? 'I made it clear that I wanted first-hand experience.' She drew a long breath. 'As you seem to be a little unsure of how to go about this kind of story, I've made an appointment for you with a Dr Gold.'

Blank look from me.

'You've not heard of him, have you? Research,' she snorted. 'Let me fill you in, seeing as you've unearthed so very little. Dr Gold is the Pacific Rim's most glamorous and highly paid cosmetic surgeon.

He's done …' and she reeled off a series of names that had even me in shock. 'And now,' she finished off contentedly, 'he's going to do you.'

Tell her, said the voices. Tell her that she's got to be kidding. That she can stick it.

'I'll call him right away.'

I dragged myself back to my desk. To face the inevitable.

I picked up the phone, biting my lip as I did. I jumped when the next thing I heard was Monica's voice bellowing poshly, 'Tamara! Come here now.'

Tamara actually ran all the way from her desk to the office. We could all hear Monica's voice.

'It's in the newspaper – people love to talk. They love to tell their stories. So where are they? Why aren't we getting this story? Find me Miss Lonelyhearts. Go see Eleanor and tell her to give you some pointers.'

Phew. At least I wouldn't have to help her. I couldn't bear it. And there was no way I could lie to Tamara. She was so sweet. God help me if Eleanor got onto it.

Anyway. Back to my *current* dilemma. I bossed myself, picking up the phone and dialling the numbers for Dr Gold's Sydney clinic.

It was one of those moments of truth. Once the appointment was confirmed, there was no turning back. It was either all the way with the exposé, or I could say goodbye to growing old gracefully.

'Hello?' I said, clearing my throat and half hoping he wouldn't be there. 'Is this Dr Gold's surgery?'

Monica had made my appointment for Monday afternoon. It was the earliest she could get, even though she told them (okay, lied) that it was an emergency and had dropped names, the receptionist informed me. Then I got back to the very important business of inviting people to come to the pre-party party.

'Why don't you all come by at about eight? You can have a few drinks and then we'll go off together at about ten – yeah?' Strangely, everyone had said yes. Which meant I was taking about forty people to the party. I was getting a bit concerned.

'No worries,' Ali told me when I rang in a panic. 'People will get sloshed and stay at your place. And it'll probably be so good they won't want to leave.'

Because I'd planned the drinks, shopped, arranged the music and cleaned the house the night before, I was both exhausted and prepared. We all went to the smelly pub after work for Friday night drinks as well as Vikram's last stand (it was probably our third farewell drinks for him – but who was counting?). Max and I were squished up against Vikram and Eleanor, with the entire home supply of boys squashed on another couch with Allison, Carla and Tamara. I was loving Max. We were becoming quite good buddies, in the way that you do with work buddies. Carla was a work buddy. We'd even mingled semi-successfully with each other's friends, and she'd used Allison for a makeover. Which, fortunately, Allison had liked.

But Max was different to Carla. While Carla and I were girls, and so had bonded through office politics, the smelly pub, make-up, exfoliators and de-frizzing serums, Max was a male, and thus could give invaluable insight into the world of men. Yes, I know, he too loved men, but that made it even better. I could find out everything I'd ever done that was wrong. (For example, high-pressure hand jobs are the way to go. No, they don't hurt. He says!)

I really wanted to get him alone for a moment and ask him about Nick. Then I wanted to tell Allison all about it. I needed the dissection. But Allison was laughing at something Dan was saying, as he gently pushed some hair back behind her ear. Max was quite sloshed and, as he'd decided it was time to revel in being in a gay-friendly town, he seemed intent on throwing sexual preference caution to the wind and having a gruesome intimate encounter competition.

'Have you ever,' Max said, sucking noisily on his Guinness, 'pretended to be a prostitute?'

'No,' I said thoughtfully. I loved rude hypotheticals. 'But I've always wanted to walk into A Touch of Class and see if I could get a job.'

'What's A Touch of Class?'

'It's a brothel. It's just up the road.'

'Why don't you do it?' Max asked.

'Yeah, just go in and see if you could get a job?' Tamara said, smiling at Max the whole time.

'Because I'm more interested in the fantasy of it. If I really go in I'll feel like a prostitute.'

'God, don't be so judgmental. They're working women, too.' I ignored Julie's ranting with a beatific smile, just to annoy her. She was getting a bit pissed, I noticed, so I took a huge sip of my lemonade, lime and bitters, just to look like I was catching up.

'So, what do you imagine happens when you go for an interview?' asked Max, eyes all poppy.

'Okay, so I imagine that one day, just out of curiosity, and the fact that I am penniless and there are no horrible jobs going at this company, I wander in.'

'How are you dressed?' Max asked.

'I am dressed like me.'

'Like an untouchable princess,' Max explained to the barman wiping our table.

'Like a fashion bohemian,' I corrected him strictly.

'Like a kid!' the big fat bartender put in.

I looked at him, my eyebrows right up around my hairline to indicate that I couldn't take him seriously at all. I won't go into how he looked. If you can't say something nice ...

'Stop it,' I said briskly to everyone laughing at me. 'Do you want to know what happens or not?'

'God, yes,' Max practically slobbered.

'Then you have to tell me something about you, okay?' I wasn't going to be the only person humiliating themselves.

'Okay.'

'Anyway. I go in to A Touch of Class and I have to go to a room and try on the wigs. I strap on high heels and false lashes and an amazing Nicholas Ghesquiere silver mesh Joan of Arc tunic.'

Carla snorted with laughter. 'It's A Touch of Class. You'd be wearing polyester crotchless underpants and a nipple-showing bra thing with a big strap-on dildo with a feather on the top.'

'It's *my* fantasy!' I protested, outraged. 'Oh yes, and lashes on my toes. And then I have to go out to the customers. Clients? Don't know the correct brothel term. Anyway, it's quite hard to walk because I've got the most enormous pair of Manolo Blahnik stilettos on. The whole 6 inches.'

'What are the customers like?' Tamara sounded way too curious.

'Well, this is the good bit. They are the entire cast of *Star Wars.*'

'*The Phantom Menace*?' Julie snorted with laughter as she said it.

'No – though I'll have Ewan and Liam. But Harrison Ford. And Mark, err, Hamill, you know, before the accident.'

'What accident?'

I ignored Tamara. Honestly. If you don't know about Mark Hamill's career being ruined by a tragic car accident that completely made his face look a bit weird and put-back-together-again but not quite correctly, well, you wouldn't last five minutes on a magazine.

Anyway. I was still telling my brothel story.

'And then I have to have sex with them all!'

'Err. Wow. Do you get the job?' I didn't like Max's doubtful tone. Did he think I was an unlikely sex goddess?

'Oh, they want me to start right away, on a huge salary, but the thing is that I don't have to take the job as a high-class callgirl because Mark and Harrison start fighting over who's going to …'

'Do you up the bum?' chortled Max.

'Marry me! Then, just as they're punching each other, Darth Vader kidnaps me, and ties me up, and Mark and Harrison have to shake hands and join forces to rescue me.'

'This is stock-standard Princess Leia fantasy land,' Chandra broke in grumpily. 'It's very pedestrian.'

'Shut up, Chandra – what happens, Megs?' Carla asked.

'There's a big fight over my tied-up naked body – which looks fantastic. I'm about 6 inches taller with bigger tits and no hair at all, except for on my head, and that's down to my bum and not frizzy.'

'It sounds like panel-van art!' Carla snorted hysterically, holding on to Max's arm.

'The fight never gets resolved. It's just me, looking from one to the other, one on each arm, getting pulled this way and that …' I drifted off.

'God. How old are you?' Chandra scoffed.

'Do you fancy Darth?' asked Max, eagerly.

'I do sort of. Is that strange?'

'Yes!' everybody said at the same time.

'Anyway, I didn't see *Star Wars* the first time it came out, if that's what you mean, Chandra,' I said.

'Mee-yow!' Max wailed.

'No,' protested Chandra. 'It's so fourteen. It could have been good – a brothel. Something dirty. But it's just about two fantasy action figures fighting over you.'

I serenely ignored her and turned to Max.

'Okay, English boy. Tell me yours.'

He wriggled deep into his seat and put his hands over his face.

'I can't, I can't. You'll all hate me.'

'No, we won't, come on – we'll all bond,' I patted his back reassuringly.

He took a deep breath and shuddered, then squared his shoulders, as if he was about to have a life-changing moment.

'I once had sex with a chicken.'

'Yuk!' we all screamed.

'Alive or dead?' Carla interjected knowledgeably.

'Neither,' he confessed.

'What?' Julie asked, eyebrows raised.

'It was frozen.'

'Dead,' Julie said.

'Does that make you a necrophiliac or a bugger? Buggerer?' I wondered aloud.

'Not sure,' he admitted.

'How did this happen?' demanded Tamara, shocked.

'Where did you meet?' said Carla, laughing.

'Well, I was about eighteen …'

'Eighteen!' Tamara blurted.

'Let me finish. I was eighteen. And I was desperate to have sex.'

'You were a virgin at eighteen!' Now Julie sounded shocked.

'It happens! And I didn't want to have a wank. I was sick of it. I'd nearly pulled it off, as it happens. No really,' he protested as we shrieked in pseudo-disgust, 'my palms were *raw*, I tell you. And I really wanted to know what it would feel like …'

'Inside a girl?' I encouraged.

'But you're …' Chandra said.

'Shut up, Chunder,' Julie interrupted.

Tamara looked panicky.

'So a friend of mine at school had told me about how inside a chicken …'

'Oh stop!' Carla said, faking disgust.

'Yes, really. Apparently it feels just the same. So I got one out of my Mum's freezer. It was a size ten.'

'Of course,' Carla spluttered.

'Big blue eyes, great legs …'

'Gorgeous, er, breast,' I joined in.

'But it was frozen. So I had to wait a while to defrost it. Have you even tried to defrost a chicken in a hurry?'

We all shook our heads.

'So, I lost patience and just did the chicken. The frozen chicken.'

We were all laughing, horrified. Drinks fell over.

Vikram fell to the floor, giggling hysterically. 'What's the bet that's what put you off girls forever,' he eventually managed to say.

Tamara looked really confused. Eric looked up at Max, a strange expression rippling across his face, then stared at the other side of the room really hard, almost like he was fascinated by how the fat barman with the voluptuous bum cleavage was spitting in the glasses he was supposed to be cleaning.

'Don't be silly. And how do you know the chicken was a girl?' I blurted, trying to throw Tamara off track. I'd tell her later.

'You didn't ask her name?' Dan thought the whole thing was hilarious.

'Okay, enough. Anyone else had any animal experiences?' I said, moving on. 'Julie? And no, not rock gods. I mean, you know, creatures ... man's best friends?'

'Nope, Max is on his own,' she said, draining her drink.

Did Carla just look relieved?

'It doesn't count, does it, if your dog licked another dog's, um, thing, and then licked your face?' Carla asked, quietly.

'No. That does not mean anything,' I whispered back. 'Unless you didn't wash.'

'Meg?' demanded Max.

'No. Yuk. No, not ever, not even a thought-wave thing.' I couldn't believe Max even asked.

'No Nancy Friday's *My Secret Garden*?' he persisted.

'Yuk! I *hated* that book.'

'I had a boyfriend who used to try to read me that Labrador story,' Eleanor confessed.

'I don't understand any of you,' Chandra said.

Carla started whispering to me in a confessional tone. The vodka must have started to hit. 'I fall in love with clothes. I just put them on and lie around. Pretend I'm in an Emanuel Ungaro campaign, and do a lot of fake masturbating.'

'No!'

'But I love clothes,' she slurred, looking at me seriously. 'I truly do. I used to write about them in my diary.'

'God, we're all tragic,' Julie said.

'I love cartoon boys,' Allison burst out. 'Like Astro Boy. Prince Planet. Marine Boy. Pokémon trainers! They're better than any real-life boy.'

'Girls are mad. How could that be?' Max protested.

'They save you. They're pretty. They're …'

'Fake!' Max shouted back.

'No, they've got beautiful souls.'

'I was in love with Kimba the White Lion,' Chandra said, wistfully.

'Who?' asked Eric.

'I could do Bob the Builder,' said Julie.

'Me too,' cried Max, transported with the delights of fantasy bonding. And lots of beer.

Tamara looked a bit teary. Time to change the subject.

'Okay, if you had to sleep with a famous person …' I began teasingly.

'Had to?' Julie asked. 'You know you want to.'

'Okay, if you could sleep with any famous person, who'd you sleep with?'

'Robbie Williams. And Björk.'

We all stared at Max.

'I just have a thing about Björk,' he said sheepishly.

'Nicole Kidman.' That was the guy with the cardigan from the art department.

'Nicole Kidman.' That was Vikram.

'Harrison Ford.' That was Chandra.

'Eeeeuw.'

'Michael Hutchence.' That was me.

'He's dead!' said Julie.

'No, he's not. It just seems that way.'

'Steve Irwin,' said Carla, grinning. We all looked blankly at her.

'He did cargos and flicks before anyone else.'

'Kylie.' That was Max again.

'God, you're supposed to be into boys,' Julie said, her eyebrows knotted together before they shot apart and she clapped her hands over her mouth, glancing in a worried way at Tamara.

'It's all about the bottom,' he explained earnestly. 'Truly, it's like a fourteen-year-old boy's.'

'Which is illegal,' Julie pointed out.

Tamara made a muffled sort of squeaky sound and sprinted from the room. Fizz got up, brows furrowed with a concerned-type expression, and galloped after her.

'I think she might be about to throw up,' I said as a decoy, thinking that spewing would at least be less shameful than revealing that she had thought Max was straight. Max, by the way, didn't seem to think anything unusual or important or surprising was going on and was continuing with an over-confident oration featuring his thoughts on famous bonking.

'I would love to shag someone famous,' he said, as English people do. 'I would love it. Fucking love to shag the most famous …' He paused, looking bleary. 'Though not Madonna … too scary. Might leave messages on my answer phone and hypnotise me into being her slave or something …

'But it would be great to do a famous woman,' he continued in a rush. 'Like Gwyneth! Then I could tell all my girly-friend workmates about it.' He said it with a sloppy, huggy lunge in my direction. I let him flop to the lounge.

Tamara, who'd returned from the toilets looking a bit crumpled and red-eyed, whimpered.

'Frankly, I'd rather hear about you sleeping with Russell Crowe,' drawled Eleanor.

'Actually, so would I,' I added.

'I wouldn't, *I* want to sleep with him,' said Julie.

We all stared – she *hadn't* slept with Russell Crowe?

'What? *What?* Anyway, aside from him, I've already slept with all the ones I've wanted to.'

'Weirdest famous guy request?' Max fired off.

We all turned to Julie.

'Piss-on-me guy!' Eleanor shouted.

'No, the poo in my mouth guy,' Max erupted, all competitive.

'No, the poo in the fridge guy,' Eleanor snapped back, even louder.

'Oh My God,' Tamara groaned.

'They're just joking,' I soothed. She looked a bit distraught. Poor Tamara. But she'd be all right. She was young. And Fizz was sitting next to her, looking all concerned. How sweet.

'One made me listen to all his music,' Julie said resentfully.

'Tommy Lee?' Eleanor asked.

'He has no music.'

'I've slept with Loveday Rooth,' announced Eleanor proudly, referring to a nineties love god we'd all been found guilty of fancying as teenagers.

'What!' Julie turned on her.

'So – what's the problem?' Eleanor demanded, eyes narrowing.

'You did not – not after we went out for drinks with him?'

'No – while we had drinks with him!' Eleanor grinned.

'Oh God.'

'He likes big women,' she slurred smugly, smoothing down her tiny leather skirt over her gigantic thighs, which were held captive by giant fishnets straining at the seams. 'Really likes them.'

'What was it like?' Allison asked, sounding a little desperate.

'Great. He loved my bum.'

'Oh God!' Julie moaned again.

'What's your problem?'

'I slept with him, too.'

'So?' challenged Eleanor. Julie's eyes narrowed.

We all stiffened. Were we about to witness the end of their friendship?

'Eskimo sisters,' they cried, and rubbed their noses together gleefully.

'Is it time to go?' I asked Allison. She and Dan were sort of eyeing each other off. She nodded at me, grinning. 'We're going – anyone want to come with us – get a lift home?' I asked.

'Oh, well, only if you're going,' said Dan, rushing to his feet. 'Nice to see you all – again,' he said meaningfully to Julie.

'Bye, Dan,' flirted Julie.

'What about me?' pouted Eleanor.

Dan and Allison went off, a bit apart. God, it was so obvious they were completely hot for each other. I stayed back to let them have a bit of a clinch and grope before I followed them.

'See you, guys – don't forget tomorrow night, hey?'

There was a chorus of affirmations. 'Are you coming home now, Fizz?'

Fizz was murmuring to Tamara. Well, he was looking at Tamara and sitting near to her on the couch. He was so tiny he was just about in her lap. She looked like she was enjoying having someone do the listening, too, in between shooting quivery, betrayed-type looks in the direction of Max.

'Fizz? You want a lift?'

He jumped up. 'See you tomorrow night,' he said, with a little wave at Tamara in particular.

'See you tomorrow,' Tamara replied.

Fizz and I just managed to pause, cough, laugh uproariously and make enough noise for Dan and Allison to break apart. Well, it looked like they did. It was hard to tell, 'cos it was very dark. I wrapped my arms around my waist and shivered in the blast of cold night air. 'It's getting cold,' I said.

'It's a southerly change,' said Allison. I noticed that her red lipstick had migrated to the bottom of her nose. Some had moved down to the bottom of her chin. 'Here,' I said, and handed her a make-up wipe.

'Oh – er, thanks,' she grinned, wiping her mouth. 'So, that was fun. Can I stay at yours? I brought my party clothes with me this morning,' she said, waving a giant carrier bag. I was astounded at how she managed to give the impression she wasn't even *thinking* about bonking Dan's brain out before the night was over. 'On the couch.'

'Gee, I don't know,' I said, like I didn't have two brain cells to bang together. 'Is that okay with you guys?'

'Yes,' said Fizz, who is lovely, but even he was getting sick of this charade.

'Dan?' I said sweetly. 'That okay with you?'

'Yes.'

'Fine then. We can all get ready together.'

'It'll be fun – like pre-cocktail cocktails. The other party's not going to be cocktails, is it?' Allison asked.

'Probably not – more like beer. Grunge.'

We pulled up outside the house. I got off Allison's lap.

'Sorry, love,' I grunted.

'Here,' I announced when we got into the house. 'Let's get some linen for the couch.'

Come on Al, I thought, if you guys are going to fake it, fake it right.

'Er, yeah,' she said, heading to the lounge room and plopping herself down on the manky couch.

'Oh, wow,' I then heard Allison saying loudly. 'Look, *Bordello of Blood* is on – it's a great movie.'

I stifled a laugh and made a vomit face at her while Dan wasn't looking.

'Is it? I might give it a whirl,' said Dan, all fake curiosity.

'Ooooh yes,' Allison gurgled enthusiastically.

God, no wonder Allison never went undercover.

I woke up with Allison in my bed again.

'Allison – how come you keep sneaking in here?'

'So no-one thinks I've done anything with Dan.'

'But if you just stayed on the couch …'

'He fell asleep on the couch.'

'But you *are* doing things with Dan.'

'Ssssh.' She giggled helplessly, curling up into a foetal position. 'I just want to keep it quiet. Anyway, it's not going anywhere.'

'So why are you being so undercover – you're usually the first one off the hussy bus? Freedom, liberate my orgasm blah blah blah.'

'It's because I like him,' she whispered. 'He's really intense. He's primal ... in bed. He's all bitey and scratchy – a bit animal.' She shivered with ... God, delight, I s'pose.

'I don't need to know any more,' I declared, covering my ears with a pillow. She wrenched it away.

'It's really good sex. And I like him,' she said again, hugging the pillow.

'So it is going somewhere?'

'God, no. I mean, if he ever thought he had the upper hand with me, he'd fuck around. Like he has with everyone else.'

Hmmn. Theory time.

'So you like a bit of rough.'

'I like that he's a guy's guy.'

'He's so not a guy's guy,' I said ominously, referring to all his girlfriends.

'No, you know what I mean. I know you know.'

'You like that he's a rogue.'

'But a very handsome rogue.'

'With very bad teeth.'

She made a noncommittal so-what kind of noise.

'Seriously, doesn't the teeth thing bother you?'

'If it did, I would have stayed with the American.'

We both were quiet for a minute, remembering the almost painful brightness of his perfect white teeth.

'Anyway,' said Allison, breaking our tooth contemplation, 'you might not even go to the party with Nick. You might meet someone here. You never know.'

She curled up and turned her back to me. I frowned. Who would I meet at my party, besides people I'd invited? She wouldn't have invited anyone – would she? Would she?'

'Night,' she said, her voice all sleepy.

'Allison?'

'Yeah?'

'What?'

'What what?'

'What have you done?' No way she would have invited any of those Lonelyhearts guys.

'Just invited a few people. Guys, you know. Don't worry about it. Just have a nice sleep.'

She pecked me on my shoulder, rolled over and passed out. You would have thought I was sleeping with a boy.

I waited till she was breathing evenly, then went to the lounge room and pulled her mobile from her bag. I quickly flicked through her text messages. Replies. Ah-ha. From man after man after man. Ten of them. One mentioned the ad.

Lk fwd 2 fnly mtng.
    At lst wl mt.

MISS LONELYHEARTS

Well, Allison, I thought, picking up my mobile and trotting out to the back yard. Two can play at that game. You invite men – bloody Lonelyhearts men?

Right then. I can't beat you, so I'll start playing the game. I'll invite women. Really, really hot women.

I chuckled to myself and called Carla. She was a night owl so I knew she would be up. She also knew models.

Really, really hot models.

'Carla? Can you round up ten super-hot girls? We need them for tomorrow night. There's going to be loads of boys.'

Smiling, I crept back to bed. I'd filled Carla in on everything and she was great. I popped three valerians just to be sure I slept.

But as it was, the feeling of contentment would probably have meant I would have slept really, really well anyway.

CHAPTER TWELVE

'There – no, there,' Allison ordered, watching critically as Fizz, Dan and their mate Eric struggled manfully with the fish tank and plonked it, with just a touch of horrible glass-scraping-across-the-cement sound, in the back yard. Except for a bit up the back, where *things* grew – things that I didn't want to know about – the back yard was mostly concrete.

'Now, fill it up with hot, hot water,' instructed Allison, strapping on a pair of long, pink gloves that somehow made her look like a hot S & M nurse about to give someone a good colonic. Not her usual Saturday-morning image, but fetching, nonetheless.

'Settle down, Allison,' I muttered as Fizz scuttled away, terrified. Dan ventured further down the yard and disappeared. 'You know Fizz is a softie – what's with you?'

'Where's Dan?' she asked, ignoring me. Pointedly.

'He's cutting the 'erb, mon,' said Eric in an appalling Jamaican accent.

'Why do boys love growing pot so much?' I

asked, starting to wash the cobwebbiest glasses, mainly to take my mind off Allison's shitty mood.

What was with her? She'd been so happy last night.

'I don't know,' replied Eric, speaking normally again. 'It's up there with fake boobs and Formula One.'

'Call yourself a guy,' I teased. He flashed me a rueful look.

'Yep. Not much of a macho man, am I?'

'Never mind,' I said, pulling him close. 'You're my favourite.'

'Awww.'

Allison was staring out the window. I stood next to her and looked. Her eyes were lasering away at Dan and Fizz, who were down the end of the long, skinny concreted-over back yard, trying to decide how to harvest their meagre marijuana crop.

'Seriously, Eric ... why do we have illegal substances in our yard?' I asked.

'That is a rhetorical question, right?' Eric replied. 'Guys like to see if they can grow it. It makes them feel out there. Wild. Plus they can show their friends.'

'Oh. So is it a bit like home brew?'

'Yeah, only better.'

I looked out at Dan in the marijuana garden. He was wearing a T-shirt that said XXXX, and baggy jeans that hung off his bottom. He was scratching his thick, black curly hair. From a distance, where you couldn't spot the teeth, he looked gorgeous.

It's all that labouring.

'He got a tattoo yesterday,' Allison said.

'What?' I felt a flash of possessiveness.

'It's some Celtic thing,' she replied, going red. 'I think it might be a name.' She looked like she was going to cry.

'Sssh, they're coming back.'

Dan and Fizz stomped back into the kitchen, Dan dragging weed, Fizz wiping his feet and looking nervously at Allison, who was washing a glass way harder than she needed to.

'It's clean, already,' I told her, as the boys headed out to the fire to dry off the herb.

'I feel sick. Dan's thinking of going back to Ireland,' she said, her voice flat and stoney.

'What?'

'Yeah. He reckons he's got some stuff to sort out.'

'What? What stuff? Who stuff? When did you find this out?'

'Yeah – exactly. It's *who* stuff.'

'He hasn't said a thing about a who.'

'No – he hasn't said anything to me either. Not about Ireland, not about a who. I was just in his room. There was a letter. Open. On the bed. Just now. And now he's got a stupid tattoo. He's probably been madly in love with her all along. God, I think I'm going to have to be sick.'

She came back into the kitchen a couple of minutes after a dramatic exit, whiter than white.

'But … this doesn't make sense. I thought you were having a thing.'

'Apparently this thing doesn't include telling me about a certain *who* – who's back in Ireland.'

'Ouch.'

'Yeah. Well,' she said, wiping her hands clean on the tea towel, 'it was fun while it lasted.'

'You *could* talk to him.'

'Talk to him? We've *been* talking. And he didn't mention *this*. I'm not going through what you went through.'

I kept my mouth shut. Ben and I had been together for a year, and she and Dan … well, it was sort of at the beginning. It wasn't the same, but that doesn't mean it didn't hurt.

'He can get stuffed,' she said with total finality. 'Anyway, it wasn't ever really a thing.'

'It was *so* a thing. It was the thingiest thing you've had for ages,' I insisted.

The boys came in, dragging twigs with them.

'Our harvest,' Dan said proudly. Allison looked away.

'You'll be hanging with T-Bro' – our spunky pothead neighbour on the right-hand side – 'next, Dan,' I said. I hated pot, but someone had to lighten the mood. I clapped a hand to my forehead.

'Oh. My. God. Have we invited the neighbours?'

Everyone looked a bit blank and couldn't-be-bothered. I started to fret.

'Well, we'd better,' I said, my voice going a bit wobbly. 'If we don't, the Christians' – our neighbours on the left-hand side – 'will ring the police, and T-Bro will call in his mates.'

'She's right,' said Dan.

'You go over, Ali,' I bossed.

'No. I'll go,' said Dan, looking all suspicious. He obviously realised she may never come back once she saw T-Bro and the guys he hung out with. I have to admit that T-Bro does have a great bod.

Allison ignored Dan and smiled a scary smile as she went to tell our neighbours about the party. I started getting worried when I saw the hard stare she threw at Dan. I think he did too, but he knew better than to try to stop her.

We heard the front door slam and sat down and waited.

And we sat.

And we waited. No-one moved a muscle. At least that's how it seemed. I think there was a bit of chat. A flicker of movement. But we were all on hold.

Ali stomped back in after about twenty minutes, all swingy and flirty.

Dan's face went all thundery.

'Nice time?' he asked over-solicitously.

'Yeah – they're great,' Allison countered, over-enthusiastically.

'They're what? Listen, don't you let them fool you with their "Hi, we're lovely boys who treat women right"' (only he said *roight*).

The temperature had just gone up in the room. I hated arguments. Hated them. And I was pretty sure I was in the middle of one.

Dan was looking more and more like his hair was curling tighter and tighter. He was a big man, but he seemed to grow a bit more with every bit of tension building in the room. Fizz, Eric and I watched them both and waited for an explosion. But before it could happen, Dan left the room. Well, actually, he stormed out. He didn't say anything, but you could see the anger rippling out of him. Eric jumped up after him and Fizz practically ran to join them.

'Allison?'

'What?'

'What just happened?'

'Er, Dan left the room?'

'What happened next door?'

'Nothing,' she said, looking at her nails. Any second now she was going to pull out a nail file and start sawing at them. Like Monica did at work. I hate that sound. All those bits of DNA flying through the air. But, thankfully, she just looked at her nails.

'Tell me.'

'Have you ever seen T-Bro with his shirt off?' she asked quietly.

I nodded, remembering the sight.

'T-Bro answered the door with his shirt off,' she continued.

Her face went so pink I could feel the heat from where I stood.

I raised my eyebrows. All was clear. I hadn't thought Ali would be the six-pack's latest victim, but who could resist its awesome power? 'Oh – so you saw the amazing torso then.'

'Yep.' She said it like she wished she hadn't.

'It is quite remarkable,' I conceded chattily. Maybe if I ignored the implication it would just evaporate.

'How can a drug dealer look so …?' she wondered, leaning back.

'I don't think T-Bro actually takes many of his drugs – but he loves other people to stuff them in,' I explained.

I was suddenly very, very nervous. Allison had discovered the best way to make Dan squirm, in the shape of a man who knows scary people and has never done a tax return.

The party started the way they always do – you break open a bottle of wine, you watch other people drink it. You feel really happy because your best friend's matchmaking plans have been thwarted by your equally brilliant boy neutralisation plan. Carla had rung the top model agencies and invited hot girls who wanted a chance to score brownie points with Go Global Enterprises (she'd hinted something about *Elegance*). You get ready with your girlfriends in your bedroom and play music, and help each other with finding the best look. You feel so thrilled you decide you might even have a drink. The first for ... well, for a long, long time.

I was moisturising my legs, watching Carla and Allison compete for the mirror.

'This is my "I'm not interested" look,' Carla showed us, lifting one eyebrow and raising her chin haughtily, managing to look like she'd be hot in bed.

'This is my "I'll fuck your brains out" look,' Ali said. She really scared me, sometimes.

'This is my hair flick,' I said, flicking my hair. It frizzed out madly. I quickly smoothed it back down.

I was going to have a great time – my friends from work were already there, drinking and laughing in the lounge room, and the plan was I was going to move on at nine-thirty on the dot to Nick's party, nicely warmed up thanks to my social success at home.

Everything was perfect.

Who knows? Maybe just one drink. To celebrate.

The music was so loud we were shouting at each other, which is why we hadn't heard the ten guys who had been knocking at the front door for fifteen minutes ... which is why T-Bro, the drug dealer, and one of the Christians had gone outside to find them standing there, yelling at each other with instructions about how to climb up the drainpipe. They'd tried madly texting Allison, but she'd left her phone in my room, and was too busy having a tense discussion with Dan, so there'd been no chance of her letting them in.

T-Bro led the lot down the side of the house, like an urban pied piper of love, ripped open a window and stuck his impressive torso right into the house.

'I've got about ten guys here looking for a girl!' he bellowed.

Diane actually stepped forward, offering herself up. Chandra, Julie and Tamara spun around expectantly. I bolted from the room, peering out my bedroom door to see who was coming in.

Allison flashed me a grin.

'Oh, Allison, you didn't!' I squeaked, feigning shock.

'Yes, I did,' she laughed. 'Come on. It'll be fun. See what they're like. They don't know who you are, but you know who they are. Perfect!'

I didn't know whether I was scared or excited – I felt oddly protected from having to do anything, the thought of Nick some kind of bubble around me. A cluster of boys who'd been in hunt of Miss Lonelyhearts were in the corner. I giggled madly. 'Hi guys,' I said, grinning like a maniac. 'Which one of you is here to meet the girl from the paper?'

They looked embarrassed.

They all looked the same-ish. A bit brown.

Nice enough. Neat and tidy.

Fortunately, the music was so loud no-one could possibly hope to talk to me. I led them all to the fish tank.

'This is a fish tank,' I shouted helpfully, 'full of alcohol, mixed into some kind of lovely drink by Dan, who's over there.' They all turned and looked at Dan, who waved, grinning and flashing those imperfect teeth. Diane waved too, hovering close to Dan.

'Goodness!' I yelled at Allison, who was looking at the boys with her eyes very wide. 'I wonder what I'll do with all these boys.'

Which is exactly when Plan B made an entrance.

'Oh look – models! Problem solved,' I grinned at Allison.

She looked stunned. That was so good, I can't tell you. I almost jumped up and down and clapped my hands. (But don't worry, I didn't, okay.)

'Fuck,' said Allison. 'Who the hell are they?'

'Just some friends of Carla. Oh, look – they're talking to the boys. Time for me to go soon,' I said blithely.

'Smarty pants,' she grinned. 'You figured it out, didn't you.'

MISS LONELYHEARTS

'Yep,' I said, grinning right back. 'I'd better go and chat a bit more to my suitors,' I said, winking at Ali. 'Who knows? Nick may have competition.'

I could afford to be gracious. I knew they'd never look at me.

Allison took another sip of her drink.

'What's it like?' I asked, like a teenager having a first drink.

'Good,' she said. I eyed off the fish tank.

'Are you going to have a drink?' she asked. 'Wow. Red-letter day.'

'Here, let me get it for you,' smarmed T-Bro, obviously making a play for Ali. Who seemed to be … sort of … *encouraging* him.

He filled a smallish glass with a cherry-red drink.

'Here. This is special. It's a partini.'

'A what?'

'Not a cosmopolitan, or a flirtini. It's a partini.'

'Thanks,' I said, pleasantly impressed he hadn't poured me a whopper. Allison held up a glass too, and we clinked. I took a sip and decided I'd better mingle.

'Hi,' I said, smiling awkwardly not really knowing where to look. All of the models had crochet tops, well, more like lots of intricate string bits all sort of joining up like a spider on acid had got stuck in an origami class; tiny little denim skirts, which most of us would have worn as belts; pipe-cleaner thighs smooth as the inside of anyone else's wrist; childlike bottoms and Kylie smiles. Only they were all tall. They could have been very elongated, rangy children. Oh, all right, they were in their teens.

And yes, they were legal. But they sure didn't look it.

'They're quite tall,' I whispered to Carla.

'Don't worry,' she muttered. 'They'll be nice.'

'Have you briefed them?' I asked, wondering at all this gorgeousness in my own beanbagged lounge room.

'Yes, and they're going to castings at *Elegance* next week so they are our slaves.'

'Good. Sorted, then.'

The power of the media had made itself apparent in my grotty house.

'Siren,' called Carla. 'This is the girl,' she said, making a gesture at me. 'She's the one.'

'Hmmn,' said Siren, looking me up and down with very turquoise eyes and very long, very red hair.

'Is that your real name?' I blurted out. 'Sorry. Couldn't help myself.'

'Yes,' she said, looking a bit annoyed.

'Hi,' said a girl's voice next to me. She was extremely pretty. 'Who *are* those guys?' She was staring at two of the brown boys, slowly dancing in a swivelling twist, like someone's dad after a visit to the cryonic defrosting centre.

'Those guys? They're my potential new boyfriends,' I giggled.

Two more models came and stood next to me. I hadn't seen so many models since the company's Christmas bash. It had been rumoured the old manager guy before the new manager guy had hired them, and invited his friends.

Yes, I know, it's *disgusting*. (And you should have heard what he did in the eighties.) I think that's partly why he is the *old* manager guy. Even at that level it doesn't pay to be so obvious.

'Fantastic,' I said to nobody in particular. Time to get ready for the party. The other party. Complete reappraisal of make-up. Nervous change of top. Allison grabbed me just as I was ready to bolt to the bedroom.

'Come on, at least have a drink with the girls. They're much nicer than they look.'

'I really have to change,' I said abruptly.

'Sure you don't want me to come with you?' she asked, looking at me strangely.

'No,' I said as I walked to my room. I opened a drawer, Lonelyhearts letters flying everywhere, before choosing a spangly skirt for a belt. And digging round for my green eyeshadow.

I shook my hair out of the ponytail it had been in for the last hour to bring it under control. It fell down in ripply waves. It was a miracle – a good hair day!

I sighed as Allison entered my room.

'I think I'm ready.'

'Come on. Just one more drink,' Allison insisted.

'Nope. I'm staying sober.'

'Oh, *please*, one won't hurt – Nick's not some kind of policeman, is he?' Allison snapped.

'No, he's great,' I said meekly as she led me into the back yard.

Allison plunged the huge soup ladle into the fish tank and poured a frothy pink liquid into a large former peanut-butter jar. She stretched her long golden arm out to me, and I shrugged my shoulders and took it from her.

Allison clinked her glass against mine. 'Here's to …'

'Things,' I said.

'So, you think he's a thing?'

'A real thing,' I quipped, taking a sip. A little molten river flowed down my throat, and a lovely warm fuzzy feeling started in my brain.

I'd had a funny feeling that tonight was going to be *significant*.

I'd thought that feeling was about Nick.

But as I caught a whiff of the mad party happening in my house, my funny feeling could have been trying to tell me that we were all hovering on the edge of disaster.

Or some such.

CHAPTER THIRTEEN

'What are you still doing here?' Carla asked me about half an hour later.

My head was swimming, but I felt I could dance to anything. Julie and Eleanor were certainly dancing to anything. Even Chandra was grooving away in a corner, with one of the brown boys. No! With Vikram. And Craig was chatting with a model who looked like she'd rather be having an aneurysm.

'You should go,' Carla advised. 'You see us all the time – don't forget about Nick?'

'Oh, Nick!' I said. 'I'm going, just after this song,' I protested, whirling round and round like a three year old after way too much red cordial.

'You're coming with me. Let me look at you.' Carla stood me under the light. 'Okay, I'm giving you ten seconds.'

She marched me straight down the hall, through the dining room and out into the crowded back yard. She took me way down the back behind a tree, where I never go, and sat me down on a bench that I didn't even know was there. What did she mean ten seconds? Ten seconds till what?

'What are you talking about?' My words floated out of my mouth and I watched them leave the back yard and drift over the fence

A wave of nausea crashed throughout my body, building in my guts and winding its way through my entire system. I staggered off the bench to the side and heaved, fertilising some of the boys' pot plants. I sat down, then stood up, shocked.

'I was just sick.' I was astonished!

'Yes. How are you feeling now?'

'I'm never sick, I've got a cast-iron stomach, and I …' I stopped suddenly and heaved again. The marijuana plants were fertilised anew.

'I don't ever drink. But I had a drink. Two drinks. I'm. So. Sick,' I moaned.

She moved closer. 'You're *green*. You've had much too much to drink.'

'Don't be silly. I never drink too much. It was two.'

I sat down on a milk crate turned upside down, feeling very peculiar, wondering why the back yard was turning slowly.

'Carla, what's happening?' I said.

'Just a sec, stay here. I'll get a glass of water for you.'

'Don't, I won't be able to have it.'

As soon as I'd said it I was madly thirsty. A hand appeared next to me, stretching out a bottle …

'Thanks,' I said to Carla, relieved.

A guy sat down. One of the brown hairs. Not that I'm brownist or anything. I actually really like brown. Chocolate, for example. But he was a brown brown. Like the brown of one of Craig's cardigans. If you know what I mean.

'How are you tonight?' he asked nicely. I looked at him, in shock.

'Oh, fine thanks.' I took a swig on the bottle and gagged on alcohol.

'So, who do you know here?'

'Well, I live here. So tomorrow's going to be horrible.'

I started laughing, then stopped when I saw his face.

'How come you're here?' I asked, trying very, very hard to be normal. After all, this was a unique opportunity to see inside the heads of one of the letter-writers. While I was sick as a pig.

'Well. I was hoping to sort of ... meet some new people.'

'Have you?'

'Yeah. There's some amazing women in there. Do you want to dance?'

'Excuse me,' I said politely. 'I would, but I just have to be sick.'

'So,' he said, after I'd vomited, returned, and sat down, 'I like your hair.'

'Oh, thanks.' What? He liked my hair?

Scarily, he moved closer. What was he doing? Why were there two of him?

What was wrong with me?

Carla arrived back, just in time.

'Hi, nothing to see here people,' she said, simultaneously moving Mr Brown aside and herding a model into his vision. Carla elbowed her.

'Wanna dance?' she lisped at Mr Brown, who did the most comedic double take I've ever seen. He looked at me (vomity, short, good hair), looked at her (mermaid hair, skyscraper legs and turquoise eyes) and kept looking at her. 'Nice talking with you,' he said. His gaze never made it back to me.

Carla handed me a glass of water. I sipped gingerly at it.

'Can you believe that? He tried to pick me up!' I held my head. 'Why would he do that – look at me?'

'You're not that bad,' she said.

'No, but I'm a complete mess,' I replied. 'I don't understand – I had two drinks.'

She looked at me. 'Come on, you're getting somewhere safe. You're a walking target in this state.'

I was stunned, but somehow not that shocked. It was cold, but I felt quite cosy. I should have been mortified, but I couldn't have cared less. It was like I was watching this entire scene from a distance – like I was wrapped in cotton wool. 'I only had two drinks,' I repeated as she led me inside. I saw Allison out of the corner of one eye, and started to weave my way towards her. 'Just want to talk to Allison for a sec,' I said.

'Come back here,' Carla ordered.

For a woman off her face I was surprisingly fast on my feet. I barged back into the lounge, where some amazing dancing was going on. T-Bro was gyrating with Allison. Dan was staring at them, his thick brows furrowed. Diane was chatting away to him, pointing out how great they looked together. Brown-haired men were dancing with models, who were really something to watch. Eleanor was shaking her great big bum round and round in giant circles, which were quite hypnotic. Even I stopped for a moment. But then a red-hot fireball of anger went through me.

'Allison!' I yelled, striding over and pulling her away from T-Bro.

'What, babe?' she slurred, hanging on to T-Bro, who'd taken his shirt off and was officially dirty dancing. I couldn't blame her entirely. He was outrageously good-looking, even my addled brain could register that. Slick black hair. Carved cheekbones. Lips as swollen as an eighties supermodel's. It should have been a great combination – get him out of the shell suit and he's an Armani model. But to me he looked like a handsome lizard, like he had a tongue a mile long tucked into that fat mouth just waiting to flick it out and catch flies when you turned your head.

Andy Garcia syndrome.

'What did you put in my drink, Ali?' I demanded.

'I have no idea what you're talking about,' she said, blurring in and out of view. 'But you've obviously had *something*,' she agreed.

I moved forward, wobbling madly. I was determined to get Allison to 'fess up.

I must have looked a bit out of control (which I was) because T-Bro moved between us, pushing me back with one large meaty hand. He was probably quite gentle, but in my state I stumbled backwards and fell on my arse into the beanbag. Even more beans dribbled onto the floor. They appeared to be dancing.

'You bastard!' Dan yelled, hurling himself at T-Bro. 'You pushed Meg!'

'Get off him!' Allison shrieked, stumbling into T-Bro, who put a protective arm around her. 'Come on, babe. Let's go.'

'No Ali, don't,' I said. 'You're supposed to come with me.'

She turned and grabbed her bag and started to walk out. Well, weave out, more accurately. I clambered out of the beanbag and went after her. Dan stayed rooted to the spot, two burning circles of red lighting up his cheeks. He seemed oblivious to Diane, who was attempting to soothe him with another drink.

'Ali, come back … you can work it out with Dan.'

She turned and her ice gaze death-rayed through me.

'He's got someone else,' she said, anger pouring through her voice, shouting, though she whispered it.

'Oh Ali, come on! You haven't even asked him.'

'Bloody hell! When are you going to realise that I'm not like you! I'm not going to get stuffed around by some guy with a girlfriend …' She broke off, shaking her head.

'That isn't what happened!' I shouted.

Allison pulled her shoulders back and flashed me a determined look. 'That *is* what happened! And you'd still take him back!'

'I wouldn't. I'm going to meet someone tonight.

MISS LONELYHEARTS

I mean, thanks for the scheming, but I'm not interested in your arranged dates, thanks. Not any of them.'

'Oh really,' she challenged.

'No! As if anyone who answered an ad would be – normal.' That was a bit mean. They were all very brown, but I'm sure they were perfectly nice men. Unfortunately, I couldn't get any of that out of my mouth at the time.

'Not your type. Right. No-one you could ever be interested in would do this, right?'

'Don't yell at me,' I said, feeling weird. This felt very, very, very unsafe all of a sudden.

Allison crouched down and said in a spookily quiet voice. 'Well, that would be why Ben wrote, wouldn't it,' she whispered.

I stared at her, feeling like I was zooming backwards down a long dark tunnel and she was getting smaller and smaller. 'Why *what*?' I may have said that. I definitely thought that. But it's more likely my mouth just flopped open.

'Here,' she said, holding a letter out to me. 'I've been keeping it safe. Didn't know whether to show you or not. But here you go. Why even fight it?'

I looked at it, then at her. 'Ben wrote?' I repeated, like a demented person. I think.

She stood up, wobbled, steadied herself, then turned and walked away, through the blurry dancing people, without looking back, T-Bro chasing her like a puppy.

Ben *wrote*?

'Good luck with Nick,' she yelled over her shoulder at me, from far, far away. I didn't think she meant it.

'*Nick!* Oh my God! Nick!' I said, panicking. 'What time is it?' I grabbed Carla's wrist and squinted my eyes and miraculously made out the time. It was only eleven. Not a good look, but at least I could turn up.

That's when the room started spinning and spinning and spinning around.

'Meg, you can't go,' said Carla, dragging me into the bathroom. 'Come on, have a look at yourself.'

I tried to focus on the bathroom mirror. The reflection in it wasn't anything like the girl I'd been before the party.

'You're off your face. You are practically green. You will, most likely, throw up again soon. Is this how you really want to see him – first date and all?'

I stepped closer to the mirror. All I could see was hair, pale skin and massive bluey-green eyes. My pupils were tiny flecks of black, like a tiny black plug in a big round swimming pool. But I was still standing.

'Don't be silly, Carla – I have to go. I just need some water.'

'If he's keen he'll hold on,' she said, turning me round and marching me out the door towards my bedroom.

'I can't just not turn up,' I protested.

She grabbed my phone. 'Tell me his number.'

I searched, no, groped around in my head, desperate for a few traces. 'I can't remember,' I said slurring.

She sighed, handed me back my phone and marched me straight into my room.

Which wasn't the peaceful oasis it should have been. There were at least four models sitting on the floor, going through my Lonelyhearts letters.

Carla went into action mode.

'Put – the – letters – down.'

'Have you any idea how hard it is to meet a man in this city?' hissed a sexy redhead, refusing to disarm. I just gaped, before slumping sideways onto the bed.

Carla stood her ground.

'Oh. Look, here you go,' said the pipe cleaner, dropping the lot down on the floor and tossing her hair as she stumbled out the door.

Was everyone at this party completely smashed?

Carla glared at them. Now that worked, and the rest of the models backed away from her. 'Honestly, you won't even miss these ones,' they said defiantly, sprinting for the door, still clutching some letters to their chests.

'They're just lucky I'm pissed otherwise they wouldn't work in this town again,' she said, once they'd disappeared. I was down on my knees, beet-red, snatching letters off the floor and stuffing them back into the drawers.

I was mortified. 'Models have been reading my letters. Going through my drawers. What next? Does everyone have to know?'

'I'd be more worried about them seeing your undies – honestly, haven't you got any pride?' she asked, only half joking, holding up a pair of grey knickers with elastic that had long departed this earth, with a look of true disgust. 'Meg, they actually wanted the letters – it's you who thinks it's weird. Everyone else is Internet dating and having sex with anyone, just hoping they'll get a relationship. You're the only one who thinks it was a stupid idea. So if you don't want them,' she said, moving to grab some. 'I'm joking,' she said, laughing, as my jaw dropped open.

She pulled off my shoes, pulled the covers over me, and left a glass of water next to my bed. Bliss. But I couldn't fall asleep. Not now. I had to read the letter from Ben.

I held it tight, snuggling into my lovely bed, struggling to focus on opening the envelope. Only my eyes wouldn't open all the way.

I passed out almost instantly. No dreams. Nothing.

One thing you can say about whatever was in the fish tank. It sure made you sleep well.

Like the dead must rest.

CHAPTER FOURTEEN

By the time some kind of consciousness cracked through on Sunday, the evening of my accidental cocktails to bond with buddies before going to Nick's party was an impressionistic black canvas streaked with bright, strange flashbacks. I should probably consider Polaroiding my every move in future, I groaned, rolled over and sipped faintly on some water. At least if I had pictures I wouldn't have to deal with wondering just how bad last night really was.

What had happened, anyway? I wondered, lying still, eyes very shut. I groped through my memory. At first all I could really come up with were random, unchronological and decontextualised glimpses of:

*Diane kissing Dan, whose eyes appear in my memory flashback to actually be pointing in two entirely different directions; both of them probably searching for Allison;

*Max and Eric giggling together over CDs, culminating in them playing and dancing to Britney Spears's 'Toxic';

*T-Bro dancing with Allison. Allison dancing right back at him, deliriously, probably due to the fact that T-Bro had his shirt off;

*Carla kissing the Christian who lent us the blender. Looking extremely uplifted. If you know what I mean;

*scores of completely unknown men looking at every woman there with an expectant expression. One even held roses;

*Eleanor, gyrating, surrounded by a circle of cheering brown-haired men;

*me with a bra for a top, vomiting near the barbecue; and

*Allison and I fighting. In front of everyone.

Oh, the shame. Is there anything worse than the paranoia that hits you with the hangover? I mean, the hangover itself is bad enough. The pain of the head. The need to eat, yet the complete impossibility of keeping anything down. The longing for lemonade, yet having no-one to fetch it. All of that is disgusting. No wonder I didn't usually drink. But the paranoia really nails the lid on it. I was so ashamed I didn't think I could even show my face in my own house, let alone in public. Bloody hell!

I looked at the floor. There was my poor little sparkly party top. With horrible post-party human fallout all over it. I shuddered – seeing it reminded me of just how messy I'd been. Made me realise just how sick I still felt.

Poor little top. I'd chosen it so carefully. For Nick. Lovely Nick. Who I'd managed to stand up.

Shit.

MISS LONELYHEARTS

I'd meant to go. I had, really, I had. But maybe I wasn't meant to go. After all. Ben's letter, you know.

I opened it and read it.

> **Dear whoever you are**
> **Everyone says they never do things like this. But this is true. I do not do things like this. I don't really know why I'm answering your letter. It's not like me to read the ads, let alone respond. But something about what you said ... called out to me.**
> **And me? A dead-end relationship and too little time to waste for the rest of my life. I want a soul mate.**
> **I want to meet you,**
> **Just tell me when.**
> **Ben.**

It was his handwriting. His style. The sort of words he used. I had his letters somewhere. I had ... hang on. I had a book he'd given me, he'd inscribed something ...

I reached over. Shakespeare's sonnets. Love poems. I opened it up. *Always*, he had written. With just his name.

Always.

The letters were looped in the same funny way, the writing sort of spidery and eccentric, straight up and down with the occasional flourish. Even in just one word.

Same writing. Same guy.

Oh. My. God. I had to get a grip. I can't deny I wasn't excited. If I hadn't been so sick, I would have been sick with excitement. But I had to think. Diane burst through the door in cosy new best friend mode.

Oh, God. It couldn't have happened. She couldn't have stayed overnight. Could she?

She obviously had. She was wearing one of Dan's Clash T-shirts and his beloved uggs. Horror. Girlfriend activity already. And why wasn't she sick?

She plodded gingerly over the flokati before thunking down on my bed. I still had letters scrambled all over the pillow, so I had a bit of a mad flurry trying to get them all under the doona. I managed. Just. Amazing how fast you can move with a hangover. Must have been flight or fight syndrome.

Yuk! She was sitting on the end of my bed.

'Are you still trying to ring Nick, Meg?' she asked, head tilted to one side, sounding terribly concerned.

'What?' I said guiltily, feeling like I'd been caught using my phone as a vibrator, or something.

'You were trying to ring for a while last night but you couldn't punch the numbers in and you couldn't tell Carla the numbers because you were really gone,' she said fondly, rumpling my hair like I was naughty schoolgirl.

I flushed. How did she know?

'You know, I can ring him for you now and explain if you like,' she said, taking my phone and pushing redial.

'No!' I yelped and grabbed the phone back off her and hit stop.

'Oh, okay, whatever you like,' she said kindly, as if I was a sad little slow person.

'I love and approve of myself,' I quickly muttered, trying not to face the reality of my life.

'Ohhhh, you've got a copy of *You Can Heal Your Life*,' Diane gushed, pouncing on my book like she'd just discovered that we both own the same really obscure pair of shoes, or are related, or have shared boyfriends, or something. 'Isn't it …' she began enthusiastically. 'Well.' She patted my leg under the covers, making a muffled chunky noise on the doona. 'I should let you find out for yourself. It is an amazing book.'

You Can Heal Your Life had actually been giving me filthy looks from the foot of the bed for about two nights. I'd even slept with it, which is a bit of a shock to a self-help virgin. I mean, it was like hearing all your friends talking about having sex, and feeling quite keen on having it yourself, and then experiencing the awful reality of actually losing your virginity. It was almost impossible to talk about it in any realistic way.

It was very, very weird … and yet … addictive.

I had tried a few attempts at the mirror work. I looked at myself in the mirror by the bed.

'I love and approve of you,' I said to myself, looking at a pimple that seemed to be sprouting from between my eyebrows.

'I am perfect exactly as I am.' I thought about how pissed I'd been and had a strange flashback of nearly kissing someone who was not attractive. At all.

Diane continued with her brand of over-familiar rhapsodising for about five minutes, which was actually really good because I sank back into the pillows and let it wash over me, as if her ravings were an inspiring wave, but actually I think I must have had a little sleep while she gibbered on. When I paid attention again she'd shifted subject.

'… Even Allison thought so, and you know what she's like – I mean, she's great, I love her to death, but she hasn't really … thought about life … as much as she's just sort of living it,' she said importantly, looking at me as though I couldn't do anything but agree with her amazing insight.

'Allison is my best friend,' I said staunchly.

'And she's great. Really free and doesn't care about what other people think – in a really good way. Like she doesn't need our approval. And so ambitious. She's going to get ahead – no matter what!'

I looked a bit pissed off.

'Oh, I know how close you are – although I had thought lately there may have been a bit of a rift … you know, she sort of said she was … a bit … well, maybe it was just that I got the wrong impression. You never know!'

'What – what did she say?'

'Just that … it was time for some things to change. She said something about you needing to boost your confidence, and, well,' she lowered her voice and looked around, 'she was going to do something about it. Whether you liked it or not.'

I didn't say anything but I snuggled deeply into the pillows, face down, to stop the tears that were starting in my eyes. Hangovers always make me feel so pathetic. When I lifted my head I got a shock.

God, she was still there. Looking at my books from where she was, sort of lying back in my bed.

'I don't want to leave you if you're upset,' she said, concerned and all kindly. I ignored her.

'Look, don't take what I said the wrong way. Allison was a bit excited a week or so back. Said something about how she'd get you back on your feet and then she could get on with things. She said something about saving you from yourself.'

'Did she tell you all this?'

'Not really. But you know what it's like when you live with people. You know things. You get a vibe.' She lowered her head sadly.

I stood up, wobbly, still in my party skirt and bra, and said, 'I just need to go to the loo.'

I went to the toilet and had a little cry. Was Allison saying she was sick of me? Maybe I had been taking up a lot of her time. She *was* pretty ambitious. And I had been kind of … well, I'd thought I'd been better, much better than when I'd broken up with Ben. But maybe she was fed up with me. Maybe we were having a friendship break-up. I'd written about them, but I'd never had one. Apparently girls never say. They just stop talking and that's that.

I dried my face on some toilet paper, flushed it away and padded back to my room.

She was still there! Fuck off!

'Um, I really need a cup of tea,' I croaked.

'Love to,' she said, jumping up.

'Can you just leave it with me? I want to sleep a bit more,' I said.

'Sure – and here's your book. Maybe you could read a little before you fall asleep. It might help ...'

She closed the door softly, and I waved, smiling in a murky half-hearted kind of way. I didn't *completely* dislike Diane. I'd tried really hard to get along with her. But I'd never quite trusted her. It always seemed like she was sneering at people who had to work for a living – 'cos she was a trust-fund girl with rich parents. Her being a hippy seemed like, I don't know, kind of an act – and she obviously felt morally superior.

But Ali had always said she was okay – really smart and funny, too, even if she was out there.

I didn't mind the out-there stuff. It was the weird feeling about ... her not being quite who she made herself out to be. Even though she was so different to Ali, I'd thought there'd been a touch of the single white females about the relationship. Like Diane was just waiting to pounce on Ali's life – without having to put any of the work in.

I'd always thought she'd been after Dan.

And now, here she was.

When I woke up again, it was because I heard someone in the hall, and I was having an awful dream that a cat was licking at an empty bowl. I pulled on an unfortunately bright pink T-shirt (freebie from Anna Sui) and struggled out of the bedroom.

Fizz was cleaning up some party horror. He was looking like a tiny sick pixie, half-heartedly sweeping away.

'How do you feel?' he asked in a deathly whisper.

'Shocking. Fizz, what happened?' I replied, looking around at the house, expecting aliens to sprout from the walls and slime me just to top everything off.

'It was a great party,' he said. Grinning slightly.

I had another flashback. Fizz grinding up against Tamara, like they were trying to squash themselves into each other.

'Is someone still in your room?' I asked in a loudish voice. I heard a funny little noise. 'You dirty dog,' I said admiringly. 'Is that Tamara?'

'Um, um,' he said, looking around in a panic.

'Where's Allison?' I whispered. He shrugged. 'I don't know. Diane's here,' he whispered in a conspiratorial tone.

So it hadn't been an awful dream. Ali was gone and Diane was here.

I sat in the hallway, wondering if I could crawl to the kitchen without anyone, apart from Fizz, seeing me in my state of ultimate disgrace. I slumped forward onto my hands to have a bit of a think about it and swayed softly, groaning for a while, until I heard the door shut behind me. It was Diane. I could tell because I could see Dan's enormous ugg boots thumping their way towards me.

'Oh look, Fizz,' I faked quickly, 'I think I've found it.' I held my own earring up. I couldn't let her think I was actually about to crawl down my own hallway, could I?

'Hi, Meg,' she gaily chirrupped, stepping over me. Ouch.

'How are you all? Great party! More tea?'

I was still in the hallway when she brought me a cuppa. There was really nothing to do except go back to bed. And listen to Diane chatting and snuffling away at Fizz before I heard her stomping in a horrible headache-inducing way down the hall to Dan's bedroom.

What the hell was going on? I asked the ceiling, which seemed to have patterns moving on it. Horror. The horror. Standing up Nick. Men in brown. Fight with Allison. Letter from Ben. Letters! Where were they?

Some were still under my doona – but where were all the ones those girls had been going through last night? They were private property! And I wasn't going to be a public joke …

I crawled over to the secret hiding place in the drawers to check them. And there were … there were about forty letters.

Weren't there more? I swear there had been about 200. Allison had practically wet herself saying so. So where were the rest? I stuck my head around into the hallway.

'Hey, Fizz, have you seen any of the, you know … fuck letters?'

He took a step back. I must have sounded a bit scary.

'The Lonelyhearts letters, you know,' I explained.

'No! You said *fuck*! We were keeping it *secret*.'

Sweet boy. So that ruled out Fizz.

What about Diane?

Of course, I thought, brow furrowing. She'd probably taken them. I knew she wasn't to be trusted. The thing was, what was she going to do with them?

By later that day, the whole house was beginning to look normal again. As in the horror of the party was beginning to morph into our normal surroundings. It seemed perfectly normal to have a broken glass with wine in it on the fireplace. It seemed normal to have the toilet not flushing properly. It seemed almost normal not to be speaking to Allison. To have Diane around instead.

Not.

Diane was acting like we were instant new best friends. I mean, friendships grow – I'd known Ali since she stopped Linda Goodridge from flushing my head down the toilet because I wouldn't smoke. But Diane was just ... she seemed to think we'd known each other all our lives. And that I'd be providing girlfriend support for Operation Dan.

'So, Meg, I've never really had much time to spend with you – I'm really looking forward to it,' she chatted at me once I'd managed to make it to the couch later that day.

'What?'

Oh. She was talking about her now-established relationship with Dan.

'Er, Diane, wouldn't count on spending too much time with ...' God, how do I say it? 'Dan is, well, you know he likes women. And aren't you worried about, well, the fact that, um ...'

'That he and Allison were having a bit of a fling? Well, you said it yourself – Dan is ... different. And anyway, everything can change when you meet the right person,' she said.

Oh, God! Everything was horrible. My life was now a strange parallel universe where Diane was the new Allison, thousands of men were interested in seeing what I wore under my skirt and instead of Geri there was a very weird and horrible person who was about to sack me for not getting plastic surgery. And I'd stood up a perfectly nice, not brown, guy. The only good thing was the fact Ben had written that he was in a dead-end relationship … with Freya! I still couldn't get my head round how to deal with that.

Amidst all the awful self-examination the phone rang. I staggered down the hall, a wave of excitement and hope and relief breaking inside me. Allison! Everything was going to be great. Life would be back on track. Next weekend would be different!

Mum. Life was awful.

'Hello, darling,' she started, 'you sound a bit croaky.'

I immediately went scarlet and tried to sound perky. 'No, just, maybe a bit of a late one.'

Why? Why do I tell my mother anything resembling the truth?

'I hope you're taking care of yourself, sweetheart? I'm just ringing to tell you all about next week. It's Tod's engagement party!' she said breathlessly.

'What?' When had my brother become engaged?

'Well, darling, it's what most people do after they've been seeing each other for a while.'

Unlike people like me, who are not normal? Who are just massively disappointing to parents?

MISS LONELYHEARTS

'Anyway, yes, darling isn't it wonderful? Finally one of you is all sorted out! Now there's only you girls to worry about, though the way the boys run after Karen she'll probably be next. I suppose it's hard when you get a bit down, never mind, darling. We'll always be here for you. And you have some nice friends,' she said, as if she was already seeing me with forty cats and a polyester nightie buying tinned food at the corner shop.

'Anyway, Tod and Lisa have set a date. It's fab, isn't it? And he's going to have a party. At the RSL.'

'So ... that's great Mum. Can I talk to him?'

'No, he's not here darling.' She lowered her voice to a confidential tone. 'He's in the den.' She said in a conspiratorial whisper.

Oh, God. My brother had managed to have the garage converted into his very own bachelor (soon not to be) pad. I won't go into the spectacular abyss my life had fallen into once I realised my younger brother had a hot sex life, millions of girlfriends and a ready-made party pad, because, my parents claimed, boys needed their privacy, while I'd still had the pink frilly room next to my parents. In fact, still had that room.

'You can stay overnight dear. Do you want to bring someone? ... Allison?' she said hopefully, when I paused.

'No, I think I'd like to really focus on meeting Lisa's family.'

'Be here at two. We can pick you up from the bus stop if you don't want the walk.'

Oh horror. The full and bloody horror of being catapulted back into my adolescence.

'Karen's coming, though she's not bringing someone. She thinks it would give them "ideas". The minx,' she said approvingly. 'They're all running round after her.'

Great. Both my younger siblings were fulfilling my mother's every fantasy, while I would arrive, sad and alone, with no prospects and in the wrong clothes and have to sit under a picture of the Queen at a table with people who would wonder what was wrong with me.

'Are you seeing anyone?' she teased, sounding somehow suggestive and coy at the same time. Mum and Dad, but especially Mum, were always hoping that I was sleeping with people. I think she wanted me to be all bohemian and wild, and maybe run off and join a cult. I was quite a disappointment, all in all.

'No, Mum.'

She sighed.

'Well, I am a bit … I just didn't want to say anything.'

Now where had that come from?

'So, I'd love to bring someone. If that's okay?'

There was a pause while my mother took this in. Probably wondering if I was insane.

'You have someone to bring – well, that's – that's a surprise. I'm just a bit, well …'

'I thought you'd be happy,' I sulked.

'I'm just a bit surprised I haven't heard about this before.' Apparently I'm supposed to tell her everything.

'Sorry, Mum – just wanted to make sure it was on

track before introducing you. We've been spending lots of time with each other.'

With who? What was I doing? I *was* insane.

'Oh, I see – is he there now? Goodness!'

Oh God. How embarrassing. My mother was thrilled I was in bed, hungover, with an imaginary person.

'Is Dad there?' I said, a bit desperately. Hopefully. 'Can I say hi?'

'Of course you can – what – don't you think your father wants to have a chat to you?

'Hi, darling,' he boomed. 'It's a great day here on the beaches,' he said, as though where they lived was a holiday resort and I was in some kind of concentration camp in the inner city. 'Well, I'll put you back onto your mother.'

Oh God.

'Well, darling, two o'clock. Will we pick you up from the bus stop? Wear something nice. Like a skirt. Nothing black. It's a happy occasion. Say hi to your friend!' she trilled.

Oh God!

'Okay, Mum. See you then.'

So that was next weekend. Written off. Over.

'Hi,' said Diane, popping out of Dan's bedroom for a moment. Had she handcuffed him in there or something?

'I'm just off home to make a lasagne. Your oven doesn't seem to work properly. I'll be back later.'

'Okay,' I said faintly, staring at her.

'Can you do a salad? No mushrooms though – Dan hates them.'

I waited till the door had closed and I heard her footsteps going down the path before I hammered on the door to Dan's room.

'Dan. Dan. It's me. Come on, I have to talk to you.'

Fizz was looking at me, worried. Eric (who spent so much time here I may as well have had three flatmates) looked up from a Freddie Mercury biography.

Freddie Mercury?

'Dan!' I opened his door. He was lying on the bed, curled into the foetal position. 'What's going on?' I said.

'I don't know. She's like a virus. Just spreading and taking over my life. And I'm too sick to care.'

Wow. Him too.

'She is. I think she's stolen my Fuck letters. Plus she's bossing me around about making salads. We eat pizza! Cheese on toast!'

'I was ambushed,' Dan said pathetically.

'Maybe we can change the locks,' suggested Fizz, who was looking ill too.

'No. Dan! You have to tell her it's over.'

'Okay,' he said faintly.

'What? What's the problem?'

'I'm … scared of her.'

'Oh, you wimp.'

'I feel trapped.'

'Have you spoken to Allison?' I asked.

'No,' he said, sticking his head round the door, looking miserable. 'Have you?'

'No,' I replied, pulling a wry face. 'I think we might not be speaking to each other. I think the party may have been one of those crucible-type things, where suddenly everything in your entire life changes in one night.'

'Maybe you can go and see Allison when Diane comes over and make things right,' Dan half-pleaded.

'But you – you have to talk to her, too.'

'I don't know. I don't think she'd want me to.' Really, boys don't have a clue!

'I don't think she'll want to talk to me, either.'

We sat miserably watching Elvis movies on TV for the next couple of hours, eating fried rice from the corner shop fetched by Fizz and Tamara. Dan actually started whimpering when he saw Ann-Margret go-go dancing.

'That's all over for me now,' he said. 'Diane's got me. She drugged me last night. Now she won't give in till I wake up one morning with her and twenty kids we're homeschooling in a mudbrick house with an organic garden.'

Eric looked up. 'She didn't drug you,' he said.

'I know she didn't. But I can't believe how sick I'm feeling. It's not normal. Everyone was totally wasted really fast.'

'I was sick, too. I only had two drinks. Really!' I pitched in.

'It was T-Bro,' said Eric, calmly. 'Had to be. He's the only one likely to introduce illicit substances into the mix.'

We all chewed on that for a second.

'So what was it? I thought it was just, I don't know, alcohol poisoning 'cos I was so pure. Or fungus from the fish tank.' I was a bit disturbed so I was making excuses.

'Well, it could have been. But T-Bro served a lot of drinks. And he made sure Allison had plenty. And she was off her dial. And he made friends with you, too – remember,' Eric said.

'And he poured me a few, too,' said Dan.

'Wow. Maybe it was … Let's not even think about what it was,' I said.

'At least we're all still here,' said Tamara, sweetly, holding on to Fizz.

Eric went straight back to his book. 'What are you reading?' Tamara asked chattily.

God, why was she so perky? Was she still too young to get truly dreadful hangovers?

Oh, that's right. She was high on love.

Eric flipped the book at her.

'*The Freddie Mercury Story*,' she said, puzzled. 'Who's Freddie Mercury?'

Eric cleared his throat. 'Actually, I'm just researching for …'

'Big Pooves Week,' Dan sniggered. Eric slammed the book down and strode out of the room.

'I was *joking*!' Dan yelled after him.

Phone! I scrambled for it. Nick? Allison? Oh God, I begged, let it be Nick! Or Allison! I felt flushed with hope, like I'd been given a second chance and everything was going to be …

It was Max.

At least it wasn't Mum.

'Oh, Max. Thank God. Listen, everything's

fucked. Life's a mess,' I babbled. He listened politely but I could tell he wasn't really taking it in …

'Meg, we can talk later. I'm coming over.'

'Oh, great … what time?'

'Can I have a word with Eric? About a CD,' he said, completely hollowly. 'I am *sooo* sick, I can only talk when absolutely necessary.'

Wow. Him too. What was going on here?

'Eric!' I called. He was standing about 3 inches from me. 'Oh, it's for you.' Max, I mouthed, pulling a surprised-looking face. 'Maybe he's got a crush on you,' I whispered, my hand over the phone. Eric went beet and sort of glared, but not at me.

'Just a sec,' I said. 'Don't you want to hear all about my problems?' I sniffed into the phone.

'Of course I do, babe,' Max said, a bit impatiently. 'But I'm going to be sick. Can I talk to Eric and share with you when I'm human?'

I handed the phone to Eric, who looked all feverish and nervy.

What is going on? I thought, tromping back to the lounge room, feeling strangely rejected.

Tamara and Fizz got up from the couch when I came back in and disappeared back to his bedroom – again. These marathon shag sessions were really depressing me. Anyway, weren't they sick?

There was a knock at the door.

'You're answering it,' I glared at Dan.

'Oh God,' he moaned. 'I'm so sick. Do I …'

'Answer it!'

I could hear Diane's voice, and she burst triumphantly into the lounge room, holding a huge picnic basket and a sack of clothes.

'Hi!' she boomed out. 'Who's hungry?'

I glared at her. If I asked her where my letters were, she'd know I had letters. Which was only a problem if she didn't have them. And I was nearly certain she had them. She'd been in my room. But … I settled for just glaring at her. I'd bide my time. I'll find out.

An hour later we all sat down and ate the lasagne, which was really delicious. Dan loved it. I gave him a look when he said, 'Mmmm, Diane, this is fantastic, I feel like a new man,' sounding like they'd been married for nineteen years. She said, 'Funny. That's exactly what I was wanting,' before snuggling up to him.

Dan cringed, then looked guilty. Traitor, I mouthed at him.

He gave me a startled look back. Guys are such moral vacuums.

I looked around the room, feeling disgusted. There was Max, giggling over some CD in the lounge room with Eric, Fizz and Tamara emerging from snog land to eat the rest of Diane's lasagne, Diane proudly overseeing the table, complete with apron, her and Dan the mum and dad of our little home, her face absolutely alight.

It was beyond horrible. I couldn't face it. So I did what all modern, assertive women do when their territory is being invaded by a predator, right?

I went and sulked in my room.

CHAPTER FIFTEEN

The party night was cold – remember? Well, fast forward two days and it was hot. And I had a cold. That's Sydney. Head towards March and watch the temperature rise for one last time, just after you've packed away all your cossies and shirts and cool summer things. You have to get back into the wardrobe and pull them all out again.

Mind you, that would be what happens, if you were Carla, or Allison, but definitely not Monica, who probably had a biseasonal walk-in wardrobe. Luckily, my clothes were handily lying all over the floor.

I sighed as I pulled on a silky top (one which, I'll have you know, I'd already said a mental goodbye to until next summer), and some skinny-legged men's trousers and my purple Converse. Godammit, I needed some comfort in my life. Forget walking. It was humid and swampy warm. Sydney's typical tropical summer's last fling, oozing sweat, heat and humidity just when the winter fashions were arriving in the shops. It was so humid you could practically lap at the air and relieve your thirst; unless it was beer or white wine you were after.

Oh. Oh, you're right.

What about Nick?

I know. I'd completely forgotten about him, well, till Diane had brought it up. *Him* up. And now I had no idea what to do. I liked him – lots. But Ben was back in my life – well, nearly, anyway, even if he didn't know it was my life he was in exactly. So if I rang Nick and said sorry, wouldn't that be, sort of, sending the wrong message?

Not that I didn't have something to say sorry for. I knew that. The guilt was like a marble albatross thunking against my boobs all the way to work on Monday morning. I started thinking seriously about what to do while I was on the train.

Maybe if I rang him, I thought in one of those irrational moments of denial ... Of course! If he heard from me now, everything would be fine. We could probably catch up later, and I could explain everything. He'd understand. I mean, surely he knew what could happen if you unintentionally got pissed and wasted, even if you never even hardly drank?

But how was he to understand that I was planning on getting back together with my ex-boyfriend? I mean, I always had, but Nick had been a momentary distraction. Maybe he'd come along to remind me that I was able to attract someone special. So therefore I could get back with Ben.

I cleared my throat and readied myself for a practice run, aiming for just the right tone. I felt almost positive. First, I'd sort everything out with Nick. Then I'd see Ben. Then I'd thank Allison and we'd finally be back on track.

Everything was going to be perfect.

'Er, hi. Nick,' I croaked aloud. Everyone in my carriage looked at me. Oops. You really do need props when speaking aloud in public, I reminded myself.

I held my phone up to my ear, pretending to make a call. 'Hi, Nick,' I started again. 'Just remembered you'd said something about a party and ... ooops!'

A wave of guilt nearly knocked me out of my seat. I mean, I'd hated it when Ben had dropped me. Just because we were probably getting back together didn't mean I could start being horrible myself. Besides. Think of the karma!

I mean, what if he'd thought I'd had an accident or something? No, he probably just thought I was a bit slack. In fact, that was very arrogant. He may not have even noticed.

That was a comforting thought.

I cleared my throat and continued my practice run, trying to get just the right expression in my voice.

'I am truly terrible for not even ... showing up to your party, which I'm sure was much better than the one I had at my place, accidentally, that night ... It started out as drinks and ended up ... something like ... carnage.' I laughed.

No, that sounded callous.

'Anyway. Feel terrible. Like a sick pig. But ring anytime. Would really really love to hear from you ... Bye!'

No way. That was appalling. Heartless soulless cow phone call. I really needed to get this right before going through with it. I had so much on that day it was unlikely I'd run into him, I rationalised. (I think it's called denial.)

I jumped off the train, walked to the office, and readied myself for the *tick, tick, tick* sounds of the Monica clones' heels, and actually smiled for the first time in days, I swear, at the anticipation of the inevitable blast of air conditioning. For once, I couldn't wait to get to work.

When I walked in to Go Global Enterprises, there was no frosty blast, forcing me to get a cardi on quick smart. It was even more hideous, if that was possible, than inside the train. The kind of heat where people pass out.

Everyone was milling about, moaning and waiting for lifts, rather than taking the stairs (we've got some very sweat-conscious people in our office). Just to be sure I'd avoid Nick, a little incidental exercise seemed in order. No-one else but a woman with an albatross for an accessory would be crazy enough to take the stairs in this weather.

It wasn't until I reached the third floor, drenched in perspiration (thanks, silk — sexy, but stinky) that I felt safe. Sweaty, but safe.

Which is exactly when Nick came bolting towards me.

'Hi,' I said brightly, hanging off the banister, thinking he'd just bolt on by.

But no. He was going to make me squirm.

'Lifts are jammed,' he said. And gave me a look.

Not a very nice look I might add. He seemed a bit angry. But it may not have been about me. It may have been the air conditioning.

'I'm so sorry,' I blurted the second our eyes met. Someone was dragging themselves up the stairs behind me, so I had to make it quick.

'I was going to ring, but ...' But what? I was too scared to leave a daggy message? I was drugged by my ex-best friend's new boyfriend? My ex-boyfriend and I might be getting back together? (Oh yes, after I contact him, that is ...)

He gave me a cool look. Sort of friendly. But wary. I don't like wary!

'Hey, no worries. Nothing to apologise for. Got to rush – so talk to you later,' he said abruptly, vanishing as Eleanor made it to where we were standing.

'But –' I blurted after him.

'Bloody hell,' I said.

'Oh my God,' said Eleanor, panting for breath. 'Was that Nick? How can he move so fast in this heat? He must be really fit.'

'I think we were just saying goodbye. Forever.'

'You're mad fucking that up.'

'Thanks. And, by the way, speaking of mad, what the hell are you doing walking up the stairs?'

'Lifts are jammed,' she explained, as if I were a complete idiot.

I just shut up. Seeing Nick hadn't made the albatross disappear and now I was even more confused. About Nick. And about Ben. The only thing I could do was try to forget about both of them – and focus on work … and Monica.

The heat, rather than cheering everyone up, was completely draining, and we flopped about the office moodily, limp as lettuce. Monica was the only one who remained on full professional alert.

'Have you been in yet?' Eleanor asked Julie, who was splashing her face with cold water in the tearoom.

'Nope. But the word is she's in a foul mood,' she said, nodding towards the art department, where we could see Craig through the glass partaking in a serious-looking power huddle with the other three brown cardigans.

'Why do you think they all wear brown cardigans?' Julie asked Eleanor.

'Because Craig does.'

'But they're revolting.'

'Yeah, but he's the alpha male. Plus, never underestimate the importance of a title. The powerful illusion it creates,' she explained as we walked back to our workstations. 'So, in this instance, Craig, who we all know is nice-looking, ordinary and probably colour-blind, is given the title of – she whispered – 'the art director, so *voilà*, obviously he's cool. And thus brown jumpers began to proliferate.'

'But,' Julie said loudly, 'they're brown *cardigans.*'

'I didn't make the evolutionary rules of office survival. It's just the way it is. Everyone starts dressing like the dominant male. Or female.'

'We don't do that,' I objected, thinking of Geri

and her supersized big-patterned Supré specials. 'What about Geri?'

'She wasn't actually the dominant female.' Eleanor stated as she left us to get ready for the Monday meeting.

Julie and I looked at each other.

'Now, who do we most resemble?'

'Oh my God,' said Julie. 'Eleanor is the alpha female.'

'It's true,' I said in wonderment.

'So Monica's not really in charge,' Julie said with a smile.

'That's a story,' I said, grabbing a notebook and scrawling down some ideas.

Which was handy, because next stop was Monica's office for some brainstorming. She was behind her desk ... looking like a queen.

We filed in. Carla, Eleanor and Chandra were already there. We all grinned at Carla and Eleanor, and avoided eye contact with Chandra. Too risky. Might lead to conversation and hard-luck stories that had been on very high rotation.

'Have you seen Dr Gold?' Monica asked, not even making eye contact.

'No, but I am seeing him ...' Why was she asking? She'd made the appointment.

'We need to move fast. This is a weekly, Meg, not some kind of monthly magazine. Get busy, or get busy looking for an alternative.'

I gulped. And blushed. And clenched my hands.

'Anyway. Next. This Miss Lonelyhearts story, Tamara. How are you going with it?'

'Well, I ... I haven't been able to find her yet ...'

'But we do have a great lead,' butted in Eleanor, saving Tamara. 'We're close.' She sounded firm enough that Monica looked like she was going to take her on, then she backed down.

'So, have any of you got anything for me? Julie? Sandra? Carla? Max? Stories? Scoops? Ideas? Pictures?' demanded Monica in bored tones, reaching for her glass nail file and sawing away at her French polish. 'I'm not getting my hopes up, mind you. By the way, your story on shopaholism,' she said to me, 'was very disappointing ...' she concluded brightly.

'I worked hard on that story,' I bristled.

'Really? It seemed quite thrown together. And was that quiz meant to be amusing?'

'I ...'

'Because it wasn't,' she snapped. I was going to say it was supposed to be both funny and informative, i.e. witty, but a savage glare had chased the words back down my throat. The filing continued. There was something scary about it.

Monica always files her nails during meetings. Eleanor's theory is that it's a power moment – she can, we can't. Hierarchy established. So where do you draw the line? Make-up, dressing, personal hygiene boundaries were in serious danger.

Chandra could smell blood, just like any award-winning supervictim, so she seized the perfect opportunity. 'I'd just like to suggest a few health stories. We've been very light on in the serious stuff lately, lacking in something that's of ... real value to the reader.'

Ouch!

'Eye care – ten ways to keep your eyesight on track. Bathing them, treating them, when to get a new prescription.'

We were all shocked, waiting for the gale of abuse for such a boring idea. But that didn't happen.

Chandra took the moment and ran with it.

'For example,' she continued, 'my eyes are like two hard-boiled eggs – it's the glare. Can you please,' she said, smiling like an evil doll, 'close your blinds in future?'

And to think I'd thought that she'd cool off now that she had Monica to really hate, but no. She was still fixated on me as well. I folded my arms and let her go. Give her enough rope, I thought.

'Perhaps a story on people who drink too much and how it affects their work,' she said smugly.

We all looked pissed off. Let's face it, that theme could have applied to everyone in the room. Even me, after Saturday night.

'And perhaps a hand story … Hand care, treatment, and how difficult that can be. I, for example, am getting RSI,' she droned on, holding up a limp wrist laden with horrible jewellery. 'It's from,' she sniffed, 'mousing. Gwen in the mail department's had it. I'm sure that's why I haven't been able to do much.'

She was acting like we worked in a lace factory and she was one of the oppressed.

Monica must have been affected by the heat because she wasn't saying a word. She just looked at Chandra, her nail file frozen in mid-air.

'And about flowers ... let's do a story on ...'

We all became aware that Monica was actually transfixed not by the brilliance of Chandra's ideas, but by the vision of Renata, the advertising chick, making hysterical gestures outside the glass partition. Monica beckoned her in to the office with her nail file.

Renata yanked open the door like it had refused her a bonus, entered, then slammed it before storming up to the couch and flopping onto it dramatically.

'Yes, Renata, what is it?'

'Phimacare,' she said over her heaving chest, 'have pulled.'

We all sat, very quietly, and I can't guarantee it, but I'm pretty sure I wasn't alone in feeling a little trickle of ice-cold sweat run down my spine.

'What? Phimacare – it's twenty million worth of business!' Monica exclaimed.

'Not for us,' Eleanor interjected.

'Well, it was one million that went to us,' Renata snapped.

It must have been a bad day for my starsign, because Renata turned the furnace blast of her frustration on me. 'I told you we should have put their products in.'

'They were toxic,' I snapped.

'They're our advertisers,' she snapped back.

Renata drew a deep breath. Once she started her rant I'd never get a word in. Time for a pre-emptive strike.

'I did put some in,' I explained very slowly, calming down, trying to stay cool, much like I was

MISS LONELYHEARTS

trying to talk my way out of a hostage situation. 'I'm not *obliged* to put any in. And I didn't think it was very … healthy to put the …'

'Oh for God's sake – we're trying to run a business here,' interrupted Monica, starting to file away at a nail extra viciously.

'Everyone, out. Except Renata, you stay. We'll sort something out. And Meg? I want that rewrite – by 5.00 p.m. And I want five product mentions in there. Advertiser product mentions. You're the bloody beauty and fitness editor – not health.'

Okay, okay. So that made a rewrite and a visit to Dr Gold's in the one day. Fine! Save me thinking about my stuff-up of a life for a few hours.

Monica was still screeching. 'I thought you used to work on a newspaper. So where are your reporting skills? And if you have none,' she interrupted me, as I went to protest, 'use your imagination,' she yelped. 'You want me to figure it out for you? That's why *you're* here. And the moment you're out of ideas and solutions and use for me it is the right time for you to start looking for another job.' Every shrill word was punctuated with a thrust from the nail file.

'Okay,' I nodded meekly. 'I'll do my best.'

'Five products, 1500 words. Five p.m.'

'Why is she so vicious?' I moaned once I staggered back to my desk, reaching into a box of chocolates (sent by some suitor or other. Don't worry. I'd made sure everyone else had eaten more than me, and I was planning on going to the gym later).

'I suppose she just takes her career seriously,' said Tamara, dangling some lingerie before her eyes.

'Career — that's a funny word for it,' Julie scoffed. 'Have any of you noticed what the average life span of an editor is?'

'I'm not *just* talking about Monica,' I pointed out, passive-aggressive to a fault. 'And Geri was here for ages.'

'Yeah, but look at *Elegance*. At *Phwoar!*. At *Look Out!*. At *Cheeky You!*. It's eighteen months max,' Eleanor stated lightly, peeling an orange.

'Don't you want a chocolate, Eleanor?' asked Tamara, holding my box out to her.

She looked impatient, shaking her head. 'The average life span of a magazine editor used to be three years — advertisers wanted stability. Now they expect a high turnover.' She popped a piece of orange in her mouth. 'Then they wonder why the readers get confused.'

'Anyway, look,' snapped Julie, who seemed like she'd heard this a few times before. 'How do we tame the bitch?'

'Should we take a chocolate in to her?' suggested Tamara.

'Only if we poison it first,' Julie said.

'She's under heaps of pressure,' Eleanor commented.

'Why? I mean, the sales are okay,' Tamara asked.

'Oh really?' said Julie, dripping with sarcasm.

We all nodded, except for Tamara, who probably hadn't noticed how much Big Boss had been hanging around lately and how much it made Monica nervous. Skittish when he was there, she was completely unbearable once he'd departed. When he 'dropped by', the door to the blue room was shut. When she knew he was dropping by, her skirts got shorter for the meetings, but she was still left with a big, fake shaky smile plastered on her perfect face.

'There's success for you,' Julie said, watching her have a mini-tantrum at Renata. 'Top of the tree and the fire's lapping the bark.'

CHAPTER SIXTEEN

If you've never been to a plastic surgeon's office, and I've heard quite a few people haven't (though now I'm beginning to doubt it), let me paint a little picture for you.

Imagine two perfectly groomed girls, a little under perfect model height, with nails that look like orange talons and which make their jobs (picking up pens, answering phones, running fingernails down lists of appointments, handing you massive forms to fill in) very, very difficult. They smile with their perfect, plush, full-blown lips, revealing bright, white teeth. Their eyes are like fault-finding machines. I stood naked, well, metaphysically, while they scrutinised me for any potential work for the good doctor.

After much attempted running of fingernails, and meaningful looks about the state I've left myself get in, they call the star of the show.

Out comes our leading man: the famous, rich cosmetic surgeon. The aptly named Dr Gold.

He had to be the ugliest man I've ever seen who's good-looking.

I'll explain. You know how George Hamilton is at the same time good-looking, yet extremely repulsive? That's what's going on with the good (I hope!) doctor.

He had black, black hair, none too thick, not overcombed, but tufty in front. Growing in, it seemed, definite patches. Brown, brown skin, with not a single line. Like plastic. Brown Tupperware containers, I thought, when I saw his face. And it was dewy. Glowing and radiant and feminine and creepy. He had smallish hands that were much too soft, that reached out to shake my hand in a limp kind of fashion, leaving a funny after-feeling on my palms. Like they were crawling.

And gold – gold everywhere. Gold, the Pamela Anderson of metals, was dangling off him, like a Christmas tree or a man awaiting his turn in the Mardi Gras parade. He was wearing all white, as befitting a doctor, attempting to symbolise all that is clean and pure and perfect. He looked like a very old cabana boy from Palm Springs who should be cleaning a pool.

There was something so ... Californian about the whole experience, I almost felt like I'd travelled twelve hours on a plane to get this appointment. So surreal, it was like I was jet-lagged.

But he wasn't.

Dr Gold was quite excited actually, all ready to go with the pitch. He was going to tell me about myself – and how I could look a whole lot better.

Before I got to meet him, I'd had to fill in an extremely long and boring form. He was holding it in his hand as he led me into his office and beckoned for me to sit down.

'What sort of work are you interested in getting, Peg?' he smiled, revealing frighteningly white teeth.

'Meg.'

'Well?'

'I'm not sure – I wanted to see what was available, but I wanted to put myself into the hands of an expert – see what you thought. I'd be interested in … a bit of a transformation …'

'You wouldn't be a proper woman if you weren't,' he sniggered. 'Well, let's start at the top,' he said, looking at my forehead, 'and work our way down.' When he finished speaking, he was looking at my ankles, which seemed to swell under his gaze.

'Now, I'm not the man for every part of your anatomy, you know. I don't work on everything. I do skin, breasts, lipo and hairlines.'

'Hairlines,' I yelped. That was a new one.

'Oh, yes. Marilyn Monroe had her hairline lifted, don't you know. One half of an inch, in the old measurements. Quite painful, back then. A lot of electrolysis. The hairline is very interesting – it can completely change a face. Give you that … elegant quality.

'Hairlines are not my favourite, though,' he confessed.

'Oh, what would that be, then?' Despite myself, I was getting very curious.

'Oh, I especially enjoy breasts,' he said. 'You can't beat an augmentation that's really worked. I see girls come in, all flat-chested and sunken, and send them away – well, bouncing and radiant. Attractive, they feel, for the first time in their lives,' he smiled, admiring his own ability to work miracles.

'Often the boyfriends come in too. I advise that sometimes, because they do seem quite keen to see how it all works.'

'Do you ever think, you know, that you should leave nature alone? That we're meant to have all sorts of different shapes and sizes?'

'Well, of course, if you're happy being sunken-chested, good for you! I always say, good looks don't matter to some people.'

Like Gwen Stefani, I thought. I mean, that was why I loved her – she was small-breasted, and proud of it.

'But there's no denying that no-one forces the women to come here. There's something so fulfilling about helping a woman reach her true potential.' His eyes glazed over a little as he said that.

I looked around the room. Impressive certificates were lined up along the walls, medical journals on his desk. On the coffee table there were magazines featuring ... well, featuring women who were always in magazines like mine. Or *Elegance*. Or *Phwoar!* for that matter.

'Excuse me,' he said as his phone rang. 'I'm waiting on something quite important.' I raised my eyebrows and nodded, to show I understood.

'Yes ... They are. We can't? Well, if that's out of the question, we'll need to look at other territories. Yes. Look I can't speak now. I'm with a journalist,' he smirked into the phone, winking at me. 'That's right, you can't be too careful.'

'Now don't be mean about *Gossip!* It's a very entertaining magazine.' He grinned at me as he spoke to whoever was on the other end. At least he was trying to be nice.

'Excuse me – I just need to …' I nodded and went outside to let him continue in private.

The receptionists were chatting among themselves.

'Why two?' I wondered and sat down to wait.

'I must see Dr Gold,' panted a girl who was as brown as brown can get with suntanning. She was practically … beef jerky with bronzer.

'I *have* to see him,' she wailed.

'Would you like to make an appointment?' one of the Barbie twins asked.

'The Laser Centre wouldn't see me,' she hissed. 'I must have this hair removed *now*.'

'Oh.'

'I've seen him before.'

'We can squeeze you in.'

'I'll wait.'

'Some of these places,' she spat, 'suck. They said I was too tanned. Dr Gold never said that to me.'

I looked at her legs. She *was* too tanned. Like old leather.

'You are a bit brown,' I suggested. 'I guess they're worried about skin cancer.'

She looked at me like I was mad. 'No, they're worried about … something to do with the laser not working. She scratched a patch on her leg that was whitish and strange. It really stood out against the brown everywhere else.

'Shouldn't you do what they say?'

'I need to look good. I'm seeing my boyfriend tonight. And he hates it when I'm pale. And hairy.'

I screwed my nose up, in sympathy.

'Miss Tooley,' the receptionist said, gesturing me back in to the doctor's office.

Interesting. So if she couldn't go there ... she came here?

'Ah – sorry about the intrusion,' said the doctor smoothly. 'Please, come over here.'

I lay down on a white leather armchair, the equivalent of a dentist's, only from some kind of Italian furnishing showroom. He looked at me closely, pulling my skin gently between his fingers, asking me to turn my head to the right, to the left. He'd scanned in a photo I'd sent in earlier, and he brought it up on a green screen sailing into view above me.

'This,' he said, 'is the site now.'

'The site?' I asked.

He chuckled. 'Your face – it's the professional term for the area we will be working on.'

'Oh.' The building site, I thought.

'Let's see what happens when we ... let's see ... lift your hairline.'

On the screen my hairline receded a little. I looked, smarter ... elegant.

'Then let's do some work on the teeth.'

Now I was getting cranky. I mean, my teeth are my pride. I am Australian, best dentists in the world, and come from a family where we weren't allowed a single sugary drink for my entire youth. My brother still doesn't have a filling. Smugly, I thought, let's see what you can do, plastic man.

He fiddled with the mouse a bit, and another astonishing thing happened on the screen. He smoothed the alignment of my front teeth, and knocked a little off the bottom of both of them. Then he cut back my gums. 'Ouch!'

'Oh, it's nothing – everyone in Hollywood's has this done.'

'Your breasts ... are quite a nice shape,' he said, appraisingly. 'I would just resize them a bit to give you a better proportion.'

And on he went.

My waist could be whittled into shape with the removal of a rib, and my hips could be sucked a size or two smaller by a small flesh-hoovering vacuum cleaner ... local anaesthetic procedure only. Reshaping of the ankles, calf implants and a bum-lift, and ... *voilà!* ... I'd be a better-looking person.

Visions of a new career as a grand-prix girl in an electric-blue unitard and silver thigh-high boots flashed before my eyes.

This would have been a dream come true when I was about seventeen. That was what Allison and I referred to as the Time of the Large Underpants.

That was when, for some reason, I started to eat a lot. And eat and eat and eat. There was never a moment when something wasn't being chewed or crunched, or sucked. And slowly and extremely obviously, fat cells gathered together and discussed the fact that my character could really do with a serious appearance crisis.

They gathered and multiplied around my bottom, my thighs, my hips and my tummy, my upper arms, my neck and my back. Strangely, never really around my tummy. And of course, my breasts (at that stage small and insignificant) were strictly off-limits to the ancient clan of fat cells. But the rest of me bloomed and expanded.

When I realised one sad day that lying flat on my back on the bed to zip my jeans wasn't going to work, and when Tod said blankly between bongs, 'God, you're so fat,' I realised I had become A Big Girl.

That was when the next phase of the strange eating program began. Instead of:

*four Weet-Bix, full-cream milk and four instant coffees with milk;

*snack of muesli with milk; and

*chocolate Moove, hamburger, chips, tomato sauce, three instant coffees with full-cream milk,

I only ate:

*one chocolate chip cookie each day; and

*one Diet Coke each day.

For seven days I did this and I lost lots of weight.

But not enough to get me back to the 48 kilos my seventeen-year-old body was used to being.

So I got serious about the whole thing.

I had heard about girls who vomited after they gorged. It sounded like heaven to me. Imagine being able to eat as much chocolate chip ice cream as you could stuff in, only to have it come back up and out of you before it could get busy keeping your hips warm for the dreadful freezing winter we were meant to have.

(I thought, you see, that the reason I had so much extra flesh gathering around my bum was because, in days of yore, or even a past life, or if you looked at my great-great-granny, who was fabled to come from County Cork, there were some very scientific explanations for this fat attack.

One was that my genes carried within them the desire to make it through another winter until spring came, when there would be enough to eat, at least more than some mouldy old turnips.

The other was that my trusty Irish-potato-famine legs had stored all available fat because Darwinism had ruled that only the piano-legged among my tribe would survive.)

Anyway, I didn't want my fat legs any more.

Allison and I read everything we could on eating disorders, so we could get one, too. I so wanted one. I could almost taste it.

Anyway, I would gamely stick my digit down my throat and get stuck into my vomiting. Oh, there were some overtures: a bit of gagging, some head spins and a touch of dry-retching, but never could I manage a proper vomit. Everything I ate went *nooo*, thanks anyway Meg, but we like it down here. We've got no desire at all to spend the rest of our days in that lovely white porcelain bowl you're worshipping.

Then I heard that spitting was good for ditching weight.

This came from watching *Top Gun*, which starred Tom Cruise, who I learnt was a wrestler in real life (stay, stay, it's all going to come clear in a second).

MISS LONELYHEARTS

Wrestlers, I learned in a fanzine, had to stay at the right weight for them to fight, or joust, or whatever strange thing it is that they do (lots of foreplay after a very big night out, it looked to me. There are those rumours about Tom, after all).

Anyway, they spit to ditch weight. Run around in hot clothes, sweat a lot and spit.

So I started spitting.

Revolting habit I know, but no worse than trying to make yourself vomit if you keep it to yourself. However, it didn't work. I think I may have got a little dehydrated but that was it.

I was a total failure.

I couldn't even get an eating disorder. Anorexics were such lucky bitches, I thought.

Of course, I know better now. Please don't get *too* offended. It's just the way it is, not only when you're young but when you're a girl, you tend to get rather unbalanced ideas about life, unless you're extremely fortunate, or have psychologists for parents (except they're the people most likely to top themselves). Most women I know, scratch a little, and you won't find a complete mess. But a bit of a mess, definitely.

Look at me now. I'm in a cosmetic surgeon's office getting a quote for a total body makeover. And that is my job. Maybe plastic surgery is just a natural progression for people who've had eating disorders? Or attempted eating disorders? Maybe it's bulimia for people who can't throw up.

Dr Gold was clearing his throat. He was obviously wondering why I'd gone quiet. 'This kind of reshaping is extremely common these days. It's not really cosmetic surgery, more like a little bit of work here and there to get you into optimum shape. Then we really only need to see you once a year to check on your progress, and you've got at least ten years before your face needs any serious work,' he explained, looking into my eyes meaningfully. 'But it's best to start early.'

I looked at the version of me he'd recreated – and she didn't look bad, I've got to say. I could have made it to the cover of *Phwoar!*, practically. It was only that she didn't look so much like me. The hair was still me though – mad and curly and out of control.

'The only thing that's the same is my hair,' I said.

'Well, we haven't touched your eyes. Though we could do a Botox lift – it would increase the arch. Hmmm. But there'd still be that excess eyelid skin. And then there's your hair – clown hair, we call it,' he chuckled, finding himself very funny.

I think he mistook my look of horror at his rudeness for a look of horror at the helplessness of my ever getting anything other than clown hair.

'Hair surgery?' I queried, sarcastically. Except he didn't realise I was being sarcastic.

'Well, look what Nicole Kidman's achieved with her mad mop.'

After that, there wasn't much more for Dr Gold to fix, so he wrapped it up and printed me out some pictures of the new and improved me.

As I left, there were people in reception who hadn't been there on my way in. One woman had lips like zeppelins and the other had bruises under her eyes. A youngish man looking like a severe party veteran, wearing black combats and a silver tank top, with buffed arms and polished skin, had a face full of acne scars. He was reading the glossy brochures about full facelifts and laser resurfacing and was definitely in for a little something. An older woman, maybe forty, sat quietly. Her face was swollen, and as she turned her head I could see ugly black stitches and angry red welts under her ears.

I stared at the quote in my hand. Dr Gold hadn't been completely upfront, but had alluded that if I wrote nice things, he could talk to his business partner about a 'good price'. But from my research I knew that even with a special deal I would be looking at a face and body with a swing tag of about $40 000.

Not that they hadn't thought of everything. They even had a pay-as-you-go plan. It was a bit like getting an education. Pay now, benefit later. Imagine explaining the surgery on your credit card statement.

But the best thing, according to Dr Gold?

'It's all tax deductible.'

The world was officially crazy. I was right to be miserable.

When I got back the office, it was practically deserted. Smelly pub! I thought, excited at the idea of telling my cronies about Dr Gold's den of facial reconstruction for the imperfect individual. I'd just check out the tanning/laser connection first.

After a few minutes online, the link was obvious. Pigmentation. If you were tanned, the laser not only zapped dark hair, it wiped out the pigment from your skin too.

Not life threatening, but not exactly aesthetically enhancing, either.

Oh well, I thought. It's not amazing, but it might go somewhere.

Anyway, why is Dr Gold doing laser on suntanned girls? He should know what happens, shouldn't he?

Still musing on the downside of suntanning, I grabbed my bag, ready to bolt, when I heard a muttering from the far corner, where the artists sat.

Max was hunched over his mobile, speaking earnestly.

What was he doing there? (Writers, you see, never hang out in artists' territory. There's been blood on the floor over less. Don't even start me on the great subs vs artists wars – they're horrible to behold and still going on to this very day.)

'Hello – David? Yes, it's about the Miss Lonelyhearts thing. Yes. Well. I'm her agent. I am ringing all candidates to appraise their potential. You may not know about the demand generated by this particular ad.'

Silence, while he made listening noises and flicked through *Elegance*. 'Yes, I am sure that you have every chance. However, to be certain for safety reasons, I must meet you first.'

I stood there, folded my arms, and took it all in. There were about four letters on the desk. Max was still swivelling in his chair, getting more and more comfy.

'Great stuff, David. Look forward to it.' He put down the phone with a satisfied thump and turned back to his pile. His pile? Of MY letters.

'Now, who's next on my list?' he muttered. 'Ben!'

Ben? No way. I had Ben's letter.

'Now he looks great,' he said, tossing a photo aside.

Bugger. I didn't have time to see it properly. But it *looked* ...

He started dialling. I coughed.

'Hi Max,' I said cheerily, swooping down and snatching the letters off his desk. It was a smooth move. I didn't stuff it up at all. I sat on the desk and looked down at him.

He went crimson.

'You're looking a bit flushed,' I said archly.

He crossed his arms defensively.

'Max, it looks like you've been a very, very naughty boy.'

No reply.

'Maybe I'll have to get ... I picked up a letter and casually read the name. 'Robert here to spank you.'

He tittered nervously. Oh no. He wasn't getting off the hook that easily.

'Max, you little shit, are you trying to date the men who wrote these letters?'

'No!'

'You don't think they'll be a little surprised when they turn up at a restaurant and find they've made a date with you?'

'You weren't using them,' he said defiantly.

'One. You stole them.'

He rolled his eyes.

'Two, Max, they didn't ask to go out with you. They wanted to go out with – me!'

He snorted.

'And thirdly,' I said, swatting him with the letters, 'you're *swat* going *swat* out *swat* with *swat* Eric!'

He yelped.

'And fourthly, how can you even think of doing this to ERIC?' *Swat!*

'Stop hitting me or I won't tell you a thing.'

SWAT!

'You'd better tell me NOW,' I said, ready to pull out the big guns, 'or Monica will find out who stole her La Mer body serum.'

'Oh bloody hell, all right,' he said, holding his hands in front of his face to defend himself. 'Just stop that. And how did you know about the La Mer?'

'I didn't. It was a lucky guess. But if you're cheeky enough to do this, you'll definitely get into the beauty cupboard.'

'If you don't tell her, I'll share the booty. I had keys made,' he couldn't resist boasting.

'Max! You're dreadful. I understand, sort of, risking your life for La Mer – after all, it was La Mer – okay, so I understand that, but my Lonelyhearts letters? That's low. I can't believe it's you.' I gave him one more swat before putting down my weapons. 'I thought it was Diane. What are *you* doing with them? And what about Eric?' I asked, perplexed. They'd seemed on the brink of something good.

'I'm not trying to date them,' he said, sounding shocked and disgusted. 'But there are so many people who are lonely, Meg. And these guys want someone. So if I could help them, why not?'

He sounded very sincere. So, obviously, I was still very suspicious.

'Why would you want to do that? Since when did you start caring about lonely people?'

He shrugged.

'What's the real reason? Come on. You can't bullshit me, Max.'

'I thought I could make some…' He hesitated, looking sheepish. 'Money,' he admitted.

Now it was my turn to look disgusted. (I do good disgusted. Max was practically quailing.)

'Well, you know what we're paid,' he pleaded, 'it's ridiculous. Practically everyone's freelancing on the side.'

'Max, that doesn't justify taking my letters.'

'But you didn't even want them,' he protested.

I opened my eyes a little wider at that.

'Eric told me,' he mumbled.

This is great, I thought.

'I *didn't* want them. But, I don't know. They're still mine.'

'Look, I went through them quite carefully,' he said eagerly. 'Some of them – they sound excellent candidates for boyfriend-hood.'

'No, forget it, it's crazy. Give them back.'

'Do you know how many girls are single?'

'Duh, yes. But these guys didn't ask to be treated like … handbags. Or meat or something. Come on. Just give them back.'

'What about my dating agency?' he sniffled.

'You can help me write the nice rejection letters,' I said, comfortingly. 'And I won't tell Eric.'

My mobile made its stupid ring. MC Hammer. Allison. Sob.

'Hang on – hello?'

'It's your mum, sweetheart. Just reminding you about the weekend. I know how plans can come up, so I'm just making sure you're both still coming.'

'Hi Mum. Yep, we're coming.'

'What's his name again, darling?'

Oh. I hadn't actually said. Damn. 'It's um. Um, er.'

'Darling? You sound a bit –'

'Hang on, Mum.'

I turned to Max, wincing at the dilemma I'd got myself into.

'Quick – my mum wants to know who I'm bringing to my brother's engagement party.'

'Me?'

'No!'

'Oh my God! Here you go – take one of these guys.'

'What?'

He shoved a couple of letters into my hands. 'Liam would be perfect! Or Tristan – have a look. I was going to keep him for myself, but …'

'Shut up,' I hissed, and got back to Mum.

'Meg! Meg – are you there?'

'Yep. Sorry Mum, still at work. On deadline. Anyway, I'm bringing, er …' I looked at the letter Max had shoved into my hand. 'Liam.'

Max nodded wildly, urging me on.

'He's great. You'll love him,' I improvised, sounding super-confident.

'See you at 2.00 p.m. Saturday then. At the bus stop. Is Liam going to be –'

'No! No, he'll just meet us for lunch. We're um, still in the early stages, you know. Don't want to scare him off.'

'We're not that scary,' she huffed.

'Got to go, Mum – bye.'

I hung up.

'Oh. My. God. You're going to do it! Ring now, before we lose the momentum,' Max insisted.

'We?'

'Go on! Do it!'

'Are you threatening me?'

'Yes I am. I know what happened at the party. You have a letter from an ex. And Allison's pissed off about it.'

I narrowed my eyes at him.

'Scary – NOT. Ring Liam first,' he instructed, his voice kind all of a sudden. 'Then come to the pub and tell Max all about it.'

CHAPTER SEVENTEEN

I can't tell you how much I was looking forward to the trip to my Mum and Dad's for my younger brother's engagement party. I would be spending more time than it takes someone to go from London to Paris going from one beach suburb to another. And all by public transport! The thrill was almost too much to contemplate. And I couldn't even bitch to Al about it. All that time to think about Nick, Ali and Ben. Fabulous!

So I sat on the bus most of Saturday morning, looking out the window as the city gave way to suburbs, which gave way to green bush, beaches and homes. Paradise, apparently. Growing up there hadn't seemed that great, even if it had been on the idyllic beach. I'd never quite cut it as a surfie girl – and I definitely never made it as a cool girl.

It was like travelling through time – watching the icons of my teenage years flash by. It rolled past the library, where I'd spent so many weekends. It went past the school, where Allison had saved me from the great toilet flushing incident. It wobbled past a shopping centre I'd had a part-time job at. That was the year I finally had sex.

I said 'finally' because I didn't actually lose my virginity till pretty late compared to everyone else at school. There was no moral basis. I was only holding off because all of my friends were supposedly virgins. I didn't *want* to be a virgin. I was actually damn keen to get into the whole sex thing. In fact I'd sneakily been on the pill for a year. I felt like such a slut – even though I'd never had sex. At that stage I'd never had a boyfriend, either.

But then years later I found out they HAD ALL HAD SEX. Every single time they'd denied it, they'd lied! They'd done it.

'Well, duh,' said Allison when I confronted her about it years later. 'Haven't you ever heard of a social contract? Played poker? No-one was going to go first and tell everyone,' she'd explained, patiently, like I was a much, much younger sister, when in fact I was three months older than her.

'But I never had sex because – because I didn't want to be the only one who did. And I wouldn't have had anyone to tell.'

'You could have told me,' she said.

Finally I got fed up and decided to de-virginise myself. But that's a tale for another time.

Mum and Dad were at the bus stop to pick me up, waving madly from the front seat of their car. I climbed out of the bus with my bag, feeling like I'd just been transported. We drove slowly back to the house, Mum and Dad talking and talking.

The weirdest thing about being home was how right and how wrong it felt at exactly the same time. I still had a white, carved wooden single bed, upon which I'd writhed – okay, in my imagination – with many a teenage boy who seen past my monster hair to the sex goddess I fancied myself to be on the inside – all those novels, you see. My bedroom still had, seriously, peachy-pink walls and mirrored wardrobes, inside of which were all of the things even Mum hadn't had the heart to throw out packed neatly away – for she was neat – into labelled boxes. Don't get the wrong idea. My room was hardly a shrine. It wasn't filled with beloved stuffed toys and favourite dollies or anything creepy like that.

It was more like it was waiting for me.

Like it had been expecting me.

Because it *was* the same ... the same room where I'd spent hours singing into my hairbrush for Allison, where we'd worn out tapes, learnt dance routines, coached each other in precisely the correct length of time to leave it before you called a boy after they'd called you. My parents had always refused to get an answering machine, so I had sat by the phone for many a petrified hour, willing it to ring, before going to the beach. Or the library. Or playing music. Breathing was just acceptable.

I'd read up to twelve books a week. Insane. Before I met Ali. There was even a picture of us in my room. We were lying on a beach; both of us perfect eighteen year olds; all sun-bleached hair, brown tasty skin, and tiny salty cossies. It was amazing how we had thought we were so fat.

MISS LONELYHEARTS

I looked at the two of us and felt sad, not just because we'd fallen out and she seemed to have frozen over, but because we'd had so little faith in how lovely and fresh and young we were. And I knew that one day I'd look back and feel exactly the same way about today.

But that didn't make me feel better about today at all.

I couldn't stand looking at the picture, so I turned it over. 'It's worse than breaking up with a guy,' I muttered to myself.

'Are you okay in there darling?' my mum yelled out. God, she had ears like a bat. 'No, I'm heading for the big slump, the black doom cloud is hovering, Mum,' I said sarcastically, flicking through some CDs that were lined up.

God, look at these. Betty Boop.

Take That.

Oh – Beastie Boys. My rap slash punk phase. I'd tried to be angry, but snarling about anarchy, wearing bin liners and kicking rubbish bins safely out of Mum and Dad's sight didn't seem very punk somehow. Not when you were sixteen years old and had sunburn and thought you were fat and knew that one out-of-control brother and one madly flirty younger sister everybody loved seemed enough for Mum and Dad to cope with. I'd put away my Smashing Pumpkins poster and taken up fighting pimples and taming hair.

'Can I bring you a cup of tea?'

Actually, that offer I couldn't resist.

'Yes, please.'

I sat on the bed holding my signed copy of Take That's first album (I was sixteen; Karen and I had lined up for hours outside the Entertainment Centre, with Mum, and Karen had scored the kiss, but I'd got Robbie's signature) and waited for Mum to bring me a cuppa, feeling suddenly very safe, if very best-friend less.

If Allison and I never spoke again, how on earth was I going to tell Mum and Dad?

Mum would have to break it to her drinking buddies.

'Well, Meg, she's going through a bad patch. Broken up with her best friend.' Mum would relish this bit of news, I thought meanly, especially as she'd had no serious boyfriend action to report for years. Finally, something to tell the girls. Tod had thought we were secret lesbian lovers anyway.

'Why don't you two just get on with it and have your lesbian affair,' he'd drawl through the crack in the door, when he'd first realised that girls can like girls and he couldn't think of any other reason we'd stay in my room for hours.

Anyway, there'd be no more of that talk. Not unless I really did become a lesbian. And I just couldn't see anything happening to get me past the pashing stage with any girl.

Mum knocked on my door – a first, and I felt like I was at a bed and breakfast when I sat up straight in bed and said, like you would to a stranger bringing toast, 'Come in.'

'Here you are,' she said happily, sitting on the bed next to me. 'A nice cup of tea.'

MISS LONELYHEARTS

I don't want you to get the idea that my mum is unbearable. She's not that, not at all. In fact, she's almost too bearable. She's almost too great sometimes. She'd be a fantastic mate. If she wasn't my mum. She's loads of fun. Very extroverted. Gorgeous. Smart. Allison loves her. Which isn't very surprising when you look at her mum.

But no matter how funny and good-looking and young she felt (was? seemed?) around my friends, okay, around Allison in particular, around me when it's just her and me on our own she somehow morphs into … such a mum sometimes.

Just when I thought I was safe, when she'd behaved in exactly the same way for weeks and weeks and I began to feel that we could get past that mother–daughter thing and be true mates and I could tell her things, like the black feelings that twisted inside me sometimes, or the urge to sleep forever, or the fear I had of never sleeping at all, something would always happen to make me realise that no, the most important thing we'll ever have between us is that she's my mum and I'm her daughter. I had to protect her from my unhappiness. Because she'd usually be looking at me like she was grateful that I wasn't as mad or bad as Karen and Tod.

At least I'd never been caught.

There are strict limits, though we act like it's otherwise.

She looked at me close, and pushed some of my hair back from my eyes.

'Are you well, darling? Your dad and I have been thinking that we haven't spent much time together lately. Would you like to come home for the Easter break? You could bring Ali if you want, so you don't get bored with us oldies ...' She doesn't mean that, by the way. My mum is not one of those oldies.

'Oh, I'd love to, Mum,' I half lied in a singsong voice, letting my monster hair surge forward again to hide the lie. And it was only a half lie. It would be nice to kick back in the pink room and be served cups of tea and laugh with Mum at the soaps and watch Oprah and Jerry and work on my Ricki Lake with her and Karen, maybe even Lisa. I could get to know her. If she and Tod ever emerged from their shag fest. But it would also be a little shameful to go home again. Home was a bit like an affordable version of the Priory, only the décor was more like the Betty Ford Center. Nothing bad can happen to you at home. It's like being a protected species, and you have a much higher chance of staying alive if you are in the zoo. You have to really look for trouble.

I wasn't ready for that kind of return to the nest. I had been released into the wild and I had to make a go of it. It wasn't time to go back to the animal shelter. Not again. Not yet.

'You know,' she semi-sighed, starting up in the gap where I'd been sort of looking at her without realising I was because I was so lost in my thoughts, 'you did before when –' and she stopped short.

'That was only when I was between houses.' Defensive. Suddenly sixteen again.

A trace of something I couldn't pinpoint flashed across my mum's soft features, all fading beauty queen and bottle green eyes.

She got brisk. Mumsy. Not like my mum.

'Yes, I know.' She knew something? My brain, always on alert, sounded the alarm. 'But ...' But what? 'It's been a while, that's all.'

What I used to do when Ben and I had broken up, but were still sleeping with each other every now and then, was head to Mum and Dad's. I'd tell Ben I needed to do some work, but really I hoped by making myself unavailable he'd miss me madly. Basically, I was playing games, because I was desperately insecure. I had so little confidence that I felt if I didn't make myself scarce, I'd become like too much stock on the supermarket shelf. So I would go home, to the 'burbs, to the beach, and I would take a book and read and read on the sand, and let the sun penetrate all the places that felt cold inside, and feel myself being heated up. Lying in the sun was like how love should feel.

Before the looming trauma of champagne popping and RSL food and sitting under pictures of the Queen, I needed some time out. Besides, I wanted to call Liam. Maybe he could sneak down to the northern beaches and I could make sure he was sane before presenting him to my family.

Not that they were sane.

So I went to the garage, opened up the ancient cupboard that still has all our antique beach towels and ancient blow-up balls and vintage cossies, and grabbed something that should fit me. I think it was Karen's but, hey, I deserved to have a little of whatever she had going on.

'Mum, can I borrow the car?'

'Where are you going, darling?'

'Just down the beach ... just to have a walk.' Just to screen my decoy boyfriend.

'Wear some sunscreen,' she said. 'Enjoy yourself darling.' She held me close and kissed me. 'I know it's not always easy for you. We love you darling.'

God, they were still worried about me then. I felt a rush of guilt through me and held myself just slightly out of her embrace.

'Are you sure you want to go by yourself?' Dad asked. 'Go on, take Karen. She needs some fresh air!'

Nooooo.

'Yeah, I'll drive,' she said, leaping up.

Shit. 'I was going to walk.'

'No come on, it'll be fun.'

No it won't. I need to ring my decoy boyfriend.

'I could come – give you two a race?' Dad sounded way too enthusiastic.

We both looked at him.

'Okay then, girls. See you later.'

Karen drove down, exactly the way we used to every weekend. Karen was even behind the wheel of Mum's mini-muscle car from the early eighties. We had done dreadful things in that car. In fact, it still smelt a bit funny.

We swung into the road, looking at all the renovated seventies flats, the trendy coffee shops. When I used to come down, every weekend, with Allison, there'd only been the one shop, selling hamburgers, Paddlepops and chiko rolls, complete with a Mad Max pinball machine you had to queue to use.

Now there was an Internet café. But the surfies, perched like birds on a wire on the fence overlooking the best break on the beach, looked the same.

The sand was the same. Thick and golden, the way it always was on the northern beaches. Stickier and thicker than its pale gold Bondi cousins of the eastern suburbs. It stuck to my feet, the water cold and a touch of frost in there, the sun still warm, the break still in the same place, a smooth curling left-hander divided by two rocks. An ocean pool glinted at the end of the point. It still had fish in it. This was where I'd caught a fish with my hands – it was dead, but I'd flapped my hands around so the fish looked alive, and we'd eaten it for dinner that night. A rock fish. Caught with my bare hands.

They must love me, to have risked themselves like that.

Tod had nearly drowned in the pool. Dad and I had been swept off the rocks. Allison and I had baked our backs for six hours straight to look good in our halterneck dresses. I crunched through the sand as I sifted through the memories. The texture of the sand felt unbelievable. Better than a pedicure at We Believe. I looked out at the ocean and, like it always did, it soothed me.

'So, what's this guy like? The one coming tomorrow,' demanded Karen, pushing perfect hair away from her perfect face.

'Oh for God's sake.'

'Okay, that means there's no guy.' She snorted with laughter. 'You've made him up.'

'I have not!' I said. Five minutes with Karen and I was getting irritated and defensive. Hello, childhood.

'Anyway, how's Allison?'

'Fine.'

She made a snorting noise.

'Okay, what is that second revolting noise supposed to mean?'

'Usually you'd be on the phone to her as soon as you got here.'

'So what?'

'So you two are fighting.'

'We are so not fighting.'

'Ah. You're not talking. Is it about this guy? Did she sleep with him?' She was *really* pushing it.

'I –'

'Did she sleep with him and you tried to top yourself?'

'What? No, she didn't sleep with him and I didn't try to top myself. Though I might top you if you don't shut up.'

We walked down to the beach. It was sunny and warm, but cold in the shade of the headland. Spray spat up and made my hair frizz up.

'Remember last time you and Allison went swimming?'

Oh God. We'd ended up on the front page of the *Manly Daily*. Allison had come to the beach with me on my birthday. And it had just been one of those incredible autumn days. No humidity. I was wearing a second-hand fifties dress; she was wearing jeans. By the time we decided to get into the water we were just wearing our undies. No bras. And …'

'You got caught in that rip. And that guy rescued you.'

'Rescued *Allison*,' I corrected. I started to chuckle. 'He strapped that thing around her boobs.'

'That's right,' said Karen, delighted. 'And you had to swim in. You practically drowned!'

We sat for a while, smiling at our sentimental memories of near-death experiences and eager lifesavers. Then Karen broke our reverie.

'So how's work?'

'Horrible,' I said, frowning.

I dug my feet into the sand. Leaving dents.

See – I'd been there. I'd made some kind of mark.

A wave came and washed them away, and I grinned.

Look, I thought to myself. Maybe I was never here at all.

'Mine's horrible too,' said Karen. 'Waiting on tables, smiling at every ugly man who sits down in case he's the head of a TV station, or a producer, or something …'

'I thought you wanted to be a psychologist?'

'I do. One of those ones on television. And imagining them seeing me on telly is exactly how I get through the day.'

You too, I thought. That means Ali *and* Karen both wanted to be on TV. The question was, could TV handle them both?

'That's why I've decided to audition for *Big Brother*.'

'Karen, you're freaking me out.' I sounded dismissive, even to myself.

We trudged back up to the car park while she explained her theory of the career path she'd follow. She'd do *Big Brother*, enrol as a psych student, finish her degree, then move into *Oprah*-style programming for teens.

I must admit it sounded good. Callous, ruthless, commercial and soulless, but it's a good plan, right?

That night I managed to sneak away for a half-hour or so – I'd offered to collect the takeaway from the Marigold down the road. I couldn't believe that for the last fifteen years it seemed my parents had ordered practically the same meal. And we would sit around the copper coffee table and eat crumbed prawn cutlets and try to use our chopsticks. With all of us there, it was like being thrust back into childhood, only being bigger.

But waiting for the chicken chow mein gave me the chance to make a couple of calls.

The first was to Liam. I was getting very nervous about having invited someone I'd never even met to meet my mum and dad in the guise of my boyfriend. A least I wanted to ring him again to make sure he was coming.

'Hi – Liam?' I asked.

There was very loud music. Was he at a nightclub?

'Hello,' he bellowed.

'Hi Liam – it's Meg. We're meeting up tomorrow. I just wanted to make sure you were coming.'

'Yeah – hang on – I'm at work,' he bellowed.

God – how to ask. Are you normal? Criminal record? Acceptable to date? Willing to pretend to be my boyfriend?

And how could I let a normal person walk into my family? Was that fair?

'Um, Liam, I should explain. My mum and dad are going to be there tomorrow. It's a family lunch thing – I just didn't want to meet you on my own. And I didn't want you to be too surprised. I hope you understand.'

There was a pause.

'Parents, huh?' He laughed. 'That's okay. I'll be on my best behaviour. Then we can head out afterwards, okay? For a real getting-to-know-you session.'

'Great,' I agreed, my voice all strangled.

I could get out of that. Plead illness. Give him the slip.

Or do the right thing and give him a chance.

I mean, why not?

I'll tell you why.

One person.

By the name of Ben.

I didn't tell you earlier because I knew what you'd think. But while at the pub with Max, after ringing Liam, and after telling Max about half of my life story, and him listening and nodding and not even laughing, we workshopped the idea of ringing Ben. And letting him know it was me he'd written to.

We read the letter again and again. How he felt stuck in a dead-end relationship, how something about my ad had 'called out to him', he said.

Called out to him!

'Max,' I said, feeling tired and tearful. 'What if this is a second chance? You know — that it *is* me he was after all the time? That it's actually ...' I looked down.

'Kind of meant to be?' he asked, gently.

'Yeah. I never really got over him, you know.'

Understatement of all time.

I looked at Max. He looked back, a world of compassion in his brown eyes.

'Maybe you need to give it a shot,' he said and sighed. 'Just one shot at a second chance.'

'I can't ring him, ' I said, holding my phone out to him. 'Can you ...?'

'Yeah, of course I will. I'll make the call.'

So now you know. What do you think?

I think I'm either insane, or it's fate.

CHAPTER EIGHTEEN

Despite the fact that I knew everything was going to be perfect, the next day at lunch I was still in shock. It's not often you end up sitting at a plastic table at the local RSL club at lunchtime to celebrate your little brother's coming of age as a proper grown-up human being.

He's engaged. It's so *adult*. Needless to say, I was having some trouble believing it. Actually I think I was refusing to believe it. If he was getting married, and that was so universally approved of, what kind of reaction were my life choices receiving? I mean, at this stage I was bringing a stranger to meet my parents and setting myself up with the ex who'd dumped me. How confident would you have been in my life choices?

Anyway, I thought, trying to concentrate on someone else for at least five minutes (what – you mean you're not self-obsessed?) and gave up. I glanced furtively at my mobile under the table to see if any text messages from my semi-normal friends had reached me. But no. The minute you step off the spinning stage everyone just accepts that you've gone into the parent zone.

My brother smiled at me over his chicken Maryland. His girlfriend, sorry, fiancée, was telling a very embarrassing story about how, when they'd met, she'd been with someone else so she and Tod had some kind of clandestine affair for a month or so. Apparently the ex had made a dramatic attempt for romantic re-entry into Lisa's life a couple of weeks ago. Now they're ... engaged, maybe because Tod's competitive urges made him up the stakes. It's all about Darwinian manoeuvres. Brown-cardigan syndrome.

Mum was beaming. I mean it. Beaming. It almost looked like her face hurt with smiling so much. Dad looked relieved. Karen hadn't arrived yet.

And that's typical. Mum, meanwhile, was passing down the myths and legends of the Tooley family to those who would create the next generation of little Tooleys. She's not big on character development. I, apparently, am 'the interesting one'. Karen is 'the good-looking one'. Tod is now 'the engaged one.'

I thought I was the intelligent one, Karen was the scary one and Tod was the pot-head.

But that's all changed now he's engaged.

'So, have you got a boyfriend at the moment, Meg?' I smiled mysteriously in reply. After all, they were just making conversation. And who knew if Liam would turn up.

'Or are you one of these single women we keep hearing about?' he leered. That's Lisa's married older brother – who's been looking down my top for the last half-hour – who was asking, by the way. Who wants to know? I sneered in my head. But she didn't get a word in – not out loud anyway.

'No,' I say truthfully. 'I'm seeing someone. He's due here soon.'

He didn't bother listening anyway.

'Never mind, we can set you up with someone. Like Earl!' They all laugh uproariously because Earl was the eleven year old sitting next to me at the table. I think brother-in-law had been thinking that one up for the last half an hour.

'Yeah, I saw how you were looking at him,' laughed my brother's intended. Was she being friendly, or bitchy? I couldn't tell, so I smiled weakly – the weak smile is a great two-way bet in the expression stakes. The eleven year old looked quite excited and laughed through his nose. Then he took a good look down my top, just like his big brother had.

I felt humiliated. Mum looked embarrassed.

'Oh, Meg's still getting over a bad break-up. She hasn't had much luck with men,' Mum explained earnestly, like I wasn't there. I certainly wished I wasn't there.

'Actually Liam's going to be here any minute,' I insisted, fingers metaphorically crossed under the table. Karen (you know, the good-looking one) had arrived while I was being checked out by the eleven year old. She snorted, with her usual respect, love and empathy for her 'interesting' big sister.

'He was held up at work,' I said smoothly.

'Oh, he works!' Mum exclaimed with delight, looking at Dad with an exaggerated surprised look on her face. Karen's lip curled in disgust. She was probably imagining an accountant with a paunch. Not that I had any idea of what to expect. My tummy began a strenuous gymnastics routine. I glanced, probably desperately, at my mobile. Thank God. He was coming. The 'Nearly there. Trying to park' SMS gave it away.

And, seconds later, an RSL club arrival managed to distract everyone from solving my single-girl problem.

That was because someone who looked suspiciously like a male stripper we featured a few months back in a beefcake-to-boardroom makeover, strode in wearing a string vest over horrifyingly defined well-done steak-coloured pectorals and stonewash jeans, Velcro straining at the sides (easy stripper action, he explained later). He looked around searchingly.

'My date,' I whispered, dumbstruck. 'Darling,' I said, moving over and giving him an awkward hug.

Even Mum was dumbstruck.

'This is Liam,' I said, rubbing stripper boy's stomach, trying to communicate intimacy. His belly was exactly the right kind of surface for a shirt to be ironed on – the string vest meant we all copped an eyeful, whether we wanted to or not. At least he was grinning, though I wish I'd had time to tone down the blush in the cheeks and hair like a World Wrestling Champion – long, tangled, wild and black. Unnaturally black.

He smiled, nearly blinding me with American soap star teeth, gave a what-the-hell kind of shrug with his Andean shoulders, and moved in for a massive passionate kiss. I came up for air seconds and seconds later, and laughed nervously, lipstick halfway round my face.

Everyone at the table looked shocked. It was like my dad had brought Pamela Anderson home and said, kids, meet your new mum.

I darted a glance at Karen. She looked like she'd been hit over the head with a hammer while sucking a lemon. I suddenly felt a bubble of happiness rise up, as out of place as a balloon at a wake. 'What the hell's going on?' the good-looking one in the family muttered, outraged at this new threat to her place in the family favourite's pyramid.

'What do you mean?' I asked, coolly, leading Liam to the table.

'Nothing. Only stoner Tod's getting married and suddenly you're having sex manual-style hot foreplay at the table.' She narrowed her eyes. 'I smell a rat.'

'Jealous,' I said, and sat myself on his lap for a second before sliding onto the seat next to him. My hunk reached out and grabbed a hunk of garlic bread.

'So,' he said, crumbs flying everywhere, 'how's everybody going?'

My mother started to cough, then seriously looked like she was going to choke on her champagne. Dad whacked her on the back and an earring flew off into the prawn cocktail. 'Stop it, Barry,' she gasped, purple, and Dad stopped thumping her long enough to give Liam a hard look.

Lisa looked pissed off. She'd better get used to being upstaged if she's seriously thinking of joining the family. Other families do Monopoly or Trivial Pursuit: our family excels in jousting for position and battling for attention.

And then the man with the abs and the hair stood up and thrust a hand forward to my dad, just about upending the table with his tree trunk thighs.

And that sight shuts just about everyone up.

'You know, the story we've all been told,' I was saying, waving my wine glass, which was full of beer, around excitedly, 'ish that girls are all each other's best friend.'

Lisa looked at me. All three of her heads were nodding in agreement. I think. After all, the only things I could really see were her lips which, she'd smudged round their outlines with M.A.C. Glamour the last time we'd been to the toilet. Which was quite miraculous, because I was quite, er, drunk. At the exact point where using the word blind made perfect sense to describe being drunk. So I was actually very, very pissed.

We were in the middle of Paddington, hours later and, as I said, I was pissed. I'd had plenty, but not as much as Karen.

It wasn't my fault. It was a creeping blinder that I was on. It had started late that afternoon after lunch. Somehow we'd escaped the parents (well, we'd just said, 'let's leave you oldies alone to get to know each other', and ran away, laughing madly) and had shared a cab into the city. We'd gone to a 'cool bar' because 'he never takes me anywhere'. I'm quoting Lisa.

Which brings me back to now. Which was about eleven at night. But it felt much, much later, in the way that all-afternoon drinking sessions warp the actual amount of time you've spent drinking till it seems like you've been doing it for days and days and days and lifetimes.

'The problem with girls ...' I took a deep breath here. 'I'm about to commit a cardinal sin – the kind you can't confesh away, so believe me, I'm expecting no absholution once I've told you ... The problem with girls is that they ...'

God, I'm such a traitor.

'Okay, the problem is, right, that girls basically have pack mentality. They compete. They attack. They brood. They let things Build Up. Then they drop you. Best friends don't. You'd think. It's not supposed to happen.'

'The problem is,' slurred Karen, who was sitting on stripper boy Liam's lap, before she ran out of steam. Probably got confused by a thought, went off to follow it, leaving us all waiting far too long. Drunk time. Stripper boy, by the way, was asleep, still with a huge meaty hand hovering in the whereabouts of my crotch. I shifted and his hand flopped onto the booth bench. He burped in his doze.

'Lightweight,' sneered Tod.

'No, no, no ... *no*.' The thought had obviously just been processed by Karen's brain, and it was now making its way out into the world.

We all turned to see what would happen next. In slow motion. Stripper boy's eyelids peeled back, revealing coffee-coloured long-lashed orbs.

I could see three of them.

'Girls do stick together. Help each other.' Karen finally said what her brain was sending to her mouth on five-minute delay.

'Yeah, RIGHT. You're my sister and you're sitting on my, erm, boyfriend's lap,' I said, drunk and snotty in the manner of a PhD-style expert on women's issues.

'I only jusht met you,' he protested weakly.

Karen smiled in an evil kind of way.

'I knew it! He's a prostitute!'

'No, he's ... oh God, he ...'

'I am not a prostitute. I asked her out. In a letter thing. In an ad ...'

'In a personal ad?' Karen crowed. 'Oh My God.'

Typical.

'Wait till I tell Mum and Dad. They knew there was something weird about you turning up with a guy.'

Oh God. Who could bother to stop her? She was just this force of nature.

There I was, with my brother, his beloved, my sister and my date – who looked like he was about to turn into my sister's latest experiment.

Whatever I'd wanted to say never even got an airing at that point, because stripper boy reached out for Karen. It was just mildly annoying. I didn't like him or anything – but did he have to start snogging my sister in front of me?

Evidently, he did.

CHAPTER NINETEEN

Monday morning at work was hell. Two full-on weekends in a row ... with alcohol. It's too much. Unless you're nineteen. I, at twenty-six, am moving into that zone where you actually don't look good with a hangover. Not really. Unbelievable as it sounds, there was a time when the redness in my eyes made them look greeny-bluer. When the effect of alcohol made my pores shrink. When I could sustain manic energy throughout an entire morning. When sleep was a boring necessity.

Not today though. And not for a long time. I was sitting slumped at my desk, watching the flying toasters go by gently on the screen's background. A Coca-Cola and a hamburger lay next to me, ready to be consumed when I could face them. I checked some emails. And phone messages. (None from Allison.) I went and knocked on Monica's office door, just as soon as I could bring myself to. Fortunately, I was still a bit drunk.

'Yes?' she said, not looking at me. I hovered in the doorway.

'I went to see Dr Gold last week.'

Her face went all … pleasant for a second. She was so pretty when she wasn't being frightening.

'It was, well, it was interesting. He gave me a full rundown of what he could do for me. I thought I could start the story with a report on …' I trailed off as she raised her face from the Victoria's Secret catalogue she'd been poring over.

'You did! Terrific,' she said and beamed. Her face went all warm, and scary. 'Start on it straightaway, won't you,' she urged. 'I'm glad to see your attitude has changed so much. You'll see I reward people who play the game, Meg. Professional people. Doing the right thing for the magazine. Not with some silly agenda to push.' She paused to fiddle with some jewellery. What was she so excited about? I wondered through my horrible hangover.

'Anyway. It could be a big job. I'll get someone to give you a hand.'

I felt confused. I'd thought I would probably just get a nail file session and then be sent off, metaphorical tail between actual legs, again.

Monica called out to the rest of the team, who were dotted around like shells on a beach. Flotsam.

'Come on in everyone,' she said cheerily. 'Let's get under way.'

God. She seemed so happy.

It was awful.

I grinned ruefully at everyone, trying to signal that I wasn't some kind of bum-crawler or arch-conspirator. I hadn't got to share with Julie and Eleanor. Or check out what time Tamara had come in (seven-thirty was her record). And I hadn't even eaten my hamburger. Plus I hadn't had any vitamin pills for days. At least I wasn't running late.

Chandra, on the other hand, was.

'Sorry I'm hideously late,' she said in her usual my-life-is-so-tough-you-have-no-idea tone when she finally arrived in the meeting.

She sat as far away from me as possible. No, it wasn't the only seat available.

'The bus driver wouldn't let me on with my hot coffee,' she explained once she'd made herself comfortable. 'It had been made too hot and then he wouldn't let me on, and then the next bus came and it was still too hot and then it started to rain so I waited under a tree and then it started to rain more and then …'

Eleanor shot Chandra a glare. Monica looked lethal.

'I'm glad you could make it to our meeting, Sandra. It's about a very important project we're going to be working on,' Monica said. Chandra blinked a couple of times – rapidly.

'I think, as fitness and beauty editor, it's only right for Meg to drive this project.' She smiled at me. I felt faint. God, Chandra was features editor. Usually she'd be in charge of these things. Was she trying to make *everyone* hate me?

Monica went on to outline the plastic surgery project – in vague and glowing terms.

'Bringing cosmetic surgery reporting into the twenty-first century blah blah blah synchronicity blah blah it's youth appeal, not anti-ageing blah blah

blah responsibility to readers blah blah ageing is so last century blah blah blah.'

'That's all,' she said, eventually. 'Meg, brief Chandra on what you expect her to do.'

Oh God. Chandra was tense and insecure enough. This was just going to drive her over the edge. All the bitterness and resentment was going to be directed at me. Instead of the usual 90 per cent.

'Chandra? Stay behind please.

And shut the door.'

We all heard the words flake, disorganised, punctual, flake (again) and useless being bandied around by our fearless leader. I wished I hadn't heard any of it.

I felt embarrassed for her. And not as grateful as I would have thought. I'd been in that room last week copping it. It didn't seem fair that there was a rotating torture system.

'Do you want to have a chat about the project?' I said softly when she finally made it out of there, her face like an Easter Island statue. She ignored me and went to her desk, where I could see her back, which had no chance of turning around. It was practically vibrating with something … Rage? Fear? Loathing?

She said nothing. But she must have heard me. Unless she'd entered a high state of hate meditation, or was actually rigor mortised, or was … just blatantly ignoring me.

'Chandra, I'm just going to make a cup of tea. Should we talk about the project when I get back?'

She kept her eyes fixed on the screen in front of her.

I made meaningful eye contact with Julie. Who pulled a face. Like she was mental.

'Just going then,' I said, sounding twelve, even to myself.

'Arrgh,' I unleashed when I got to the tearoom. Julie was already there, swinging her tea bag like a pendulum.

I leant my head against the wall. 'What am I going to do?' I hissed, my back against the freezing cold tearoom wall. Eyes darting everywhere to make sure Chandra wasn't coming.

'I don't know. I'd deck her,' Julie said and laughed.

'Then I'd end up in HR with a lawsuit slapped on me,' I moaned. God, I was so feeble, I couldn't stand myself.

Julie shrugged. 'She's taken me to HR.'

'Really?'

'Yeah. For being rude.'

Oh. 'Cos Julie was rude.

'But you're just …' I sought out tactful words. 'Like that.'

'I think it was about calling her Chunder. What did she call it?' Julie mused coolly. 'That's right. She called it "psychological undermining".'

A shadow fell over the doorway. I cringed. Julie kept blithely dishing the dirt.

'Shhh!'

It was Eleanor.

I should have known. She casts a giant shadow.

'You have to get a hold of yourself, Meg,' she said, quietly, for her, 'and learn to be strategic. Don't expect fuckwits to do the right thing. Sometimes, when people are bad, you have to take back your own power.'

I blinked. Where had I heard that before?

Not in *You Can Heal Your Life*, surely?

'It says in my book that everyone is a reflection, a mirror. So this wouldn't be happening …' I explained.

'That is the most arrogant thing I've ever heard. You make people behave the way they do? Like you're the robot master?' Julie snorted.

'No. I meant more that everything is always my fault,' I said.

'Same thing – can't you see? Some things are not your fault. They have everything to do with that person. You don't control everyone. It's just not possible,' Eleanor explained.

Julie nodded wisely.

'The only person you actually have control over is yourself,' she said, backing Eleanor up.

'But what is the matter with me – why is everything such a mess?' I moaned melodramatically, pleased to have so much attention.

'Life, Meg. It sucks, then it doesn't.' God, Eleanor was wise!

Chandra wasn't at her desk when I got back. 'Where's Chandra?' I asked Tamara.

'I don't know,' she said nervously, looking away. God, no-one liked to get in the middle of these things.

Who could blame them?

Well, me, actually. I blame them. Take sides. Act strong. Then I won't feel so scared and all alone.

Through my hangover, I wrote up the outline for the plastic surgery project – the plastic surgery botch-up package that is – then started fleshing it out. I was pleased with how it was shaping up. I'd found somebody whose tummy tuck had never healed (gross, I know) and someone who reckoned she had migraines from Botox. The girl I'd met in Dr Gold's had pigmentation damage from where the hair-removing laser had burnt away the colour in her skin. I'd rung Fantasia, the self-injecting stripper, but she seemed not to be talking to me after Allison's piece. I'd keep trying. But all in all, it was becoming a great package. And maybe it was a godsend Chandra wasn't talking to me. I mean, what if she told Monica what I was *really* doing?

Anyway, I had other distractions to take my mind off the Chandra situation.

Liam had called.

Several times. And he'd done me a favour coming along to my mad family's thing.

But he'd ended up going home with Karen. Probably. And I *really* know I had no right to be suspicious.

Only I hadn't thought he'd ring. Not the day after. I mean, he hadn't even scored. Not with me, anyway.

I sighed. There was nothing for it.

I sighed and dialled his number.

'Hello, is that Liam?'

'Hi – Meg?'

'Great night last night. Thanks very much. Look. I was wondering …'

I waited. Here it came.

'Have you got Karen's number?'

Happens every time.

CHAPTER TWENTY

I sat in the fading pink and gold light, staring down at my lap, where I'd hidden my hands. I willed them to be still. They stopped shaking for a second. Good. Then they started trembling again, ever so slightly. I looked up, and around the café again. Inside were already three or four tables with happy-looking groups of people at them, laughing and drinking in the sunset. No girls on their own. No confusion then, I thought. I was the only girl here alone. Ben would have to realise. Maybe not at first, but ... well, if he didn't, I had the letter ready to show him. But I'd save it for just the right moment. I'd pull it out and hand it to him. That is, if I could stop my hands shaking long enough to pull it out of my pocket. I tried to think soothing thoughts. Everything was going to be beautiful. Any minute Ben would be here and we were maybe one hour away from the rest of our lives. It wasn't as if I was even the tiniest bit nervous.

So why was I shaking?

Not that anyone could actually see. And not that anyone in particular was actually looking. I was in one of those huge cavernous Balinese-style beach cafés twinkling with tea lights (glam effect, but really a clever ruse to hide the festering décor). On the other side of the window were Tibetan prayer flags flapping away in the breeze, girls with belly buttons on display, and the shiny, shiny sea. It was really strange we'd arranged to meet at Bondi – okay, not so weird seeing that Max, acting as my dating agent, had arranged it, but very weird that Ben had agreed to it. It was the sort of place Ben *hated*. It was just the sort of place he'd spent most of our relationship avoiding. He'd preferred tiny, stinky, nicotine dens with brown drinks, bolted windows and hard-core bands due to come on after ten. Before then, you drank. And smoked.

But this was light. And comfortable. And the sea was a pretty twilight mauve and the sky was silvery pink and gold and everyone looked like they were on holidays.

Only he hadn't arrived yet.

Which was okay, so far. In fact, I'd been a bit early. I'd really worked hard to look perfectly couldn't-care-less good, but I still worried I'd overdone it. Everyone at work had assumed I was dressed up because I was meeting Nick. (I hadn't seen him since our encounter on the stairs … and I am sure I hadn't crossed his mind since.) Except for Max, who'd promised to phone at seven to check on my progress. But I still felt overdressed. You have to know Bondi. I mean, there were people here in towels. As long as they were nice towels, stylish towels from, you know, Orson & Blake or somewhere, that was fine. And thongs were fine, especially if they were those high-heeled practically million-dollar ones from Sigerson Morrison.

Anyway, I'd sort of tamed my hair – taken hours in the work toilets – and I'd raided Carla's beauty cupboard. I was wearing a sparkly top that slid just the right way off one shoulder and a great pair of jeans, and not too high but high enough to make your legs look longer heels. I was cold, but it was worth it. That's why I was sitting in the light, the windows folded back, a warm, salty westerly softly blowing straight in and out the other side.

No petty revenge fantasies filled my head. No flinging wine in his shocked, humbled face. No saying, sorry, but it's never going to work out. I was about to get the moment some people wait their whole lives for – a moment of truth with their first love. And it was bound to work out. It had to. Otherwise *nothing* made any sense at all.

I had thought and thought about it. It had all been meant to happen this way. The whole thing. Allison's idea (okay, mine) to sort me out. Which then led to the Lonelyhearts letters. Which led to Ben's letter. Which led to 6.00 p.m. Now. Sunset, Bondi Beach.

It had all been a test, you see. It all made sense now – even the heartache with Ben the first time around. Nothing works out without a struggle, does it – nothing good, anyway. Why did I expect that my relationship with Ben would be any different? It was supposed to be that way – because here we were, about to meet and realise that the person he'd always wanted, after all, was me. He'd written to me. Without knowing who I was.

We were going to get a second chance.

A sweet-looking guy with dreadlocks was staring at me from the corner table. He raised his beer glass, and I smiled, but shook my head. Thank you God. Nothing makes a girl waiting for the boy who dumped her feel better than being saluted by a cute alternative. I couldn't even get flustered. Poor guy. He was lovely – he'd find someone one day, I thought. Maybe even find his way back to someone. Like Ben and me had.

I was still trying to slowly work my way through my enormous beer. I was determined not to drink much – I didn't want to be fuzzy-headed, I just wanted to take the edge off. I wanted to remember absolutely everything about this moment. I wanted to be able to retell it in perfect, vivid moment-by-moment detail, over and over again, to our grandchildren one day.

I looked around, beginning to feel a bit worried. Where was he? He'd always been late, but that had been for me – not for the girl of his dreams – the girl he'd written to. I wondered if I should take a little walk around, when I saw a skinny guy nearby sort of searching his way through the crowd. His eyes looked a bit confused when he saw me, and then I waved.

He looked around, and a huge grin broke over his face. The grin just grew as he moved towards my window seat.

I clutched the table and bit my lip. I didn't care how it looked. This was it. He was still as gorgeous as ever. Plenty of straight brown hair, pale skin, rain-grey eyes and full lips. I sighed, happiness filling me. Exactly the same as he used to be.

I didn't say anything, just stared at him.

He moved forward, close, reached a hand out and held mine for a second, then let it go.

'Hi,' I said quietly. I wanted to savour the moment of realisation, the exact second it hit him that I was the girl he was looking for.

'Hi,' he replied, looking at me, with a sort of lost-and-found expression on his face. I felt a rush of fondness for him – there he was. Here we were.

'Um. Hi. I'm meant to be meeting someone,' he mumbled, with a half-grin.

Too right you are. I smiled enigmatically.

'But you're here instead,' his eyes drifted over me – and came back to my eyes. It was like being hypnotised. He had this way of making you feel so important when he looked at you. He had always been very big on eye contact. I'd always been a sucker for it.

'You look well.'

'I am well,' I said, sounding chirpy. Bugger. Why couldn't I purr? Allison would have purred – and twirled her finger along the rim of her glass. Me? I chirped.

He was still staring at me.

'Anyway.' I leant forward, trying to look sort of sexy and mysterious and suggestive. 'How are *you*?'

He looked at me, eyebrows raised, brow furrowed. 'Wonderful.'

God, had he always been this seductive?

'You still living at, um …' It seemed suddenly crude to be straightforward. It was so complicated communicating with him.

'No. We're at Bronte.'

We. Who was we? Must be flatmates – those guys who'd been in the cool band. She would never have gone to Bronte.

'Bronte?' I asked. I used to try and de-beachify myself. Now he was living at the beach?

He shrugged, and grinned. Adorably. What did the shrug actually *mean*, I wondered?

'I changed. I needed fresh air, and I don't know … It didn't seem weird any more, hanging out at the beach. It seemed … I don't know. The air. The sun. Everyone zooming around. It was all uplifting. Light. Space. Great Art Deco buildings.'

He leant into the remaining light, and I could see sun streaks in his hair.

'In fact, you won't believe this. I've been surfing. I've got a Malibu.'

I must have looked shocked. 'You've changed,' I said. I didn't know what else to say.

'You haven't,' he said, just a little tenderly.

I blushed.

'Oh? How would you know?' It was meant to sound flirtatious, but it came out ever-so-slightly nervous. I laughed to cover it up. 'I guess I'm sort of the same. Lots has happened though.'

I came to a halt as I realised he was busy looking around again. Time to bite the bullet. Was he still with … her?

'So, what are you doing here?'

'I was meeting a friend. Yeah. But ... looks like they're not turning up. Hey – how weird that you're here.'

'Are you ... you know ... seeing anyone?' he asked.

'No,' I said truthfully.

'That's good. I'd be a bit jealous.' I blushed again. God.

I had to ask. I mean, he'd said it was a dead end. But were they breaking up, or what?

'Are you ...' I had to make sure I wasn't hearing voices. Suddenly delusional. I mean, with me there was a fine line. So many imaginary conversations – and this one just wasn't going right.

'Sorry. Um. Are you still living with her?'

'Yes,' he said, looking ever so slightly caught out. 'Sometimes it feels weird, you know, you forget just how special it was. Then I see her, you know, just doing something ordinary, like brushing her teeth or something, and I get this big rush of love and remember that we're soul mates.' He grinned, apologetically, almost.

A little flame lit inside of me. Soul mates? That's not what his letter had said. 'Can you excuse me a moment?'

I went straight to the bathroom and sat down on the loo. I ripped up the loo paper into tiny little shreds till I felt I had my temper back under some kind of control again. I splashed my face and took some deep breaths, crossed my arms and let myself just be bloody furious.

The pig!

I had a few things to say, but I wanted to make sure I could get through them all without dissolving into tears. I nudged around my feelings, the way a tongue searches out a sore tooth. Everything seemed okay for a major rant. I was pissed off – extremely – but I wasn't going to cry.

I took his letter out and looked at it. Right. Time to go back and face up to – everything.

I sat down, popping the letter in my pocket. He saw my face, and flinched.

'So, where were we?' I said cheerily. He relaxed a little. 'That's right! Wow. Soul mates.' I nodded my head, trying to look impressed. 'You're lucky. Not everyone feels that good about relationships. Apparently things can go a bit stale.'

'Yeah, well, we have to, er, work at it.'

'Some people,' I said thoughtfully, 'can feel caught in dead-end relationships. You know. If they've been together for a while.'

His ears pricked up at that one.

'And sometimes they feel like someone's just called out to them ...'

A funny look scrambled across his smug face. Hah! I raised my eyebrows. Oh this was good. This was ten million times better than throwing wine in his face. Or getting back together.

'Some people feel so ... compelled that they write to people they don't even know. Can you imagine?' I said, taking the letter out of my pocket and placing it just out of his reach.

I was feeling ruthless. It was exhilarating.

'Like this one. Here,' I said, friendly, 'have a listen. See if this strikes a chord.'

He winced when he saw what I was holding. 'Meg, what's going on?'

'No, no listen. You'll like it. I really think you will.'

He actually looked a bit frightened. Good. I cleared my throat, and a few people started looking over.

> **I don't really know why I'm answering your letter. It's not like me to read the ads, let alone respond. But something about what you said ... called out to me.**

I read it out in a warm, strong voice, adding lots of emotion for extra effect.

'Isn't that beautiful!' I remarked, shooting a soulful glance at him. His face was bright red.

'Meg, just ... that's enough.' He sounded a bit angry. Well, not as angry as me.

'No, no, let me go on. It doesn't finish there.' He reached out to snatch it. I stood up and moved back. More people were looking now, interested in our little soap opera.

> **And me?**
> **A dead-end relationship and too little time to waste for the rest of my life. I want a soul mate.**

Everyone was listening. Even dreadlock boy was having a good look.

You called out to me.

'Wow. He's pouring his heart out, Ben, isn't he?'

'What is this? Meg. Some kind of set-up?' he growled. 'You're only embarrassing yourself.'

'"What is this?" That's a great question, Ben. I mean, it sounds like a guy writing to a girl because he wants to have a relationship. But what I think it actually is, Ben, is a guy writing to a girl behind his girlfriend's back. Seeing if he can still pull the chicks. You know, like he used to.'

'Come on, Meg,' his face looked anguished. 'If I'd known it was you I'd never have said those things.'

'Like that's a news flash,' I laughed, though I was beginning to feel a little weird. The elation was feeling slightly hysterical, now. 'Well of course you wouldn't have.' *Dickhead*, I added silently. 'But it turned out to be me, Ben.'

Everyone was positively enraptured. Theatre on the beach.

Another hard, straight arrow of anger ran straight through me, shot out the other side and made impact with Ben's conscience. Finally.

I could see it on his face. He was ashamed. He flushed. Gotcha.

'I'm sorry,' he mumbled, holding out his hand to me and hanging his head down.

Too right he was. Sorry he was in so much trouble.

I took pity, sort of, on him. I shut up, and put the letter away again.

'You're lucky. I could show this to Freya,' I said,

shaking my head. 'Why'd you do it, Ben? Do you cheat on her lots?'

'None of your business,' he muttered, sulky.

Maybe it wasn't. He wasn't my business. Not any more.

Poor Freya.

'Look, I'm sorry I treated you so badly. I have thought about you often.' He reached out and grabbed my wrist. Tightly. I didn't like it. I didn't like him.

'You know,' he said, looking all emotional, 'when I think about you – the feelings come back.'

Nice try.

'No, Ben, I won't give you the letter,' I said, softly. I pulled my wrist away from his hand, and turned around to gather my things.

'You have to give it to me! You can't show it to Freya.'

I looked at him, shocked. I had no intention of showing it to Freya – I didn't want to hurt her feelings, which I confess came as a bit of a surprise to me.

But let him sweat.

'Why not? Give me one good reason,' I said defiantly, swinging my bag over my shoulder.

'Because we're …' He choked. Couldn't get the words out.

'What? You're what, Ben? Come on. Out with it.'

'We're getting married.'

I walked along the beach for a while before going home. There was so much light pouring from the houses, the Icebergs and the car park that the beach never really got dark. I sat there, jeans rolled up, knees hunched together, looking at surfers packing up to go home, staring at the big golden moon rising up into the sky. Maybe it was all the feel-good endorphin-boosting negative ions at the shore, maybe it was the moonlight, but I felt really clear. What a waste of time it had all been. All the crying and worrying and fretting over what was wrong with me. Nothing had been wrong with me. He'd been right. He was the problem. And he had told me so.

God, all those exhausting hours of self-examination. Was it my hair? My suburban background? My height? Nope. All the wrong reasons.

And you know what? He wasn't the person I'd thought he was. He wasn't some kind of genius hero who I'd let slip away because I wasn't clever enough or pretty enough. He dumped me. Maybe Allison had been right all the time. The truth, that he'd liked me, and had been ashamed of it, hit me.

Wanker, I thought, stifling a giggle as I thought of his face when I'd started reading his letter.

Allison would love to hear about this. She'd be proud of me, I thought, hugging my knees.

Hell. I was proud of me.

CHAPTER TWENTY-ONE

I might have had a moment of clarity on the beach, and I definitely had my moment of triumph at the café. But that didn't mean it didn't hurt that night, or that I didn't have a bit of a cry, or feel tempted to guzzle some wine, just to put me to sleep nice and fast.

The truth was, I was disappointed. But I knew I'd get over it.

'Just get angry,' Max said.

'That's what my mum says,' I said to him. 'Have you been taping *Oprah* again?'

He ignored me. 'Listen to Max. When you feel pissed off, just go and thump something. But not a person,' he elaborated worriedly.

'I'm not a psycho, Max,' I said. I gave him a hug. After all, he'd got me tissues when I'd cried. 'Anyway, I'm not angry all the time. It's actually … I dunno. It's a relief. It's kind of over. Finally.'

But he was right. From time to time I got really, really pissed off. So I took his advice. Every time I felt a wave of anger threatening to overwhelm me, I went to the toilets and kicked a bin and splashed cold water on my face. The third time I snuck off and booted the bin, I started to giggle.

'Meg, you're worrying me.'

I turned around to see Eleanor standing in the doorway.

'Fuck it, Eleanor! Don't sneak up on me like that!'

How the hell *had* she snuck up on me? You could usually HEAR her coming a mile off. Something was changing – and it was Eleanor. Like snow on the Kilimanjaro, her fat was … vanishing. Someone else had actually got into the tearoom this morning – while Eleanor was in there.

As well as looking, er, smaller, she was standing there, staring at me, her head to one side, her eyes all concerned.

'What are you doing?' she asked in a suspicious drawl.

'Nothing,' I blurted, turning away.

'Have you been crying?'

'No!'

'Something's up, Meg. Your eyes are red.'

She stepped a bit closer, all motherly and concerned.

'Do you think you might be – pushing it a little?'

That wiped the fake smile right off my face. 'What? *What?* Eleanor, *you're* the one who vomited out my window during the night of the Long Island iced teas, remember? The one who passed out on my bed during the Oscar festivities … The one we dragged away from …'

'You just look hungover.'

'Well, I'm not. I haven't been for a day or two now,' I said sarcastically.

'*And* Monica's on the warpath. And ...'

'*You* drink Eleanor. You *and* Julie and Max and ...'

'Yeah, we do. But you never used to.'

'I did when I was nineteen,' I corrected. 'Then I did again during a bad break-up. Which is why I didn't any more. But then I saw the guy again and I did. But it's finished now, so I won't. Understand?'

'Perfectly,' she said, backing off carefully.

Step *away* from the nutter.

I made it through the rest of the day – feeling okay, actually. There was a scary meeting with Monica and Chandra about my project, which I survived, but during which I was petrified lest Monica berate me about the plastic surgery thing again, but she'd probably decided it was too much even for her to bring it up in front of other people. I was probably supposed to go and get it, then she could say that I'd wanted it all along. Bloody hell. All the manoeuvring was doing my head in. But nothing was said. In fact, she was nice to me. Which would have alarmed me had I been fully operational. 'You don't look well,' she said. 'Why don't you take off a bit early today?'

Excuse me, but wasn't she meant to be on the warpath today? She was so damned unpredictable. I'd prefer to know she was just a bitch, so I could know how to react to her all the time. But she has these ... moments where I *almost* warm to her.

Yuk. She was her very own good cop–bad cop team.

Chandra's face fell a full five floors at that comment.

I ignored the temptation to feel like shit once again and nodded.

'Thanks, Monica, I will.'

Was it my imagination or did she look a bit pissed off?

Was I meant to resist the opportunity and counter the offer with the typical over-ambitious mantra of the magazine work junkie: i.e. *no no no* and then stay back till midnight just to prove how much I was needed?

I might have been, but I wasn't going to. Not any more.

Thankfully, the Monica meeting was followed by a fairly cruisy advertising gathering, where I had to be nice to people who made dodgy chemical soft drinks, which was followed by another suck-up session at a beauty briefing, where Carla outdid herself charming the pants off people who put fresh roadkill collagen into eye creams and called it a miracle anti-ageing treatment. Renata was appeased for another day.

Maybe this seems basic to you – for me, the day had all the hallmarks of a breakthrough. Without any costly therapy! By the time I escaped the office, I was tired, emotional, and strangely elated. Corner turned.

Time to get on with things.

When I got home, Eric was sitting out the front of the house, staring forlornly up at the second-floor window.

'Hi,' I said, walking up to him, pulling my jacket closer around me as the wind cracked down the hill. 'What are you doing out here? It's freezing.' He looked at me, his lovely face troubled.

'Er, I'm just …'

'What? Checking out the traffic?' I teased. 'Come on.'

Fizz was leaning out a side window. Smoking! It was like seeing a pixie flashing, or something. It was *wrong*.

'Is that …'

'Yes. It's an after-sex cigarette.'

'Ohhh. That's why you're out here.' Poor Eric. It can be awful when your best friend suddenly hooks up with someone. Even though Eric and Max seemed to be getting along very well indeed.

'Have you heard the noise they make? Actually, don't answer that,' he said, blushing.

'I will. It sounds like a bowl being licked by a cat.'

'Through a giant sound system,' Eric added.

Max popped out the front door, his face lighting up with a manic grin, and joined us on the front step. I wasn't sure how he'd beat me home but I wasn't going to ask. He sat down next to Eric and hung his head on his shoulder.

'I feel terrible,' he cried dramatically.

None of us said anything.

Disappointed, he took up his own thread. 'I should never have let them watch that video.'

Okay. Now I had to ask.

'What video?' I said looking at Fizz, still curling smoke like Jean-Paul Belmondo out the window.

'Well, Max said one way to really sort people out was to test them with …

'Hi,' said Dan, calling from an upstairs window. 'Got any more of that gay porn?'

I looked at Eric. '*Gay porn?*'

'Have you *seen* any?' Dan yelled down. 'It's *fantastic*!'

'Oh God.' The Christian neighbours briefly stopped washing their van and glanced over, then started washing again, really, really hard. I waved to them, feeling like God was going to bust me big time, and walked inside the brothel formerly known as my house.

'What's happened here?' I sang out to Dan. 'We're talking gay porn. Post-coital ciggies. Max! Explain yourself.'

Dan ran down the stairs and clutched my arms. 'Gay porn is the best thing ever invented, and I'm including every drug, every drink, every kind of mind-altering substance known to mankind. Maybe even food. Water. Air.'

'Explain.'

'Don't you understand? It worked – it worked. My life has been a Diane-free zone for two days. No meals cooked, no cuddly toys on my bed, no planning our weekend getaway.'

'What did you do?'

'What didn't I do? I belched. I farted. I rolled over and fell asleep. I purposely didn't make her co –'

'Enough!' I clapped my hands over my ears. '*Lalalalalala.*'

'And he pretended he couldn't get it up,' bellowed Max with considerable glee.

'That was my idea,' Fizz said proudly from upstairs.

God the walls were thin. Mental note: remember *never* bring Nick home. (Where did that thought come from?)

'And then I showed her some gay porn. She ran! It was fantastic.'

I stood there watching Dan do some kind of Irish jig with the biggest, stupidest grin on his face. He didn't hear the front door open – but the look on our faces made him stop.

I couldn't believe what I was seeing … it was Diane, looking as if she owned the place. My house. I was the alpha female here. Maybe not at work. Definitely not in the family. Absolutely never in any of my relationships.

But in this house I was the alpha woman. And Diane was about to hear me roar.

'Good to see you,' she said, struggling in with three gigantic bags from House of Fetish, Pussy Galore and Bad Boys Whippit Club. She dumped them on the floor, and came over and gave me a big undeodorised hug.

'Wait till Dan sees what I got for him,' she laughed, winking at me. I was in shock. Following right behind her was Allison.

Diane either ignored my awkward pause or was oblivious as she prattled on.

'Allison and I thought it would be good for her to pick up some of her stuff,' Diane said.

'You know — now I've got some of my own,' she added, pulling a studded leather bikini top out of the first gigantic bag.

'Oh.' I felt really sad. All the fight just drained away. 'You do?' I asked softly, peeping at Allison.

She nodded, not meeting my eye.

'I might as well,' she sighed.

'Oh. Well, it's nice to see you, Allison.'

'Meg.' We nodded at each other.

Dan was standing behind Diane, pulling faces like an epileptic gopher. I cleared my throat and attempted communication.

'What's been happening?' It was directed at Allison but Diane jumped in.

'Weren't you in a hurry?' she asked Allison.

Bad move, Diane.

'Dan totally inspired me with some very raunchy little films. He's probably been wondering where I went off to.'

'He sure did,' I murmured.

'So. How was your family? Was it okay?' she was practically stroking my hair. Next she'd be knitting me something.

'Look, I started knitting this for you while you were at your Mum and Dad's,' she said, holding up a weird beige and brown beanie thing from the second bag. 'I saw it in a pattern book and I thought it was *really* you.'

I looked at her, wild-eyed. All the fight flooded right back in again. Welcome! Round one — Ben over and done with, packed up and put in the emotional recycling box, to be pulped and used for better things. Is that just a fancy way of saying chalk him up to experience?

Maybe. But tapping into the rush that was my Ben triumph was inspiring me to do great things on the Diane front.

'Anyway – hope you're okay,' she said, all concerned. 'Families can really push your buttons. Some have a lot of unresolved issues. I was a little bit worried about you.'

Ali raised an eyebrow at me as she made her way up the stairs to get her stuff.

Enough.

'Diane,' I said in a dead-straight voice, 'can I have a moment with Allison?'

She laughed, lighting a pongy stick of incense and shoving it into an orange and putting it on a side table where the phone was. That's my side table. My phone. My orange. And, even if she did shit me, and even if she wasn't perfect, even if she had hidden Ben the bastard's letter from me, and even if we never ever talked again, Allison was My Best Friend!

'Sure,' she said, taking the longest, most frustrating time on earth to pick up her enormous bags and stagger away under the weight of her kinky gear. I thought I was going to scream.

Finally she shoved off. In slow motion.

'Anyway, we have some things to get organised for the long weekend, don't we, Dan?' Dan looked like a condemned man.

'The long weekend?' Shit, it was out of my mouth before I'd had a chance to check in with my brain.

'We're all going away to my folks' place,' Diane explained. 'You know, up the coast.'

'We?'

'Yes. Eric and Max, Dan and Fizz and Tamara are coming. All the new couples. You'll come, won't you?'

'I'm not in a new couple,' I snapped, crossing my arms. She was a social Darwinist, plotting to make us all her friends, leaving Allison exactly – where?

'Oooh, who's being all mysterious? We know about Nick,' she said, one eyebrow raised in a carbon copy of Allison's favourite expression.

I almost laughed in her face at that one.

'Come on. It's the Byron Blues Festival,' Diane said. She was obviously on an entirely different wavelength as she seemed sure everyone was going with her … when only ten minutes earlier they'd been telling me that they'd finally got rid of her.

'Is Allison coming to Byron too?' I asked Diane.

'Er, well, I haven't asked her.' She lowered her voice to a clearly audible, booming whisper. 'I just thought it was best if she came and got her things.'

Not a good plan, Diane, if the look of sheer hunger Dan directed at Allison was any indication.

I put my hands on my hips. I think I even stood with my legs apart, like some big, manly warrior-type creature.

'I'll go if Allison's going.'

'Well, of course I can ask her,' Diane said.

'Great,' I replied. I pushed in front of her and yelled up the stairs.

'Allison – do you want to come to the Blues Festival?'

There was no reply.

'In Byron?' I heard her drop something.

Still no reply.

I kept my back to Diane and made like Allison was answering me.

'Oh. Okay – great,' I said brightly. 'Yes, she does,' I said definitely. Diane looked confused.

'*I* didn't hear anything.'

'Sometimes smoking a lot of pot will do that to you,' I said innocently.

Diane looked even more confused. Ha!

God – alpha female, hear me roar.

Allison exited Dan's room, clutching a few T-shirts and undies, looking miserable. 'They're my best ones,' she said aggressively. 'Otherwise I wouldn't have bothered.'

Dan thrust his head into his hands, looked down and groaned.

'Don't worry, Allison – T-Bro will love them,' consoled Diane.

'I'm not talking to you,' said Allison through her teeth.

It was getting hard to find any room to sit down. Our lounge room was full of couples.

'She's gorgeous.' Tamara was gushing over some fashion shoot in *Vogue*, or *Bazaar*, or *Elegance* or something.

'She's not,' said Allison, sitting down next to her.

Diane moved a bit closer to Tamara, her leather mini creaking. 'She's not, you're right. It's all cosmetic surgery and computer touch-ups,' she said, wriggling closer to Dan. Somehow the comment seemed aimed at Allison.

'What I meant was, she's a bogan,' Allison explained, a flicker of impatience crossing her face. She flicked a page. 'See? Bogan,' she said, pointing. 'Bogan. Bogan.'

'I see what you mean,' Tamara said, flicking a page. 'Bogan.'

'Yep.'

'I don't,' pouted Diane.

'Look,' said Tamara, patient to a fault. 'Dyed blonde. Meanish face. Lots of make-up. Lots. Big tits. Add it all up and what have you got?'

'Bogan?' Diane replied.

'Like what's-her-face. That one who goes out with that actor,' said Eric.

'Yeah – the one who sings – she's such a bogan,' Max said.

'What about that one who was in the American telly program – she's a bogan, too,' I had to get my two cents in.

'Don't they all live in Coffs Harbour?' Max asked.

'Where that actor lives?' Eric added.

'Yes!' we all snapped. Boys. Duh. No celebrity radar at all.

Diane sneered. 'Well, they're not sexy, anyway.'

'No! They are sexy – bogans are really sexy,' said Allison.

'But they're bogans.' Diane obviously didn't understand.

'Aahh,' Max said. 'I get it.'

'We should do a story,' I said, looking at him. 'Bogan Beauties.'

'No, no … Beautiful Bogans.'

'Yeah. There's her, her and her.'

'And then there's wog beauties,' Max was getting excited.

'No, that's *wrong* …'

'And it's not mean making fun of bogans?' Diane exclaimed, ready to see a cause.

'Yeah, it's about time we made fun of bogans,' Max said.

'Definitely. I'm a bogan,' I said.

Everyone was silent.

'It's all right,' I said. 'I'm a bewdiful bogan.'

'I thought you were Greek,' Fizz said.

Everyone looked at him.

'We can visit Boganville on the way up – it's on the way to Byron,' Eric said, grinning a lovely grin, the kind where the sides of your mouth go straight off your face. Somehow it seemed the idea of going to Byron and free accommodation outweighed the Diane-is-slightly-deranged factor.

'So you're coming to Byron then, Ali?' I asked looking at her like I was trying to will her to say yes.

'Definitely,' she nodded her head vigorously, sending tousled red fringe and thick ponytail everywhere.

'Do you want to bring T-Bro?' chimed in Diane, practically creaking with enthusiasm. 'Oh bring him, go on – he'd really enjoy going to the beach.'

Everyone looked at Diane like she was mental. Which of course, she was. I mean, we lived at the beach.

'Now, just because Ali's fallen for someone you all consider a little outré,' she admonished. 'Everyone, except me and Dan' – who assumed the cringing schoolchild position.

It was all that leather. She'd whack a cane down on the coffee table in a minute.

'He's the local druglord, Diane,' spluttered Dan, who had seemed to have temporarily lost his fear.

'Oh, come on, Dan,' said Diane lovingly. 'You grow pot. You must bring him. If Ali's coming, T-Bro's coming too,' Diane said, the glimmer of a knife edge in her voice.

It was like watching two people fight it out at the OK Corral.

They stared at each other.

We stared at them. No-one moved. Fizz's face twitched.

Allison shook her hair out of the ponytail it had been in. 'Are you hot?' she asked sweetly, taking off her jumper.

Still no-one moved. Fizz's face started twitching a lot. This was a major challenge.

In response, Diane clambered onto Dan's lap. His eyes bulged, and he bit back a whimper.

'Anyway. No. T-Bro won't be coming. That's off,' said Ali, leaning forward, bosoms brimming up over the edge of her pink Bonds singlet.

Dan looked like he was going to have a heart attack.

MISS LONELYHEARTS

'Oh, no! Really? But you're great together,' Diane pouted, wrapping herself around Dan tightly.

'Actually, he's a bit of a creep, Diane.' A pale-pink strap fell off one creamy shoulder.

'No – he's just a rebel – you like that kind of guy. You'd be bored with someone who wasn't breaking rules, wouldn't you?' she asked, moving closer to Dan (if that was possible).

'Well, it's over, permanently,' Allison said, cool and pointed.

'But whyyyy?'

'Forget it, Diane. He's not *fucking* coming.'

'Oh, you heartbreaker.' Diane laughed nervously from her position on Dan's lap. I think he was worried about whether he'd still be fertile when she stood up. 'Never mind – there'll be loads of guys in Byron for you.'

I felt a little flare of pure anger go up.

'Diane –' I warned.

'Meg, I'm sure I'm just saying what's in your heart too. Ali,' she said, adopting the manner of a concerned careers-guidance counsellor. 'Are you sure about this? This T-Bro thing. This could be commitment-phobia raising its head – again. You can't just see one guy after another guy after another and another and another …'

Allison looked like she was going to throttle her. I jumped up and down on the urge to whack Diane over and over again with a big leg of ham.

'Well, thanks for the invite. But I'm busy!' Allison ambled off, swishing her behind like a secret weapon.

Dan blanched.

So did I.

Dan swayed. She was using very heavy artillery here.

'Where are you going?' Diane demanded, panicked.

A feeling of peace and tranquillity flowed through me at the thought of Diane's agitation.

Yep, things were finally getting back to normal.

'Come here.' I took Allison's arm. 'You've got to pick up that book you lent me.' I marched her into my room, leaving Diane gobsmacked. I closed the door gently in Diane's face, wobbling away with its new leather cap.

'Sit down,' I said stroppily. Allison obeyed, her lips looking a bit pinched.

'What's going on with us? We haven't spoken for *ages*. This is an all-time record!' I shouted, my voice going up and up until it ended in one of those hysterical squeaks. I started pacing around her like a cop during an interrogation. Anger made me energetic.

I ignored her horrified 'you're a looney' look by changing the subject.

'Look – why don't you come to Byron?' (Somehow I was now entertaining the idea of staying at Diane's folks' place. The world really had gone crazy.) I didn't add, 'So we can save our friendship that's just hit a massive iceberg and is sinking'. But that's what I meant.

'What for? To see Dan and Diane together? To hear all about you and Ben?'

'Ben? I saw him, and I really want to tell you about it …'

'Oh, shut up,' she snapped. 'I know you saw him. I suppose you blew Nick off.'

'How would you know?' I yelled at her, filled with righteous anger. This was so unfair!

She looked at her lap, twisting her hands into pretzel shapes.

'Things have been weird since you … since you broke up with Ben. If you're even thinking about getting back with him …'

I sat down next to her.

'It *was* an accident, Ali.'

She looked at me like she didn't believe a word I was saying.

'I'm sure it was,' I said, nodding wisely.

'Crap,' she replied, miserably. I hated arguing with her, so I didn't. But it had to be said.

'You, er, told my parents.'

'You made me keep it a secret! That's it! There're too many secrets. Can't mention the fact you swallowed half the –'

'Shut up!'

'Medicine fucking cabinet –'

'Shut up!' I screamed this time.

'And you hadn't moved for three days!'

'Look, I …'

'And you crashed my car,' she said.

'SHUT UP!' I roared. 'I already said I was sorry about the car!'

'Why should I? You tried to …'

'It was an accident! You should never have said anything to Mum and Dad!' I was still yelling.

'Why not? I'm not a social worker or a psychologist or ...'

'I went to a counsellor, remember – I told you.'

'Oh, that's right, I remember now, something else I couldn't tell anyone about.'

I'm sorry. I'm sorry. It must have been hard. I thought it. I nearly said it. But something stopped me.

'Oh piss off!' I shouted instead. 'That was ages ago.' Good one Meg, be a grown-up, I thought.

'Forget it!' she yelled back at me. 'Byron,' she roared, stalking away, 'stinks, anyway.'

CHAPTER TWENTY-TWO

You might have realised that I've glossed over a few things. Like the depression thing and the drinking thing and I don't think I ever mentioned the crashing-car thing.

Sorry 'bout that. About not telling you everything, I mean. I'm also sorry about how worried Ali was for me. And thanks to her I'd gone to stay at my parents and had time to sort myself out. But she didn't need to be worried ... if only she'd let me tell her about Ben. Loser Ben!

I wasn't sure how we'd fix things but I knew I had to. And what was that she said about Nick?

(Oh. By the way – I just want you to know that Allison actually doesn't think Byron Bay stinks. I know because Allison and I went to Byron after we finished high school. We were going to the Gold Coast. In fact we did go to the Gold Coast. Schoolies and us did not go together. Everyone was out of control – where was the fun in that? We hired a Mini Moke, drank ourselves silly, bought low-fat yoghurt, plastic low-fat cheese, low-fat everything and some apples. And a lot of white wine. And we drank. And danced. And pashed. In fact, we'd had a contest – who could pash the most guys. There'd been a list of conquests on the fridge. (And, somehow, I'd won.)

We had history, Ali and me, so I wasn't going to let my momentary (okay … so it went on for a couple of months) slide into the black hole damage our friendship. Somehow I'd make things right. Wouldn't I?

Somehow, my going to Byron was like a planet being sucked into a black hole: it was practically inevitable. When I got to work the next day there was a phone message from Dr Gold's assistant inviting me to a Botox conference the same weekend, only fifty minutes away from Byron on the Gold Coast. Once I told Monica about it, the days off were a done deal, as long as I came back with a Hollywood forehead. But Max was banned from the out-of-office field trip.

'You can't all go,' Monica said without looking up. When Max, Tamara and I attempted to organise a team story. That hardly seemed fair. She was going off on her very own super-smarmy office ra-ra team spirit–building course the next week. She wanted to make sure everything was up to date in the office while she was mud-wrestling, or whatever they do. She was taking some extra time after the conference, too, and we weren't allowed to contact her there either. Whatever. She was the boss. I had to reassure her that we'd be working.

'Just so you know, Monica, I've hired someone to come in and work on my stories – I've got them under control, he'll just make sure they're fine, do a fact check. I worked back to make sure they were in good shape. That way I can concentrate on the Botox conference.' But I think it would be good if I had the others with me.

She looked at me like she wanted to tell me not to be a smart-arse, then thought better of it.

'And why does Tamara need to go?'

'She has to cover the vox pops while I cover the operations. I'm certain I could do both, it's just unfortunate I can't be in two places at once. It's the sort of experience that will help her cut her teeth as a reporter, though.'

She nodded, impatiently.

'And Max could cover the men's angle.'

'Why? We're a women's magazine. It would help if I could rely on you to remember that.'

I knew when to stop pushing. I shrugged at him. He pouted. Sorry, I lip-synched.

'As long as the two of you come back with a story, then,' she said, glancing up at Tamara and me.

'Thank you, Monica,' I said, not at all sarcastically.

I mean, I could write what I found, couldn't I? And she'd be away at her weirdo conference thing. And Eleanor and I had organised for Vikram to come in. It had taken hardly any pleading – he thought it was funny that we needed him back already. Besides, I think he was missing Chandra. I'd always thought he had a soft spot for her – and he'd asked if he could sit at my desk.

Interesting.

Monica looked a little concerned that she was leaving the office for an entire week and was having to rely on Eleanor following her instructions to meet the deadline, given away by the one faint line creasing her smooth-smooth forehead. Her eyes narrowed just that little bit, like when people who thought they were in complete control suddenly realise a little crack has opened and you might just be wiggling to freedom through it. She looked at me like I might just be a little bit less predictable than she thought I was. I couldn't possibly be making some kind of crazy escape bid, could I? I could see the thoughts forming and evaporating, being rejected, one by one, and with each rejection the barely perceptible little creases and frowns somehow making their way through the Botox creamy smoothness of her skin disappeared. Even I could observe the process, despite all the interference. Time to sigh heavily and look worried.

'I'm a bit concerned though – I know we're going to have you away, even though I'm sure the conference will be amazing for us all.' I glanced at her. No, she didn't think I was going too far.

'It'll be especially hard for Eleanor. But I've tried to make it as organised as possible. And the story needs reporting, I think.'

Monica looked all self-assured again.

'Just make sure it's better than your last effort.'

Ah, the turn of the perfumed knife. Strangely, I couldn't even feel it.

* * *

After Monica dismissed us I headed back to my desk for an hour before the notion to exercise came over me.

It's very strange, but sometimes I actually enjoy the pain of working out.

'Gym?' I asked Carla, stretching back.

'Yep,' she nodded.

We changed in silence. It's like that sometimes. You just want to get into it and unleash the exercise beast. Sweat out the toxins. Suffer, to atone for your sins.

I ran, I sweated, I belted the bag. Parched and a little out of breath, I went over to the bubblers and drank and drank and drank, feeling refreshed.

'No, Milla, you do it this way,' I heard someone saying. I knew that voice. I looked up, pushed the hair out of my eyes, and saw Nick gently help a tiny waif-like creature curl a set of dumbbells to her chest. His voice was unbearably tender.

If it had been another man and another woman, I would have been touched at the cherishing way he was coaching her through the moves. I would have related to the way she looked, so grateful, the way she tilted her face up to him like a flower to the sun.

I stood still as still could be. He hadn't seen me. Even though I wasn't moving, I actually felt my heart rate go up. And up.

I saw him crouch down and give her a little talk, and nod his head. Their faces were close together, and he was looking right into her big, moony eyes. I couldn't stop staring.

'Meg,' Carla said, suddenly by my side, dragging me over to the treadmill, pushing me on and shifting the panel's pace up. 'Don't look.'

'Ice queen?' I said, forlornly.

'Just do your workout. That's what you came here for,' she snapped.

'He looks like he likes her!'

Carla looked at me witheringly.

'Is he –' God, I nearly gagged – 'is he holding her hand?'

'Yep,' snapped Carla, who must have had terrific peripheral vision. 'He's helping her with the waist thing now.' I saw Carla's eyes flare a little.

'What's going on?'

'I think she's fainted or something.'

'Lightweight,' we both said. I had to look. Nick helped Milla, pert-pretty-boy's-bum Milla, over to a bench, got her a drink of water, then turned and caught us staring.

'God.'

He wandered over.

'Hey girls.'

'Hi,' I mumbled, looking down.

'Good workout?' he asked.

'Not as good as yours.' I wanted to bite. I smiled, one of those corkscrew ones that nearly kill you to pull off.

Carla said, 'We're just leaving actually.'

I gave him a look, and he was still looking at me as Carla dragged me off. He must think I'm mental, I thought. I like him! And look how cute he is in his gym shorts. Look how nice he is to Milla. Uh-oh. Look how nice he is to Milla! Oh, shit.

'What are you doing?' I gasped at Carla as we reached the showers.

'Ice queen,' she said. It was completely silent in there. 'Ice queen? *Why?* What's going on,' I groaned dramatically.

'I *had* to get you out of there,' she explained kindly, like I was a sad little person. 'You were just about to say something ridiculous.'

'How do you know? I could have been pithy, witty, charming.'

'Your tongue was hanging out. You would have said something stupid.'

'*Stupid?* I didn't get a chance to …'

'And you need to roll your tongue back up next time you see him at the gym.'

The shower stopped. I walked out.

'Anyway,' Carla continued. 'He's obviously interested in you. You can easily get him off the pipe cleaner.'

'What?' Honestly. She so didn't have a clue. Hadn't she seen the way Nick was looking after Milla? I really had to do something about my friends' crazy ideas about me and men.

Thank God I was getting out of town for a few days. Then I could think about what to do next.

What to do about practically everything.

CHAPTER TWENTY-THREE

Byron Bay is paradise. Yes, I know, it's overrun, there are backpackers everywhere, it's more expensive to live there than in Sydney, and the people who do live there are even more obsessive about the ever-increasing price of real estate than people in Bondi, but there is a very good reason for all of this.

It's heaven on earth. Truly it is.

There's a beach carved in the shape of a sickle and pointy, magical-looking mountains as its backdrop – with turquoise water and dolphins that slip in and out of the waves that curve around the white shoreline. That's the bay. It's as far east as you can get in Australia. Its water is mild all year round, like the temperatures. Whales and sharks are there. Hippies are there. There's a smell of money, and dope, and something like love in the air. The coffee shops are good, the local coffee being the hot crop, after the macadamia plantations that were established in the nineties.

I know all about it, because one day I want to live there. One day.

MISS LONELYHEARTS

Diane's family was north-coast loaded. Which meant they had an old Queenslander nestling on the beach at Belongil, just one sand dune and plenty of sandbags and stakes away from king tides, and 4 metres away from the lake. Which meant mosquitoes.

Somehow Diane had talked us all (except Allison and Max) into the trip and we'd already spent a day getting on each other's nerves. Dan was the most annoying because he kept whingeing about Diane – but he was still sleeping with her and staying in her parent's house. Men – pathetic sometimes.

There was a slightly irritated air in the house, made worse by the fact that the wind had come up. And I'm a beach plus wind combination loather. Cannot abide it at the best of times (i.e. indoors drinking a large glass of white wine). But on the beach. Outside. No way.

Sorry. I know exactly why French folk reckon le Mistral sends them crazy and agree with Van Gogh that ear-chopping is the only sensible solution to that hideous whistling thing.

So, anyway, Eric and I were sheltering from the nasty blustery squalls and torrential rain in our new hang, the beach café. It was better than being aggravated by everyone at the house.

We had to walk there and back along the curve of the beach from Belongil to Main Beach, so we justified scoffing pancakes (wholemeal, I'll have you know) with the fact that we were actually building a workout into our feasting like pigs.

I reckon there could be a story in it — saint and sinner in the one day — the balancing act every modern girl needs to know about.

Eric was finishing his chat to Max and turned off his mobile. 'Max says hi — and ring Max.'

I grinned. 'What's he doing — apart from calling you?'

'He's been doing some story on some star's dieting disaster, plus a story on someone or other's new affair, plus there's some kind of attempt to find Australia's Posh and Becks — he's doing a poll.'

'God. Poor thing.'

'He's got Kylie and Jase, Kylie and Michael. He had Heath and Naomi but then he found out they'd broken up again, so he thought he'd save them up for a story on yo-yo daters. Oh — he mentioned that Monica was really fired up — his words — about your plastic surgery piece.'

'Oh, really?'

'Right.'

'Ha!'

'You're not getting any, are you?'

'Any what?'

'You know. Bits rearranged. 'Cos I could do that for you,' he grinned, giving me a playful thump on the arm.

'No, silly.'

We went quiet for a minute.

I'd been dying to ask him. So I bit back the urge not to and just went right ahead. 'When did you know?'

'Know what?'

'That you and Max ...'

'Oh, you know, pretty early. He's funny. It wouldn't have happened for ages if it hadn't been him.'

'Do your mum and dad know?'

'Nope. My sister does. She's cool. In fact I think she wishes I'd camp it up a bit so she could brag to her friends about her cool gay brother and so I could sneak her into clubs.' She was fifteen. Just so you're in the picture. 'But I haven't told my mum and dad.'

Which seemed a bit odd, so I said so.

'Isn't that a bit ...?'

'Strange? Not really.'

'But they're both – well, they're ...'

'Face it – you can say it – they're very socialist worker. But ... okay, you don't know this.'

He had a sip of water.

'I had an older brother. He's dead. Stupid car accident, at least ten years ago. So, I don't know, I don't think they're ready yet ... to hear my news. They'll never get over it. But they thought I might get married have kids, or move in, accidentally have kids.'

'Have a one-night stand, have a kid.'

'And I haven't the heart to tell them it probably won't happen.'

I nodded.

'Where're Tamara and Fizz?' he asked, changing the subject.

'Last seen heading for the sand hills.'

After the café we wandered around for a few hours and then found a tapas bar. More food! I clocked at least forty boys without their shirts on, and it was not like when men on Oxford Street take their shirts off. These were surfie boys.

A backpacker asked me directions. I must have looked like a local.

When we got back, Dan was sitting in the lounge room, looking pensive. Good.

'Why are you staring at the phone?'

'Can you take Diane out for a drink or something?' he whispered. 'I have to ring Allison.'

'To say what? "I'm in Byron with my new girlfriend."'

'No, to straighten things out. I've made up my mind. I'm going to talk to Diane tomorrow.'

Typical ... get another bonk and don't spoil the weekend mentality.

'I'll see what I can do.'

I went in search of Diane and found her in the main bedroom, straightening a dolphin poster on the wall.

'Diane?' I sat on the bed and looked down, rearranging my face into innocent, yearning-type features, before looking up at her beseechingly.

'Do you think I need cosmetic surgery?'

'What?' she yelped, whirling, Diane-fashion, around. She sat down on the bed and took my face between her hands. 'You *know* you don't.'

I couldn't say anything, because my face was all scrunched up. But I mumbled, and cast my eyes around, trying to say 'But don't you reckon I'd look better with ...'

'No,' she intoned, stretching out a hand dramatically. 'No more. Come with me.'

She marched me in front of a (shell) mirror and said, 'Look at yourself.'

I looked at myself.

'Say "I am beautiful, exactly as I am". Say it. Come on.'

'No!' I said, wriggling. But she had a firm grip on my head.

'Say it,' she said, in tones that brooked no contradiction.

I looked at myself. Scruffy, sun-kissed, and no skin, yet, peeling from my nose.

'I am beautiful, exactly as ...' I started to giggle, and stuck my fist in my mouth.

'A lot of emotions come up for people when they first begin to look within,' Diane explained gently.

Oh, I thought, cottoning on. She thought I was crying. Duh. I sniffled away.

'Would you like me to do some mirror work with you?'

I looked at her. 'What about you? Do you think you need cosmetic surgery?'

'As if. I'm proud of who I am.'

'Why?'

'Because I just am. I am good enough, exactly as I am.'

'Are you?'

'Well, yes.'

'So, do you want to go to a Botox workshop?'

'Haven't you been listening to anything I've said? You know I would never, never subject myself, or support that kind of barbaric sexism that ...'

'I know, I know. You've heard about my boss?'

'Sort of.'

'I have to go to this conference. I sort of have to have plastic surgery.' I thought she might explode, she looked so angry.

'You cannot go alone. That would be wrong. I must go too. I'll tell them all how insane the notion is.'

'No!' I yelped. 'Honestly, Diane, I think it would be overkill. Tamara's coming, anyway, so …'

'Perfect!' she said. 'Tamara can go to the Blues Festival, and we can go to this … Botox thing together. Honestly, you need someone there to make sure you don't do anything silly. Like get something done.'

'But I wouldn't!'

'You don't know how powerful the group mind is. I'll just be there to keep an eye on you, and do whatever Tamara was supposed to be doing. It's perfect. This way she gets time with Fizz, and you get the job done, and I …'

'Yeah, what do you get?'

'I get to have my say,' she said, with a glint in her eye.

Later on we wandered down to the Station Hotel for a drink so we could talk through what she called our non-violent peace strategy. The pub was packed – the Blues Festival was massive, and people from everywhere were laughing and chatting. The vibe was so laid-back it was only minutes before we ended up talking to a group of gorgeous people hanging near us. One of them, Marley, who was quite cute in a wholemeal kind of way, looked at Diane the whole time she was speaking. Hmmm.

'So, what do you guys do?' I asked. They rolled their kohl-rimmed pot-reddened eyes.

'We're focusing on getting our organic garden up and running. Then I'll be painting,' said one girl whose name, I think, was Ariel.

'Meg works for a magazine,' Diane said, half apologetically, half ... proudly?

'How's work going?' Ariel asked importantly.

'It's great,' I joked. 'After all, I'm not there.' The hippy wasn't laughing. Diane smiled. Sort of. 'Does your magazine have ads?' Marley asked slowly.

'Sadly, yes,' I laughed. 'We can't do without them.'

'Meg works for a trashy magazine,' interrupted Diane.

I gave her a hurt look. Hey! I knew it was trashy, but the way she said 'trashy' made it sound like something I should be ashamed of. I'd been kind of ... kind of liking Diane, truth be told.

Marley looked a bit disgusted.

'Magazine, hey,' Marley said, all the while looking at Diane. In fact, it was obvious that he was still staring at her. Interesting ...

'Bummer. Hard to sell your soul like that,' he said, still looking at Diane.

'Yep. It's a living,' I said, getting a little reckless. 'And I am one of those people who have to make one.'

'Meg is the health editor for *Gossip!*,' Diane elaborated.

'Health editor! Editor of bad body image. It's magazines like yours that help women think they have nothing better to do than look good, get married and breed,' Ariel stated, shaking her bright pink head disapprovingly.

Marley, looking at me with concern, changed tack. 'Maybe you could switch allegiances. You actually could work on that other magazine, the one in the weekend paper. The quality one. With the good articles.'

They all waited expectantly.

'The one with the ads?' I asked innocently.

Marley gave up on me and moved his attention back to Diane. They were soon caught up in a fervent conversation that combined cell food, auras and ascended masters. It was kind of sweet how into it they were. She was really enjoying herself. He was too.

'Diane,' I interrupted, 'I'm going back to the house, okay?'

'Oh. Maybe I should …'

'No, you stay here. You're having fun.' I was genuinely liking her. What was going on?

'You can stay with us, Diane. There's a film about reiki on in the back room in a minute.' Marley said, his eyes boring into hers.

'Oh. That sounds great. Meg?' She was beaming. I smiled. It was impossible not to.

'No, thanks. I'll see you a bit later then. Have fun.'

Hmmmn. Interesting. Very interesting.

* * *

MISS LONELYHEARTS

I don't know this for sure, but I think there'd be pretty good odds that Diane looked unlike anyone else who'd ever attended one of Dr Gold's conferences. She had proudly reinstated her tie-dyed hair scarf for today's anti-Botox protest, and she'd somehow managed to have an 'I love my facial expressions' T-shirt made up in town.

She looked incredibly out of place. And so did I, in jeans and a sparkly top and a lick of lipgloss. The problem was I just wasn't looking old enough, no matter what my mum had said about sun damage.

Diane gawked at a peacock strutting by on the green lawn dividing the office from the hall where we were to meet our saviour.

'God – Dr Gold says he's going to introduce a new breakthrough in dermal fillers today – one that has eight patents pending,' I said, reading the shiny brochure featuring models telling us that we could look like them. 'I wonder what it's made of. It doesn't say anything about it. Maybe it's some kind of animal product.'

'Surely they couldn't do that?' gasped Diane. 'Harvest animals for human consumption!'

'Oh no?' I said. 'Remember the hamburger? Now,' I warned, stopping her for a second. 'Just don't carry on.'

'Meg, I'm here to support you,' she said, all sincerity as she watched me step up to the ticket-taker.

'It's Meg Tooley from *Gossip!* – I'm here for Dr Gold's conference,' I explained. 'This is a friend of mine from another publication. Can she sit in?'

'Welcome, Meg,' said a girl with an impossibly smooth face, big fat lips and tattooed eyebrows. 'Not a problem, enjoy!'

She ushered Diane and I into the darkened hall to watch an introductory video.

It was actually quite interesting, I thought. Objectively, what could be wrong with women getting a little boost? God knows people are hard enough on us about our looks. Who wouldn't want to look better? I thought of all the cellulite cream I'd slapped on my thighs, all the control briefs I'd met and rejected, and all the times I'd tried to de-frizz my hair.

Was this really so different?

Diane had not uttered a word. But when I had a look, her fists were clenched and the sound of her teeth grinding was going to annoy somebody very soon.

'Diane,' I whispered. She jumped. 'Just calm down. We've got a while to go.'

She sighed gustily and didn't grind her teeth any more, but even in the dreadful light I could see her moony face getting redder and redder. She was just bursting. Hold it, Diane. Hold, hold.

When Dr Gold strode out onto the stage after a particularly gushing testimonial from a woman who claimed he'd saved her marriage, there was very warm applause. There were even some wolf whistles.

After a bit of a speech, where he displayed the charms of a lesser Eddie McGuire, he asked if anyone was ready to try a 'a little freshen-up'.

Hands like spears shot up everywhere.

One woman, with a youngish face, was beckoned to the stage, and we all settled back to watch the enormous overhead video screen of her being 'refreshed'.

'This is barbaric!' said Diane, aghast.

I had to agree with her. My cosy thoughts after the video were banished by the first sight of the needle heading towards her skin.

The woman winced and her lips bled as the needle was pushed through the skin. Tears started in her eyes and one ran down her cheek.

'God. That hurts,' I said.

One woman behind me said, 'Oh, that's nothing. Wait till you see the bruising that happens.'

'It looks like you've been punched by Russell Crowe,' added another.

'What?' I said. 'Do you bruise more with Botox or collagen?' I asked, pulling out my notebook and beginning to jot this down.

'Collagen,' claimed one confidently.

'No way. Botox,' said the bruiser. 'And the bruising's not the worst of it,' she continued. 'Once the left side of my face was ... paralysed,' she leant forward and whispered.

'And they don't tell you this either,' hissed another one in clandestine tones, 'but you can sag with Botox. Sure it freezes your muscles, but have you ever seen anyone in a wheelchair? Their muscles are frozen too. Do you really want a face like Christopher Reeve's legs?'

'I'm sorry, but just why do you do it, then?' I asked, pen poised.

'It doesn't hurt as much as wrinkles.'

'This is terrible,' said Diane huffily.

'Ssshhh,' I hissed. 'Let me get the info. That's the only way to do a good job. Otherwise I won't get anything and you'll just make these women – okay, people,' I corrected myself, seeing some smooth-looking guys gossiping over their brochure in the corner, 'feel bad and then they won't trust me.'

Diane looked like a bull ready to charge. She snorted and pushed her hair back and rolled up the sleeves of her horrible T-shirt. 'Sometimes, Meg,' she said, getting to her feet, 'you just have to take a stand.'

While I was trying to calm Diane down, Dr Gold finished his 'refresh' on his volunteer and an assistant helped her walk off the stage and back to her seat.

'Look, here's another volunteer,' yelled Diane, waving. Dr Gold stopped mid-charm session about his new filler. 'Over here. Take me.'

'Diane, what are you bloody doing?' I demanded, grabbing her arm.

She pulled away. 'Peaceful protest. I'm going to tell them all the truth, then lie down and refuse to move. Like Gandhi. Non-violent. They'll have to get the police to move me,' she said, her face agleam with a martyr's glow.

'Diane, this is *not* about you,' I said sternly. 'Sit down right now and behave,' I ordered. A few people were glancing our way, wondering what the drama was about.

But Diane knew when she had a shot at sainthood. No-one could stop her.

'Oh, don't worry, Meg. You'll have your story.' She broke away, moving faster than I'd ever seen her, towards the stage.

'No – Diane, stop!' Everyone stared at me. God. I sat down, breathless.

What the hell would happen next?

'I am here,' she announced evangelically, 'for all women. To say to all of you, we don't have to put up with this!'

The crowd looked confused. Then little ripples of explanations made their way through the throng.

'Put up with what?' I heard one exfoliation addict ask.

'Why, getting old, naturally,' gasped another.

'You're right,' one said, leaping to her court-shoed feet. 'We don't have to take it. We don't have to grow old – naturally!'

Diane, blissfully unaware of anything except a reaction, really thought she had them. She was single-handedly going to get every woman over fifty to reject cosmetic surgery.

Like hell she was.

'Now I am going to lie here and *not move*,' she bellowed. The crowd roared. She lay down on the chair. She opened her mouth. The crowd hushed.

'And why am I here today?' Her voice a theatrical whisper. Dr Gold looked confused. The nurse was poised, syringe in hand. He reached over and took it himself. What was that about? I wondered.

'I am lying here today,' Diane started up rousingly, 'for the good of all women who have been sold the lie that youth is beauty.'

As if programmed, the Stepford wives went wild. About a thousand age-spotted pairs of hands started clapping rhythmically.

Dr Gold smiled down, and made a quick gesture. A nurse darted forward and rubbed what must have been anaesthetic cream on Diane's mouth. It must have been very fast acting, because even though her volume went up, suddenly she became a lot harder to understand.

I managed to make out 'Until I get to do what I came here for …' Everyone applauded wildly and began stamping their shoes on the floor. They probably rattled their jewellery, too.

Meanwhile, Diane's lips were becoming frozen. A loud noise was coming out, but who knows what she was saying?

Despite the strange turn her speech had taken, her new fans surged forward, keen to see their heroine receive the new procedure.

'No!' I shouted, trying to hold them back. 'She doesn't *want* anything. She's protesting!'

Nobody seemed to hear. Way too much jewellery clattering happening.

I ran towards the stage, but was held back by a crowd of excited fifty-somethings who thought they were about to see a miracle. Helplessly, I watched Diane slowly realise she was at the mercy of a mob who'd got the wrong idea and a doctor with a syringe full of God-knows-what. I imagined her mouth trying to form the words peaceful protest, but nothing coming out. Overhead on the enormous screen her eyes got wider and wider as the syringe filled with Dr Gold's eight patent-pending wonder filler headed her face's way and smoothly punctured her epidermis. I winced.

'That's good, dear,' soothed the doctor as his surprised patient visibly shuddered. '*Very* good.'

Exactly one second later, Diane started to scream.

CHAPTER TWENTY-FOUR

Make her answer, I prayed, to something, someone (that I hadn't realised I'd believed in) from the squishy confines of the helicopter that was throbbing its way towards Brisbane. I crossed my fingers, tightly. *Make her be there.*

No answer. I hung up and punched the numbers in again, way too hard, feeling desperate. As if jabbing was going to make a difference. But the phone didn't care, had no intention of helping me out and just rang and rang. And rang a bit more.

'Shit, shit, shit,' I exploded.

Oh. I hadn't thought that bit, which is why the ambulance officer was frowning at me. I squeezed Diane's hand. I think it was beginning to turn blue, her grip was so tight. She obviously still had plenty of strength left.

'For God's sake, help me,' hissed Diane.

I looked down at her swollen, blotchy face, and smiled in a funny, twisted, I-don't-really-feel-like-smiling-but-I'm-doing-my-best-to-make-you-feel-better way at her. I really did feel like a prize shit.

Diane was in pain, and I felt responsible. She wouldn't have been there if I hadn't told her about my story.

Diane whimpered again, interrupting my self-flagellation.

I squeezed her hand, wondering if it would be callous to try the office again.

'You're going to be okay, really,' I soothed, completely hypocritically. It seemed best to lie at this stage.

'Mumph blurgle snuffler.'

'What? I – it's my ears, Diane, they're a bit funny with all this noise. Can you say that again?' I leant in really close, practically squishing her ear.

'Mlurble fernoopha?'

'Ohhhh. No, you look okay – really, considering. It's actually not that noticeable.' May God forgive me.

'Beeweelly?'

'Really,' I said confidently, with one of those definite little nods of the head that seem to make people feel better. She started to cry again.

'Don't start, Diane,' I begged, willing her to quiet down. 'Remember how the doctor said it would make the swelling worse?'

She stopped, only erupting with the occasional explosive sniffle.

'That's a good girl,' I said, rubbing her knee absently. 'You're being really brave.'

Which was the absolute opposite of how she'd behaved, actually, but hey, I'd never had such a dramatic near-death experience, so who was I to talk? I looked meaningfully at the ambulance officer again. 'When do you reckon we'll be getting there?'

'Jeez, as soon as this air traffic clears up a bit, miss.'

'Isn't there anything we can give her?' I asked, feeling desperate.

He shook his head, slightly. I think he'd heard that one before.

Diane snuffled out 'Pwease! Oh Gobh!' And he shrugged.

'Go on, Katie,' he drawled, 'give her a blast.' The blonde ambulance officer applied the gas.

That shut her up.

Relieved, I hit *Gossip!*'s number again. I knew Eleanor was working over the weekend to iron out a few glitches. This time it was picked up immediately.

'Hello, sex sells … Buy me.'

'Max – oh, thank you God. It's Meg.' Eleanor had obviously drafted some slaves.

'We're only answering to our porn names now. Yours is Candy Fresh. You like?'

'Put me on to Eleanor, Max, would you? Now,' I demanded, impatiently.

'Eleanor? Oh, you mean LickaLicka Lushytrousers,' he corrected.

'Max!'

'Say Lickalicka and I'll get her for you,' he drawled, annoyingly.

'Max! Get …' Oh, hell, what was the point. 'Get LickaLicka – *now*!'

I glanced around – everyone was frowning at me, even Diane, who was wincing in her gas-induced sleep. I turned my attention back to Max, who was prattling away. What was he *on*?

'Hello – Meg?'

'Eleanor, something really bad happened at the Botox conference.'

'What? What happened, Meg? – are you all right?'

'I'm fine – but Diane isn't.'

'Diane? What was she doing there? Did you get a story?'

'Look, I can't tell you all about it, we're on the way to the hospital in Brisbane – and I'm really, really sorry but I have no story. It's rooted. I mean, it wasn't rooted, it was going to be very fine, but then Diane decided she was going to protest and nobody realised – they thought she wanted to try the stuff and she had, I don't know, a reaction and … and so, I thought I'd better let you know.'

'*Why* are you going to hospital, Meg? *What's* actually wrong with Diane?'

'The Dr Goldenfiend person stuck some new dermal filler thing in her face and it's blown up to truly horrible puffer-fish size!' I shouted, sounding just the wrong side of hysterical.

'Blifcht!'

'Sorry, Diane,' I said apologetically. 'The real problem is she can't breathe,' I whispered into the phone, suddenly feeling close to tears.

'Meg! Which hospital, Meg?' I could hear Eleanor tapping away at her keyboard.

'Are you typing something?' That's what I did when I wasn't actually listening to someone. 'I can't believe it. I practically am having a heart attack here and you're writing – maybe emailing someone!'

'Is it that bad?' She sounded quite excited.

'Yes – I hate heights and I'm in a helicopter. And then there's, now what was it? Oh yes, there's Diane, choking on her own face, which is the size of those pumpkins Americans leave out on Halloween every year. Oh, and I'm on deadline and my story's rooted. But everything's fine, apart from that,' I said, savagely.

'Which hospital, Meg?'

'St Tandrelle's.' Some static cut into our conversation. 'Oh do you mind?' I shouted at my phone and, miracle of miracles, it cleared.

'Look, we're landing soon,' I shouted into the static. 'I'd better be going. Don't want to crash the helicopter. Really sorry about the story but I have to stay with Diane.'

'Look, I have to make a couple of calls,' Eleanor said, by way of goodbye, I suppose. 'I'll be in contact.' The static interrupted again and crackled over her voice.

'Eleanor, sorry. I know this sucks, especially with Monica away. Or maybe it's better with her away. Anyway.'

'Don't panic, okay. And don't turn your phone off, whatever you do.'

'Look, can you tell Monica – shit, I don't know what you can tell Monica. I resign?'

'She's not contactable. And anyway, the story's not necessarily rooted Meg. You just need to …'

But the phone cracked up and left me listening to

a trail of electrical noise. Eleanor had been consumed by the static. Gone.

Damn. I looked at Diane, whose eyes were still visible, slightly; tiny, pink and bright in the vast swollen puff pastry of her head.

Oh shit, Diane, I thought, panicked at the size of absolutely everything above her neck. *Why did you do it?*

The chopper wobbled down and the noise, which was like Marshal stacks playing *Apocalypse Now* back at me, abated slightly.

'What now?' I screamed over the noise at the ambulance officer, who was looking at me. I was feeling kind of elated – adrenaline, I thought.

'She's having trouble breathing,' Katie the ambo said.

Oh Diane, you great big hippy pain in the arse, I'm so sorry, I thought, feeling desperate and guilty. The fact that she looked like her head was three times the size it should be wasn't exactly my fault, but it felt precisely like it was.

'Okay, here comes trouble,' the ambulance officer said.

A tight, wiry, balding photographer was closing in on the chopper and taking pics.

He flashed a press pass at the ambulance folks.

'Oh, piss off,' Katie said, pushing past him, but not before he snapped Diane looking glazed, bloated and terrified on her stretcher bed, her long hair blowing fetchingly around the threadbare nylon pillow.

I stood there, mouth open, looking equally ridiculous.

'Where are *you* from?' I snapped when I'd completed gaping duties.

He gave me a wink, and whispered, 'I'm on your side. Ooh, here comes the filth. I'm off. Thanks love, great shots,' he said to Diane, who looked like she was trying to smile weakly. 'You look great,' he said. 'Only kidding.' Then he burst into nasty cackles and strode off as fast as his super-tight sprayed-on black ball-crunching jeans could carry him.

The guards, consisting of one tall, thin bloke with a tan and a really huge nose and good teeth that looked false, dwarfing a stumpy, freckled, sandy-haired guy, came up to me.

'Miss Tooley,' – that was the skinny one, flashing his badge – 'we need you to come with us for questioning.'

Oh, great. Just, well, fabulous really. I mean, after a helicopter dash for life and a surrogate near-death experience and potential job loss and career shame, I really needed to get ready to spend the rest of my life in prison with a large shaven-haired tattooed protector between me and certain death.

'Can I make a phone call?'

'We're not police officers, miss. The doctors just need to talk to you.'

'Take care of her, okay?' I said forlornly to the ambulance folks, who were already wheeling Diane off.

'Mlargheee ...' she choked out at me. Her eyes

looked desperate. She grabbed a little piece of paper and scribbled something down. I took it and read it.

'Call Marley 066 978 765 ...'

Marley! Not Mum. Not Dad. Not Dan. Marley! This was significant.

'I really don't think I should be leaving her.'

'Miss Tooley?' said a nice-looking tall man. I nodded. 'This way, please.' He led me to a room and closed the door behind me, before pulling out a chair. The kind you might pick up from the side of the road. If you couldn't get a milk crate. Or a floor.

'Thank you.'

I sat down on the nice brown chair on one side of a nice beige desk.

'So,' I said. 'What do you need to know?'

A couple of hours later I emerged into the Queensland heat. There were about three messages on my mobile, which I listened to while I waited for a taxi to pull up at the deserted rank. I called Marley, filled him in on Diane, and then called Eleanor at the office.

'Meg – thank God – I've been trying to reach you. We got some pics back ...'

'What? Was that vulture guy at the airport *you*?'

'*Us*, actually. Freelance vulture guy. Great pics. You look a bit pale, by the way, thought you'd been in Byron, but they're ... they're sensational.'

'Sensational *how*?' I asked, a bit narkily, as a cab pulled up. I hopped in.

'Um ... I need a nearby hotel. Cheap-ish,' I said. 'Sorry, Eleanor. Just arranging my emergency accommodation.'

'Diane looks *dreadful*.'

Things started to click and whir inside my very heavy, tired head.

'Are you thinking there might be something in this?'

'Oh, yes! There *more* than might be something in this. Whatever you've got planned for tonight, kill it. I need you to pull together a story by 8.00 a.m. – sharp.'

'Oh, there go my plans to eat alone in a hotel room and watch some bad TV,' I laughed. 'But tomorrow? It's' – I looked around and checked the clock on the dashboard – 'it's already four o'clock, Eleanor.' Hey – four o'clock on a Saturday? Why was she still at work? Wasn't that smelly pub time?'

'I know. Look if it's too much for you …'

I frowned. What was she insinuating? That I couldn't hack it? I could hack it with the best of them.

'Well, of course I can *try*,' I snapped. Did Eleanor think I couldn't write a bloody story? I grabbed my notebook out of my handbag, ignoring the vitamin tablets that scattered everywhere. 'For which issue?' I asked, getting ready to write.

'It will be the cover article in the next one.'

Next week's deadline. 'No problem,' I sighed, a feeling of relief working its way through my body. Now I could watch television till I dropped. Excellent. It wasn't such a rush after all. Typical editor, telling you to get your piece in a week early, when all the time …

'Meg,' snapped Eleanor, interrupting my internal rant. 'It's for this week's deadline.'

'Pardon?' I asked, feeling suddenly confused and disgustingly tired.

'The one we practically finished *last* week. The one that's going to print *Tuesday*. Got it! I'm holding everything till we get *your* story. I had to change some of the back of the magazine – that means I can change the front, too.'

She was right. The way stapled magazines are bound means that the back bits are joined to the front bits – pull one apart and you'll see what I mean. There was only one thing to say to this little piece of news.

'You're changing the cover. Oh my God,' I gasped.

'Not that you need to worry. Let me handle that. You just get me the story, okay? By tomorrow morning at EIGHT. And I don't need to say that means EIGHT, not TEN, like some people think EIGHT is.'

'Oh shut up LickaLicka slavedriver,' I heard Max gripe in the background.

'So that's why you're not at the pub.' I knew something was happening. She laughed in agreement. There was something I had to clear up.

'Eleanor, look. About Monica …' I took a deep, gusty breath. 'Monica, much as I despise and murder her every half-hour or so in my imagination, will have every right to saw you in half when she finds out you're planning on changing her cover.'

'I know. But it's something I have to do – and I know precisely how vomit-making that sounds, trust me. But there it is. The other joy is that she will be totally isolated at the conference. They're not allowed any contact with the outside world at all, unless, I suppose, someone dies or something. So we're safe.'

The driver had pulled up at a nice blond-brick building with – joy! A swimming pool. I gave him a ten and jumped out, headed for reception and did a lot of smiling and nodding at the elderly couple behind the counter while half listening to Eleanor raving on about the bliss of Monica being away for the next week. I handed over my ID, signed something and said uh-huh into the phone a lot. The joys of multi-tasking!

'I just don't want you to get the sack,' I explained, a bit more nicely once I'd cleared reception, made it up the stairs, and found my room. I opened the door into a really sweet room with orange thready bedspreads and flowery lamps. There was a frangipani tree blooming outside my window.

'No, you dill, I'm not going to get the sack. *This* story is great and the cover we have *sucks*. It won't sell, and this will. I don't know how or why I know but I just *know*. So make your piece about 1200 words – every single one of them brilliant and must-read. Give me a quiz – you're the best at those – witty but factual, multiple choice …'

'I know how to do a quiz, Eleanor. I *am* Quiz Queen, remember?' I smiled into the phone. Brilliant? Must-read? It'd been a long time since anyone demanded such a tall order of me. It would be a stretch after party frocks and vitamin jabs. Could I actually pull it off?

My heart started to beat a little faster, even though my body was begging me for sleep.

'Just bang it out. It'll be great,' Eleanor said.

'I think,' I said clearly, 'I can do a bit better than that.'

I'd given Eleanor my address, and she said she'd organise a laptop and a fax to be delivered to my room in an hour, so I went and bought a few things – like a cossie and toothbrush – and had a quick swim, then started making notes in my room. Room service had hooked me up to a virtual intravenous drip made up of a low-burning caffeinated mix, and I was feeling particularly Lois Lane (if you overlooked the fact that I'd changed into my jammies).

So very up-and-at-them reporter girl-ish. Just had to write the effing thing.

I jotted down the bare bones of what had happened, worked on a dramatic, gripping, in-your-face crime and sex and glamour novel-style intro to hook our readers into the story (*It could have been your face. Or your sister's. Maybe your mum's. Only this time it was Diane's* ...), then rang the hospital to get all the correct medical descriptions of what had happened to Diane, then went online to our website. Eleanor had posted the shots so I could caption them – dramatically, wittily ... and correctly. I gasped when I saw them – she'd been right. They were amazing. Diane's face looked like a soufflé that had got stuck on the rise button. I winced and clicked back to my Word document. I fleshed out my story a bit more, describing the drama of the helicopter ride and the potential criminal charges — against a certain Dr Gold.

I read over it quickly, then once again carefully, slowly, and felt a heat light up inside me. It was really getting there.

I think I was having fun. Really — when you're in there and it's clicking and you're not second-guessing yourself and you just know where to put what and how to say it, sensing what must go and what to add, imagining the readers when they really feel the impact and get swept away in your story, when they feel something because you put it just the right way — it's a great feeling. The best.

I zoned out for a while, as you do, losing myself in shaping, rearranging, refining and checking my facts, to the point where figures, statistics and telephone numbers and emails began to wobble and twinkle in front of my eyes. It wasn't like me to be so anal about everything, and I knew Vikram would be onto it as soon as I emailed the story. He never let an error go by — spelling or grammatical or factual. That's why we'd called him the cleaner — a human spellcheck, with soul. But if I buggered this story up it could mean the whole cover and the premise behind it would collapse — it'd be a beat-up with no meat to it, a teaser, not an actual piece of — God, was this me really thinking this way, getting all evangelical and John Pilger-esque about *Gossip!* journalism? Well, stuff it! I didn't care if I was a big embarrassing try-hard. I had to get it right — there wasn't any room for mucking anything up.

MISS LONELYHEARTS

I wiped my forehead, rubbed my eyes and stretched slowly, like a cat, moving my hunched-up shoulders in loose semicircles, lengthening the tight, shortened muscles all the way down my arms to my wrists and my fingers. I glanced in the mirror and screwed my tired face up at the state of my hair. Typical, I thought. Somewhere there were people drinking cocktails and eating delicious whatevers and getting late-night caviar pedis in the luxe spa … Look at me, I thought – and I'm loving it.

Ah well. That could come later. In another lifetime. I looked at my watch. Eleven o'clock. Time to eat, you need protein to keep going, girl.

I rang and ordered Atlantic salmon, grilled, with spinach (EFAs – smart food, and iron – stamina – and mash – for slow-burning carb energy).

I ate and sat back and thought and thought about what I could do.

The story was pretty much there. It was shiny and smart and just a little sexy. It was pretty damned good, and I felt completely able to say that myself.

I could just send it, and have a bit of a sleep.

Yeah, I thought slowly, feeling fatigue weigh down my limbs. Why not leave it, and get the police to clean up the mess that was Dr Gold?

Because that could have been you on the stretcher, said a jarring little voice.

Not her again.

It could have been you. Or Allison. Or anyone else. Do you think he should just walk away from that?

Oh, shut UP!

What if this is supposed to happen? What if you're the person who's supposed to do something about it?

Why me? I thought wearily. I'm just a slack tabloid health/beauty writer with a cow of a boss and a deadline I've just managed to meet. Bugger off.

You know you can make it better.

Why should I bother?

Because it's come your way. Use it.

OKAY, SHUT UP. PISS OFF THEN AND LET ME GET ON WITH IT, I yelled silently, seeing my grim face and clenched fists in the mirror. *Ooo-er*, I thought slowly, total looner alert. I sat up, breathed slowly and quietly for a few breaths, shook my head to clear out the sleepy feeling. How long had I actually been asleep?

Not long enough.

That bloody annoying voice.

I'm still here.

Okay, I'll do it, I thought, hardly believing I wasn't going to get to pass out on the nice fluffy bed.

I wiped my face with one of those hotel towelette things, popped some Visine into my eyes, brushed my teeth, drank a whole lot of fizzy water, went to the toilet, then sat down at the laptop again and started digging.

Something had to turn up.

People like Dr Gold don't leave a trail, they leave a great big stinking mess. It was up to me to find out what he'd been up to.

I went online to find out what I could about Dr Gold. Went to all the search engines, one after another, and typed in every variation of his name I could think of.

Hmmmn. Doctor Gold had no matches under Google or Yahoo, but a certain Dr Goldenfield – wow! – had been written about quite a lot. In his native South Africa you could say he was a bit of a star. Famous, even. In the nastiest sense of the word.

Was he my man? Time to search for pictures.

I love the net. You have to check everything, but the things you can discover. It's access to the world's libraries, only a click away. There was information sitting there quietly, waiting to be found. You just had to ask the right question.

It turned out he had no real qualifications – not as a plastic surgeon. Sure, he was a GP. Maybe even a very good one. But cosmetic surgery? Dr Gold was just making it up as he went along ...

Fantastic.

I found an article from the *Cape Town Times* where he elaborated on his exciting plans to help women with his 'innovative, technologically advanced and superior quality dermal fillers'. Dermal fillers – what kind, I wondered, chewing on the end of a pen as I scribbled some web addresses down. I scrolled down another story – bingo.

'My own patent,' he claimed proudly.

Wonder how much work the journo had after that little puff piece was published? I asked myself. I shouldn't be judgmental. Maybe somewhere in the world there was another boss who made her staff spruik cosmetic surgery. Anyway, I didn't actually have anything against the notion. Nah – if my nose was three times the size it was, who says I wouldn't have it reduced? If my boobs were enormous, to the point where I had back problems, I probably would get them halved. And one day, if I had a chin like a melting ice cream maybe I'd do something about it. Hey, I was definitely getting my teeth whitened, one of these days.

But the slicing and dicing and mutilation stuff? The pulling of muscles into tighter shapes, leaving it up to someone else to play God and decide the contours of your face. To be frozen in a bad moment? It was like the old tale about the wind changing and your face staying the same – but this time it was in a wind tunnel. Nope. It was as bad as bulimia – and a whole lot more expensive. And surely big melon breast implants are the new millennium equivalent of shoulder pads.

Don't be bitter, I ordered myself. Take action.

So. He was making his own dermal fillers. Even better.

I headed to a legal site, waited and waited and trawled and hunted, until I was rewarded – his patent papers. *Voilà!* I thought. You are so busted.

Bovine.

Nothing weird there, I thought. Everyone uses cow collagen.

British cow …

Hang on.

British?

What about?

Oh great. Mad cow link, I thought. Shit – what about Diane?

MISS LONELYHEARTS

I read over my story – it still needed so much work. I grabbed the phone and dialled the hospital. Time for a Diane update. And maybe some details, this time.

'Diane – how is she?'

'She's okay. She's breathing assisted, but all her vital signs are good. She's hungry – that's always a good sign.'

I felt slightly less worried – Diane was always eating. She had the opposite of all the abstaining eating disorders. She had a cramming disease. She just couldn't fit everything in, she felt so empty on the inside.

'You got her to us just in time, Miss Tooley.'

'Thanks – look, what was wrong with her?'

'Massive allergic reaction to the filler.'

'Can you tell me what was in the filler?' I pushed.

'We've been in contact with the doctor's assistants, who gave us a sample. It's with the lab. But there's almost certainly some kind of animal product in there.'

Oh God. Animal product. And Diane was a vegetarian.

'Look, can you test it? I think it's bovine, for sure, but I'm worried the origin may be Britain. I know it's a long shot, and it sounds mad. I just think it's worth checking.'

'I'll let the lab know.'

'Good,' I said to the phone, and put it down. Right away it started shrilling.

'Meg, how're you going?' Eleanor sounded a little weird.

'Fine,' I said carefully. This was usually the point when your editor tells you they've changed their mind about using your story. But thanks anyway.

'Look,' she said cautiously, 'the plan's changed a little.'

'Shit, I just spent ...'

'Shoosh. Look, Julie, Chandra and me are working on some colour stuff to go with the story, some overseas celebs whose faces are ... you know. A bit messy. But your story's what we need to peg it on Meg. When is it getting here?'

I looked at my watch.

It was 2.00 a.m.

'It'll be there as soon as I can ...'

'Okay. I'm leaving the office now. We've mocked up the layout with the shots.' She quickly ran me through the images she was using – Diane's arrival, a panel with star before and afters and what went wrongs, and some portraits of Dr Gold.

'Is she going to be okay? Don't forget to check in on her status before you deliver the copy.'

I sighed. 'Yep, got it.'

'It's going to the lawyers at 10.00 a.m. So ... I know you won't let us down. If you happen to finish early – just send it through to my home email, okay. It's got some auto alarm on it, so it'll buzz me awake. Nifty, huh?'

I hung up and sat back down, wrote, then smoothed, rearranged my pars, did a stats box on accidents that had happened – do you know how many people die from walk-in/walk-out lipo – and it was ready.

I sent it then.

Eleanor rang back twenty minutes later.

'It's great …' she said, cautiously. Holding back.

'But?'

'It needs something else. Something to fire it up. I guess quotes from someone else who's seen the doctor – who's had this sort of thing happen. Then we can nail him. Can you do that?'

'I can only try. Just because it's nearly three in the morning, and everyone is asleep, except for us, shouldn't be too much of a problem.' I was beginning to feel pissed off and was slightly sarcastic. This was serious overtime, and that was something we never got.

'Just try, okay.'

I rang Fantasia's number. It picked up.

Deep breath. Quick. Get into it. Don't let her say no.

'Look Fantasia, I'm really sorry to be ringing you so late. It's Meg Tooley here. I met you at a *Phwoar!* party. I wonder if you've heard of a Dr Gold? He's done some work on a friend and it went wrong. It would really help my story to …'

'What magazine's it for?' a not-even-sleepy voice replied.

'You know I work for *Gossip!*.'

'Will I look like an idiot?'

'This time no, I swear. I know you don't want to know about subs changing people's words and mean editors, but it wasn't my fault, and this is important.'

'Okay – Dr Gold was my doctor and I know another girl who'll talk to you – you won't be wasting your time. He tried to feel her up while he thought she was out from the anaesthetic. Her name is Cookie.'

Oh this just gets better. 'Thanks Fantasia, that would be very useful. Now, I'll ask you a few questions if that's okay?'

Brilliant – quick, get into it, before she changes her mind.

'Would you say you were informed of the possible side effects of the procedure?'

'No,' came the quick reply.

'Well, he did say that it might sting a little.'

'What about after care – any explanation?'

She snorted.

'How much were you charged?'

'Five hundred dollars, for three applications, over three months. By the second month it was starting to come out.'

'How did you know?'

'I was kissing my boyfriend – he's not my boyfriend now, the bastard, but he was kissing me and he could feel it.'

'You couldn't feel it?'

'Oh, I'd always felt it. I'd said it felt a bit funny after the stuff went in, but he said it would settle down.'

'Did it?'

'It got worse. I could feel it every minute, every day. It made it hard to do my job, dancing, 'cos I have to smile at the guys, you get more tips that way, and the thing was that if I smiled I could feel it sort of pulling my face in one direction. So I looked weird, like I was snarling.'

'What else – how did it feel in your skin?'

'It was always hot. Anyway, it felt a bit like a spring in a couch or something that might come out.

'It was Gore-Tex, right? Like a little pipe cleaner under the skin, yeah?'

'That's it.'

'Did he say that you should go for this kind of implant?'

'Well, I'd always gone for the other one, the one I'd had for years. Dr Gold said this was his own – that it was superior – high quality – stuff like that. And that I'd get it cheap.'

Bingo.

'My lips were weird for weeks and my job's all about looking good – okay, looking sexy.'

'Look, thanks Fantasia. I won't do the wrong thing by you. Oh – one more thing – have you any before and afters?'

'Yes. Why?'

'Can we use them?'

'Suppose you can. Can you put my mobile number in, for a bit of business?'

'Yeah. Look, I've been writing this up as we speak, I'm sending it through to you now, you're on email, yeah? Great. I'm just going to email this through to you. Make sure it's all right.'

God, had I overplayed my hand? What if she thought it sucked, changed her mind, or didn't ask her friend Cookie to ring me?

'It'll be there in five. Will you read it as soon as you can? Please?'

The desperation must have gotten through because she sighed and said. 'No probs. I'll just get up and make a coffee.'

I sat there, sweating on the return phone call.

People often tell you things, on the record, too, but establishing trust with a contact, then maintaining that all the way through to publication – maybe even beyond – is damn hard.

Nobody seems to like seeing what they've said in black and white.

They wrote what I said, Joe DiMaggio complained once. They should have written what I meant.

When the phone rang, it woke me up.

'Hello. It's Cookie here. Fantasia said I had to call you.'

'Thanks, Cookie. Do you mind telling me what happened with Dr Gold?'

'I was having a walk-in walk-out lipo thing, you get twilight sedation, two hours, 600 bucks if you pay cash, you know,' she confided.

'So I had the twilight and was just sort of laying there, in my undies, on the table thing,' she said gently. I winced. How vulnerable they were.

'And just before he started with the incisions and suction thing' – I winced again – 'I think he – um.' She stalled. This was normal. Patience, Meg. Keep her on the line. Don't freak her out, I told myself, fighting back my desperation to get this story over and done with.

'I think he …' She stopped again, making a weird, gaspy sound. Hold, Meg, Hold.

I took a deep breath.

'He might have …'

'He *what*, Cookie?'

'I don't know for sure, I was very woozy. But I think he sort of, you know?'

'No, come on, Cookie, what? Just say it!'

'I think he sort of kissed me. No,' she corrected herself in her dazed, singsong voice, 'he *did* kiss me. And sort of, you know ...' She lowered her tone to a whisper. 'Touched me.'

'Can you give me some more detail, Cookie?' I asked gently. 'People can't just touch you.'

'Well, actually they can – if they're doctors – and he's one. But the lipo had nothing to do with my boobs, right?'

Oh gross. And *great*.

'This is a pretty serious thing you're talking about. This is assault, Cookie. Did it go any further?'

'Assault, huh? Well, you know, I'm a stripper. We get groped all the time.'

'But that's not supposed to happen, is it, Cookie, not on the job. Not anytime. Not without consent.'

'But I guess it's an occupational hazard. Like getting sunburnt if you're a gardener or something.'

I felt impatient. 'But surely you don't ...'

'I know,' she interrupted tartly. Not so sweet. 'You do not pay a doctor so he can have a go.' I could practically feel the anger being freed.

'What did you do?'

'I tried to push him off me,' she said in a hard little voice. Good girl! 'I thought I might have just been muddled, and he said I was confused when I asked what he'd been doing.'

I glanced at the time.

It was 4.00 a.m.

'Cookie, thanks a lot. Sorry for getting you up at this hour.'

'It's okay', I was just going to bed. Dance clubs stay open late, remember.

I promised to email her the copy, then wrote it, sent it off, waited, and rang her back.

'It's perfect,' she said, voice sweet and childlike. 'The prick.'

I read over the lot and felt … elated. Absolutely stoked. Could not wait. I was holding a time bomb. A real story.

I danced on the spot with excitement, waving my arms around.

'Dr Gold is Dr Goldenfiend – and he's been very very bad! And I'm about to bust him! Yeesss!' I cried victoriously. 'This is good,' I thought, exhausted and elated and tired and wired from too much bad coffee. Really bad and extremely caffeinated coffee. Ugh.

I hit send and blew a kiss to the sexy laptop's screen as my masterpiece went fizzing off down the electronic highway to Eleanor.

'Have a safe trip,' I said, waving, as the little clock closed down. As soon as it had been confirmed, I flopped backwards. I groped around in my handbag, swallowed two magnesiums, drank a litre of expensive minibar water, ordered some cheese on toast from room service, and passed out in my clothes, a sheet over my head, waiting for the sun to come up and bite me with its heat.

Shit. I hadn't rung the hospital to check on Diane's progress. And I had to ring Dr Gold. Don't think I wanted to.. But it's not fair to just go and publish something without at least giving someone the right of reply.

So I pulled myself together and called the mobile number on Doctor Gold's brochure. He answered straight away despite the time and I went straight into my spiel. 'Doctor, I have been informed of some very serious allegations being made against you by several women.'

'Do you know what hour this is?'

'I'm on deadline. I'm sorry to wake you up. But I feel you should be given the chance to respond ...'

A woman's voice cut in and said, 'Dr Gold will get back to you.'

'It's Meg Tooley from *Gossip!*.'

'Yes, Meg. He will get back to you.' the voice said, as if she was doing an in-store demonstration.

'It's very important.'

'He'll call back when he can.'

Bloody hell. They were blowing me off.

I gave up when I heard the receiver being put down. Fine ... no reply. I punched in another lot of numbers.

'The swelling's abating slightly,' the doctor told me. 'No long-term damage.'

'But could she have died?' I asked, scribbling down his words in my really, really bad shorthand.

'Yes. Swelling – in that region – she could have choked.'

'Doctor, can I get five more minutes of your time? I just want to make sure I have everything absolutely correct when I'm quoting you.'

'I'm surprised you even check,' he said, just the wrong side of patronising.

Once I would have sighed, maybe said, *Please doctor*, and then listened to his protest, understanding all of it, feeling smaller and smaller and less and less worthy of answers, of being taken seriously. But not now. Really. Even I was surprising myself.

'Look, why don't you think about it this way,' I said in this really confident, strong, but not at all ball-breaking voice. Like a newsreader! 'The bottom line is that people should know, agreed?'

I gave him a chance to make a grudgingly assenting grunt. 'If this story even makes it to a daily newspaper – and it won't, not at this stage – it'll be a tiny piece – they'll bury it up the back, and no-one who's likely to be hurt by this sort of thing will have the chance to read it. Now, you may think what you like about my magazine, but one thing that you cannot dispute is that 800 000 women will get the message. It's your call, doctor. Are they worth reaching?'

'I'll …' he replied, taking a deep, deep breath. 'Give you a few more quotes,' he finished, clearing his throat importantly. 'Take this down.'

Forty minutes later I was stretched out, fully clothed on a hotel-room bed, the last email sent, gently snoring.

I know this because I woke myself up, before rolling over, groping for some magnesium, and fading out again.

CHAPTER TWENTY-FIVE

I slept for twelve hours.

Do you know how amazing that is? For me, it's extraordinary.

The only reason I didn't sleep for fourteen hours was because the phone ringing woke me up.

It was 5.30 p.m. I felt – well, gluggy-brained and drugged, like I was sleepwalking.

'Hello,' I said, slowly, cradling the phone like a pillow. I put the phone down. Immediately it rang again.

'Meg?'

'Eleanor? God, I've been dead to the world – how was the story? Was it okay? Did you get the update?'

'Yes, yes and yes. Very nice work. Look, I'm just ringing to tell you it looks great. Your material was excellent, but wait till you see what we've done with it! I'm going to make sure no dummies or advance copies go out till I can't hold them back any more. But whatever happens, it's a great story.'

'I practically wrote it in my sleep.'

'It doesn't matter. That just means you're a pro. Vikkie got rid of any glitches. Not that there were many.'

'Are we going to lose our jobs over this, Eleanor?' I asked – not desperately at all. Curiously, I wasn't panicking. Where was all this inner confidence coming from? Is this the miracle of a good sleep? I wondered. Because usually I think those sorts of things but I never, ever risk anything by asking them.

'No, that's too yellow,' I heard her saying firmly. 'Take it back. It's not about them looking jaundiced. They ...'

'The skin tones are horrible, though Eleanor.' I could hear the whole thing.

'That's right. Keep them that way. Please.'

'If you want 'em that way, love, I can do it. It's just not what ...'

'I know. Thanks.'

'God, what does it look like?' I couldn't help but ask. 'He sounded shocked.'

She was silent, then said 'It actually looks ... pretty different. Hey, no, NO! I can't talk now, Meg, there's something up with the back section – some pubes or something are showing – we'll have to do a rough job here to get rid of them. But you'll see. Really really soon.'

'So, are you planning on freelancing?'

She snickered. 'Freelancing' was code for getting shafted, or having a breakdown and running away from the madness of magazine office politics.

'Oh yeah. Freelance managing editors are highly sought after. Not. Who knows? But you needn't worry. This was my decision to make. If there's going to be a head rolling down the aisle, Monica will make it mine.'

'You think?'

'Possibly. Maybe. But unlikely. Anyway, don't you worry, you selfish bitch,' she chuckled. 'If it happens, it'll be me.'

'Bummer,' I said. 'I could do with being sacked.' I sighed heavily. 'But nothing nice ever happens to me.'

We laughed.

'Look, when you need to come back, just ring and give Tamara the details. Take your time. We're okay till next week. I've planned out the follow-up issue already.'

'But I don't have anything to do. Shouldn't I come back?'

'Er, no, it's fine. I'll see you next Monday. But leave your mobile on.'

How weird. Oh well. Time out for a couple of days. I put down the phone and there was a knock at the door.

I opened it up, and Allison was there.

She threw her arms around me. I hugged her back, then broke away.

'What the bleeping hell are you doing here?'

'I heard you were in hospital. I flew straight up. Are you okay?'

'Who told you that?'

'Dan,' she muttered, avoiding eye contact.

'Nope. *I* wasn't in hospital. Diane still is.'

'Oh God. I flew to Brisbane to make sure you were okay.'

I grinned and nodded. 'Come in then.'

It was early evening by the time we'd gone through the whole Diane scenario.

'So she's not going to, um, die or anything,' Allison asked.

'Nope. And there's some guy called Marley who's spent his whole time at the hospital. I had to ring him yesterday to let him know. She wanted me to. She didn't say anything about Dan.'

'Oh, well,' she repeated. 'You said Eleanor told you to take it easy. So that gives us at least two days. Let's hire a car tomorrow – Byron?'

'Byron stinks, I hear.' I wasn't going to let her off the hook too easily.

'Oh no, don't believe it. Sun! Surf! Men with big boards.'

'We can go to the tea-tree lake!' I crowed happily. Just like old times.

'We're go-ing to By-ron,' she sang, practically skipping with excitement. She did a little run on the spot. 'I love it there,' she yelled to the world.

Road trips are fantastic. I've always liked them because you get caught in between – you're going somewhere, but you haven't arrived. Ali and I had done it once before. We'd driven meanderingly up the coast when we'd finished our HSC, and I still don't know what was the most fun, the driving, or the holiday itself. After we'd given up on the Gold Coast, we drove back down the coast, waking up at a beach car park, running out straight into the ocean for our shower, hair stiff with salt for three weeks, skin toasty brown, dancing madly, pashing boys, and putting together The List.

Ali threw me the car keys just as I was settling in for a great daydream about Nick.

'It's time you drove, don't you reckon?'

'I can't drive.'

'No, you *don't* drive. You got your Ls didn't you?'

'Yeah.'

'Then you got your Ps, right?'

'Yeah.'

'Here they *aaa-aaare*,' she sang, holding them up. She'd obviously forgiven me for crashing her car.

She pulled over and swung her long, sunburnt legs out of the car we'd hired.

It's too embarrassing to tell you. Okay.

It was a Charger.

Allison looked amazing. She'd put her hair in bunches, high up on her head, and shoved a floral-sprigged sun visor over the top. Her legs went up up up until indecency was cut short by tiny-tiny cut-offs, smudged with real grease.

'Shorts, Ali,' I'd said when I'd seen her.

'Getting into the right mood. Anyway, I haven't worn these since …'

'High school. You make me puke.'

She swung her legs round the car and bent right over, gaffer-taping the P plates to the front and the back and nearly causing a pretty serious head-on between a car loaded with surfies and a truck loaded with pigs.

Her head suddenly appeared next to me, bits of long red hair whipping about in the wind, green eyes boring into me.

'Come on. Get behind the wheel.'

I must have gone white under the sunburn. I know I crossed my arms and shook my head.

'You can do it. Nothing bad's going to happen.'

Sulkily, I shoved the car door open and slowly climbed out. She jumped in and scooted over, patting the seat playfully.

'Come on, babe. You know you can do it.'

I can't swear it happened, but a tumbleweed might have blown down the highway right about then. It felt like one of those quiet, too quiet moments in westerns, when a massive decision was at hand. A choice had to be made. A road had to be gone down.

It was a turning point.

I stood there, feeling my heart rate rise, feeling sweat breaking out under my armpits.

Was I excited, or was I going to drive us off the road?

There were kangaroos to hit.

And what about the wombats?

Australian roads are really, really scary – particularly the Pacific Highway. I gritted my teeth. I could do this. I started off shakily but on the right side of the road. Allison ignored my grimace and relaxed into the passenger seat.

'Oh. I forgot. I've got this, for the trip,' Allison said, holding up a tape.

'What?'

'Look – it's an ancient love token.'

'Where'd that come from?' I asked.

'There's a card …'

'Don't read it, just keep driving. I'll read it to you …'

'"I thought you might want some tunes to listen to over Easter. Wish I was there. Dan. PS, track three."'

'Oh my God, Allison – he made you a tape!'

She said nothing.

'God, Allison, that means he's serious.'

'Serious. The very word is like a bucket of cold water being thrown over my head,' she said and tossed the tape onto the dash.

'No it isn't. He must have sat at home the night before we came up to Byron to do this. For you.'

'He probably had it sitting around.'

'Why am I more excited than you?'

'Because you've got nothing to lose.'

'Oh bullshit. He's into you. Get used to it.'

'I don't want to get used to it. It's at exactly the point that you get used to it that it all goes wrong.'

'Oh. So eternal vigilance is your love motto.' She grimaced.

'What about you? "Treat 'em mean." Nice.' I'd told her about Nick. And Ben.

I decided to let the red herrings just swim on by. Before I cunningly started up again. 'Anyway – how can it go wrong when it hasn't even started yet?'

She stayed shut up. After all, I had a point. Except that it was way beyond not starting.

It had started. He knew it and she knew it too, which was why her hackles were up.

'Maybe it always goes wrong, because that's just the way relationships are.' Allison said. 'It's a natural law, some kind of human physics. Chaos theory of humanity, trying to get it on without hurting each other. Immutable. Cannot happen. Does not compute.'

'Once again: bullshit! Can I remind you that *you're* not the only one with the psycho family?'

She said nothing but grabbed the tape back.

'Has he written the songs down? What's track three?'

'Nope. Nothing here.'

'We'll just have to listen,' I said, glad she was going to find out what song he'd meant.

'No, fast forward or whatever it is you do with tapes.'

'Wait – it says something else on his card.' She grabbed it and read it out.

'"PPS, Don't fast forward."'

So we drove and listened.

Track one: 'TNT', AC/DC.

We turned to each other and screamed as the heavy-metal sounds of western suburban Sydney circa 1975 careered through the car. Our heads snapped forward, and lashed back, and we laughed till the tears ran. I drove on the empty road, feeling free.

'I bet you want to have sex with Bon Scott,' Allison laughed at me, hair plastered across her face. She picked some out slowly from her sticky, juicy mouth, smudged with gloss.

I ignored her. Because she was right.

'What's next?'

'You have a definite necrophiliac dead-star thing going.'

I ignored her again. Waiting for the next song to begin, getting quite excited that we were getting to track three.

'You know why you like dead stars?'

But I never heard her answer, because, thankfully, track two – the Offspring – started. 'Pretty Fly for a White Guy'.

'Eeeuw.'

'What is he saying with this?' I shouted at her. I turned the music down to hear her answer. There was none.

'I think it's a joke,' I said. 'Isn't it?'

'Yeah, I think he's being self-deprecating.'

'Good.' That's the trouble with being at the beginning. You can interpret everything *soooo* loosely – sometimes too good, sometimes bleakly. You can be way off the beam, just as long as it fits into the pattern of Mister Guy You Like.

Track three: 'I Want You'. Elvis Costello.

We said nothing till the last sounds had faded out. We sat there, wind whistling though our hair.

Allison hit the pause button. 'Now *that's* beautiful,' she said, eyes all teary.

I didn't say anything.

She slapped me.

'Meg!'

It had made me think of Nick. There was no way this little hiccup was going to crack me. *There will be no falling in love.*

'He sounds like a stalker,' I bitched.

'Excuse me. It's my tape and track three is definitely *not* about a stalker.'

'Yes it is. It's weird. *I want you*,' I whispered in a creepy voice.

'No, it's about someone loving someone so much you could peel all their skin off and get inside.'

'Now *you* sound like a serial killer.'

I hit the pause button, and whatever it was she was about to say was drowned out with Dido's 'Thankyou'.

I hung my arm out the window and listened to the rest of the tape, before Allison rewound, looking for clues. I just wanted to listen to 'I Want You'. I was rewinding it for a third time when Allison threatened to throw the tape out the window. I settled for another tape she'd brought with her.

I watched my arm slowly turn pink, then red as the morning passed. It was probably just the heat, 'cos there was no real sun hitting me, but I didn't care.

'Do I look brown yet?' I kept asking Allison.

'Shut urrrp,' she said. 'You're red. Should we break out the sunscreen yet?'

I shook my head. I wanted a tan, and if I was going to have to burn to get it, so be it.

Ali took over driving. I'd had enough after one hour, could feel the weights dragging my eyelids down.

Allison smoked. I made her blow it away from me. I dozed in the sun and felt myself relax. Slide into that trancey, semi-conscious state you can get into when you're on the road.

We drove in companionable silence, past tiny farms and fields with sugar cane, meadows with cows, and all the time the massive crook of Mt Warning came closer and closer into view from the floodplains.

When we finally pulled into the caravan park, I was a bit disappointed. I guess Diane's house had spoilt me. I hoped Dan and the rest had left her place tidy – I'd asked them to leave my stuff on the verandah so I could pick it up.

'Are we going to have a schoolies reprise? Another pashing list?'

'This break's going to be different,' she said, sliding an Air CD into the player and pressing play. Haunting sounds filled the caravan. 'This time, we're going to detox,' she said, opening a bottle of wine.

'What?'

'We're only going to eat well. We're not going to drink. I'm …'

'Opening a bottle of wine.'

'We're drinking tonight to celebrate arriving.'

'Do you want to do a dolphin workshop?'

'I'm thinking about doing some reiki. Or … I dunno. Lithos therapy!' she said, flicking through a magazine we'd picked at the caravan park office.

Ali lit up a cigarette. 'What are you doing?'

'It's a clove cigarette.'

'It's a cigarette. Besides, it stinks. Go outside if you want to smoke.'

'It fits right in,' she said, opening the tiny window and leaning out and gesturing at the expanse of sand. And blue.

'Look out there.'

'It's so beautiful,' I said.

'It's so peaceful,' she replied.

As soon as the words were out of Ali's mouth someone started drumming on the beach.

'I hate those people.' She leant out and yelled. 'Shut up!'

The drummer turned around. He was gorgeous. Allison was gorgeous. They had one of those beautiful people mutual admiration moments.

The drummer started drumming again, but very low, walking away backwards.

'Fuck off you fucking hippy!' Allison muttered, sexily.

'Feeling relaxed?' I couldn't help asking.

'Not if there're any fire-twirlers about.'

It was like an entire summer had been shaken, stirred and served up in a tall glass containing the perfect cocktail of three hot, clear burningly bright days.

There were no bluebottles bobbing about waiting to sting us while we splashed and bodysurfed in the clear aqua seas, and the small foamy waves spat us up onto the soft, sandy shore. Sand did not form penis-like structures in our bikini bottoms when we were dumped because we were borne, like mermaids, towards the shore.

Our thighs did not wobble when we walked from the water. I did not go salmony-pink, and not a single annoying bit of skin peeled off my nose. Like I said – perfect.

There were only good-looking and nice-mannered surfy men and women of Byron around us. There was no sexual harassment or drunken hordes of footy blokes yelling things about our tits or lack of them. The drugs people had taken for the Blues Festival had a lingering potency that rendered them effectively love machines hugging in the street.

We looked prettier.

My hair didn't stick out at the back in a giant fuzzy cloud that I didn't know about until I caught sight of the extra head growing out the back of mine.

I think my legs grew longer.

Everything was easy – even sleeping. Even dreaming. No *tick, tick, tick*s to be heard this side of the pillow, and believe me, almost a week without a visit from the dream-bomber was a long, long time in my world.

We had the *best* time. We made a pact not to talk about Nick or Ben or Dan or any male from back home.

We walked. We played. We talked. We started conversations with people we didn't know. I even had sake at a Japanese restaurant, not as much as Allison, but enough. We laughed till our heads collided in the centre of the table. Which then made us cry with laughter, until that made me snort, which made some other people in the restaurant ask us to keep it down, which made some gorgeous surfies tell them to shut up, which made us shriek, so we left anyway.

All in all, a terrific evening.

Reminiscent of school dances, opening bottles of wine with our stilettos and throwing tampons at unsuspecting passers-by one tragic night when we got drunk for the first time at fifteen in a theatre restaurant with waiters who'd tried just that little bit too hard to pick us up.

Okay, to pick Allison up.

We did all the things you do on holiday – when you're nineteen. At twenty-six, it was even better to request stupid Abba songs and dance around our handbags at the Beach Hotel in full view of the slightly bemused Celtic-tattooed dreadlocked surfies and the full disdain of the Celtic-tattooed and dreadlocked eastern suburbs cool kids who'd made Byron their second home.

We bought bikinis together – and even looked at each other under the fluoro lights in the change room and didn't laugh out loud!

Of course, we had the great suntan race, which, Allison being a redhead and all, I won within three hours, and she thankfully admitted defeat and took to the Nicole Kidman-esque full-length swimming cossie.

'If ever I make it big I can get my skin bleached,' she said.

'You'd look like Michael Jackson,' I replied, dripping on her towel.

'No, I'd look like a gorgeous creamy redhead with No Freckles. Anyway, Michael Jackson's black.'

'Not any more.'

The best thing about those days (which I managed to stretch because Eleanor okayed me staying away until the following Monday) was that I remembered all the reasons Allison and I had been friends for so long, and we got back to what it was all about. Laughing. Digging into each other's psyche which, I admit plainly and fully, we had actually stopped doing during the recent second Great Ice Age. Exploring. Knowing.

We had aura photographs made. Had a crystal reading.

'What do you make of all this stuff, then, Ali?' I asked as we sat in the café next to the Crystal Castle, staring at our aura pictures.

'I don't know. Mine just seems a bit red.'

I looked up at the code print-out we'd received.

'That means you're passionate, dynamic, angry and stubborn. Stressed. Violent?'

'But it's got a love-heart shape in it. Which must mean something. What colour's yours?'

'Blue. Means ... here we go. Apparently I'm wise, calm, a teacher.'

She snorted.

'You're just jealous. At least it's not brown.'

We flicked through the local paper, which had fantastic stars. I made a note. I mean, these were brilliant – funny and smart, and somehow soothing. They made Madame Staria's seem, like her name, totally hokey.

'Do you think we've been conditioned to be addicted to horoscopes?' Allison asked one morning in another café.

'Probably. We don't have religion. We have starsigns. Auras. Psychics.'

'I have to be careful of this stuff. If I get a great gig on a current affairs show, I could also suddenly become the target of sleazy tabloid rags populated by jealous hackettes feeding rumours to their readers about my pathetic addiction to psychics.'

'We're on holidays – and don't worry. Even if you do get to be the face of some morning show where you make ministers squirm, I'll never tell.'

'You're reading your stars, are you?'

'Yes.'

'Crap,' she said pointedly. I looked over – everyone else had left the room. 'You're a Pisces. Your eyes were top right. Pisces's are bottom left. You're obviously reading Nick's!'

I blushed.

'What is he, anyway?' she asked.

'Why don't you guess?'

'Scorpio, Aries or …'

'Scorpio.'

'Really? Oo-er – watch out.'

'Why? It all depends on your rising moon sign, or something, doesn't it?'

'Scorpios – sting in the tail. Sex-addicted. Secretive.'

'Thought you said it was all crap?'

'I'm still educated.'

'What's Dan, then?' I knew, but I wanted to know if she knew.

'Oh, You won't believe what Dan's is.' (So much for no talk of the men back home!)

'Try me.' Hee hee.

'Virgo!' she whispered, triumphantly.

She was right to be so triumphant. Dan was like the Anti-Virgo.

'What?' I said in feigned disbelief. 'Tell me again. Did you just say *Virgo*?'

'Yep.'

'What!' I spluttered again, gleeful. Allison was *so* into him. She'd never before known a guy's starsign.

'I *know*.'

I ticked off Dan's un-Virgo characteristics one by one on my sunburnt hands.

'*Not* neat. *Not* tidy. *Not* obsessive.'

'But it's true.'

'Not a virgin!'

'Absolutely not. In fact, it's in the area of non-virginity that he's actually something of a perfectionist.'

'And he has worry-wart tendencies,' she added.

'What about that tattoo – that's not very Virgo. What about going back to Ireland?'

'That's so Virgo,' she said.

'Why?'

'I'm not supposed to say anything …'

I assumed an innocent air. 'You mustn't tell me if you don't want to.'

'Can you keep a secret?' she said, looking around furtively.

'NO! Enough bloody secrets. I've been in trouble for saying exactly the same thing.'

'No, seriously, Meg – can you? Just for the time being.'

'He's going back to Ireland to be Very Virgo.' I rolled my eyes.

'Let's say he needs to clean up.'

'Yeah, duh, he had that letter from his ex-girlfriend. He's got a relationship thing to sort out.'

'Well, a bit more than a thing.'

She passed me a picture of a freckly, dark-haired kid – a girl.

'He's got a kid!' Her face was shining.

'Are you serious? Dan's a dad? He's Lord of the Rings with his pants down and he's a dad.'

'The two often go together, Meg.'

'It's disgusting,' I blurted. She gave me a pitying look.

'Meg, he only has a kid – he hasn't killed anybody.'

'It's serious,' I objected. 'That's a person and a life.'

'You don't know all the details, so I don't want you getting all worked up about this, okay.'

'I'm just flabbergasted. Dan – a dad. Does Diane know?'

'No – nobody knows. Look, I can't tell you anything else – it's too long a story. And he didn't tell me until all this stuff came up.'

I shut up and sat quietly. Dan a dad. Interesting times!

CHAPTER TWENTY-SIX

Sydney was much cooler than Byron. Giant thunderstorm clouds were brewing as we landed on the Sunday afternoon. *So* Sydney. Freeze, sunny, then hail down on you. I didn't mind. It was easier to think in the cool, biting air.

We hailed a taxi, which took us back to my place. I felt like I was in a limo – such a contrast to the train or bus. Or walking. I stretched my legs – they were hankering for a good thump around the block.

I turned the key softly, and walked in.

Dan let out a huge cheer and flung himself around Allison. Fizz threw his skinny arms around me. Tamara smiled and Eric stuck his head out from the kitchen and blew me a kiss.

'Oooh, prodigal daughter alert!' cried Max, lingering outside the bathroom door in a towel – of the stringy, beige variety. Hmmmn. I wondered if Eric had been using my bedroom again.

Ali looked all teary.

'Got something in your eye?' Dan teased.

She thumped him.

'Don't get cheeky. Just because I care.'

She cares, I thought. I raised an eyebrow. 'You care!' I said archly, a huge grin breaking over my face. At last!

'Oh shut up,' she muttered, turning red.

'You care!' I sang under my breath. 'And you're blushing. So are you two going to turn into those really smug people who are all "I'm so single" one minute then completely and utterly "we'd" after that?' I teased.

'Uh, Meg,' said Max. 'There was a call for you.' I winced. Bloody Ben.

'Can you just throw the number away please?'

'Okay,' he said, crumpling up a piece of paper and throwing it in the bin, grinning.

'Thank God,' I said.

'I thought you liked Nick,' Dan asked, puzzled.

'Nick?'

I scrabbled around at the bottom of the bin.

'Oh my God,' I said, holding up a crumpled Post-It note that didn't have his name on it. I flung it aside in disgust. 'Where is it?' I turned to them, gleeful. 'Oh my God! He rang.' I was practically dancing around – and for once, I wasn't even embarrassed at myself. I wanted to be wild with joy – I wanted to be swept away.

'He rang. *And* rang,' said Dan.

'And rang,' said Max, doing that meaningful eyebrow action he's made all his own. 'He thought you were ill.'

'He did! But he doesn't know I'm back, right?'

They all shook their funny heads. My home!

'Great,' I sighed, flopping down onto the nearest beanbag. 'So tell me all,' I begged, looking at them affectionately, feeling all warm inside.

'Nothing,' they said, looking at me, puzzled.

'Oh, come on. Eric, what music have you been playing this week?'

'Oh, hard-core thrash, 1993.'

'Mmm – take me back,' I grinned as Fizz handed me a drink.

'Mmm, thanks Fizzy,' I said. 'What else?' I asked, taking a big sip.

They were all staring at me, looking a bit odd.

'What?' I demanded. 'What? Have I got something in my teeth?'

'You're so *frustrating*,' said Allison.

'Why?' I asked, totally blank. I spotted the wine glass. 'Is it this?' I asked, waving it at her. 'Because you have nothing to be worried about. I was just having one glass of wine. Truly. Not one splash more – honestly. Those days are gone.'

'No, you berk – Nick! Aren't you going to ring him?'

I shook my head. In response, she threw herself on the floor, rolling around, clutching her head, faking agony.

'AAAARGHHHH! I *have* to know,' she bellowed. 'I can't STAND waiting to see what's going to happen.'

Hmmmn. Very interesting, I thought coolly. So, when it came to me, she just had to know. In fact, look at them – Max looked furious, Tamara looked like she was going to burst, Eric was gaping and Fizz was puzzled. They all had to know. My life was their soap opera – and, admittedly, I'd made it that way. And yet they all wanted to carry on their romances in secret.

It was sweet, it may even have been partially my fault, but that didn't mean I had to tell them anything. Besides, I had nothing to tell, and they definitely weren't witnessing the phone call.

I didn't say anything. I needed to think. Obviously, up till then, I'd invited them to be my audience in virtually every aspect of my life – it was going to be like withdrawing from a bad drug.

'You don't know what it's been like without you two here,' said Dan, bored with Ali's rolling around. She dusted herself off (it was our floor, after all), sat down, and resumed pleading.

'I need to know what the climax is going to be,' she whined.

'It's like if *Bold* was cancelled at work,' interjected Max, sounding all reasonable. For once. 'What would we do?'

'You have to ring him,' piped in Tamara. 'Do it for us.'

I tried not to laugh, and took a bit of a breath. 'Look guys, *Bold* hasn't been cancelled. But it's moving to one night a week, and tonight's not scheduled,' I said, all firm. I understood, really. But I wasn't budging.

'I just need a moment,' I explained. 'It was nice not obsessing about all this for a couple of days. I'm not ready to ring him yet.' It was true. I needed a moment or two where I could sip the cool, cool wine and have absolutely nothing going on inside my head.

Fizz smiled and gave me a squeeze, understanding.

I love my boys, I thought with a contented cat sigh, sinking back into the luxury of my beanbag.

Besides, there was tomorrow to deal with.

When Max and I walked into the Poisoned Palace at 8.45 a.m. the next morning, I felt like a deer in the forest with a target stitched to its back. I took a long look around the lift. It was different, now that I'd been away. It seemed ... smaller and it seemed ... stinkier, somehow.

I looked at myself in the mirror in the lift, not caring that the girls from *Elegance* were doing their staring and nudging routine. Hmmmn. Let's give them something to talk about when they hit the fifth floor, I thought. I stood up close to the mirror and gave myself a good, long stare.

Yep, there was some evidence of metamorphosis, definitely. Head was held higher. Sparkle action going on in the eyes. Hair sort of curly and thick and lustrous, not mad. Well, not *that* mad. Not as mad as I always imagined it looked, anyway.

So I *did* look different.

I was certainly acting different, judging from the muffled giggles behind me. I turned around.

The twin fashion plates were making 'check her out'-type eye contact. Not that I was worried. It was about as threatening as being laughed at by two Darrell Lea chocolates.

And the smell of their perfume was overwhelming.

I smiled at them cheerfully. They nudged each other again. I just didn't care.

I strode into the office, feeling ... elated. Still! Yet nervous. However, life seemed to be carrying on as usual. Max plonked his bag down and went off to the tearoom to fire up some morning coffee. Tamara was in already. Normal. Chandra would be unpredictable but her desk would be covered in spiky plants and any other feng shui stuff she could ... Hang on. Not happening.

Not normal.

Hmmmn. Her desk was actually visible. And while there were flowers and an oil burner and some crystal thingies and posters of Nicole Kidman (the divorced woman's ultimate pin-up girl) it looked quite – well, normal, would actually be the word. There was still the line of kooky pot plants though. Good to see some things remained the same.

Apart from that, nothing seemed to signal anything was wrong. I had actually arrived early. I sat down. I started going through my messages, taking down any notes. I heard a rustle from next to me.

'Meg?' It was Chandra. Arriving. Just before nine. How weird.

'Oh, hi,' I said, and I didn't even wince. I gave her a smile and then got back to work.

She moved two of her plants a little way apart.

She cleared her throat. Before she could say whatever it was she was about to say, Eleanor came through the doors and came over and gave me a squeeze. I stared at her. This time my new cool demeanor fell apart.

Firstly, she hadn't crushed me.

Secondly, she had – goddammit – tears in her eyes.

Thirdly, she'd lost weight. This time you couldn't mistake her for someone who hadn't seriously embraced either a fitness routine, systematic purging or maybe, just maybe, a balanced and sensible approach to eating and exercise.

Finally, she had her sensational cleavage on display. And this time it wasn't scary. Not at all.

'How are you?' I said and grinned, looking her up and down.

'Fine. Really good. Nervous, though.'

'Not surprised. Monica's going to shit herself when she sees you looking so gorgeous. You are sensational!'

She smiled and blushed nearly as pink as her hair.

I'd seen too much lately not to ask the question.

'You haven't ... you know, had lipo or something, have you?'

'No! What would I do that for? It's dangerous!'

'It's just you look ... amazing, and it seems to have come off really fast. You're only supposed to lose 2.2 kilos a week, you know.' I sounded very bossy.

'Meg – it's okay. I've only lost 24 kilos. It took about five months. I didn't start last week, you know.'

'But it looks ...'

'Sudden. It's not. It was exercise and not eating the shit in the office. And drinking light beer at the smelly pub. Okay? Satisfied?'

'Er, yes.'

She walked back and addressed everyone, all quite professionally really.

'Look, we're not having one of those meetings this morning. Monica called and said she had been delayed so she'll be in on Wednesday. We can't contact her till then.'

'Oh,' I said, heavy with the sarcasm. 'How awful. I won't get to be humiliated in public.'

'Well, you wouldn't have anyway dopey, because Monica's not here.'

'You just called me dummy – I'm going to HR.'

She snorted. 'Actually, I called you dopey.' She grinned a devastating, megastar-type grin. I was feeling quite starstruck.

'Anyway. You know that story on dress sizes you were talking about …'

And so it was that we started talking about the summer issue.

'Chandra,' she said shoving aside some more pot plants, making the fence between us practically non-existent, 'can you get some women in their forties who've got real change-my-life success stories?'

I braced myself for the hissy fit. But there wasn't one.

Chandra looked … respectful.

'Of course,' she said purposefully, not even shoving her plants back together.

'If you need to get any numbers,' I started, helpfully.

'I'll be fine, Meg,' she said firmly, but without the usual bitterness. 'I've been doing this for a while.'

Okay, so we wouldn't work it out overnight. I could live with that. In fact, the rivalry was beginning to kind of ... tickle me.

Tamara, who'd just wandered in, sat down and started booking flights for Julie. 'Hi,' she said, happily.

Now what was weird about this picture – everyone was definitely themselves – give or take some major weight loss – but there'd been some kind of bizarre change of atmosphere while I'd been gone. They all seemed kind of happy and, you know, what's the word?

Oh, that's it – they were working, not actually trying to not work, or stay all day on a fortune-telling website or read a paper or check personal emails ... Well, it *was* early in the morning but that made it even weirder. Usually we came in at nine, but work hadn't started till around eleven since, well, since Geri had gone.

Something was happening here. I was almost tempted to ask Chandra about the office's collective horoscope, or some spell-casting she may have had some luck with. But busy noises were emanating from her desk, so it didn't seem the right time.

'Guess what?' Tamara said. 'Julie's going on tour with Kylie.'

'God – who will she have sex with?'

'The dancers!' Julie replied, deadpan.

I looked at her – had she learnt nothing?

'I'm JOKING,' she said when she saw my concerned face. 'I know they're not going to sleep with a *girl* – duh,' she said, a bit like she couldn't believe how naive I was.

'Anyway, she's taken a vow of celibacy, and Elle's joining Kylie and Nicole for a party in London in honour of Australian women – and we're covering it. It'll be such a cool story.'

'Very.' But one thing puzzled me – how did we get such a cool story? We were usually chased away from prestigious gigs like the magazine lepers we were.

More weirdness. More changes.

More things working.

Curiouser and curiouser.

Apart from that though, and the building tension due to the imminent return of Monica, we just got on with things, Tamara got us coffees, Julie cracked a few jokes, we discussed some story ideas, but it was all pretty informal. And some really good stuff was coming out. Until the inevitable happened.

'You guys!' cried Eleanor. 'It's here.' She quickly cut the string on a bundle of issues and triumphantly held up a copy.

There was a collective outing of pent-up breath.

Bright. Wild. Brave.

It looked *sensational*.

'Oh my God,' said Craig, the designer, clutching his head in his hands and peeking through the gaps. 'It's how I always knew it could look.'

'You just needed to be allowed to do your job,' Eleanor said with authority.

'Oh Eleanor.' He grabbed her and whirled her around in his big meaty arms. 'I don't even hate you any more.'

'It's sen-fucking-sational,' said Julie, smiling warmly at him.

Craig? Julie? Smiling? Come to think of it, Craig wasn't even wearing a brown cardigan. He'd been set free.

We all grabbed copies and dived in, head-first, no safety warnings, no holding back.

On the cover were about four celebs, all of whom were sporting some pretty bad and extremely fascinating before-during-and-afters.

'The during is a brilliant touch,' said Chandra.

'Thanks,' said Eleanor, shy and proud, like a mother accepting compliments about her baby.

Pride of place, in the centre right of the cover – the absolute to-die-for prime position on any publication – was Diane's face, swollen and bruised, at once a caution and a heroine.

HOLLYWOOD'S GREATEST LOVE AFFAIR IS OVER. (The 'over' was underlined and italic.) THE TRUE STORY ON WHY THE STARS ARE DUMPING COSMETIC SURGERY – AND WHY YOU SHOULD, TOO, with a giant bright-yellow arrow pointing at Diane's face.

I flicked through, excited – for the first time in ages. It was surprising me! It was inspiring me. It was totally *Gossip!*, yet totally unlike anything we'd done before. There were stars, there were real people, there was the 'ten ways to look ten years younger without going under the knife' story I'd written and had sitting on the back-burner since Monica's arrival.

We had stars who had surgery versus stars who didn't, and ones who just grew older. We had recipes that were yummy-looking – a salmon anti-ageing diet; fashion for budget-savvy girls; a workout program that looked, well, real, funky, and fun, that I was already dying to pull out and stick on my wall and turn into a funky dance routine; and a lucky money scratching section printed right inside the front page. 'Win a million dollars?' I asked, incredulously.

'It was just a few phone calls,' shrugged Eleanor.

'It's a fucking million dollars,' I practically screamed. 'Oh my God – this is excellent! It's so good, I'd, I'd – I'd actually buy it!'

'I just had a few ideas. She said to run it as if I were an editor.'

'Which means "make me look really good",' said Julie, wryly, checking out her pages. 'What you've actually done is blot out the sun. It's a total eclipse. These shots are *amaaazing* – where'd we get them? We didn't spend any money, did we, Eleanor?'

'A bit,' she admitted, making a funny face.

'And it's … *how* many pages, Eleanor?' Julie continued. Oh, she was ruthless.

'It's 204 pages,' Eleanor said, her voice muffled by the fact that she'd collapsed into a chair and smothered her head in her arms.

'You *added* pages?' I gasped.

The head in the hands nodded.

We all looked at each other, stunned. You *never* added pages – unless someone died. Like Diana. Or Michael. Or Paula. Or …

'I just thought it gave it a better weight,' she moaned.

Max burst through the office door, flustered and pompous with his takeaway coffee. 'I heard it's here.' He stretched a demanding hand out, turning his head away as if shielding his eyes from the potential horror.

'Show me,' he demanded dramatically. Then he snatched his hand back. 'No don't! I can't look.'

'Get you own copy, coffee boy,' I snarled. He grabbed a magazine from Eleanor, and gasped.

'Oh My God. It's hideous. It's fabulous. It's horrible. It's irresistible.'

'Anyway,' said Eleanor, coming out of the foetal position. 'There are things to do. This issue is on its own now. We've got another one to send off into the world.' She sounded all confident and inspiring, which rallied us all, but then I heard her muttering to Julie.

'Wonder how many holidays I've got if I get sacked,' she said, chewing a cherry-red nail.

'Shut up,' I said, thinking she was joking. Couldn't she see how good it was?

Apparently not.

'I've probably got about twelve. I can have a couple of weeks to find a job, then maybe I can …'

'Shut up,' we all yelled at her.

'Sorry,' she said quietly. 'I'm better now.'

Throughout all of this, Chandra was working feverishly, but with a sly grin on her face.

'You know, what do you think? This story about – I might have a famous person who can do it …'

'Who?' I demanded suspiciously. Eight months of horror are not that easily forgotten. Besides, Noelene Hogan or Tara Moss just wouldn't cut it.

'Well,' she said casually, looking at me out the corner of her eye. 'I might have Sigrid. And maybe Jerry. Hall. Not that Spice Rack thing. And Joan,' she whispered, leaning in.

'Collins?' I barked. 'If we could …'

'Get her sex secrets …' Chandra finished my sentence.

'Chandra – can I ask – are you … well, obviously they're your contacts or you wouldn't say anything.'

She nodded solemnly.

'But how?' I burst out, waving my hands around. 'Sorry, but really! These are remarkable.'

She touched the side of her nose. 'Let's just say between my Women Scorned support group and my Goddess workshops, it's amazing who you meet, and just how much you can have in common,' she said coolly.

'Right,' I said faintly as she started to tap away.

'Um. I've got the details of a sex therapist who's treated some pretty big stars,' I offered, gingerly.

'Have you?' she said, smiling so that it reached her eyes.

'Yeah, here,' I said, copying a number down and handing it to her. Our hands nearly touched, and I didn't even pull away. 'She's pretty saucy – gives great quote.'

She took it from me, smiled, sat down, smiled again before moving the plants back.

There was a definite sense of anti-freeze in the air.

MISS LONELYHEARTS

* * *

I went to a bar by myself after work and watched people for a bit, nursing a mocktail, just thinking. I didn't feel like talking to anyone. The smelly pub was too intense. Home was full of nosy friends. I just wanted some space to think

The issue was going on sale and I was probably going to have to find a new job once Monica came down from the roof and sacked us all.

Shouldn't that have freaked me out? Because it didn't.

Somehow, it felt okay. If I could do that story, I could do others.

My mobile rang. 'Yep?'

'Meg, it's Eleanor. Look I sent out a press release about the story – can you go on the *Morning* program tomorrow? It's an early start.'

'How early?' I asked nervously, reaching for a pen and paper.

'You have to be at the studios at 6.00 a.m.' She sounded really excited.

'Oh My God. What will I wear?'

I could practically see Eleanor beaming. 'Don't fret – Carla's got it all worked out.'

She hung up and I finished the last of my mocktail as the butterflies did somersaults in my belly. The *Morning* program … six in the morning. I felt like a grown-up!

CHAPTER TWENTY-SEVEN

The next morning I was sitting in the *Morning* program's strange studios, wearing a suit. Sort of. Or very, depending on your point of view. From mine, it was a very. A YSL black satin tux with a Collette Dinnigan lace bit of gorgeous fancy nonsense under it could have looked stupid. But the reactions around me – door opening, taxis stopping, weather clearing up with no humidity thus ensuring frizz-free hair – declared otherwise.

'You look *soooo* lush,' cheered Carla when I'd put them on at home that morning. She'd arrived at 5.00 a.m. with an armful of gorgeous things. I felt like Nicole Kidman must have during Oscar week – fancy having incredible outfits brought to your door.

'I'm wearing about six thousand dollars, Carla – don't you think people will think I'm some kind of rich bitch?' I said nervously, twisting my hands together again and again. Carla slapped me.

'Stop that! It makes you look guilty,' she ordered. 'Remember – open palms make you come across as trustworthy.'

'Okay,' I said, and immediately started fiddling with my hair.

'But do you think this is the sort of image we should be projecting at *Gossip!*?'

'Your hair is curly and your face is adorable, so they won't think you're stuck up – you're too sweet-looking for that. Plus you smile all the time. That helps. The suit could be anyone's – it's gorgeous, but it's smart, and you look like you know what you're talking about. If I send you out there frou-frou or silly-looking everyone will think you've made it all up. If I send you out there plain and frumpy, everyone will think you have an axe to grind with surgery because you're a frumpy feminist. Sorry,' she said, seeing the evil look I shot her. 'It's true. You have to look serious and smart – yet adorable. A girl's girl.'

I am a girl's girl, I thought, smugly.

'Anyway, it's not about you – this suit says this issue is serious and I'm not scared to stand up for what I believe in. It also says *Gossip!* can be taken seriously. Plus you look hot. So shut up and get used to it,' she said, sternly.

'Go away, scary lady,' I sniped, only half-jokingly.

'You'll be loving me before this is over,' she said, completely seriously.

I had another glance in the mirror. I was feeling the love already. I did look very ... lots of warm brown hair and green eyes and a big mouth and a great suit and a sexy lace thing and – oh, shit. I looked down. Curse my short-legged Irish forebears, even if stumpy limbs had seen us through the great potato famine.

'My pants,' I wailed, 'they're about a foot too long.'

'Duh, that's what I'm here for,' she said, whipping out a cute little package of Hollywood tape and expertly taking my trousers up to just the right high-heel skimming height.

'Now, that won't move. Nothing can get your pants down now.'

Except Nick, I thought wryly. Pity.

After catching a taxi with Carla, who was my official hand-holder and make-sure-the-silly-bugger-gets-there-without-egg-on-her-face minder, I was escorted to make-up, to have my face done – MY FACE DONE, just in case you think I've suddenly got used to this star treatment – by somebody gorgeous called Eva, who was married to somebody famous, with soothing hands and a nice smell.

'Here, sweetheart. Close your eyes and relax. I'll just get you a peppermint tea.'

I sat back and let the goddess do me. It was like being at We Believe. Carla was a bit of a nazi – no, do not give her too much lipstick, no something lighter, softer, that one's all red and mean, we don't want Cruella de Vil – God, I was in great hands, and between the two of them I looked ... pretty good. I actually blushed at one stage – when Carla and the make-up artist, Eva, had finally bonded, Eva had whispered a bit too loudly, 'It's so nice to work on someone young and pretty and fresh. You wouldn't believe the old boilers we have in here.' So, okay the old boilers bit kind of reduced the pretty and fresh bit – but she had said those words. Fresh and pretty.

MISS LONELYHEARTS

About me. And they were given considerable weight by the fact that Eva was young and gorgeous.

I felt all glowy, no doubt a side effect of the fresh and pretty mantra running through my brain. I never said I wasn't shallow – and it'd been a while between compliments from a professional make-up artist.

I'm pretty. I'm fresh. And I can write! I thought, as we were led towards the green room. Lucky me! Easy girl – don't get a big head. You still have to get on that stage thingie and somehow not make a complete twat of yourself in front of, oooh, maybe one million viewers, including my housies, my bestie, and possibly by this stage, thanks to Ali's diligent though forbidden phone calls, my family.

Somehow the idea of Karen seeing me on telly looking not at all like a half-baked potato in a bad frock made me feel quite good about the whole thing.

Until we were ushered into the green room, that is. Stars buzzed about, chatting knowingly, those tight, special little clusters that say 'back off, pleb'. Carla must have sensed me getting wobbly, or maybe it was the fact that I was hyperventilating that gave it away. Anyway, she was great – like some kind of TV-debut coach. She said all the right things. 'Think. Breathe. Nicole Kidman on *Oprah* being asked about life after Cruise – again and again and again. Cherie Blair hiring Peter Foster – without even knowing he was Samantha Fox's ex, plus the other stuff. Think Clinton dealing with the Lewinsky thing. Think Jennifer Lopez explaining her divorce body count – to her mother. Come on! You think *this* is pressure?' she whispered fiercely. She was good.

I straightened my shoulders and stopped white-knuckling. Obviously inspired, she went on with the cheerleading. I thought she was about to start striding round the room.

'It's true. This is a piece of cake. You know what you're talking about. You haven't done anything wrong. You're a journalist. It's your job – your craft – your profession to tell the story – and tell it well, or I'll never have a cosmopolitan with you ever again,' she hissed.

I breathed in, focusing on the distance out the window, where stars were clambering out of the station helicopter. 'I'm feeling a bit better,' I said to her, squeezing her hand.

'Good. Because we're relying on you. Just pretend you can do it,' she instructed, 'and you can.'

'I'm definitely feeling better,' I said, just a bit sarcastically. Just like vomiting, not like throwing myself out the window and ruining my suit and the make-up artist's fine work. This was a chance, I said to myself. Look at this as an opportunity to be remembered for something other than being the girl who Ben dumped. Karen's sister. Ali's friend.

'How are you?' asked Carla, probably a little worried by the faraway look in my eyes.

'Fine!' I said brightly. Whoa – faking it is easy, I thought. So that's how everyone does it. They're not actually super-cool, self-controlled, confident masters of their domain – they just act like they are.

'The soft hair, smart suit thing really works for you,' said Carla, obviously thinking her way through a new fashion story.

'You're so good at this,' I said.

'I am,' she agreed.

My heart was hammering so loud I thought the microphone and the cute guy who winked at me while strapping it on would have to be picking it up. I looked around. As I said, we weren't the sole residents of the salmon sandwiches and super-stocked mini-barred green room. A man with a golden tan and familiar golden-brown hair was reclining on the one couch, his long legs sprawled lazily over the coffee table, fawning lackeys (okay, assistants) dancing attendance.

Dr Gold. I felt shocked. Surely we weren't meant to sit together politely before verballing each other into career hell. What were they thinking?

I looked at Carla, panicked.

'The strategy is to get the chemistry going before you go live,' she explained quietly, making constant eye contact with me

'So what should I do?'

'Face him,' she ordered, giving me a little shove towards the scary gang. 'Beard the lion!'

'Can you tell me what that is actually supposed to mean?' I demanded, panicking. She was pushing me closer! 'I never got that saying and I really don't get it now,' I complained. She stuck her face right in my face.

'If you don't tackle it now you could lose your confidence out there.'

I walked over, holding my head high but with a polite and friendly we're-all-in-this-together-so-let's-be-civilised-about-it type expression on my face. Or then again, he may have thought I had a carrot stuck up my arse.

'Hello,' I smiled, unsure of what the etiquette was here. 'I'm Meg Tooley. I wrote the *Gossip!* story.' What now? Didn't politicians always shake hands before tearing each other to shreds? I held mine out and he looked at it, amused. He took it in his soft, golden-brown hand, and turned it over.

'Yes,' he said, looking at my hand, like it was a specimen. 'Some nasty sun damage going on there,' he commented to a minion.

I flushed, and snatched my hand back.

'Why don't you talk to my assistant — come in and we'll have a look at whether we can help you.'

'Or at least call a hospital,' said one blonde and brown person, meanly.

They both turned away and laughed.

I stood my ground.

'I came over to wish you luck, Dr Gold,' I said. 'I think you're going to need it.'

I turned away and walked stiffly back to Carla, who was nearly punching the air with glee!

I sat down and stared at the back of his head. If evil thought messages could make things explode, his head would have been all over the room by now.

'Who does that hideous man think he is?' asked Carla loudly. 'And why were you being nice to him?'

He turned back to me, gave me a look that didn't so much imply as impale me upon its icy glance, and shook his head very slowly, from side to side. Tch, tch, tch.

'Meg – phone call,' said Carla softly. 'I grabbed it, still staring at the doctor. Keep it together, I thought, my hands trembling with rage.

I could barely focus. Should I pretend it was my mum and I had to go because something had happened to the cat?

'Er, hi!' I said, enthusiastically in case it was someone I should really have known.

And it was.

'It's Diane. Look, I'm out of hospital but I'm not coming back to Sydney for a bit' – she lowered her voice – 'and I'm going to stay with Marley for a while. He was there, the whole time in hospital. He sent me energy, and I'm sure that's what saved me. I just wanted to let you know I was better,' she said, her voice a bit funny.

'That's great, Diane. How long are you going to holiday for?' I asked.

'Er. I'm not sure. I'll see. It might not be a holiday. Marley said I could come stay with him ... to have someone take care of me. Anyway, thanks. And good luck on telly!'

'Thanks.'

I rang off and felt energy surging through me. This was what it was about – Diane, and all the Dianes and the Mums and the Karens, and maybe even in their darker moments the Eleanors and, impossible though it might seem, maybe even the gorgeous Alis and everyone who thought they needed stuff – we all thought about lipo (come on, if you're over twenty-five you *know* you have). We didn't. Dr Gold was getting richer by the day, cashing in on our fears that our bums were definitely way too big in those jeans.

Time to say stop.

I must have looked how I felt. A professional-looking blonde bob walked towards me and held out her hand for a firm shake.

'I'm Anthea – the segment producer. Ever done this before?'

I shook my head.

'Well, you look very impressive,' she said warmly as she looked over at Dr Gold.

'Hello, Doctor,' she said brightly.

'Hello,' he said, taking her hand and shaking it mechanically, all the while glaring at me.

'See, he's rattled,' whispered Carla.

'You've both met? Ready for the stoush? We want sparks flying! Good TV!'

A wave of nausea crashed through me as we were led to the set. I found myself shaking another hand, this time that of the *Morning* program's smart, tough and sexy-looking presenter, Justine Marks.

'It'll be interesting to see what you two have to say – give us something to really get our teeth into this morning,' she said and laughed, shaking hands with us both.

'Ready to go, people?' asked Justine.

'Yes,' I said, clearing my throat.

'Certainly,' he grinned.

A studio person with headphones and jeans and long hair held up a clapperboard thing and went 'three, two, one and – go'. He waved his arms around and pointed straight at us.

MISS LONELYHEARTS

It didn't phase Justine, who smoothly swung into breakfast-news-host mode.

'You've seen it on the stars, you've read about it in magazines. You've maybe even had it yourself. Yes, tinkering with nature – playing God with our faces – that's plastic surgery, and it's today's hot topic. As a doctor performing voluntary procedures for more and more Australian women, Dr Lewis Gold says that it's a life-enhancing tool that's a positive side of modern medicine's advances. Meg Tooley, journalist with *Gossip!* magazine, challenges that notion. As a reporter, and a friend, Ms Tooley says she has witnessed the other side of cosmetic surgery.

'Doctor, can you tell us what it is that you do?'

'I'm a surgeon. I enhance people's looks. Sometimes these are minor procedures, sometimes they are quite complex. All are performed with the full consent and knowledge of each patient. Basically, I'm providing a service that in twenty years, maybe even less time, will be considered as necessary as going to the dentist.' He smiled smoothly. Goddammit! He sounded so reasonable.

'Meg Tooley – what's your take on Dr Gold's statement?'

'Justine, I think that it's time someone pointed out the dangers of surgery – that it's not the same as applying lipstick or trying a new perfume. If it's surgery, it's surgery, and we have the right to be treated safely, regardless of whether it's optional or otherwise.'

'Would you ever have plastic surgery?'

'Well, I have, actually,' I said. Justine and the good doctor looked aghast. 'I had an accident when I was young, and had a skin graft to reduce scarring. I don't actually have anything but praise for true surgeons who work to help people. And I have no gripe with surgeons who decide to go into the beauty trade. But I do,' I said, looking at Dr Gold, who was looking far too comfortable, 'have a major issue with GP's who perform surgery that demands years of training. I want to know why Dr Gold is performing operations that only a surgeon should be permitted to perform. And,' I said, as he broke in to reply, 'I want to know why he isn't breaking the law by doing this.

'We have,' I went on quickly, my voice going up a notch in volume, 'harsher controls on vitamin companies, on farmers, on people wanting to run cafés, than we do on these so-called professionals altering people's faces. And that seems strange to me.'

'You're being a little over the top,' Dr Gold said and laughed, smiling conspiratorially at Justine. 'We all know that feminists have a problem with these things.'

'This is not a discussion about my opinion – it's a fact, isn't it, that you are qualified only as a GP?'

'Is that so, doctor?' Justine was beginning to look curious herself.

'Yes, I am. I studied and trained and worked in South Africa,' he said, sounding like he'd spent all his time helping end apartheid. 'But not as a surgeon,' he added.

MISS LONELYHEARTS

'I just need to make sure this is right. No qualifications at all – not even any training – as a surgeon?' I was sitting forward, my words strong, my face a little heated, but I was not flying off the handle. I was not wimping out. I was in there. The zone. It was exhilarating. And the best thing was that he *had* to answer my questions.

He laughed. 'I have performed over 3000 facelifts. I have –'

'Without,' I interrupted, 'any training for surgery. Don't you think it's like a very good vet giving me heart surgery?'

'I am a doctor!' he said with carefully constructed indignation.

'That's right. Probably a very good doctor. And yet, you injected these women with a new substance at the conference a couple of weekends ago on the Gold Coast.'

He momentarily looked startled, then his eyes narrowed, and he collected himself and smiled darkly, teeth gritted.

'Of course I didn't.'

'You had advertised your event as a Botox conference – is that right?'

'Yes, that's right,' he said, sounding relieved. 'Botox,' he chuckled, playing to the camera, 'is legal.' He rolled his eyes.

'But it wasn't Botox that ended up in Diane Worthington's face, which led to her being flown to hospital with a life-threatening allergic reaction. How many women in this country have been tested –'

'Women have been tested,' he said, his smile looking more and more like a snarl.

'Can you just confirm for me — tested in this country?'

He said nothing, but he looked like he wanted to give my voicebox some Botox right there and then.

'Is it true you pay women in Third-World nations to take —'

'This is a fiasco!' he spluttered at Justine.

'… to be paid to inject, actually, all sorts of compounds into their faces, so that *we* can safely fill in our wrinkles?' I felt really angry, but the kind of icy anger you feel when you feel about as close to right as you probably ever will be.

'Yes. Again, it's legal. This questioning is offensive and ridiculous. Any pharmaceutical company does the same. I provide major benefits to impoverished communities.'

'But isn't it true that these women at the conference did not know that instead of the Botox you'd offered, you used a new, untried, untested …'

'It was tested.'

'In Africa. By women. Who need. To feed. Their children. Who may have no medical back-up once things go wrong.'

'Can we get back to the topic, Meg,' Justine said, sounding a little bit like she wished she didn't have to be a fair and reasonable moderator.

'Wasn't this in fact the fourth time you've had a patient react badly?'

'I can't remember.' He shifted in his seat, looking as though he'd like me to burst into flames.

'Four, doctor. Is it four?'

'Doctors like me are just doing what women – most women – want. So you can't blame us.'

'But Diane could have died. And people die from liposuction.'

'People die from bee stings,' he said and laughed – but not too convincingly. 'Let's kill all the bees!'

Time for me to change direction.

'Dr Gold, are you a bad doctor?'

'No,' he spluttered. 'I am an excellent doctor. I am better than anyone you could ever hope to see. People wait for months for an appointment with me, to be operated on by me. I am a busy man because I am a brilliant doctor.'

'So, Dr Gold, you are a fine doctor. So in the hands of other, less proficient doctors, all of whom are legally allowed to perform surgery, the results could even be worse?'

'What!'

'You can't have it both ways, doctor. Either you are a good doctor and you take the greatest care with great knowledge and rare talent, and thus you have a minimum of patients who experience side effects and we should hold you up as an example. Or you are a bad doctor, who experiences a high level of mishaps.'

'I am a fine doctor.'

'What are you getting at, Meg?' Justine asked.

'Dr Gold is a great doctor. And my friend nearly died. How safe is it for anybody *not* in this doctor's hands? Because there are a lot of other doctors out there performing serious operations, who Dr Gold admits are probably not as skilled as he is. There are a lot of shysters out there.

'And if this doctor – this very good doctor – sent a friend of mine to hospital yesterday' – I turned to the camera – 'what could happen to you?'

'Thank you, Dr Gold, and thank you, Meg Tooley of *Gossip!* magazine.'

'Just one last question, please, Justine.'

'Meg?'

'Dr Gold, what's the connection between suntanning and lasers?'

'What?'

'You do know that there's a problem with people who are suntanned having laser hair removal?'

'Of course!'

'What is the problem?'

'Skin cancer, of course.'

'No, doctor. It's pigmentation. And you give patients at your clinic this treatment even though it is outside the guidelines recommended by the Plastic Surgery Association.'

'After the break,' Justine started to say, 'the fascinating relationship between dogs and humans', but the rest of her words were drowned out by the ringing in my head. I sat, a bit dazed, with my hands clenched. I unfolded them and flexed. No need for fists any more. It was over. We went to an ad break.

'Thanks, Meg. Doctor. You were both brilliant.' I smiled weakly at Justine Marks and shook her hand. God, had it worked? It felt like it had.

Dr Gold looked hard at me, then reached out a

hand and grabbed my wrist – twisting it slightly in his grip.

'So,' he hissed nastily, 'Monica Drawmer gets breasts then sends the office girl to screw me.'

'What?' I said, shocked. Monica had had what? Oh God.

'You'll be hearing from my lawyers.'

'She's away,' I whispered after he and his entourage walked away. 'She's at a conference,' I shouted after him.

'She's been at my private clinic for the past three days,' he spat back, stalking further away on his long, lean legs.

I raced off after him and caught up, panting.

'Don't bother,' he said. 'It's too late. I'm going to unleash hell on you and your little magazine.'

'Dr Gold, are you saying to me that you had an arrangement with Monica Drawmer? Some sort of cosmetic surgery for comment thing going on?'

He laughed. 'Don't pretend to be so naive. You know how this industry works.'

'Did you?'

Nothing.

'Please, Dr Gold, answer the question.'

'Talk to my lawyers. And stay away from me or you'll be slapped with an AVO faster than I can make a 58-year-old feel like she's thirty-four again.'

This time I grabbed his arm.

'What about Cookie?' I said to him. 'What about what happened when she was under?'

'That,' he said right into my face, 'was my tip.' And he strode away, down the antiseptic corridor and into a waiting limo. I followed him out, and a taxi pulled up.

Carla opened the door. 'Come on – back to the office.'

I couldn't move. Monica had got breasts in return for a flattering story?

She looked at me. 'You were *sooo* great. I'm really proud. The girls rang before and said they were watching – the office sounded like the smelly pub!'

I sat there, feeling a bit stunned.

'I think he was a bit shocked,' Carla said.

'He just claimed Monica had him do her breasts!'

'Oh My God,' she said, throwing her arms around me. 'You're so clever! How'd you get that out of him?' The spongy-brown interior of the cab began to spin round and round before I could remember – how *did* I get that out of him? And why wasn't my head working any more?

'Carla, I feel weird.' My voice sounded all far away.

'You're just hungry – now shut up and have some juice – your blood sugar's probably low,' she said, handing me a carton of orange something-or-other and passing me a massive packet of cereal.

I looked at them sceptically.

'They're preservative and additive and colouring and all the good stuff like sugar free – I checked,' she said impatiently. 'Eat. Drink. Or spin out!'

I ate, I drank and slowly the taxi stopped cartwheeling and my head gradually cleared.

'So I was good?' I asked, as soon as I was capable of speech. I just wanted to hear her say 'yes'. I know,

I know, but tell me you've never done it (remember 'does my bum look big in this?') and *then* and only then will I feel silly.

So you have asked, when you knew you were pushing it?

Right then. Glad we sorted that out. I'll get on with it.

'Yes, you were great,' Carla said, giving me a little shove. 'Really alive and sharp but warm, too, and caring.'

I settled back, letting the glow creep over me. I smiled – probably a bit smugly.

'Pity you let him call you a feminist – not very good for the magazine.'

I should have known not to push my luck ...

The same day I became a TV star, I did twenty-eight radio interviews and thirteen print – and my condition of interview for *The Echo* and all affiliates was that Allison had to be the journalist assigned. And I demanded she get a picture byline. It caused serious problems with her chief of staff, who thought the story should go to one of the boring ambulance chasers, but I made sure she got the piece – the best quotes and the most time. She looked hot in her pic. After hours and hours of talking, I was buggered. Once I started saying the same things over and over again, only lying face down on the floor under my desk, Chandra told Eleanor she'd better do something. Eleanor stepped in and took over, but it was a bit annoying, apparently, because they'd all made a bit of a fuss about wanting to talk to me.

After the heavy-duty non-tabloid-type newspapers had picked up the story, Diane's protest gone wrong had practically made her a national celebrity.

'Diane is going to be famous,' Ali said to me, incredulous. 'And so am I – thanks to you …'

'What I find really weird,' I croaked into the phone while still lying under my desk, clutching my copy of *Gossip!*, 'is that Diane is now a covergirl. Sort of.'

'Fancy her being on a cover of a box of toilet paper, let alone a …'

'Look Ali, we should give her a break. She really was sick.'

'I know. Poor thing,' she snorted, and we both started laughing. Or rather, she laughed and I made a horrible rasping sound like I'd slept rough and smoked twenty packets of Winnie reds a day.

'Honestly though – I can't believe she's a vegan and she got animal bits injected into her face,' Ali chortled, once I'd finished rasping.

'By the way – the editor thinks I'm *very* hot. And,' she whispered, '*The Real Story* called.'

'Oh My God. It's happening!' I practically yelled, I was so excited.

'Well, it's a screen test. But *The Real Story*! Oh My God.'

Later that night when I got home, Ali was already there – I'm not sure whether it was me or Dan that was the attraction. Either way, it didn't matter because we were back to normal. I collapsed immediately on the floor in the lounge room. Because she hadn't bothered leaving since we'd got back, my clothing supply was running dangerously low.

'What a team,' she said, sighing contentedly and sinking into the beanbag.

'What a team,' I agreed. 'Pity it all has to end when Monica comes back and finds out what we've been up to. Maybe I can go back to newspapers,' I said, making a face.

'Poor you,' said Ali.

CHAPTER TWENTY-EIGHT

The next day the entire office was at breaking point. Shitting ourselves. Eleanor had already sent off the next Monday's issue the night before – using a lot of Chandra's contacts they'd done a great follow-up. But the tension was held in nicely. We actually managed to have a civilised meeting about the next issue. We tossed ideas around, snickered at Max's jokes a couple of times.

'We've been getting loads of calls,' Julie said. 'From the distributors.'

'Why? Are people flinging back their copies at the newsagents' faces?' Carla asked.

'No! They want more copies, apparently.'

'God,' I said.

'What time is Monica supposed to be back?' asked Tamara nervously.

'Today,' said Eleanor. 'But who knows when.'

Face it.

We just had to wait. For her wrath *and* to see if she had bigger breasts.

MISS LONELYHEARTS

Carla was the only one actually working, albeit in the fashion cupboard. She was trying to hunt down free things to give to Monica to appease what we assumed would be her horrible reaction.

'Do you think she'd like these?' she asked anxiously, holding up a pair of shoes that were about the same price as a small house in a coastal village.

Our plan was to present Monica with an irresistible bunch of freebies once she'd seen the issue. We thought that way she might be furious, but at least she'd be distracted enough to forget to sack us all.

'Oh shit, wrong size.' She flung the shoes down, savagely. I'd never seen Carla looking so stressed. She never treated shoes like that.

'What about these?' She held up a pair of new season Prada boots.

'They're too big for her. Unless the management course was like *Survivor* and her feet swelled up after an exotic insect bite or she has had a reaction to silicone.' I was trying to be helpful.

'Look, just give her the Chanel, Carla,' ordered Julie, perched on a chair lining her eyes with kohl. Again. With a shaky hand. She'd already wiped off the wiggly line she'd applied with unsteady hands three times, and it wasn't even ten o'clock. And, for a change, the shaky hands had nothing to do with alcohol. We all knew, like birds before a thunderstorm, that trouble was brewing. And everyone's nerves were twitching in different ways.

'Do I have to?' Carla wailed.

'Yes,' everybody said, stonily.

'Shit.' She went and got the make-up she'd been stashing in her not-so-secret make-up cupboard that we all wanted to break in to, but never had. Because Carla would kill us.

Probably.

'I thought once, just once, I might actually get to keep something I wanted. I hate giving this to her. Why do I have to sacrifice the Chanel? She can afford it.' She slumped in her seat, clutching a couple of products close to her chest like they were babies being ripped away from her arms. 'Fuck it. I'm keeping the lipstick.'

'Give her the lipstick,' Julie said emphatically.

'Why?'

'Do you *want* to lose your job?'

'All right – I'll give her *one*. There must be a horrible colour – there always is.'

'Or,' said Tamara wisely, 'just pretend they're horrible colours. Or that they were made from animal torture.'

'Yes – think of the dolphins,' intoned Chandra in a spooky voice. 'I'm joking,' she said, exasperated, when we all turned and stared.

'I can't choose,' Carla muttered, frantic, grasping the lipsticks.

'It's not exactly *Sophie's Choice*, Carla. Just give her both of them if you can't decide and shut up. The rest of us have to put up with it,' said Julie, impatient with nerves.

'It's okay for you – you don't have to give her anything.'

'Bullshit. I have to give her my tickets to the Stones' intimate concert,' said Julie.

'Not anything nice, then.'

'I had to give her exclusive gym memberships,' I said, biting my nails.

'I had to give her my holiday,' said Craig.

'Not exactly Chanel,' grumbled Carla, but she shoved the lipsticks back in their box and stomped over to Monica's office and practically threw the products onto her desk.

'Okay, here's the rest of the stash,' said Julie. 'She's got the Chanel. A weekend at the Golden Door. A sound system. A body/mind/soul realignment program. Three years' free membership at the Crunch gyms – anywhere in the world. Plus a week in Paris. Surely that will be enough.'

'Are you serious?' demanded Max. 'It'll keep her busy for about ten measly minutes.'

'Why are we even trying?' Carla asked, looking reckless, obviously thinking of the Chanel. 'Let her spit the dummy.'

'Say that to her face, Carla,' said Max, 'and I'll be scraping you off this carpet in little, tiny pieces.'

'So what are *you* going to do?' Carla demanded, crossing her arms.

'*I'm* going to call her by her porn name! So she's simultaneously insulted *and* part of the team, so she'll be conflicted about her response and uncomfortable!'

We must have looked impressed. I was stunned at Max's brilliance.

'Now, what should it be?' he asked.

'Titty Boombox?'

'Abby Normal?'

'Clitty Litter?'

'We're not doing that,' said Eleanor, all stern.

'She's not going to sack us,' said Chandra.

'No, Chandra's right,' said Eleanor. 'She's going to sack *me* ...'

'Why should you get special treatment?' Chandra asked.

My phone rang.

It was Ali, checking I was okay.

'What are you doing tonight?'

'Drowning my tears – oooh rewind. Can't. No more getting totally wasted. I guess I'll just be looking through *The Echo* for a job?

'At least it's going to be over soon. Plus that doctor's fucked.'

'How's Dan?'

'Great.'

'See you tonight, babe.'

''Kay.' I grinned and hung up.

After that call all we could do was keep waiting. But it was doing our heads in.

Finally, just when Tamara was near to tears, Chandra was starting to close blinds and act like an uptight bitch again and I'd downed enough magnesium to tranquillise a sea cow, we heard a posh voice singing down the long beige hallway.

There was a collective intake of breath, and a feeling that something very, very significant was about to happen.

Monica strode into the office. In fact, her breasts barged in before the rest of her.

Let's just say they were bigger.

Let's say they were *much* bigger.

Oh shit. Let's just say she suddenly had enormous knockers.

Right on cue, when the rest of her finally made it into the room, the storm broke. A frenzy of fake typing broke out.

'Don't worry, don't worry everybody,' she beamed. 'Mummy's back,' she trilled unnecessarily, looking around her, practically rubbing her hands. 'So don't worry, it's all going to be fine,' she said.

'How was the conference?' Eleanor asked in a flat, down, colourless and extremely non-Eleanor kind of way.

'Can't you tell?' Monica stood back and extended her arms.

She had a smart white suit on, with lethal translucent stilettos that set off her (fake) perfect tan, which her face matched, and her hair was freshly frosted and iced into place. She still looked like the Ice Queen from Narnia, only in tasteful creams. She was the glamour girl of beige.

'I'm back and the conference was … inspirational. Tough. Primitive. Plus,' her voice dropped to a whisper, 'I lost five kilos.'

We were all meant to say 'oooh', I think. But we just stood there, awkwardly waiting for our working lives to end, trying not to stare at her breasts.

'Team! Team. Gather around me. There're going to be a lot of changes round here. A lot. But first – I have to share the experience. Meg? You'll never guess what I did! You'll love this. I walked over hot coals – blindfolded! I had to hold someone's hand, and it did hurt, and of course I can't be seen in sandals till I've made a visit to We Believe but – I now know I can do anything. I have walked the fire.'

Were we meant to applaud?

'Now, team, where's a copy of my magazine? I deliberately waited until I was back in the office to look,' she demanded. (She didn't tell us that she'd been holed up in a private hospital recovering from an operation – and probably too woozy to worry about anything.) We all looked at each other. Eleanor nodded and went to her desk, opened the top drawer, and handed one over.

'Oh my baby,' she cried, hugging it to her chest. 'How I've missed you …' She held it back and stared at the cover. 'OH! No, no, no, no, no … this can't be right – get me my magazine, would you sweetie? Not this, this is … well, I don't want to be rude, but it's just awful – someone's having a little joke, I expect. It's, well, a joke, so – well, whatever it is, just get the right copy.'

Obediently Eleanor walked back to her desk and got out another copy.

'Isn't she gorgeous?' Monica said indulgently. 'It is great to have a big woman on staff. She's like a big, gorgeous goddess or something.'

We were all beginning to feel a bit sick.

'Here you go,' said Eleanor, handing her over the same copy again.

'Is this a joke?' asked Monica, her gaze laser-beaming Eleanor's head off and kicking it out the door. 'Because it's a bit funny …' She held two fingers a millimetre apart and her voice developed icicle action. 'It's about this funny. Ha! Ha! Ha! There you go. Now please,' she lowered her voice to the demonic whisper we'd all come to loathe, 'get me my magazine.'

'That is the magazine. That's this week's edition.'

Monica's mouth suddenly needed shutting. Eventually she closed it herself.

'No, no, no, where's the date there ... Oh My God, a terrible thing's happened. What's happened? Somehow an entirely different cover ...'

She turned on Eleanor, and I was suddenly very, very glad it was her in the firing line. You could feel the tension spike in the room. My temple started to throb.

'Didn't you go out to the presses like I told you? What have they done – those barbarians!'

'Yes, I did go out to the printers. This is the cover.'

'This is the cover – and what's happened to the inside?'

'It's meant to be that way,' Eleanor explained quietly, looking like she was getting ready to be hit.

'Who,' Monica asked in lethal tones, 'made the decision to change this cover?'

No-one moved a muscle. Not even a twitch. We were paralysed.

'Who pulled *my* edition?' she screamed.

We all jumped. Bugger.

'I did,' said Eleanor, softly (for her), moving forward lightly (for her).

'You? How dare you. You took my magazine and produced this ... this ... travesty. This is not team work! This is a mutiny!'

She shook her head, like she was trying to get something annoying out from between her ears.

'I see what's happened. I've been away a week and you took your opportunity to undermine me. Take over. Sabotage this magazine's recovery. Out of what? Some misguided idea that you could do it better. You must be … mentally ill! A normal person would never do that! Do you realise what you've done? Any idea at all?'

'Hang on a minute.' I couldn't believe I'd opened my mouth.

I stepped forward, and stood next to Eleanor, who was looking a bit shocked.

'That cover, those changes, they're my responsibility too,' I said.

'No, that's not true. It was my idea,' Eleanor said.

'Okay, so not exactly. I didn't come up with the idea. But I wrote the story. And I knew what it was for.'

'You both deliberately threw away your editor's brief.'

'And reported what happened,' I said, looking her right in the eye. Then dropping my eyes to her boobs. They really were very large. I fixed my gaze on them for a good three seconds, then looked her in the eye again, defiant.

Something in the room cracked, and I felt the pressure shift a little. Monica looked a bit puzzled that I wasn't trembling with fear.

'I did the research,' piped up Tamara.

'I came up with all the star nonsense. How

couldn't you love that?' Max was practically filing his nails.

'And I felt it was time to redesign,' said Craig, who was sporting some very groovy facial hair.

'So it's ... well, all of us,' Chandra smiled, coldly.

Monica rallied fast, I'll give her that.

'You heinous little turncoats. How could you? Unprofessional. No standards. Disgraceful. You've degraded everything I've worked so hard to achieve. And to think that I entrusted you with this magazine. My magazine. Well. I'm afraid this will have to go a great deal higher than myself.'

She whirled and turned and the *click clack* of her heels was still echoing in my brain.

Tick, tick, tick. The heels in my dream had merged with the heels here.

'Whatever happened to Baby Jane? She's Joan and Bette cloned and merged into one horrible creature. It was fabulous!' Max said to break the tension.

He started to do a fantastic impression of her, writhing around on the floor, hugging himself in ecstasy. 'Team! Oh team! Your leader has returned! I love you all! Do you love me, no, don't answer, I know you worship the coals my hot little Manolos walk upon. Now, show me – who changed it! You're all sick! Twisted! Perverted! What have you done – you're all abnormal! Diseased! I hate you! And to think I loved you all. Ingrates.'

'God, I thought she was going to say she had to go without make-up for days in the wilderness,' Carla said. 'But check out those boobs she brought back?'

'She's going to fucking carve us up,' Julie said, peeling long strips of black polish off her nails. 'Oh well. I'd had enough of rock stars anyway. Need to stay in a bit.'

'Stupid bitch,' grumbled Carla, pressing her nose to the glass door outside Monica's office and gazing with longing at the box we'd left as a sacrifice. 'She didn't even notice the Chanel.'

'Nah, no more rock stars,' continued Julie, her voice sounding suspiciously like she was holding back tears.

'They're such boys,' agreed Eleanor, who was fiddling with a bit of pink hair.

'I was thinking of making a change, anyway,' said Carla, defiantly.

'I liked my job,' sighed Tamara. 'Oh, well. Maybe Fizz can get me a couple of shifts at the pub.'

'Should we all just make a run for it now?' I asked, feeling a bit sick. 'It's just going to be loads of abuse and then we'll get the sack.'

'I think we should stick together,' declared Chandra.

'Why give her the pleasure?' countered Max. 'We could just walk out. At least it'll be talked about. The editor no team would work with,' he said, and laughed.

'The point is, we made the changes, so we shouldn't be gutless now. We have to stick by our work. Are you really unhappy with what we've done?' asked Chandra.

'Why don't I hate you any more?' asked Julie in a wondering tone, walking round her slowly.

'Yeah, Chunder, what's got into you — are you one of those alien walk-ins or something?' Carla was looking at her with a mixture of amazement and respect.

'I just think Eleanor did her job. Very well. We should see what happens. Besides, I've put certain ... elements into place. It should be okay.'

'Oh, now I'm feeling reassured,' scoffed Julie. 'My fate, my mortgage and my sex life is in the hands of a rose quartz crystal and a $2.95 feng shui twinkle thingy. Oh, that's fine. Let's get back to work. What was I worrying about?'

'Shut up, Julie,' said Eleanor. 'She's right. We should stick by what we've done. Unless you don't want to,' she said to us. 'But I'm staying. It *is* mainly my fault.'

'But aren't you glad we did it? Aren't you the least bit proud of what we pulled off?' asked Carla.

'It's all going to be fine. The pink ray says so,' says Chandra, getting off her online oracle.

'God, I thought you'd gone normal on us for a second,' said Carla.

'Anyone who leaves right now won't find out a thing,' said Max. 'It'll kill you, not knowing how we died.'

'I'm staying.'

'I'm in.'

'Me too.'

'I already was sacked, so it is immaterial to me,' said Vikram.

We shut up as we heard a door in the distance slam, and one set of very spiky heels heading our way.

Tick, tick, tick.

'Oh, look, decision's made. Run, if you want,' said Max.

Everyone sat down. Nobody even bothered pretending to work. We watched Big Boss, Monica and another new HR bloke enter the room.

'It's over to you,' Monica said bossily to Big Boss, whose eyebrows raised ever so slightly in … disapproval? She shook her head sadly at us. He started to speak, but Monica drew a huge, gusty breath, raised a manicured hand and silenced him. He looked a bit annoyed. Interesting.

'I thought I could do something with them,' she said sadly to him, like we were juvenile delinquents and she was a social worker. 'But as you can see, they're past saving. It's just gone too far. You've no-one but yourselves to blame for whatever happens now,' she admonished.

Big Boss drew breath to speak, but she held her hand up again and continued.

I'm sure I saw his face go red.

'Here's what they did. That one, who I entrusted with everything. And the rest of them. Just look at it,' she groaned dramatically, shaking her head like she was looking at a three-headed alien baby.

'Monica,' said Big Boss, looking, for once, like the unruffled business genius with half a brain he'd once been rumoured to be. He placed a not very avuncular hand on her shoulder just that little bit too heavily. If she doesn't get that that's a signal to shut up, this will get even better, I thought, feeling a little spark of hope flicker in my belly.

'You had nothing to do with this. Is that right?'

'That? Nothing! My cover was gorgeous. New! Fresh! Elegant! *Desirable*. And it would have scored us thousands in advertising.'

'Nothing at all to do with this cover, you say?'

'Nothing,' she said emphatically.

'Then,' he said, turning to her, 'you'd better come with me.'

'What is going to happen? You must do something – they have undermined me, taken …'

'All right. We'll talk. Here, in front of everyone, though I think you would have preferred the privacy I offered you.'

Ooo-er.

'This issue,' he said, grabbing the copy from out of my hands, 'has spiked in sales. Translation, please Monica.'

Monica's eyes were enormous.

'Monica?'

'Spiked in sales?' she repeated dully, slumping. Gravity can do awful things to people's faces. Seriously, she staggered sideways in her heels.

'Oh no,' said Tamara, half wailing. 'Spiked. Spiked!'

'Spiked,' Big Boss repeated.

'Impossible,' Monica snapped.

'Spiked,' moaned Tamara, letting her head hit the floor three times gently.

'Maybe you should translate,' he growled again at Monica.

Monica grabbed the piece of paper from his hands, and snorted derisively. 'Well, really. I mean, this is obviously some kind of mistake. Maybe even for the issue the week before,' she said desperately. 'Stats – they stuff things up all the time.'

'I think I can help,' Eleanor said.

'Does that mean we've sold out?' she asked Big Boss.

'Virtually.'

'And that means we're reprinting?'

He nodded, breaking into a grin, and starting to applaud.

'Reprinting,' she repeated, wonderingly, as the rest of us broke into screams, whoops and whistles, dancing round and giggling madly.

'So we've sold …'

'We've sold out,' Big Boss said with a smile.

'Oh God.' Monica sounded like a wounded animal.

'Did you hear that?' said Eleanor and she grinned and grinned. 'It's going off,' she said.

'So, if you had nothing to do with this …' Big Boss said to Monica. 'You have some explaining to do. Come with me.'

'I won't stand for this type of treatment. I won't be spoken to in this fashion. Marcus?' She whimpered at the man in HR. 'I've discussed this with you, haven't I? That I cannot allow myself to be abused in this fashion?'

Big Boss ignored her comments and said, 'Your job, Miss Drawmer, has been to get this magazine back on track. It is finally, finally doing what it was meant to do. And according to you, while you were away on a management course you persuaded us to send you on, at great expense, this objective was actually achieved. So I suppose the management course can't really be called a complete waste of time.'

'Come on, Monica,' said the HR man. 'It might be time we talked about that package. Again.'

Monica shot us all a lethal look.

'I hope all of your chickens come home to roost,' she said in the manner of an ancient oracle invoking a deadly curse.

Her heels ticked away.

Tick, tick, tick.

And faded out to nothing.

We all just sort of looked at the ground. And then stood there for a bit more, saying nothing.

Eleanor broke the silence.

'Shall we keep going on the next issue?' she said. 'Or go to the smelly pub and do the planning there?'

We all grinned and filed to the meeting room.

'Hang on,' she said. 'Start as you mean to continue. Let's,' she cried out, triumph in her voice, 'go to the smelly pub!'

The next day we started to panic. We hadn't actually done any planning at the smelly pub. We hadn't been able to settle after the firestorm. We were all still shell-shocked when we arrived on the Thursday morning. We'd managed to have a couple of debriefings outside the tearoom and then Eleanor had been called to a meeting with Big Boss, so we couldn't possibly do anything until she got back.

She finally wandered back in looking dazed and teary.

'I've been named editor,' she whispered to Julie.

'Not even acting ed?' asked Julie, kohled eyes widening.

'No. I'm *the* editor. We met, he said some things, I have no idea what because I too busy wondering whether I was hallucinating, or if Max had put glue in my tea, and then he shook my hand, and then I walked back, and I think that's it. I think it's just happened.'

We were all sitting there, in shock.

'I mean, this is good news, isn't it?' asked Tamara, looking like she might be about to cry.

'I suppose,' said Eleanor, looking tired. 'I didn't actually mean for this to happen,' she said, blinking and rubbing her eyes. A large mascara stain worked its way down her cheek.

'Oh my God, you're going to be earning so much money. Drinks on you!'

'Shut up, Julie. It's going to be hard work,' said Chandra, hovering protectively.

'She's right. It's going to be hard work,' Eleanor said, and then smiled. 'For everyone. It's actually pretty fucking horrible – we were so damn successful with that issue. It shouldn't happen that way. Expectations are supposed to build gradually, not …'

'You don't think we can actually do it again?' Max asked.

'Yes we can,' Julie soothed.

'How?' demanded a shocked Eleanor. 'We don't have the resources – we don't have access to the stories. We don't have a mega-budget. I have no idea what's going to be hot next week. Do you?'

Julie shook her head. 'Nope.'

'See?'

'So? Prediction is what we're all about,' said Carla, who was wearing the Chanel lipstick.

'Look, we'll do what everyone does, what we always used to do. Only better. With a twist,' agreed Julie.

'Twisted magazine,' chortled Max, before clapping a hand to his forehead and shrieking.

Eleanor stood up and strode out of the office. Then she turned around and came back in. She cleared her throat, and looked a bit sheepish.

'Okay guys. I have a couple of things to announce.'

'Right. First. Sorry for losing it back there. It was all taking a while to sink in. But now that Julie's been a complete bitch I've seen the light. I won't chuck any more wobblies – promise. Except maybe on deadline.' Julie looked smug.

'Now, I am making a couple of appointments. Immediately.' Julie looked interested.

'Julie, you're going to be my deputy ...' Julie looked like a stunned mullet, then like a twelve year old about to meet Justin Timberlake.

'Yes!' she screamed, jumping up and down and clapping her hands.

'Rock journo?' Max raised his eyebrows at me.

'She's excited – she's allowed to be silly.'

I was feeling excited myself. What would happen next?

'And Chandra, you will be the co-deputy ...'

'What?' Julie had stopped jumping and had returned to the stunned-mullet stage. They stared at each other, alternate surprise and disgust wriggling across their faces.

'You'll just have to learn to … respect each other's differences. Seriously. Because I need both of you. Everyone's relying on me. And I'm going to be relying on you. Both of you.'

A great big balloon of dead air went up.

'Please?'

They leant in, narrowed their eyes at each other, then crossed their arms tightly across their very different chests.

'Okay,' said Julie.

'I will,' said Chandra solemnly. I tried not to snort, but something escaped and I copped a glare.

'Thanks guys,' said Eleanor, shaking her head at Chandra.

'Thought you'd never ask,' said Julie, moving back to her desk.

'It's going to be okay,' said Eleanor, moving towards a chair and sitting down.

'Anyway, now we should talk about the next issue.'

'Where?' Chandra asked.

'Here?'

Eleanor sat down on the floor and kicked off her sandals. We all followed suit, feeling a bit weird. 'I'm staying on my chair. And keeping my heels on,' Carla said.

'Sit on this,' said Tamara, offering her a cushion.

'Ta.'

They smiled.

Not *more* new friendships and bliss – was there going to be any creative tension left in this place?

MISS LONELYHEARTS

'Tamara, can you' – Eleanor fumbled around in her pocket and dragged out twenty bucks – 'can you please go and get fruit and pastries, for those who need their sugar hit. And coffees. We won't start till you're back. Thanks.'

When she stumbled back in and we were all happily eating grapes (Eleanor – who would have thought) and mango (me – too much sugar by yum), the new editor began.

'Just let's go through what we need to do for the day. Meg, you're doing that story on health problems of the stars? It has to be finished by tomorrow so Vikkie can sub it, then ...'

'Vikram?'

'He's coming back, part-time. Just on the heavy days.'

'Thank God. I hate relying on spellcheck,' gasped Tamara.

Chandra looked happy, I thought. Hmmmn. Interesting.

'Meg, I need you to go to the bumcrawl for dollars thing – the advertising lunch. It won't be too bad.'

'It's fine, Eleanor.'

'Carla, you're ...'

'Going to the beauty shoot – how to look like a film star. It's going to be fun. Audrey Hepburn,' she said, looking all dreamy. 'Tiffany's cigarette-holders ...'

'Don't you think a cigarette-holder's a bit ...' Max queried.

'It's for atmosphere!'

'We'll airbrush it out if you use it,' said Eleanor firmly.

'Awww. Youse guys are fucked.'

'Carla – you sound vulgar,' Chandra sounded startled.

'It's the new black – swearing, and being crass. And sounding really Australian.'

'I blame Steve Irwin,' Chandra sniffed.

'I love Steve Irwin. He's so hot!' cried Carla.

'What?' I said, looking at her.

'What?' Chandra echoed, incredulously.

'Duh, magazine mavens. You probably think some pop star's the hot new thing. Not! It's all the way with Irwin. Apparently he's influenced the styling of the launch this afternoon,' she explained knowledgeably to me.

'So why don't I do the interviews in khaki?' I asked.

'Funny. Right, here you go,' she said, plonking all the stuff on the desk in front of Eleanor.

'What's that?'

'It's the make-up from yesterday's product shoot.'

Eleanor looked simultaneously bewildered and bedazzled. 'I don't think I actually need all this. Tamara, can you divide half of it up. If you all put in twenty bucks we can divvy it up. We'll donate the money to charity.'

'Rotating first dibs?'

'And I want this,' Eleanor said, grabbing a lipstick.

'Err, that has to go back,' Carla said, apologetically.

'Oh. Anyway. Can everyone get me their revised stories – fast. I read everything last night. There are notes in the hard copy. And about the lead story – I think we just need Chandra to …'

'Already have it. Wacky new religions – stars and their bizarre spirituality. It's a killer. And wait till you see the budget breakdowns.'

'You know, I think everything is going to be fine,' said Julie.

'Cover?' Eleanor queried.

Craig whipped out three bright, blazing covers.

'I like this – what do you think?' he asked.

'It's loud, it's cheap, it's just the wrong side of tacky. Not my first choice. Hmmm. How about taking the yellow off and substituting pink – keep it tacky *and* pretty,' Eleanor suggested.

'Like the hottest girl in the trailer park,' Craig got it straightaway.

'Exactly! You're very clever,' Eleanor complimented. Craig beamed. He didn't look brown at all any more. He was beginning to look … quite hot.

And Eleanor was looking quite … what was it? *Appreciatively* at him. Like she fancied him.

Obviously egged on by her admiring glance, Craig swallowed, then dared to ask what all designers secretly long for.

'Can we go fluoro?' he whispered.

Fluoro was the holy grail – it cost a lot extra, and nearly always made sales lift.

'Use it,' said Eleanor, definitely. 'Every issue from now on.'

'Like cheap gorgeous clothes,' Carla stated.

'Cheap is chic now,' said Julie.

'Speaking of money ...' Chandra started. 'I've done budget-saving ideas.'

'And I've already gone over budget,' Eleanor said and laughed. 'Not too much,' she corrected quickly. 'On things that matter. That readers will notice. Oh, and we'll be having a slap-up lunch once a week. If we make targets.'

'No, no, no. Eleanor, it's advertising who get taken out for lunch and given Louis Vuitton luggage and big fat crates of poncey champers and cheesy weekends away for two when they meet their targets,' said Max.

'Which is why they hassle us so much. And hate us when we don't put their stinky clients in,' Carla explained, patiently.

Eleanor raised an eyebrow. 'Look, anybody willing to spend money with us, I like. But it's time we got celebrated too.'

'We'd better do it while it lasts!' We all looked at Chandra when she said that. 'Well, while the budget lasts at least,' she added.

'Oh. Didn't I say? The slap-up lunch is at the smelly pub. Got to stay close to our roots,' Eleanor pointed out.

'That's where so many great ideas are born,' I agreed.

'Including my first groupie column,' said Julie, grinning.

'You know, I really don't know what I was so freaked about. This is looking ...'

'Hot,' said Craig.

'Like the best-looking girl in the trailer park,' admired Eleanor.

'Who's desperate to get into the suburbs,' drawled Carla.

'And there's nothing, nothing at all wrong with that,' said Eleanor. 'So. That's the guts of the issue out of the way. But what's our lead? What's our sell?'

'Porn names of the stars – plus their shameful backgrounds,' Max threw in.

'Shameful backgrounds of porn stars, aren't they *supposed* to have shameful backgrounds?' asked Tamara, bewildered. 'I mean, isn't that *why* they're porn stars – and isn't being a porn star shameful anyway?'

'Duh, no, shameful secrets of the stars, the stars – and their porn pasts if we can find them out,' said Max.

'You're evil,' said Julie, admiringly.

'Isn't that a bit tacky?' mused Carla. We all deflated. 'And isn't tacky the new fabulous?' she concluded, punching the air with a perfectly groomed fist.

'No, no, no. They're just not right. They're brilliant ideas. But that's too close to next Monday's issue. We don't want to come across too puritanical. So save that for about seven weeks down the track. Someone's bound to have done something disgusting by then,' Eleanor said.

We all nodded, remembering the Pammy and Tommy Lee video, with varying degrees of fondness.

'But this week we need to surprise the readers. We need a real-person story. Something, I dunno – everygirl. Romantic, but weird enough to sell.'

'Like a ... romance issue. But with a twist?'

'Something soft and spicy. Last week was very hard and its follow up had the same edge. And it was a bit out there. We have to go very mainstream for this one.'

I suddenly thought of something.

'Um, I have an idea ...' I said.

'Shoot.'

I pulled a face. 'Can I talk to you alone?'

'Don't be silly. We're not going to start acting like that now.'

'Um. Okay. Do you remember this?'

I took a faded clipping out of my wallet and handed it to Eleanor. It was Allison's Lonelyhearts follow-up.

'That's my clipping!' Max shrieked, glaring at me. Well, he'd stolen my letters.

'What if we do a follow-up on this girl, and a huge romance and single stars-type issue? We can match up single stars with perfect boyfriends, and write up Lonelyhearts-style pieces for them. Maybe get a psychologist to explain where they're going wrong – and we can predict the use-by dates for stars' current relationships ...'

Eleanor frowned.

'I know it's a bit old,' I said, going to put it away again.

'No, it's excellent. But no-one could find her, Meg. It's great – I love it – but we couldn't track her down, remember? Tamara tried really hard.'

'Er. You can track her down. I know how.'

'How?'

I took a very deep breath, let it out in a huge gust, then started to tell my story.

CHAPTER TWENTY-NINE

After I'd explained everything to Eleanor, and Julie, and Tamara, and Tamara had got cranky then calmed down when Eleanor said she could interview me, and Max and Carla explained to everyone that they already knew, I practically had to run to my advertisers' appointment. A lingerie launch, of course. Just as I was feeling like we'd symbolically pulled the Poisoned Palace down and won some kind of massive victory for all femalekind, it was off to the boob and bum luncheon for me. Straight back on the bus.

As we ate our lunch (raw deep-sea, wild-harpooned salmon, organic wild-seeded strawberries, French champagne, and some kind of fungus that was the new anti-ageing rage) the pole dancers wound themselves like snakes in Eden round the silver poles impaling each table. Jungle vines and real snakes were twining themselves round the girls' shoulders, and the fantasy make-up was, although reminiscent of early Duran Duran film clips, amazing.

The dancer at my table looked very much like a parrot.

MISS LONELYHEARTS

If the parrot was practically naked and had breasts and long, lean legs. And wore shoes. With feathers on them.

'She's not nude – she's ...'

'She's in her underwear,' the woman sitting next to me said.

'It's green see-through underwear and I can tell exactly who's fresh off the plane from Brazil,' she added.

It was very odd, looking at someone's bikini line while downing a bit of seaweed and talking shop.

'God, this is so chic,' purred one of the girls I recognised from *Elegance*. The *Phwoar!* crowd were there, too. I glanced over at their table. I noticed Milla out of the corner of my eye. Was Nick here? I couldn't see him but a familiar face performing at the next table saw me and came over. I didn't have time to analyse the sad feeling that crept over me when Nick wasn't there.

'Hi,' I said.

'Hi,' grinned my friend Fantasia. I hadn't spoken to her since she'd given me the brilliant quotes.

'How did it go? I read it, you know. All my friends bought one.'

'Really – thank you. It sold out!'

'S'all right.'

'No, I have to thank *you*,' I said.

'Ahem,' said Miguel, glaring at Fantasia, 'if I could just show you this flowchart.'

'Miguel, this is Fantasia. 'She got me out of a really tight spot with a story. I just want to have a word. Then I'm all yours. Really.'

'This is not the time to develop a social life,' hissed Renata, the evil advertising chick.

'Oh, chill out, Renata,' I said. 'It's work. This is important.' I gave her my best stony stare, and turned my back.

'Look, Fantasia,' I said.

'You don't have to thank me again,' she grinned. 'I got this gig 'cos you put my number in the story. It goes for six weeks – $800 a day – cash in hand.'

I put my hands over my ears. I didn't hear that.

'I have to get back to work – that's Cookie over there, by the way.'

I waved at a goddess straddling the ceiling, green-and-blue feathers trailing from her behind.

'God, you're fit,' I said admiringly. 'Can I do a story on you both?'

'Another one?' Cookie said from upside down.

'I'll call you,' I mouthed and headed back to the bossy Renata and the indignant-looking Miguel.

'Start crawling, Meg,' hissed Renata. I turned and looked her straight in her narrowed eyes.

She looked very pissed off. But if advertising want us to slave for them, demean ourselves, play out their fantasies, it's time the relationship became symbiotic. Neither parasitical, but both interdependent.

'Miguel, can I say how refreshing it is to see real women in these lingerie campaigns. They were just telling me how extraordinarily comfortable the line is – even when doing something as outrageous and strenuous as this. I think a workout spread featuring your line …' I said, tapping my pencil thoughtfully against my notebook. His eyes bulged.

MISS LONELYHEARTS

'I'll let you know. But the way sales are going, it could be a very, very strong way to reach your public. Your real public.'

He nodded, enthusiastically.

'You know rich women won't buy this line. It's chicks you want. And you need a magazine that delivers to those girls.'

He nodded again. Renata's frown was beginning to decrease. But she still looked annoyed.

'Take a look at who's reading us. I'll have some research in a couple of weeks. It's up to you – you're the expert. But I think you'll be very surprised.'

'What do you think?' Renata asked Miguel.

He didn't have to say anything – besides, he could barely talk, given the stretch of the ear-to-ear grin taking over his face.

'I didn't suck, did I, Renata?' I asked sweetly. She just sat there, looking stunned. Time to hit home.

'So you'd better start working for those freebies – because Miguel's going to let everyone know why he's just booked $100 000 – that's for starters. You'd usually get 10 per cent, wouldn't you?' She shook her head violently. 'I'll take that as confirmation. Not off my back any more, you greedy little extortionist.'

When I got back to the office I reluctantly gave Tamara the undies.

'Sadly, I don't think I'll be needing them,' I explained, dropping them on her desk.

'Crikey, thanks,' she gasped, obviously taking her cue from Carla. She was used to being at the bottom of the office pecking order for freebies.

'It's fine. I'm sorry for not telling you about Miss Lonelyhearts.'

'That's okay. You just have to give me a great interview.'

I nodded.

I did feel a bit smug and enlightened, not to mention good karma'd and decluttered. Except I also felt deflated. I wasn't *really* giving away gorgeous and undeniably hot knickers because I was a nice, soulful, generous person; it was because it pissed me off looking at things I wouldn't get the chance to wear. Or remove.

Around Nick, goddammit. I'd stood him up, been busy as hell, and had wasted a whole lot of time thinking about an ex-boyfriend. I hadn't returned his calls, emailed or anything. And he hadn't called again. Why on earth would he have any interest in me after all that?

But wasn't it worth giving it a go?

Oh boy. My annoying inner voice was right. Maybe it was my turn to make a move.

And maybe I was channelling Oprah.

I felt a bit silly (okay, really, really silly) walking up to the *Phwoar!* office, but hey, Nick had done the same for me.

I made sure it wasn't easy by torturing myself with humiliating situations I could encounter once I was there. What if I interrupted a meeting with cheerleaders? Would he invite me in, then continue organising some kind of mega-deal for himself and a lingerie model to fly around the world?

God, get your mind out of the gutter, I told myself, nearing the glass dividing doors with Bond-girl silhouettes etched onto them.

The doors swooshed apart and I walked in. Milla was at reception, laughing prettily into the phone. She caught my eye and smiled warily. Still on the phone, she turned and bent over a drawer, looking for papers.

From the back her twiggy little legs were ... were looking kind of meaty. And fleshy. Like legs, not twigs.

She bent over to the side and a little roll of fat flowed nicely over her skirt — at the back.

Oh my God. Milla had back fat. She hung up and smiled at me.

'Hi Milla,' I said. 'I saw you at the launch thing.'

'God, how weird was that?' she snorted. I love people who snort. Who would have thought Milla was a snorter? With back fat?

'You look great.'

'Oh, thanks,' she said, nervously, smoothing her skirt down.

'I've been ... working out and ...' She paused, sizing me up as a confidence-keeper.

Eating, maybe, I thought.

'And eating,' she said wryly.

'Eating?'

'He said he'd let me stay on if I joined a program ... you know. A lot of models ...' Had she just shrugged in the direction of Nick's office?

'Oh, you mean Nick,' I said, like I knew. She nodded. How many hats did Nick have on? He'd be canonised if he carried on like this much longer. 'Well, you look gorgeous. Heaps better than – I mean,' I bumbled awkwardly

She snorted again. 'I was a skeleton. I'm working on it,' she said.

'Drop down some time. We can have a coffee – or cake,' I said, grinning at her.

'Yeah. I want to hear all the gossip from upstairs.'

I rolled my eyes.

'Well, we'd better have that coffee soon – things are moving so fast.'

'Seems that way. By the way – I really liked the story.'

'Thanks,' I flushed. I wasn't used to compliments from girls I'd formerly felt threatened by. 'Um, Nick isn't here by any chance is he?'

God, it was so different to *Gossip!*. At *Gossip!* people just walked in and found you – the only person guarded had been Monica. But Milla was like the tiny elfin protectress of all that was *Phwoar!*. Even the guys who looked like bikers.

'Nick,' she grinned. 'No, he's on a shoot.'

I turned around, shoulders slumped. 'Oh, okay. Well, thanks, I'll, um. Oh …'

And my words just faded away. Because Nick was walking towards me. He had a jacket thrown over his shoulders and his hair was a bit longer. His face was a bit paler. But his eyes were still the kind of blue you can see at forty paces.

It had only been a couple of weeks.

'Meg,' he said, frowning and smiling at the same time.

I blushed again – badly. The crimson kind of blush that must send your temperature up a few degrees at least.

'Have you got a second?' I asked, in a mumbled kind of fashion, hoping Milla wouldn't hear. She was filing, but I could practically see her ears changing direction as they strained for details.

'Sure,' he said, shrugging in the direction of his office. 'Come in.'

We went into his expansive room and he gestured towards the couch. And it was like when you are looking at the thing you always wanted and never admitted to yourself you wanted because you never thought you'd get it, and then you realise you only had to try and it could have been yours. And then you realise how much you always wanted it. Still want it. Every single gesture of Nick's, every movement, filled me with a kind of ache. Which I kept tightly under wraps because absolutely everyone in the office had blatantly stopped work and was staring at us. I felt like I was in *Big Brother*. Or a shop window. Everyone stared at us without actually trying to disguise it.

'What are they waiting for?' I asked, nervously. 'What do you usually *do* in here with women, Nick?' I said, trying to be all light-hearted and witty and winning, but tearing myself into little shreds on the inside.

He looked up and glared at them, and they all started to do something else very energetically. Then he sat down opposite me, our knees bumped, and I thought my body would spontaneously combust.

I cleared my throat and started talking. I just had to say it, escape, then I would cringe, have closure, and maybe one day, if I was very lucky, I would meet someone as nice as Nick again and I would think back to this day and remember not to stuff it up.

'I saw Milla at lunch. She looks great.' He ran a hand through his dark hair, which flopped back into his blue eyes immediately. 'I keep forgetting what a small world it all is.'

He just raised his eyebrows. So, I stumbled on into the open space. Note: never leave cover when in the firing line.

'Um, I was just wondering ... if you weren't too busy or something, if maybe you'd like to go and ... have a coffee. Or something?'

Silence.

I panicked, hurrying into my next sentence, which spluttered into the next one, which was due to collide with the next thing out of my mouth very soon.

'I thought you might want to. But ... anyway, I shouldn't have assumed. Anyway. Sorry. I'll just go now.' I pushed my chair back and started backing away.

'Um, Meg. I'll think about it – okay?'

He'll think about it. I shot him an angry glance.

'Oh.' I went beet-red. 'Right.'

He leant back. Sexily. Got a very nice shot of his crotch. Delicious. I realised I was still staring at it when he cleared his throat.

'Bye,' I said, drawing myself up to my full height and feeling very much like a tall, dignified skyscrapery person. Only short. Time to go? Right note to finish on?

He was still staring at me.

I walked over and thrust out my hand. 'Well, no hard feelings.'

We shook hands, him looking vaguely amused.

I'd done what I came to do, I thought. Now get out of here before you ruin it.

I said, 'Well, goodbye', and gave a cheery wave that made me feel about as sexy as, oooh, let's see, the Queen.

I walked out with my head stuck high up in the air, pushed the lift button and waited. I hate that. I needed to escape before something happened that wrestled this whole thing right out of my control again. I pushed again. I pushed again. I turned and pushed the fire escape door open and went down, practically running down the stairs to get away.

At least, I panted, pushing the door open on my floor, that was over. I walked through the foyer and a lift pinged open. With bloody Nick inside of it, leaning sexily against the wall.

Oh God. It's awful when you think you've settled everything with someone then you have to see them again. It would be so much better if there was no further contact.

He reached out, grabbed my arm and pulled me in.

'We've got some unfinished business, you and me,' he said.

And the lift doors closed. He pushed 120 and we started going up.

'What?' I said, looking nervously around. 'Hey, you're holding my arm.'

He still hadn't let go of my arm.

'Shut up. What are you doing tonight?'

'Did you just tell me to shut up?'

'Do you need me to say it again?'

'I'm not doing anything tonight. Telling people to shut up is rude, you know.'

'Come to Swanson's at' – he checked his watch – 'bugger, I can't make it till 8.30. Is that okay?'

'Is this a – you know, getting-to-know you type thing?'

The doors pinged open. Big Boss and the HR man were standing there with a tearful-looking Monica. I couldn't really feel sorry for her, 'cos she was clutching what was probably a very big cheque.

'Sorry,' I said.

'She's not,' said Nick, grinning, and shut the door again by pressing my floor's number.

'What are you doing?'

'I'm seeing you home. Ingrate.'

What now – some kind of creepy sex thing in the lift? No way.

'Look, I wouldn't ask, if I were you, and if you were in the least interested in finding out,' he said.

The door opened.

'This is your floor, isn't it?' he said.

'Yes, but you haven't let go of me.'

He leant over and spoke very close to my mouth.

'Shut up. I'll see you at 8.30.' Then he let me go.

I walked away, then turned and stared at him and the doors moved together. I was angry.

And I was excited.

'So it *is* a date,' I called out to him. 'Face it.'

Everyone was staring at me.

I slunk back to my desk, elated and embarrassed, and kind of floated home, even though I was on public transport and thus there were approximately fifty people in the space normally set aside for ten. But I was so happy it was ... okay.

Fizz helped Carla and Allison with my hair – putting it up, in a semi-sophisticated undone ponytail kind of thing which showed off my ears, which had delicate little antique earrings hanging from them. They arranged one long tendril thing at the front, to fall into my eye, to make me look flirty. And to hide behind. 'I know what you look like,' Allison said, pleased with my progress. 'It's got a vestal virgin kind of feel about it.'

Carla snorted. Allison glared. They were getting along beautifully.

Make-up. Lipstick seconded from the beauty cupboard, thanks to Carla. Chanel, nude and soft, with peachy tones. Lots and lots of not-there-at-all make-up in varying shades of creamy golds for my eyes so they looked bigger and greener. Then about eight coats of mascara, thinly applied, so it just looked as though my lashes were naturally that thick and gorgeous. Brown – black is the key there – use black and no-one believes those babies are yours.

Shoes. Hmmmn. Had to be high, but no toes showing – no time for any maintenance. But high satin slingbacks with true stiletto heels made my legs, normally a bit lumpy-looking I'd always thought, longer and more muscly and defined. God bless high heels!

Okay, God bless Carla and the fashion cupboard at work. Carla coming to my rescue was beginning to be a habit.

'Here you go, honey,' she said, handing me an indigo blue sparkly thing.

'Wow – what a beautiful top!' I gushed. It was. It was shimmery and sparkly and fragile and delicate, but the colour was bold and dramatic and the cut was daring. Gorgeous.

'It's not a top. It's a dress. A dress-dress kind of dress. Go on – put it on. It won't bite.'

It didn't bite, and it didn't suck. It was beautiful, and shimmery, and deep-watery, and made my eyes look amazing, and my skin look clear and glowy. Well, that and the make-up.

'It's beautiful,' I said, pulling on my jeans.

'What are you DOING!' shrieked Allison.

'No, let her,' said Carla. 'It sort of makes her own the look.'

There's no way I would have worn it as a dress ... I'm not down on my upper thighs, but that doesn't mean I feel comfortable actually trying to sit down in a tiny dress thing.

With my faded jeans, with shreds and grey-blue moments, and this incredible top, I felt both beautiful and comfortable. Wow. Perfect combo.

When the cab pulled up outside the house, Fizz and Dan and Eric and Max and Allison and Carla and Tamara all stood outside waving me goodbye. I was so touched. It was beautiful. Like a real family.

Only my parents and Karen had never yelled out, 'You look gorgeous', like Dan did, and Dad had certainly never made pelvic thrusts at my departing taxi. Fizz just waved and grinned, and Eric managed an incredibly authentic wolf whistle, an ancient art and tradition I thought had died out since men everywhere had morphed into their dithery and uncertain modern selves – I mean, what would happen if a bloke broke into rampant wolf whistling. What they thought would happen was that a mythical and highly secret storage space of thousands of hairy arm-pitted and very angry indeed feminist terrorists would burst open, allowing the said crazed feminists to dash out and beat them about the head with copies of *The Female Eunuch* – yes, because Germaine Greer's still the only feminist most guys have ever heard of, and definitely the only one they're still scared of. I was glad to see that at least one man amongst the millions could pass on the respected traditions as a member of the man tribe, and took it as a tribute.

Now I don't want to drag this out, because I know you are dying to hear, so I'll just tell you what Nick said.

'You look really lovely.'

He gently guided me to a table which looked out a window. Which had pounding surf.

Sorry about the symbolism.

I have no idea what the restaurant was like, because I didn't give a stuff.

I think it was nice.

I drank one glass of wine. The whole night.

Yes, I did.

And he didn't drink but we ate a lot.

Oh, all right, we ate oysters. And complicated delicious things. And had truffle and oyster shots. Chilled.

And then, after some talking about stuff that neither of us were in the least bit interested in, and after we'd both ignored our mobiles, and we'd had really fantastic chocolate cake – the best part of the whole meal, if you want my honest opinion, he paid – *he paid!* – and we got in a cab.

'Yours?' I said, not looking at him.

'Mine,' he said, reaching over and taking my hand.

And in case that's making you vomit, don't worry. I was beside myself.

When I got back to Nick's house, I more than half felt like running away. It didn't help that he lived at the beach. It was heavenly. Cold, but fresh, and heavenly, with a sea-salty smell streaming gently through the wide open windows.

Maybe the sea air was why I felt clear-headed – oh, that and the fact that I'd had one pathetic glass of wine.

It was just too perfect – *and* his flatmates were away.

So I was in his flat – open plan, ocean glimpses, boy stuff everywhere, not too foul at all, really. I'd decided I was making tea for us, and my hand started shaking as I passed him the cup.

As soon as he took it I turned away, feeling impatient. I seemed to spend so much of my time with him feeling irritated. Not *at* him, but at how I felt when I was with him. Like it was so good it had to evaporate or shatter any second. The tension was horrible. Awful. Could I run? Or should I just chat a bit more? But then nothing was going to come out of my throat without sounding like I was filling in time. Avoidance. I was here. Everything was obvious. There was absolutely nothing to say.

So why wasn't anyone making a move?

He was standing close behind me. He ran one hot finger down my back.

'You know, I really want to …' And he reached over and kissed the back of my neck. It was utterly swoony.

I found my voice.

'And then what?'

'I don't know,' he said quietly.

He moved closer. I could literally feel the heat from his body. I could feel where he started, an inch or two from his body. I reached behind and pulled him to me. He was hard along his thighs and between his legs.

'I don't know what's going to happen.'

'No-one does,' I replied, feeling the cliff fall from under me.

Sometimes, when you first sleep with someone, it's just … weird. Not awful, not bad – just … new. So awkward. Polite, even. You first, no you, oh that's a nice bra, I do like those leopard-skin undies you're wearing, nice pube shape. Goodbye, thanks for last night, like it was a nice cup of tea you'd been sharing.

And so you've got no idea what the sex was really like. Whether it was the start or the finish of something.

I didn't have time to think about that.

He wanted it to be slow, but I couldn't wait.

'Don't, don't,' I begged, as he tried to kiss my belly and work his way down.

'Now,' I said. 'Now.'

He pulled back and looked at me. He grabbed a condom, ripped it open with his teeth and rolled it on. Very fast. Very impressive.

'Now,' I said, nearly losing my temper and striking out at him. He knew I wanted him. I reached out and grabbed his shirt and pulled him towards me. His shirt between my hands, refusing to let him move. I moved myself to where he was hard and straining and pushed myself onto him. He gasped.

I am a girl who loves penetration.

He pushed me over and moved deeper into me with every thrust, my knickers to one side, my top on, my jeans down, my back hurting against the bricks on the wall, his hair in my hands.

It didn't take very long.

We hadn't even kissed. I looked at him.

He was staring at me. I could actually see the flecks of gold in one iris, before his pupils dilated abruptly, swallowing the gold with an inky darkness.

It was much too close.

I flinched.

'Look at me.'

And he was hard again. I wouldn't look at him.

'Look at me.'

God.

It wasn't tender or sweet, or angry and urgent.

It was much, much longer. And we kissed this time.

'What now,' I said, a while after we'd finished for the second time and I was stroking his chest with the back of my fingers – something I never do, by the way.

'I don't know,' he said again. 'But we could start with sleeping together at least five nights a week.' I smiled, and weirdly enough I actually fell asleep seconds later.

I'd just like to run you through my usual night, so you realise how significant the fact is that I slept with this man. Actually *slept* with him.

First three months with Ben: slept about two to three hours a night when he was in the same bed. He made me … nervous.

Nights with myself: try hot milk, every valerian tablet, passionflower extract and deep-sleep promise on the market. Still only sleep a few hours deeply. The rest of the night is so fitful, it's like all the anxieties come at once, all my night harpies, all the black horses and demons and petty hatreds and revenge fantasies and worries. Worries. They crank through my head like some unstoppable silent film, with me, the worst me, narrating. They are cranking through my head at exactly the time when I have nothing to do but pay attention.

So *sleeping* with this man was … well, it was a first in many ways.

The next morning I got up before him, and I felt amazing. Like someone had just discovered some kind of wellness and had given me an extra large dose while I slept. I looked at him. Mine, I thought. Mine? I thought again, feeling nervous by how possessive I felt.

No, mine. I can tell, said some other, more certain part of me.

I pulled back the sheets – which were fresh, 100 per cent cotton – went to the bathroom, which was clean, showered, and looked at my body – amazed.

He loved it.

I climbed back into bed, and put my cheek against his back, and rubbed it softly up and down.

When animals are born they actually rub against their mother, they imprint. I felt reborn, and I wanted to spend the day rubbing myself against him. So he couldn't get the smell of me out of his skin. You can wash clothes, you can scrub skin, but you can't take away imprinting.

You know what it's like after the first time you sleep with each other?

Let me clarify.

The first time you *sleep* with each other. And it isn't a disaster.

Because this wasn't anything like a disaster.

It was fucking fantastic.

Was fantastic fucking.

You know.

And the whole next day, *you're on fire*. Alive. Energised. Positive.

If I could write my world for that morning it would be a series of exclamation marks, followed by loads of ellipses. For all the incredibly private moments.

I had woken up, again, before him, and snuck off. I loved that. I looked over and thanked whatever gods were looking out for me that day that men were such deep sleepers, and that I wasn't. Because I got to stare at him, arms flung out and throat way back, and look. And look. And look.

He didn't wake up and catch me staring. Which was good, because I actually moved some blankets and things around, just to refresh my memory. And anyone who thinks penises look stupid just … well, his wasn't anything less than gorgeous. And a beautiful chest. And a taut belly, hard thighs, longish legs. He was a lanky man.

No fat on him.

Except where it counted. (Sorry.)

Then, when it looked like he wasn't going to wake up, I pulled on my clothes, looking over my shoulder every moment to see if he was secretly checking me out, which he wasn't, then took the opportunity to check him out one more time.

I didn't want to wake him. In case I saw something in his eyes that I hadn't seen last night. Some kind of look that indicated disinterest, disenchantment … boredom. I checked my memory for hints that I could have imagined it being as right as it had been. But in my memory it had been fantastic. And my body was practically singing, except for my head, which was humming with the sex buzz. I felt very, very, very good.

CHAPTER THIRTY

When I got to work, the fact that he was somewhere in the same building as me made every moment alive with opportunity. I could run into him at any second. It felt different to liking someone who you had little chance of running into, and every chance of waiting for their call. The only thing I had to hang out for was the inevitable – seeing each other.

It made me feel incredibly ... secure. But excited.

And nervous. Yet exhausted. It's hard to be ready for *that* moment every minute of the working day. It's hard to concentrate. It's hard to do any work.

I had it all planned. When I saw him, I would look at him with serious intent. And it would be hot. Hot. We'd whisper things like, 'Meet you at the water cooler in fifteen.'

I'd worked myself up into a right state.

And it wasn't like those times when some guy had asked me out for a joke when I was sixteen, and I'd waited at the bus stop like he'd said for me to do, and I'd borrowed Karen's best tight, shiny, red dress (without asking her – even in her early teens she was a flashy dresser), and he and his friends had driven by, in their dad's Commodore, and laughed at me sitting there, waiting.

I'd spent all day getting ready.

Karen was furious.

I thought about that. It always came back to haunt me whenever something new was starting. A job. A boy. A friendship, even.

Was this for real, or was it a joke?

Because there *were* malicious people in the world.

But something in me said Nick wasn't one of them.

He felt good. And he was sexy.

And he had slim hips. And he was tall. And he had thighs that were hard. And hair that was dark. And blue eyes.

And then I did run into him, and I practically turned and ran the other way.

My face flared red, then I looked at him. He was looking dark, and angry. 'Come with me,' he murmured, taking my arm and walking fast.

I was a bit alarmed, but in a completely fantastic way. What was he going to do?

(I couldn't wait to find out.)

We made it to the tearoom on our floor, and he kicked shut the door and pulled me to him.

We had a mad kiss, me clawing around under his shirt, him shoving his hands up my skirt, both of us greedy. We broke apart after a couple of minutes and stared at each other. It was like when you're eyes lock together when you hate someone. And time moves *veeery* slowly. Adrenaline. It makes time grind to a halt so you can figure out what to do to save your life.

So I felt exactly the same way I'd felt that time I'd crashed the car.

Clear and still. No air. No sound.

It was like we'd just had a major fight or something, the room was that brick-thick with tension.

'What happened to you?' he demanded, angry, dishevelled. Time suddenly sped up again. I felt very dizzy. And very weird. His eyes were a darker blue than they'd seemed to be last night, even when his pupils had been completely dilated.

'I ... I had to get in early,' I lied. Lamely.

(What was I going to say – I ran away?)

I moved in to kiss him, to shut him up.

But he was quite determined. Not the kind of man to be disarmed by a pair of lips heading his way.

'What would you think,' he said in my ear, after he'd worked his way up there by kissing my neck, 'if you'd woken up, with me in your bed the night before, and I'd gone.'

I nodded. 'I got nervous,' I said, taking the chance to glance at him. His eyes had lightened just a little. 'I thought you might wake up and be one of those guys who asked for numbers then never rang.' His eyes changed back to navy. And he bent down and grazed my face with his lips.

God, he was intense. But not scary intense. Intense like he cared intense. Not serial-killer intense. Though how would I know? If someone even rang me I thought they were too intense.

I stared at him, trying to figure out why his intense was good intense, even though it was far

MISS LONELYHEARTS

more intense than guys I'd rejected for being too intense.

'I have to go,' he said, yanking open the door again.

'Okay,' I said weakly, and he stormed away.

I stood there, clutching the sink, feeling horny, and happy and irritated that he'd excited me least when I could have any expectation of satisfaction.

There was another feeling as well: panic.

I've stuffed things up.

Nah – we'd been about to have sex in the tearoom. You don't do that with someone you're never going to see again.

Do you?

I remembered Ben.

We'd had sex when he had no intention of seeing me again. Except maybe to have sex.

And what was this tearoom sex caper anyway?

Was this the first time he'd ever been passionate amidst the instant coffees?

Probably not.

Maybe he'd been in here with Milla!

In fact, he worked on *Phwoar!*, so how was I to know this wasn't some kind of completely normal carry-on? In fact, he was probably under oath to have sex in the tearoom.

And then tell them all about it.

And then write an article rating my performance.

Comparing it with what's-her-face. Milla. What was she like in the tearoom? Maybe there was even more than one Milla. Maybe there were what's-her-*faces*.

Who were all fantastic in the tearoom?

I exited the horrible tearoom, shoving past Eleanor on my way. No way could I handle the real world of my desk at that moment.

As it turned out, there was no need for the paranoia festival. I shouldn't have worried. Nick rang me at five, and took me out for coffee and cake. Then he drove me home. We hung out with everyone and then he got to see my bedroom. Our house was a regular den of iniquity. There were now three active couples making noises all over the house. The weekend was one of stumbling-about bliss, going out for breakfast, smoochy walks and a movie. And lots of bed.

Heaven.

There was only one thing I hadn't told him about. The Lonelyhearts story.

I'd started up a few times. But it seemed stupid, way too early. I thought it would be best to actually see if he stuck around. Then I could hit him with the embarrassing stuff.

So by the next Monday at work we finished up the Lonelyhearts issue, and by Tuesday we were thinking about the next one.

Everything was perfect. I was just about to check Cainer's website when I was called in to Eleanor's office.

'It's about your …'

'Hair?' I said, smart-arse, to Chandra.

'No, come in here,' said Eleanor, looking a bit jubilant. 'Look. Here's the dummy of the new cover. How good does this look?'

I stared at it.

WHAT MAKES THIS GIRL
AUSTRALIA'S MOST WANTED
THE ROMANCE ISSUE YOU CAN'T AFFORD TO MISS

'It's excellent. I think. God, I hope it sells,' Eleanor said.

'It will. I'm sure it will,' Chandra replied.

'Well, Ali's doing a piece on it for *The Real Story* tonight.'

I stared at the dummy cover again. 'Can I have this?'

'Yep – don't take it out of the building though.'

Oh My God. I'd better make a phone call.

'Can you come down and see me for coffee? I have to show you something before you see it on the stands.'

It's a year since that issue came out and weekends are no longer my favourite things in the whole world. Because I think my favourite thing in the world right now is actually something that happens when Nick and I have taken all of our clothes off. Well, usually. Sometimes we actually do it with quite a few of our clothes on. Depends on how much time ... but you don't want to know. Way too much information. And, besides, I haven't even told Allison, and if I was going to make anyone squirm with the details, it would be her. God knows she deserves to squirm. How about that for newly established healthy boundaries?

But we still love hanging out. In fact, I'm in a shop right now in Bondi with Allison and Nick and Dan, and we're looking at a groovy sixties retro-style set of Alessi scales and they are so gorgeous. They're adorable. They're old-fashioned and have one of those spinning hands, it's not digital, and the numbers are massive.

'Which is good,' Allison points out, 'because then you have nowhere to hide.'

I stand on the scales and watch as it swings round to 56 kilos.

'How the hell is it doing that?' I ask her. 'You lie!' I scream at the scales, and Allison laughs.

'I swear I was 52 kilos at home.'

'I rigged it,' Allison smiles. She does these things on her TV program, too. She didn't stay with *The Real Story*. *What The Papers Wouldn't Print* offered her a better deal, so now she's doing shocking TV tabloid journalism. And she's so good. She's scary. She's probably going to get the Gold Logie in a year or two. It's just a bit weird when we're out, 'cos everyone's always looking at her. I mean, they always did, but now she has this extra glamour.

I look at Nick. I feel … like I could just hang out with him for hours. We take a day off every month and stay in bed all day, figuratively speaking. A sexy flexi day. We don't necessarily stay in bed. We may use other rooms. The floor gets a good cleaning. I swear, if we attached sponges to our backs. His back, mainly. Sorry. I wasn't going to go into details.

Anyway.

I think I'm really, truly in love.

He keeps asking me to move in with him. I think the idea of moving in is great. And I will. If we're together that long.

'Don't buy them, honey – not if you're going to get obsessed with them,' he says while I frown at the scales.

'I want them,' I said. Just to prove to myself that I don't have to stand on them every day.

I'm still in my place with the boys, for the moment, but it's bursting at the seams with all of us couples and Nick and Max are always there as well and we all know it has to end sometime. So we're hanging out as much as possible because it hasn't disintegrated into bickering or anything yet. It's still fun. Dan and Ali are definitely setting up house – but that's after they go to Ireland. To meet the kid. And Diane's still in Byron, with Marley – we get postcards, with dolphins and rainbows on them. She felt really bad about leaving Dan so suddenly, she says, but when you have a near-death experience, you have incredible clarity. And really she thinks everything obviously worked out for the best. I might even drop in and see them both one day, next time I'm up there. Nick and I keep talking about a road trip, maybe taking a couple of months off work and going all the way to the Top End. If we can ever get away. It's hard when you're both doing … okay. All right, more than okay. But I'm still getting used to this success thing. I'm not entirely comfortable with it yet.

'When are you and I going to move in together?' he said later that night, after we'd done what's possibly my new favourite thing in the whole world.

'When you ask the right way,' I said teasingly.

Seriously, it frightened me a bit. I wasn't going to take things that seriously.

'What if,' I said sleepily into his back, 'I say "now", and you go, "ha ha, only joking. Tricked you!"'

'Hmmm,' he said. 'I'm going to have to earn more money so you can get lots and lots of therapy ... What about I get down on my knees at breakfast, give you a key to our new home in a cupcake or something.'

'No!' I shrieked. 'Seriously, just ... let me think it over. It's a big step.'

As I said, it's over a year since we got together, you and I, not Nick and me. Remember? Allison, Lonelyhearts, world gone mad, new boss, Dr Gold, etc etc etc?

Oh, you want to know how Nick reacted to me being Miss Lonelyhearts. Did I have to convince him I wasn't a big loser?

Okay. This is what happened. Technically known in the business as a flashback.

I was sitting at the café wondering whether maybe I should have just shut up and let Max start his funny little agency, or run away, or ring Nick and break up with him, when the man himself interrupted my panic-stricken reverie and handed me a letter.

'What's this?' I asked.

'It's just something I wrote for you,' he said.

I ripped it open and a hand-drawn love heart on a piece of white paper looked up at me.

'To Miss Lonelyhearts.'

I gasped. And grinned. And punched him in the arm.

'How did you know?'

'Max told me.'

'Max!'

'And Allison.

'And Carla.

'And Eleanor.

'Oh. And Diane.'

'Oh My God. I thought – well, I was going to show you this.'

I handed him the advance copy of *Gossip!*. With the article in it. This story sure had done the rounds. Note to self: put magazine in scrapbook. For future reference.

He smiled. 'I thought I'd better get in first. You're in demand.'

I swatted him with my hand.

'Ow!' he said, laughing, then reaching out he grabbed my hand, pulled me on to his lap, and kissed me.

God, he was sexy.

He looked at me, seriously.

'No more dates.'

I agreed, loving this.

'No more dates!'

'No more freaking out.'

'No more freaking out.' Well, I'd try, anyway.

'No more Miss Lonelyhearts.'

'Deal.' That bit was easy.

We snuggled for a bit. It was very warm and cosy being squashed up against his chest. Mmmm.

'One day, if you play your cards right, you can even be a Mrs Lonelyhearts if you like …'

I snorted, and then laughed, but there was a look he gave me that was a bit serious. Like maybe he meant it. Or meant something like that.

Oh My God.

And then, as we made plans for that weekend, and the next, and the next, I really did think that everything might be going to be all right.

And it still is.

And it probably will be for at least a while yet.

That's pretty good, isn't it? To be in love with someone who's in love with you. At the same time?

To be happy?

That's all any of us can ask for. Don't you think?

ACKNOWLEDGMENTS

I'd like to thank my Mum, for being so lovely and brave, my daughter, for being bliss personified, my dad and my brother for being supportive and never ever making fun of me (at least not since I was fifteen.) I do need to thank everyone who ever gave me a job on a magazine, and all my colleagues and bosses for being not at all like anyone at all in this book. No really. Not even a bit.

Mostly, I'd like to thank everyone at HarperCollins. Fiction publisher, Linda Funnell, for being so patient and encouraging and for laughing at all the right bits; Vanessa Radnidge for being the angel of editing, the ironer-out of glitches and the picker-up of hitches; the heavenly Jenny Grigg for the cover (and for the magazine memories) and utterly everyone at Cameron Creswell's, but mostly the much-missed Annette Hughes.